BLOOD & DUST

JASON NAHRUNG

CLAN
DESTINE
PRESS

First published in Australia 2015
by Clan Destine Press
PO Box 121 Bittern
Victoria 3918 Australia

Copyright © Jason Nahrung 2012

First published by Xoum Publishing, Sydney 2012

National Library of Australia Cataloguing-in-Publication entry

Nahrung, Jason.

Blood & Dust

Vampires in the Sunburnt Country 1

ISBN   (pbk) 978-0-9942619-2-2

         (eBook) 978-0-9942619-3-9

Cover Design: Motivating Marketing

Design & Typesetting: Clan Destine Press

Printed and bound in Australia: Lightning Source

www.clandestinepress.com.au

For my father, Frank,
who slept on the west bank of the Warrego
and, as is the custom,
has ever yearned to return.

ONE

Dawn was one of Kevin's favourite times of the day, second only to knock-off time. It was cool and quiet, and things hadn't had time enough to go wrong yet.

From the far end of the house, where the bedrooms overlooked the servo and the main road, came the radio news theme. The strident jingle shattered the stillness like a chainsaw on full throttle. Six o'clock. Shit. The oldies were awake, and Kevin was running late. He scooped tea leaves into the pot and plonked two mugs beside it then pressed the switch to re-boil the kettle.

Voices, the flush of the toilet, then his father appeared at the end of the hall. The fluoro flickered before flooding the kitchen in harsh light.

'Standing in the dark, son?'

'Mornin',' Kevin said, then slurped his coffee.

His father, dressed for work in shirt and overalls, walked over to the bench. 'Forecast says rain.' He peered out at the breaking day, as though expecting it to pour at any moment, but the only clouds were a pink-tinged band to the west.

'And we might win the Ashes, too.'

'Miracles do happen, eh.' His father lifted the kettle to gauge its weight of water, then hit the switch, making it burble.

'It just boiled,' Kevin said with a grin and a shake of his head. Every morning, the same ritual.

His father glanced at the calendar hanging from a nail by the fridge. January, it said, underneath the blonde girl in perfectly ironed denim and fresh-from-the-box Akubra, the horse at her side looking slightly bemused. Thursday, with a red K penned in one corner of today's square.

'Your turn to open, isn't it?'

'Just heading down now.' Kevin waved his half-drunk coffee in defence.

His mother came in, her blouse and jeans a faded, imperfect version of the rodeo queen's spotless country style. 'You had brekkie, son?'

'I'll wait for smoko.' He wasn't hungry, just nervous now they were both here.

'Late night, eh?' his father said.

'Thomas,' his mother said. She reached for the breakfast plates, her fingers long and calloused and tanned against the china.

Kevin's parents had the same eyes: crow's feet in the corners, a permanent squint forged by years living in sunshine, blinking against the memory of flies, alight with the humour that helped them persevere.

His father replied with a cheeky grin. 'Just an observation.'

'I was at Meg's,' Kevin said. 'Watching some movie. Went longer than I expected.' He blushed. They had had the TV on – the TV in her room. Some old werewolf flick, lots of howling, a couple having sex by a campfire. Their attention had been on other things.

'I've actually been thinking, you know, maybe next time we go to Charleville, I'd, well, go check out the jeweller's.'

They looked at him, expressions hovering somewhere between a resigned knowing and concern. It reminded him of when he'd bought the Commodore and his father had been all, 'Yeah, it's a great car but what about the mileage', and his mother had said she liked the colour – white – and then got all worried because it had had only the one airbag.

'What do you, um, think about that?' he asked as the silence stretched out.

'Meg's a good girl.' His father reinforced the statement with a squeeze on Kevin's shoulder.

'She is; we both like her a lot,' his mother said. 'And you can bring her around here to *watch television* any time you like.'

Damn, his face was as hot as a barbecue plate.

'But you're only young, Kevin,' she continued. 'You've got time. You should enjoy being young. You don't want to do something rash. Just look at your father and me!'

'Make your own bloody tea, woman,' his father joked, even as he poured the two cups.

'It's just that her folks are talking about selling up and moving to Brissie,' Kevin said in a rush. God, his voice had a whine like a Land Rover's diff picking up speed. Made him sound like a kid. But he and Meg had been an item since they'd *been* kids.

'Brisbane, eh,' his father said. 'Quite a drive.'

'Yeah, fuckin' Brisbane.'

'Kevin,' his mother scolded. She didn't tolerate swearing, not in the house. What happened in the garage, well, that was the place for it. Skinned knuckles, shit in the eye, machinery rusted tight and unmoving, parts they waited weeks for only to find out the morons in the city had sent the wrong ones.

'What's so great about Brissie, anyway?' he said. He'd been there, once, two years ago when the cricket team made the regional finals. That was back when they had enough bodies to make an A-grade team, before the Thompson boys both went off to ag college and their best fast bowler planted his ute in an irrigation ditch on the way home from the pub. All those towers, crowding out the sky, looking as if they were about to fall and crush everyone in the bitumen canyons below. Everything so grey and cold; the air so thick with noise and exhaust that he could barely breathe. Meg would hate it there.

'I don't know if getting engaged is the answer to that particular problem, but you two are old enough to make your own decisions,' his father said.

'And we'll be here for you. Always,' his mother said.

'Always,' his father agreed. 'But right now, let's get to work. You open up and I'll be down once I've had a bite to eat. We'll have a proper chat about it later.'

His mother's encouraging smile followed him onto the landing. It could've been worse. They could've given an outright no. Still, he thought they might've been a bit more excited. A bit more supportive. A kookaburra cackled, mocking, and Kevin glared in its general direction as the stairs juddered under his steel caps. He loved Meg and she loved him; nothing was going to change that.

The blue heelers, Bill and Ben, scuttled out from under the stairs, snuffling around his heels. The wire gate rattled closed behind him as he strode out on to Barlow's Siding Road and headed for the service station. The building squatted in one corner of the T-junction facing the scrub-lined B-road, a route favoured by semis and buses looking to make up time, and grey nomads looking to take it slow. The sun, red and swollen, was still low, lone trees throwing long shadows across the barren flats. The heat was starting to settle, like a big open griller, reducing the horizon to a shimmering, silvered mirage. Underneath his overalls, the first beads of sweat stuck his Metallica T-shirt, black faded to grey, to his back.

The yard at the back of the servo was a tussocked graveyard of rusting car bodies and pieces of farm machinery butting up against the paling fence. The dogs nosed through the patch of native garden, bordered by whitewashed rocks his mother had planted to welcome the occasional tourists, and explored a roofed timber picnic table and a fake well his father had never quite finished. One of the locals had painted a crescent-shaped yellowbelly on the side of the service station, its faded scales flaking and crusted with dust. It leaped through the station's name, King River Road House; though roadhouse was a bit of a grand title for the old timber servo and the tin-walled garage tacked to its side.

He couldn't blame Meg's folks for wanting to go to the big smoke. Half the shops in Barlow's Siding were closed, half the farms sold off and sitting fallow and unstocked, half of everyone gone down to Charleville or east to Brissie or the coast. The town would end up like that old Ford truck out back: abandoned, slowly falling apart under the sun, while the world drove past without a second glance.

It was just that he – everyone – had always assumed that he and Meg would be together. This was their future, out here. Someone had to keep the place alive. The Siding was his home; damned if he'd let it die without a fight.

He unlocked the servo door and flung it open so hard it banged against the wall. Bill yelped, then looked at him accusingly, head cocked. Kevin grabbed a chocolate bar from the fridge as he went through the routine of opening up – cash register, pumps, his nemesis the coffee machine – then headed through the side door to the garage where a four-wheel-drive waited.

The voice on the radio droned on about the chance of rain tomorrow and Kevin snorted; the clouds came and the clouds went, but it'd been a long time since they'd dropped anything heavier than a galah's piss on Barlow's Siding. Should've put a CD on, made the most of it before his father arrived and tuned into ABC Country for the rest of the day.

Kevin scrambled into the pit, the Land Cruiser making a metal ceiling over his head. If he got cracking, maybe he'd be able to shoot through early and catch up with Meg. She'd seemed nervous last night, unsure; they had a lot to talk about.

The screech of braking tyres in the driveway announced a vehicle pulling up in an awful hurry. The bell dinged and the dogs rose from the shade by the garage door and yapped. Kevin looked out through the gap between the garage floor and the four-wheel-drive in time to see someone enter. Trousers and a pair of polished black shoes, dulled with red dust. City slicker.

A man's urgent voice: 'Anyone here? Hey, you under the truck – I need your help.'

Kevin climbed out slow and made a show of wiping his hands on his overalls.

The man stood at the door, a dark shape against the daylight. The dogs whined. 'C'mon, kid, I don't have all day!'

If it hadn't been for the anxiety in the bloke's voice, Kevin would've told him to bugger off. He was no kid. Hands in his overalls pockets, he strolled over to see what the problem was, ready to point out the pumps were self-service.

The sight of the stranger pulled him up. Thirtyish, solid, short back and sides framing a slab of face. Fresh scars on his cheek and forehead; hands stained with scarlet; trench coat hanging open, tie dangling loose against a blood-spattered white collar. And was that a bulletproof vest? A pistol nestled under his left armpit? A city copper? Out here?

'C'mon, kid – move!' The man's eyes flashed red, like in a bad snapshot.

Kevin blinked, stunned by the apparition. Then he was staring at space as the cop ran outside. Kevin followed, pulled in the man's wake.

Bill and Ben stood with legs wide apart, giving occasional barks as though sniping from out of kicking distance.

A heavily tinted four-wheel-drive sat in the driveway, steam hissing from under the bonnet. Rough silver haloes patterned the black bonnet like stars; a constellation stretched down the side of the vehicle. The side windows looked as if bricks had been thrown through them. BMW. Custom job, riding heavy on the shocks. Someone had messed it up good. *Jesus.*

The cop reefed the passenger door open and beckoned Kevin over. 'Give me a hand, here!'

Kevin moved in a daze. Blood all over the seat and the dash, big smears of it like a kid had gone nuts with paint. Slumped in the middle of it a man, his hair plastered to his face in blood so thick it might have been sump oil.

'Let's get him inside.' The cop heaved on the wounded man. Another cop, Kevin guessed: same haircut, same vest. Kevin moved in to take an arm, feeling moist stickiness against his face as the dead weight bore down on him.

'You got a couch or something?' the cop asked.

'Up at the house.'

'On the floor, then. C'mon, we're running out of time.'

They manoeuvred the injured man through the internal door into the servo and eased him down on the lino between the racks of fan belts and fuel additives. The man made the quietest of groans.

His mate leaned over him, shouting into his face. 'Dave? Can you hear me? Dave, you still with me, mate?' He swore when he got no response from the lolling face, Dave's mouth open and slack, his eyes showing white through the slit lids.

'What happened?' Kevin asked.

'Is there a hospital? Shit, there isn't, is there.'

'Charleville's the nearest.'

The cop shook his head. 'C'mon, then.'

Kevin followed him to the rear of the four-wheel-drive.

The cop paused to take a long, hard look at the road, the paddocks, then fumbled with a padlock as big as his hand before working a steel bar to open the door. A body lay there, dark in the gloom.

The dogs went mental; the cop shouted at Kevin to shut them up and Kevin shouted at them to shut up and eventually they retreated, growling their concern.

The guy in the back was dark-skinned, dressed in jeans and T-shirt and leather jacket. Matted hair curled about his shoulders.

'He ain't gonna cart himself in,' the cop said, and grabbed

the body under the armpits, leaving Kevin with the feet. Biker boots, cracked and dusty. He took the man by the knees, as though he was driving a wheelbarrow. The biker's jacket fell open, hanging down from his shoulders like limp wings. Something glinted on his chest, but Kevin couldn't get a good look as they jostled him inside and plonked him down beside the wounded copper.

The cop felt his mate's neck. 'Hang in there, Dave.' He looked up at Kevin, his sweaty brow tinted pink with blood and dirt. 'You got something we can tie this bastard down with?'

'We got some chain,' Kevin said. 'Some fencing wire.'

'Bring it here, quick.'

Kevin went into the garage, aware of the curious scrutiny of Bill and Ben, wishing they could do more than just stare and whine – like go fetch his dad; that'd be bloody handy right about now. He grabbed a length of chain, a coil of wire and a pair of pliers.

The cop considered the chain, then said, 'Cut me some of that wire. A good couple of feet's worth. Then cut the same for yourself and wrap it tight around his ankles. Real tight. I don't want the bastard to be able to so much as scratch, you got it?'

'You wanna tell me what's going on?'

'Just get a move on.'

Kevin did what he was told, making sure the biker wouldn't be able to move. Not that that seemed like a problem – the guy hadn't so much as twitched since they'd dragged him in. Kevin wasn't sure he was even alive.

When he was finished, he handed the pliers and a length of wire to the cop, who used the pliers to pull the wires around the biker's wrists as tight as he could. Kevin's respect for the cop went up a notch – he wouldn't have expected many city slickers to know a Cobb & Co. twitch.

The cop added a pair of handcuffs that looked solid enough to bind a gorilla.

'Jesus,' Kevin muttered.

'Yeah, he's a bad one, this one. All right, stand back.'

Kevin watched as the cop checked the wire around the biker's ankles and gave a satisfied nod, then hefted the pliers. They were a big pair with a bull nose. He stood over the biker's chest and Kevin could see clearly what had caused the glint – the man had a piece of half-inch steel protruding from his chest.

'Jesus,' he said. 'Why did we bother tying him up? He's gotta be dead.'

'You'd think so, wouldn't you?' There was no humour in the cop's voice as he grabbed the end of the steel and pulled. For a moment, nothing happened, then the metal gave, slowly inching out of the biker's chest with a low, wet sucking sound.

The biker coughed, groaned.

The cop pulled a big-arse knife, a Bowie or something like that, from under his jacket as he told Kevin, 'Get me a bucket or a glass, anything that's clean. Hurry!'

Kevin brought the first thing he could find – an oversized souvenir mug from a stand near the front door. It bore a picture of a fish and rod with a logo reading, 'Welcome to Barlow's Siding, yellowbelly country'. He wiped a swatch of dust off on his sleeve and handed the mug to the cop.

The guy paid it the barest of glances, just said, 'Hold it for a minute' before crouching over the biker.

'You know what I want, Taipan. Give it up.'

'Go fuck yourself.'

The cop seized the man's jaw. 'I can take your head right here. Your only hope is to stay useful to me.'

'Until we get to Brissie and I lose it anyway. No time like the present, eh?'

Dave's breath rattled wetly.

'I don't have time for your games, Taipan.' The cop plunged his knife into the biker's shoulder.

Taipan barely reacted. 'It don't hurt, y'know.'

'If Dave dies, you're next, and I swear to God, it *will* hurt.'

'Swear to whoever you like. I ain't doin' nothin' for you, Hunter.'

'Push his sleeve up,' Hunter told Kevin. 'Don't worry, he can't hurt you. Just don't look in his eyes. You never know what mojo they're packin'.'

'You wanna tell me what the fuck's going on? My dad's gonna be here any minute.'

Hunter's eyes were two massive pupils of glowing red ringed with bands of gun metal grey – an animal in the headlights. 'Just hold this bastard's sleeve up for me. Do it, or my partner's gonna die here on your floor, and you can tell your old man you let it happen.'

Kevin did as he was told. The biker's skin felt cool and smooth, tight with corded muscle.

'What's your name, fella?' he asked Kevin. The guy acted so relaxed, sprawled there as though on a sun lounge waiting for his cocktail to be served, but there was a hint of cold in his dark brown eyes. A touch of snake, watchful and deadly. 'Handy under the bonnet, are ya?'

'Don't look at him,' Hunter snapped, and Kevin jerked his eyes from the biker's and watched, fascinated and confused, as the cop ran his knife down Taipan's forearm. The skin parted, showing as red as a steak done rare. Blood trickled from the cut. Hunter punched the wound. 'Let it down, you bastard!'

The biker stared hate at him.

Kevin backed away. 'Jesus Christ, what kind of cop *are* you?'

'He ain't no cop,' Taipan said, his voice filled with disgust.

'Hold him steady, damn you!' Hunter turned back to the biker. 'Sun's up, creep. You choose.'

Taipan smiled, teeth very white. Blood ran in a thick burgundy stream from the wound in his arm.

Hunter manoeuvred the mug to catch the pitter-patter.

Kevin backed into a shelf, rattling containers of oil and coolant. 'What the hell are you doing?'

Hunter didn't answer. When the mug was brimming, he crawled to his partner and raised the man's head onto his knees. 'Here, Dave, this'll put you right.'

The dogs yapped and the door buzzer sounded and, for one frozen moment, no-one moved at all.

TWO

Kevin's father stood in the aisle looking confused indeed. He raised his hands – one clutching a lunch bag, a peace offering from Kevin's mother, no doubt.

The cop had somehow managed to put down the mug and draw a squat pistol in the time it had taken Kevin to say, 'Dad, something's seriously fucked up here.'

'Special Branch,' Hunter said. 'Let me be and I'll explain.'

'Explain why you got two injured men on my service station floor, or why you're holding a gun on me?'

'Both. But I gotta do this or my partner's a goner.'

Kevin's father dropped the bag on the nearest shelf and folded his arms across his chest, his lips tight with restrained anger. 'Well, be quick about it. I could have customers any minute.'

'Yeah, it's peak hour out there.' The cop left the pistol close at hand as he picked up the mug again. He dipped a finger in the brew, pulled it out dripping and said, 'Still warm.'

Bile burned in Kevin's throat as Hunter forced Dave to swallow the blood. Twin streams trickled from the sides of the injured cop's mouth. Hunter let Dave's head down gently, then tore away his shirt to allow him to pour the remnants of the mug's contents onto a puckered wound on his chest.

Hunter reached for his belt, swore, then asked Kevin, 'You got a hammer?'

'Huh?'

He nudged the spike. 'This isn't gonna put itself back in.'

'Cunt,' Taipan snarled.

Hunter holstered his gun, stood and fished a packet of cigarettes from his pocket. 'You get me a hammer, boy, and you – what's your name?'

'Thomas Matheson. This is my service station, and that's my son you're pointing that gun at.'

'Well, Tom, I'm gonna need a vehicle. The faster the better. What've you got?'

'I got a car. Up at the house.'

'So, the kid here gets me that hammer so I can secure my prisoner, and you get me the wheels. I'll see you're compensated.'

Kevin's father frowned then nodded for him to do as the cop said. 'I'll watch you *secure* your prisoner, and then I'll get you your wheels.'

Kevin ran into the garage – a lighter sparked behind him, sounding like a knife being sharpened – and returned with the first mallet he found. 'You really gonna hammer that thing back into him?'

'Fucking oath.' Hunter took a deep drag on his cigarette.

Taipan pulled himself into a sitting position. His sleeve slid back down.

Kevin stared at the man's arm, wishing he could see through the cloth. He'd glimpsed a thin blood trail, but he hadn't seen the gash. It was almost as if… But that couldn't be.

Hunter flicked ash and put his cigarette back in his mouth before gesturing to Kevin to hand over the mallet.

'Hear that?' Taipan said. 'That's your death comin'. Alla youse.'

'I don't hear nothin',' Kevin said.

Hunter cocked his head. 'Good set of ears, this bastard.' He nodded to himself. The dogs whined outside. 'It won't do you any good, Taipan.' He poised the stake over the biker's chest, then gave it an almighty whack.

Taipan jerked as the spike sank an inch into his chest. He spat blood across the cop's face. Hunter ignored it and brought the mallet down again. The biker spasmed once more, then lay still, eyes staring, a trickle of blood worming bright and viscous from the corner of his mouth. Hunter sat back, wiped his face with a handkerchief and tucked it back in his pants pocket. 'I need that car, sport. Kid, keep an eye on Dave for me.'

'Jesus,' Kevin said. 'Look at that.'

The injured cop was breathing regularly. Even had a bit of colour in his cheeks.

Kevin's father stepped closer to look and said, 'Just what in the hell is going on here?'

'Ah, crap.' Hunter walked over to the window.

'What's that noise?' Kevin said, hearing a low rumble. 'Bikes?'

Hunter motioned with the pistol for Kevin's father to move. 'The car, sport, quick now.'

'How about an explanation first?'

Kevin got a folded tarp and put it under the injured cop's head. The man seemed to be breathing okay, shallow but regular. The wound in his chest, he reached to move the sodden shirt out of the way, looked as if–

The roar of bikes filled the room. Shapes moved outside the window. The dogs barked furiously.

'Shit.' The cop ground out his cigarette on the floor and drew his pistol. 'Get down; away from the windows.' He ran to the nearest, cuddled up to the wall and peeked out. 'How many doors?'

Kevin's father pointed them out: 'Front, rear office, garage. Is there a risk – to the house, I mean?'

'They got no reason to go up there. What they want is here.' He stretched to kick the biker, the man's foot wobbling unconsciously under the impact. Fresh sweat glistened on the cop's forehead. 'We need that front door locked and those garage doors down. Right now.' He looked at Kevin.

Kevin took a moment, then ran for the garage.

'I've got the office,' his father said.

Kevin tried to call the dogs in but they were out near the bowsers, barking at people across the road. Four or five bikes sat under the power pole. Leather-clad shapes huddled around them, like a flock of crows picking over road kill. Kevin rolled the doors down, then ran back inside to lock the servo door. It and the top half of the front wall were all glass; he didn't see that locking up would help. It was just the three of them at the servo and his mother up at the house. No-one between here and town, twenty minutes down the track, and only the one cop, Smithy, on duty, anyway.

'We're cut off from the house but they seem to be leaving it alone,' his father said, re-entering from the office. He pointed a shotgun at the cop.

'I'm not the enemy here, sport,' Hunter said. 'Trust me – your missus will be safe enough if she keeps her head down. Unless they try for a hostage trade, of course.'

'You better start talking, or I might just be willing to do a trade of my own.'

Hunter stared out at the bikes making idle circles on the road. 'Is that the only gun you got?'

Kevin's father braced, the gun firm into his shoulder, the barrel locked on Hunter. 'You aren't Special Branch; there isn't one, not any more, not for years. And your prisoner isn't exactly human, is he? So you tell me, right now, what's going on here?'

'Jesus, Dad.' Kevin, feeling useless as the shit got ever deeper, looked for a weapon. Nothing but the pliers and the mallet discarded on the floor. *Great.*

'Just stay back, son, his father said. 'We'll get out of this.'

'No you won't,' Hunter said. 'Not if you don't help me. You've got no idea what's going on here.'

'Just hand him over. You caught him once. You can catch him again.'

'That lot won't be happy with that. They want blood, you can bet on it.' He checked his watch. 'I'd give my left nut for the chopper right about now.'

The window disintegrated. The cop crouched, shouted for them to follow suit. The timbers shuddered under the impact of bullets. Metal pinged where slugs tore through the garage.

The dogs barked like Gatling guns. One gave a short, sharp yap of surprise. The barking stopped. The shooting continued.

Kevin's ears felt as if they were going to burst. He kneeled, hands over his head as glass rained across the floor. Through the door to the garage, he saw a chance.

'The Cruiser,' he said, pointing. 'We could take the Tojo.'

'You finish it?' his father asked.

'Nah, but it'll get us to town, no worries.'

Hunter hadn't returned fire yet, just sat behind one of the fridges. He checked his automatic's magazine for the second time and swore again before slamming it back home. 'Wouldn't get a mile.'

'I got the keys.' Kevin stood, a hand in his pocket.

'Son, wait!'

Kevin was thrown to the floor. Try as he might, he couldn't stand up. His whole body felt numb.

His father appeared over him. 'Kevin? Son?'

The gunfire ceased. A piece of glass shattered like a chime. Kevin couldn't talk.

'Get him in the back,' Hunter said. 'Safer there.'

His father dragged Kevin into the office by the shoulders. Kevin felt nothing, puzzling over the view of the wrecked servo from this angle. Broken glass and tins everywhere, motor oil splashed over the floor, a fridge light fritzing like a bad strobe. His father, upside down, looking scared.

Hunter said, 'Help me move these two.'

'No. We can drive him to– We can do a deal. We can–'

'There's no coming back from that wound. We gotta see to ourselves now. Don't forget your missus up there at the house.'

'Damn it, he's my son!'

'Help me bring those others in here, before the bastards start lighting us up again.'

Don't leave, Kevin said, or thought he said, but his father left, following Hunter. The room wavered, darkened, and he was choking, like a mouthful of Coke had gone down the wrong way and was coming out his nose.

His father returned, huffing as he dragged the biker beside Kevin. 'Use this bikie's blood, like you did on your mate.'

Hunter hauled Dave in. 'Your kid's a lot worse off; a lot worse. Me and Dave, we got a little something extra going on, gives us an edge. I'm sorry, sport, but I could really use you with that shotty out here. They'll come in next time, I reckon.'

'Let 'em. I'm not leaving my son.'

A shout from outside drew Hunter's attention.

'Stay here. Keep that gun handy. I'll see what they want.'

Kevin had no idea where the shotgun was. His father kneeled over him, both hands pressing on his chest, and Kevin could see the scarlet leaking out through the fingers. Despite his father telling him to 'stay with me', he felt the world spin like some crazy show ride and the darkness pulled him down, right through the floor. He thought he heard screaming; and somewhere far away his mother was saying he was only young, he had plenty of time…

His eyesight is blurred beyond seeing, his body a cloud, but he can hear real good. There's a constant background rumble of bikes and there are two men shouting, but he can't make out the words. He thinks there's a lot of swearing. A gunshot, answered by many, like hail on a tin roof.

And then he hears his father, right next to him, and he blinks and blinks until he can see him, crouching with the shotgun pointed at the biker, who's on his back and looking at his father

21

with what is, if anything, amusement. No sign of Hunter; still out the front, then, trading bullets with the gang.

'I seen what you did for this copper here,' Kevin's father says, gesturing at Dave. 'You can do the same for my boy.'

'So I fix him up, and then what? You gonna shove that spike back in me?'

'There's a car in the garage and I got the keys. It's all yours, I don't give a damn. Just save my boy.'

Taipan holds his bound hands out.

Kevin's father puts the shotgun down and hefts a pair of pliers. Must've grabbed them when he dragged the biker in. Cunning as a shithouse rat, his old man. He ducks back, quick smart, as soon as the wire snaps.

'What about me feet?' Taipan asks. 'And these?' The handcuffs rattle.

'When my boy's safe, I'll get you out of here. You've got my word on that.'

Taipan snorts, drags himself to lean over Kevin. 'He's plenny far gone. This ain't gonna be pretty.'

'Just do it.'

And then, from far, far away, there's a tearing pain in Kevin's throat. It sparks a moment of extra clarity, of seeing past the bobbing black hair and cheek of the biker to the ceiling, dusty cream and water-stained in one corner, and his father hovering by the door, naked fear on his face, shotgun clenched in his bloody hands as his tense gaze darts between Kevin and the front of the servo where things are quiet again.

'What in the bloody hell are you doing?' his father asks, voice low and hoarse as he takes a step closer.

'I told you it wasn't gonna be pretty. You should just let him go. Sometimes, death is better, eh.'

'He's only eighteen.'

'More than some.'

'Less than most.' The shotgun barrel motions the biker to continue.

Kevin's consciousness flickers as his body turns icy; he can just make out Taipan's whispered, 'It won't hurt for long – unless you survive.' The biker pushes up the sleeve of his leather jacket, the action clumsy, restricted by the handcuffs. There's a faint, moist ripping noise and Taipan holds his bleeding forearm over Kevin's mouth. Kevin tastes warmth, a salty heat flowing through him like rum. It hits his gut: fish hooks are tearing at his insides, through his lungs and behind his eyes, all the way to his fingernails and toenails. He thinks he hears a didgeridoo moan, deep down under a cockatoo screeching that might be him or might be something else again, a squealing fanbelt, perhaps.

An explosion shakes the floor and the walls. A blast of heat and fumes. Figures – silhouettes against the flames – grapple and grunt. Gunshots crack amid the popping and banging, and something heavy hits the floor. Then the white glare of daylight blinds him, and when Kevin's eyes have recovered, he sees the back door is open and the filing cabinet is on its side, papers spilled everywhere.

Smoke billows, thick and greasy. A shape passes across the doorway, and he thinks that Dave has been dragged out but there's still a body there on the floor, reflections of flames on leather boots. Kevin hauls himself away. He wants to hide in the dark, but there is no dark, just the hungry waves of heat from the fire and the scouring burn of sunlight outside the door. He scrambles toward the lesser of the two deaths. Outside, groaning under the lash of the sun, he finds the cool relief of darkness, folds it around himself like a blanket, sinks into it like a bed made of dough. A cockatoo shrieks, and rumbling explosions and collapsing timber shake the ground, and that didgeridoo moans, moans like a man caught in a nightmare in which his world is coming down around his ears.

Finally, as the darkness takes him, it all fades away, drowned in the slow, desperate thudding of his heart.

THREE

One minute, Reece was covering the mechanic and Taipan, ranting at the dumb bastard for having let the rogue off the hook, for having let him do *that* to his son. The next, he was on his back and the building was an inferno and it was all he could do to haul Dave's sorry arse out of there. He found some cover amongst the car wrecks, enough to confirm Dave was still alive, but the building was aflame and he needed distance. It took everything he had – courage and muscle power – to heft his mate and get him over the fence and up to the house. It was only when he lowered Dave to the ground that he realised he'd been giving the fireman's lift to a corpse. Somewhere along the line, the Night Riders had fired a parting shot and Dave had taken the hit. Not even a red-eye could come back from a headshot.

A thin, middle-aged woman, face tight with fear and fury, emerged onto the landing and stepped cautiously down the stairs. She clutched a rifle but seemed uncertain whether to point it at Reece or the departing bikers. Together, they watched the gang flee, a roar of bikes flocking around a very smart Monaro, heading north.

The garage went up, the hot flash and detonation making them both cringe, and she lowered the weapon and all her defiance crumbled as she said two names through quivering lips: Thomas and Kevin. 'My boys.'

Reece shook his head and reached for his smokes, and a series of new explosions rolled across the flat and he felt the heat and smelled the noxious smoke, and her eyes reflected the red of flame and black of smoke and showed nothing but despair. He asked if he could use her phone, since his was still in his vehicle, but she'd already called for help; the police were on their way. But not *his* police, he told her, and she let him go for it.

Message delivered and orders received, he washed his face in the kitchen sink, then returned and sat next to the woman and offered a cigarette. She ignored him as she clutched the rifle, the butt on the step, her forehead resting against the barrel as she watched the roadhouse burn.

'You hit any?' he asked.

'A couple fell down,' she said, not taking her eyes off the pyre. 'They… they got up again, though.'

'Jackets,' he said, indicating his own, and they swapped names before falling into uneasy silence. He wanted to tell Diana Matheson that it was for the best. If Taipan had done what he suspected to her son, then death was a mercy. But he just sat and smoked and wondered what he was going to tell Mira when she arrived.

Reece waited with her while half the town congregated to watch the fire burn itself out. The local copper, a green constable called Smith, came over, his eyes staring and the blood draining from his face at the sight: burning servo, distraught hausfrau, bloodied copper sitting on the front stairs with a dead body covered by a coat at his feet. The constable was keen and not too dumb.

City folk had a habit of thinking their rural cousins were a bit slow, but Reece knew from experience that they could smell bullshit a mile off. Which was, he suspected, the real reason his own outfit didn't like leaving the big smoke. When your whole world was founded on bullshit, you wanted to stay where people respected it.

'I'll call for back-up,' Smith said, and Reece told him not to bother, he'd already called it in. Smith took their statements, his hands shaking, the pen jerking like a needle in a seismograph machine. It was a relief when a woman and her daughter rescued the widow from Smith's questions, and Smith from the widow's rising anger. Who were those people, she wanted to know. What were the cops doing?

Bikies, Reece confirmed for Smith's notebook. Amphetamines. Heroin. The works. He and his partner had been tracking them, and the gang had rumbled them when they'd pulled in for fuel and a cuppa. The hunters hunted, and Smith shared that look that said to lose a partner was a hell of a thing. His sergeant was laid up in Charleville after a traffic accident and he still didn't have a replacement. Probably going to close the station anyway, he reckoned, and Reece thought it was a shame for the cop that they hadn't, because if the young constable got wind of the real story, well, an accident and some sick leave was the absolute best he could hope for.

'Narc, huh?' Smith asked, and Reece said, 'Yeah, kind of,' more interested in getting Dave looked after than playing nice with the plods. Smith, after several attempts to convince Reece to a) see a doctor, and b) stay with him in the station's residence, gave him a lift into town.

In tourism brochures Barlow's Siding could be called quaint or historic, but in more general conversation it'd be called a shithole. Two pubs sat at either end of the main street as though keeping the place from blowing away in the next dust storm. He noted a post office outlet, a half-dozen shops selling nothing you'd want if you had the choice, a takeaway with 1970s plastic strips on the door to keep the flies out. The cop shop was a bungalow at the crossroads where the statue of a Digger stood permanent watch atop the war memorial. The empty shops outnumbered the open ones.

Smith pointed out the all-purpose general store, in case Reece needed painkillers or cough drops, but Reece said he would be all right, a little flash burn on the face, some singeing, smoke inhalation. He'd take a room at the hotel, not that he didn't appreciate the offer of a bed, but his people would want their space when they arrived. Smith dropped him at the hotel with the better rooms to wait for his people from Brissie. It'd be interesting to see how the firm handled it. What smoke and mirrors bullshit would VS pull on this clusterfuck?

The bar was already filled with conversation, and in the time it took for them to realise who he was and go quiet so they could listen, he'd heard enough.

How was Diana Matheson going to cope? Where were they going to buy their fuel now? It was an hour to the nearest garage at 'Nancy' and the fella there was a half-arsed mechanic, not like Tommy Matheson; even his son was pretty bloody handy by comparison, and not even twenty. It was a bastard shame, so few young folk staying around as it was.

They tried to ask him, the copper from the big smoke, but he pleaded exhaustion and retreated to his room for a drink, a room-service steak and a good lie down. Might as well make the most of it. And with Mira coming out this far west of the ranges, it could mean only that things were going to get worse.

At least the newborn had gone up in smoke. That was some consolation. Kevin Matheson was one loose end they didn't need to tie up.

FOUR

Kevin awoke to darkness and to silence. The world stank of diesel, ash, dirt. He was starving and aching, his mouth dry and his eyes itching. A suffocating weight pinned him down. He felt the grit under him, on top of him; dug into it with his panicked fingers. Gasped it in as he realised he'd been buried alive!

Choking, he flailed upward. Soil cascaded from him, leaving his skin – his entire body – feeling as if he'd been sand-blasted. Blazing heat and brightness scorched his naked body as he dragged himself like a newborn calf into the nearest shade: the rusted shell of the Ford truck. All around, the grass was burnt and littered with wreckage. The service station was a tumbled ruin, blackened timbers thrusting toward the sky amid sheets of buckled iron and tangles of wire. A listless line of yellow plastic tape hanging from short iron pegs bordered the devastation.

Across the singed fence, he saw his home, sagging wearily on its posts. Meg's little Suzuki soft top was parked out the front near his father's work ute. His Commodore and his mother's sedan were vague shapes hidden by the slats that walled in the ground floor.

He clambered over the fence. Fire had sneaked through the

palings and scored the lawn; a few scorched patches showed where embers had landed but failed to spread. He crawled more than walked, sheltering in the shade of the sparse, threadbare fruit trees and two towering gums, their bark hanging shredded and curled as though from torture. Sheets hung limp on the Hill's Hoist. He barely noticed the ash spotting them before he yanked one down and wrapped it around himself, grateful for any defence against the sunshine that baked his skin.

The dogs didn't come out to greet him; there was no sign of either of them.

He grabbed the rail of the rear stairs like an old man clutching a walking frame and hauled himself up, one painful, lead-heavy step at a time, until he reached the shade of the verandah. He went to open the back door but his legs gave out and he lurched into it; the door fell open under his weight and he sprawled on the lino near the dining table.

Voices came from the living room; footsteps; gasps. Hands rolled him over, and tears soaked his mother's cheeks as she looked down on him in shock and wonder.

'My God, Kevin, they said… The police said they looked *everywhere*. Where have you been?' She hugged him, her body painfully hot, and he clung to her, shivering.

Meg stood nearby, hands to her face, eyes wide. She was in jeans, T-shirt and cardigan, her hazel curls bouncing loose around her face.

'Let's get him into the bedroom.' His mother's voice faded in and out like a radio off-station.

They helped him to his room at the far end of the house. Meg drew the curtains, blocking out the cracked and shattered windows, the view of the devastated service station.

'Meg, go call for an ambulance,' his mother said.

'That's two hours. Maybe we should drive him ourselves?'

'Just go call triple-0.'

Meg left and his mother told him, lullaby-style, to lie still; to tell her if *this* hurt; or this, or this. His mother's hands probed and lifted. 'I think you're all right, under all that dirt and muck.' She sounded surprised through the sniffles. 'Let's get you cleaned up.'

'Mum?' he mumbled, reaching tiredly. 'Megs?'

'Relax, Kevin, you're safe now. Safe. I'll be back in a jiffy.'

She brought a bowl and some towels. When she'd washed him down and pulled the blanket up, she sat by his side, holding his hand and feeding him sips of water. It didn't bring much relief. Maybe it was the smoke or maybe the dirt he'd swallowed, but the thirst just wouldn't go away. His throat was so raw and tight; the water hurt like pebbles going down.

'You're cold, Kevin,' his mother said. 'You want more blankets?'

'Hot.' He took another sip of water, choked it down.

'You're okay,' she told him, sniffling, her eyes red and puffy. 'Dehydration, sunburn. Shock.'

'Where's Dad?'

His mother dabbed at her eyes with a bunched tissue. 'He's gone, son.'

'Gone?'

'Found him in the servo, after they'd put the fire out. So they think. Took him to Charleville, to be sure.'

She sniffed and pulled herself straight. 'Thought you were in there, too. The policeman, he said you were both... He said he'd seen you both, before he dragged his partner out, before it burnt down. Thank God he was wrong.'

'I don't understand.'

'They even killed Bill and Ben.'

Kevin closed his eyes against the memories, the scarlet-tinged playback of his world falling apart: his father and the biker talking, gunshots, the sound of Molotovs exploding, the rush of heat and smoke. Boots, pointing to the ceiling, over by the door; scuffed and stained, a split in the side – his father's most comfortable pair, 'still a few miles left in them'. That cheeky grin.

'A gang, the police said. The Night Riders.' His mother pronounced their name as though it was a foreign language; something curious. 'They wanted to get their leader back. Bad luck, the policeman said. Just bad luck.'

'The leader, he was–' More memories: dark skin and white eyes and even whiter teeth. Kevin kneaded his temples as though he could massage the thoughts into some kind of sense.

Meg came back and sat by his side, her brow creased, those honey-brown eyebrows almost meeting. 'I rang Smithy. He's on his way.'

Kevin heaved himself into a sitting position. 'Did he say anything about that city cop, Hunter?' The more he thought about Hunter and his partner Dave, the more he thought that maybe calling the cops wasn't the best idea.

'No, Kev, just that he'd be straight out,' Meg said.

'What about Hunter? He tell you about that bikie? About what happened to Dad and me?'

'Just what I told you already,' his mother said, plucking at the fallen sheet. 'But I don't think Hunter was his name.'

'And I'm okay?' He examined his stomach, his chest, his throat. 'I haven't been, like, shot or cut or nothing?'

'No, nothing.' Her brows wrinkled with concern as she touched his forehead, her hand like a branding iron against his skin. 'A touch of fever, maybe.' She dabbed him with a wet cloth. He was so thirsty! He could suck that towel dry. He reached for it, but his mother had moved away.

'Take it easy.' Meg patted his arm. 'It's okay.'

He caught her hand and pulled her in, her scent wrapping around him, but she extricated herself from his desperate pawing and stood up.

'Rest now, Kev. When you're better, you can tell me what happened with your clothes, eh?'

A kiss on his forehead and she was gone, they were both gone, leaving him alone in the dark, a vague hunger gnawing at his insides, fevered exhaustion smothering him.

As the weariness claimed him, the loneliness swept in; swept him up and threw him, litter in a willy-willy, and dropped him on a different bed, in another house, in another time.

A white woman straddles him in a room smelling of violets and the heavy, sweet aroma of sugar cane. It's him, but it's not him; his skin is black, and yet it *is* him. Sweat beads on her lip and dangling breasts as she gasps above him. Then her teeth grow, mesmerising in the candlelight, four fangs gleaming. Nails, clear and sharp, slice into his chest where, in another age, he might have worn the charcoal-filled scars of manhood. His mind screams at the wrongness as she bends over him, breasts pointed and firm, stomach flat, hips wide. She pins him, then latches onto his throat. He flows into her. He is in her and she is in him and it is rapture, rapture that tears his soul as a cockatoo's scream slices across their panting. She bleeds for him, binding him to her – for now but not forever.

A flash of white by the bed. A girl – Willa – in bleached blouse and skirt, a ghostly presence in the fluttering candlelight.

'Welcome, Chris,' she says, and places a hand on the woman's sweaty shoulder where her hair sticks like weed on rocks. 'Welcome to the family.'

He screams in fury. In shame. In hate. Then he is free. Free to run. Free, too late.

Kevin jerked awake, fighting the bedclothes, his chest heaving. What the hell was that about? He grabbed the bedhead for support as he levered himself up. Still a bit weak around the knees. And very, very thirsty. Running a fever, maybe, like his mum said. Is this what having concussion meant – weird dreams and a cold sweat? It was so quiet: midnight quiet. He cracked the curtain – just gone sundown. He shook his head – hadn't been out that long, then – and dug jocks and jeans and a shirt out of the drawers. A crow's call rasped like a rusty hacksaw as he left the room. The hallway light was on, making him squint against the brightness. The house was still, like a museum. It felt as if they were leaving, as if everything was just waiting for the removalists to come. It was not a happy move. Tea. He could smell tea. Hear the chinking of china; murmured conversation interspersed with sobs. Voices: his mother and Meg.

He walked faster, bare feet making barely a sound on the threadbare runner, its burgundy faded to brown. To his left, the familiar sofa and armchairs and television, the front door; straight ahead, the breakfast bar with the kitchen beyond; and to his right, the dining room, just big enough for a cabinet and table. The women were at the table, his mother facing him at the kitchen end, Meg on the far side from him near the back door. His father's .243 leaned in the corner behind his mother with a box of bullets nearby on the bench. Strange, to see the rifle there instead of in the gun safe. Strange to see it there without his father holding it.

'Mum?'

She jumped, knocked her tea over. Swore, dabbed at the mess, then ignored it to hug him. She smelled of English Breakfast and sweat; she wore sorrow like an overcoat. The lines in her face had never seemed so deep. Fresh tears brimmed and she gestured for him to sit at the table. It was as old as he was, big enough to comfortably seat six though there'd only ever been the three. Knife cuts, coffee stains and teapot burns marred the timber. Looking at it now, running his fingers over that abused surface, it was as if he'd never seen it before.

Meg fetched a cloth and mopped up the spilt tea where it puddled around the little glass vase in the centre of the table; a single rose curling to brown drooped over its lip.

'You should be lying down, Kev,' his mother said. 'How do you feel?'

'Just hungry.'

'That's a good sign. I had snags out for dinner.'

'Don't, Mum, it's okay.'

'Don't be silly. We have to eat.'

She went into the kitchen and dug out utensils.

Meg pulled up a chair next to Kevin and said, voice low and anxious, 'Smithy only let us come back to collect some stuff. We weren't meant to stay.'

God, she was beautiful. That tanned skin, smooth there on her chest and the side of her throat where her pulse bobbed. His throat constricted, his stomach tightened with love or lust or both. He needed her, needed to bury himself in her smell and her heat and –

A sharp clank made him jump. He swallowed, aware of the tension in his muscles, the shame of his distracted daydream; here she was, all care and concern, while he could think only of jumping her bones. And with his mother standing right there, too. With his mother standing right there, and his father not.

Meg lifted her hand to reveal a set of keys. 'Smithy gave us these. Found them out the back of the servo. Yours, see – the key ring I gave you. It's not scratched up too bad.'

He mumbled an embarrassed 'thanks', his fingers lingering on hers as he took the keys, the Holden emblem unmarked. He shoved them in his pocket. Keys to a servo that didn't exist, but he'd take them off the ring another time. When he could do it without crying or smashing something.

'We're going to have your mum stay with us for a few nights, at least until the police are finished down at the servo,' she said. 'You can stay, too. Mum and Dad won't mind.'

A car drove past, slow, its headlights glaring against the front windows.

'Is that the ambulance?' his mother asked as the sausages sizzled in the pan. The room filled with the smell of meat frying. 'Or Smithy?'

'I'll check,' Meg said. 'If it's Smithy, let's hope he's got good news.'

FIVE

Reece, barefoot and shirtless, cradled a stubby of beer and forty years of regret. He took in the massive wall of storm clouds building in the west; the humidity had thickened during the day to be almost choking. His body ached all over, as if he'd been dragged here from the roadhouse behind Smith's Land Cruiser rather than in the passenger seat.

He felt bad for Diana Matheson. She was an impressive woman. If his own mother had been that strong, that stoic, well, maybe he wouldn't have joined the cops. If his mother had stood up to the drunken thug of a husband of hers, maybe Reece would've gone on to a respectable public service job, or even, who knew, if he'd stuck with the schooling, to university. Now that would've been funny. It might've been him brandishing a sign on the street march instead of taking names and busting heads. Maybe he wouldn't have had to drive over to the morgue and ID his sister, just another overdosed prostitute dredged up from a Valley gutter. Or maybe it wouldn't have made any difference at all.

The story about the Night Riders being drug traffickers wasn't a line. Taipan's bunch would sell anything, do anything, if it meant staying a step ahead of the Hunters. Whereas drugs were the one thing that the Von Schiller organisation would not touch. Despite the lure of big turnover, Maximilian would have nothing to do with what he described as pollution in society's bloodstream. His people had carte blanche to deal with drug dealers any way they felt fit, as long as it didn't come back on the firm. Reece had done his share, and it still hadn't made up for the loss of his sister. Hell, he'd never even found out who'd sold her the junk. That'd been the spring of '71 and he'd been on Springbok duty. His path had crossed with Mira's and, well, here he was. Smoking and shooing flies on the back veranda of a decrepit pub in a dying town, waiting for the axe to fall. Him and everyone else here, by the look of the place.

A presence tickled at the edge of his brooding mind. Mira. It was never a good sign that her control had slipped enough to allow that sensation to filter through their bloodlink. Hunger stirred, different to the steak and eggs he'd polished off. Pavlovian, that's what it was. Needing that taste, needing it today more than ever to ease his many pains. How angry was she? He blew his concerns out with a last lungful of cigarette smoke and ground the butt out.

Back in his room, he checked his pistol where it lay on the bedside table, then rinsed his face, pulled on shoes and buttoned up his bloodstained shirt. He'd just double-checked that the internal door into the pub was locked when someone knocked on the verandah door. He didn't need to look through the window to know who it was. He could feel her, a seething thunderhead; could see in his mind's eye that boot tapping impatiently on the floor. He opened the door before Mira could kick it in, then stood back with a bob of the head and a muttered 'Strigoi'.

Mira stood, dark and electric, eyes glinting green from the shade of her hood, her custom Driza-Bone draped about her like bat wings. 'What happened, Reece?'

'We lost him.'

She hovered on the threshold, as though waiting for an

invitation, considering her options, perhaps, to bleed him or not to bleed him, and he wondered if he had time to get to the bedside table, if perhaps he shouldn't have had the Glock tucked into his belt. Futile, when she was this close. She entered, her shoulder brushing his chest, and flipped the overcoat across the single chair. The material snapped like a matador's cape. Her driver followed, looking boyish in a pants suit, a black ranger cap pushed down on her tightly pulled-back hair. She cleared a space on the small table for a duffel bag, then removed her mirrored sunglasses and tucked them into a pocket. Ponytail, freckles, wide shoulders. Familiar, but he didn't think they'd worked together. 'Nice place,' she said.

'Penthouse was taken.' He checked who might have seen them arrive – no-one – and locked the door before, as casually as he could, edging closer to his pistol.

'I've just spent an hour convincing the redneck coroner in Charleville that your partner died from a bullet to the brain and that no further inquiry was necessary.' Mira wiped the corners of her mouth with her thumb. 'He reeked of body odour. He ate tomatoes, raw, with salt, like they were apples. It was disgusting.'

The driver stood with her back to the veranda door. Reece caught the flash of a shoulder holster through her open jacket.

'I had to pay through the nose for a charter flight. Drag Felicity here off the GS roster with no notice.'

He re-appraised the driver. A jackal? Yeah, she was Gespenstenstaffel all right – no collar flashes, but she had the economy of movement, the hint of cherry glazing across the eye when the light caught it just right. And she was on first-name terms with the boss. The girls had obviously bonded during the journey.

Mira shed her suit jacket and began unbuttoning her blouse. 'Hire a vehicle. Sort out those witless fools in Charleville, then drive up here, wherever here is. I am hot. I am tired. I am *sunburnt*.'

'Dave didn't mean to get killed.'

Mira stopped at the last button, her open blouse revealing a black band of bra, a hint of rib cage and a flat stomach. She gave him a look that said her patience was stretched as thin as his luck. The Strigoi didn't appreciate being interrupted. 'And *I* would not have expected the retrieval of one Rogue on ice to have been so problematic.' She stared at him, her presence filling the room. 'I needed Taipan, Reece. I needed him and you let him go.'

'You should've sent the chopper.'

'The chopper's out of commission.'

'Would've been nice to know that before we came out here with our arses bared.'

She arched an eyebrow and he felt Felicity tense. He thought, this time, finally, he'd gone too far. But to hell with it. Dave and he had driven twelve fucking hours to collect Taipan from holier-than-thou Jasmine Turner, only to be kicked out before sun-up with nothing more than a slice of cold shoulder – straight into the Night Riders' ambush. It should never have happened; he wasn't wearing the blame.

'We could've brought some back-up, at least,' he said. 'We were completely outgunned. Who knows where they got that much firepower.'

Mira held his stare, her purple-tinted eyes examining, divining, weighing. Then she blinked, and he breathed again as she shook her head, rubbed her temples, her eyes flashing green on the way back to their natural brown.

'Strigoi?' Felicity asked, poised but uncertain.

Mira removed her blouse and draped it over the chair. Above the lace of her bra, the rust-coloured pentacle tattoo on her left breast glittered with silver streaks, like fish swimming in a stream. The sight triggered the familiar constriction in his throat, the dryness in his mouth, the tightening of his balls. Damn her.

'Long day, Reece?' Mira said.

'You could say that.'

'And you've been smoking.'

'And I've been smoking.'

'And drinking.'

'Medicinal only.'

'How's that wolfbite?'

'It isn't. We were in the car most of the time. Just got a bit toasty in the roadhouse, that's all.'

'It was unfortunate timing, Reece. The helicopter's upgrade is taking longer than anticipated. And as I said, the mission was routine. We tried to handle it quietly and it blew up in our faces. Now, we have to deal with the fallout. Felicity – my belt.'

Felicity retrieved Mira's weapon belts from the duffel and stood with them at the ready. One held a sidearm and ammunition pouches, the other a long knife and a curved sword in their scabbards. That hit Reece like a splash of cold water – Mira had brought her blades. She meant business.

'Show me.'

He opened his shirt and turned his head. She drew the smaller of the blades, as long as her forearm, and sliced the side of his neck. He flinched; the cut had gone deep. She handed Felicity the basilard to clean, then bent her lips to the wound. The pain spiked as her fangs tore at the lips of the wound, her tongue probing, lapping, and then he groaned with the familiar sense of himself draining out as she swallowed him down. 'You taste like a brewery,' she murmured, 'and smell like an ashtray.' Mira stepped back, deep purple eyes staring as she sifted his lifestream. Blood smeared her lips and chin. A few drips made short, languid lines near the tattoo over her heart. Reece wanted desperately to lick her chest clean, but he stood still, a hand pressed to the wound in his neck, blood trickling through his fingers, feeling woozy.

'You're sure about the boy?' Mira asked. 'Taipan brought him across?'

'Not for certain, but it looked like he'd gone through the motions. Needless to say, I didn't go back for him.'

'Shame. The grease monkey could've given us a valuable link to the gang. I expect more flexibility from my Favourite.'

'Standing orders are to destroy all unauthorised newborns,' he said, unable to put much fight into it. He'd been running on empty before she tapped him. He lowered his hand from his throat, letting the blood flow down his chest. His gun was on the table, the hall door locked, Felicity barring the exit with a sidearm and two blades in her hands, not counting what she was carrying herself. He was royally screwed and, honestly, too exhausted to give a damn. The kid would've thanked him, if he'd any idea what Taipan had done to him.

'Basilard,' Mira ordered Felicity, who handed her the dagger once more.

Reece smelled the girl's anticipation, saw it filling her eyes like a kid's on Christmas morning. He could've told her to hold her horses, the ambitious little bitch. He wasn't being retired just yet. He hoped.

'Come here,' Mira said as she ran the blade across her forearm. The skin parted, just above two vibrant scars circling her left wrist, and dribbled crimson. 'Have a drink, Reece. It's medicinal.'

He was on his knees, sucking down her blood, aware of Felicity looking on, all but panting, when his phone rang. Felicity answered it. 'He's in the loo... *Yeah*, I'm his *secretary*... What do you want?'

Constable Smith, she reported after she'd ended the call. Diana Matheson's son had turned up at the house, hardly hurt at all. Smith would let Reece know if he found out anything when he spoke to the lad.

Mira pulled her arm away. 'So, not dead. That changes things.'

Reece leaned against the bed, waiting for the rush to subside. It was taking longer to kick in each time; each time, it ended too soon. Through that delirious haze, past the burning itch of wounds healing, he heard Mira tell Felicity to contact this Constable Smith – no interference. No cops, no doctors, no *verdammt* reporters. Reece would handle it. Make it sound good.

'Get cleaned up,' she told Reece. 'Felicity's got a new kit for you in the car. I haven't decided yet whether the cost should come out of your wages – or your hide.' She scooped scarlet drops from her chest and licked them from her finger tip, then rubbed her temple again. 'Everybody just needs to be quiet for a moment while I think this through. We might be able to salvage this yet.'

Reece headed for the en suite. He felt sorry for the mechanic and his family, sorry he'd pulled in there and achieved nothing. Dave had died anyway; Taipan had escaped; and now the boy had a death warrant hanging over him. Usually it was Reece's job to defend the herd, or avenge them. But this time, he'd brought hell to their door, and now the devil had come to sweep up the mess.

SIX

There was a knock at the door and Meg answered it.

'Well, hello,' a male voice said, and Kevin's mother looked over from the pan and said, 'Sergeant, what is it?'

'Constable Smith told me your good news, so I had to come out and see for myself. Hope you don't mind.'

Hunter walked into Kevin's line of sight. A faint rash down one side of his face. New clothes, same scruffy coat. Same raggedy bullet-proof vest. Belt bulging with pouches, some kind of baton.

His mother twiddled with the stove and then moved to the kitchen entry. 'I was just cooking–'

The chair scraped a rude interruption as Kevin hauled himself to his feet, using the table for support. 'What the hell are you doing here, Hunter?'

The man held up a hand and Kevin stayed where he was. 'Calm down, sport. We're here to sort it all out.'

A woman in black walked in behind him. She wore an ankle-length skirt and a blouse under some kind of wide-shouldered, hooded Driza-Bone. Her hair was cropped close to the scalp, her face all angles, tight and hard, humourless, the mug shot of someone who'd blown up a bus. Her eyes glimmered green, like a cat's. Something about her reminded Kevin of Taipan.

Meg closed the door and walked over to hold his arm tight. He pulled her to him. This was not going to go well.

'My, quite the welcome home party we're having,' the woman said.

'My, um, supervisor,' Hunter told them. 'From Brisbane.'

The woman studied Kevin. 'Well, our star attraction's up and about. How do you feel, boy?'

'What's the story, Hunter?' Kevin demanded. 'What the hell happened? What happened to my dad?'

The woman glanced at Hunter when Kevin said his name, an eyebrow arched in inquiry, faintly amused or annoyed, he couldn't tell. Who wore a 'Bone out here in summer, anyway?

'Kevin,' his mother said. 'Stay calm, son.'

'He's fine,' Meg said. 'But the ambos are on their way from Charleville. I think he should be under observation or something.'

'Oh, definitely *or something*,' the woman said. 'In fact, I think he should come with us.'

'With you?' Kevin's mother said.

Meg tightened her grip on his arm. 'He hasn't done anything.'

'He is a material witness to the death of a policeman,' the woman said.

'And my dad,' Kevin added.

'And your father.'

Kevin pointed at Hunter. 'This bloke knows more about it than me. He brought that biker to the servo. He left us to die in there.'

'That's not what happened, sport.'

'Don't *sport* me. I saw what you did to that bloke's arm. I saw–'

'Oh, Reece,' the woman said, reaching inside her coat.

'Wait,' Hunter said. 'Mira.'

Mira gave him the look of a school teacher being told bullshit about homework not done, then walked toward Kevin's mother. She picked up a photograph of Kevin in his cricket whites, leg streaked with red from his bowling stint that netted his first five-for. 'You must be very proud to have such a fit son.'

'Very proud.'

'I like you, little mother.' She closed her eyes and breathed in deeply. 'You smell of strength. Not here.' She squeezed his mother's bicep. 'Here.' A hand on her chest, dark-coloured nails glinting. His mother stood, as straight as a crowbar. 'Strength and anger. A little bit of fear, too, I think. The smells of the peasant, leavened with dirt and sunshine.' Mira's hand slid down, over his mother's stomach.

Kevin held Meg closer. He could smell his own sweat. Realised that the sausages were starting to burn, the sizzling growing louder. His pulse reverberated in his ears. Meg radiated heat beside him; a trick of his hearing made it sound as if he could hear her racing heartbeat, too, feel it thudding against him where their bodies pressed together. He could see only Mira: her face so close to his mother's cheek, the crown of her head reaching only to his mother's nose; that hand, spread wide as though to sense a baby's kick.

'Stop it,' he said, but she ignored him, lost in some kind of reverie.

'I, too, was a peasant once,' Mira said. 'So, dirt and sunshine, I understand, though I have left them far, far behind. But I do like to taste them sometimes. It is good to be reminded of where we come from, don't you think? Of our heritage. Of the blood in our veins.'

'I don't know what you people want. Sergeant, what do you people want?' his mother asked, shuffling away from Mira.

'Yes, *sergeant*, tell these good citizens: what is it we want?'

'We just need to talk to your son, Mrs Matheson.'

'Mrs Matheson? It was Diana this afternoon.'

Mira looked at Hunter, amused. 'The night changes everything, does it not?'

'Mira!'

'They know you, *Hunter,* and now they know me.'

'We know nothin',' Kevin said.

'Oh, but I think you do, boy; because you don't look very well at all.'

'I'm all right.'

'You have no idea what you are.' Mira cocked her head, listening. 'Is that the Night Riders I hear? Do you hear them, Hunter? Coming to clean up their loose ends.'

'Not necessary, Strigoi. These people–'

'The boy is officially dead–'

'The constable knows he isn't. And who else by now? You can't make the whole town go away.'

A frown. 'No, I suppose not.'

'Cut our losses, Strigoi. Take the Rogue and go.'

'I was thinking, cut and run.' A finger nail drew a thin line of blood down Kevin's mother's cheek. She tried to pull away, but Mira held her firmly by the upper arm.

The smoke alarm sounded. Mira, flinching, told Hunter to take care of the pan. Smoke spiralled over the stove as Hunter stepped toward the kitchen.

'Run, Meg, run!' Kevin pushed her out of the way and charged.

Mira shoved his mother. She smacked into the table and tumbled to the floor. He lashed out but Mira side-stepped his clumsy, distracted punch and her stiff arm slammed into his chest like a cricket bat. His feet flew out from under him and he hit the floor so hard his vision turned black, lit by fireworks. When he could see again, the woman had him pinned under her boot, the chunky heel grinding into his diaphragm, the evil snout of a pistol pointed directly at his face.

Hunter helped his mother up. Meg stood petrified, backed against the table. His mother found her feet and yanked her arm from Hunter's grip. Blood smeared her face.

Kevin pawed at the boot holding him down, but Mira shook

her head at him, the gun barrel mirroring the action, and he forced himself to lie still, the anger seething inside him.

A squawk and Hunter stepped back to answer the two-way radio at his belt.

His mother grabbed the rifle. Worked the bolt and levelled it at Mira.

Hunter snapped his pistol to her forehead. Murmured into the two-way, 'Gimme a minute.'

Mira chuckled, shook her head ever so slowly. She lifted her foot, just a little, and in that ease of pressure Kevin thought he was free. He began to sit up. Her boot pushed him down again, this time grinding across his throat so hard he choked.

'Don't,' she told him, and her eyes flashed green behind the huge tunnel of the gun barrel.

'Step away,' Kevin's mother told her. 'Let him go.'

'Diana,' Hunter said, his voice so calm he might have been reading the news. 'They get up. Remember? They get up.'

Near Kevin's ear, water dripped from the table to the lino, keeping time wet and slow, slower than the clock on the wall, drip, drip, drip, puddling beside the dead rose on the floor. The smoke alarm kept its own shrill time, barp, barp, barp. In the background burning meat hissed and popped. The harsh stench of it made it even harder to breathe.

Above him, Mira's skirt hung open to reveal her leg above the rim of her knee-high boot, black tights shrink-wrapped around her thigh. It might've been sexy if she hadn't been killing him.

'They get up,' Hunter repeated. He took his pistol away. Put the radio down. Reached for the rifle.

'Who are you people?' Kevin's mother asked, her voice the barest of whispers. She let him take the rifle. She stepped back, shaking, and Meg hugged her, pulling her into a knot of arms and terrified expressions.

The radio squawked again and Hunter swapped the rifle for it. 'Go.'

He then stalked into the kitchen and took the pan off the stove. 'There's company coming.'

'Riders?' Mira asked.

'Probably.'

'How many?'

'Too many, would be my guess. Unless you got something a little extra tucked away under that coat.'

'Then let us see what the newborn knows. Take the women out of the room while I *talk* to him. Keep them quiet.'

'Mira–'

'I mentioned my sunburn, did I not?'

'Ladies.' He re-slung his radio. 'This way, please.' He motioned with his pistol.

'Don't hurt him,' Kevin's mother pleaded.

'Only a fraction more than he finds pleasurable, I assure you, little mother,' Mira told her. When the women had been shut in the nearest room, Hunter standing watch in the hall, she holstered the gun and hauled Kevin to his feet. He pedalled backward as she bulldozed him into the wall. His vision burst with a new set of flashing lights.

'Kevin?' his mother yelled, and Meg shouted too, a fearful 'Kev!', and Hunter kicked the door.

'He's okay. Just stay where you are.'

Mira held Kevin tightly by the throat, her face next to his. 'I understand you've had an intimate meeting with Taipan. Is that right?'

'What?' he croaked.

'I just need to make a blood test. It will hurt, but I promise you, you will like it.' She bit his neck and he cried out, the sound a strangled, pathetic hiccup under her carpet-snake grip. She sucked on the wound in his throat. The room spun, as though she was the centre of a whirlpool and he was a leaf caught in the swirling current.

'You getting anything?' Hunter asked.

'He's too weak. Barely had enough to get him across the line.'

47

Hunter sounded resigned when he asked, 'Cut and run, then?'

'Plan B,' she said, her gaze fixed on Kevin as though he was some new kind of bug and she was trying to identify him. 'How far out is that Night Rider?'

He talked into the walkie-talkie. 'A couple of minutes. Taking it real careful, Felicity says.'

'Enough time to put in a trace.'

'They'll find it.'

'Only if they taste him, in which case, they'll finish him off for us. But maybe we'll find out where they are. I don't see a downside.'

Mira pushed Kevin to the floor and pinned his arms with her knees. She was incredibly strong; like an anvil sitting on his chest. 'You like the view, boy?' Her tongue, so pink against her sharp white teeth, her lips glinting. She reached back to his cock and squeezed until he groaned. 'You *do* like it. Here, taste me.'

She bit her left wrist and he heard the flesh tear, smelled the blood flow, thick and metallic. He turned his mouth away, but she bled on him, splattering his lips, and he tasted her, steaming hot, and he was licking and gulping and trying to lift his head from the floor toward her, and finally she laughed and lowered her wrist till he could suck her down. A voice in the back of his head was screaming NO but the blood drowned it, drowned it completely as what felt like an electric current ran through him. Such delicious electrocution.

'Careful, don't make a mess. We don't want to leave tell-tale stains, do we? Your girlfriend might not like that.'

Romanian, he realised. Her name was Mira and she was Romanian, but that had been a long, long time ago. And the cop – Taipan had been right: he was no cop. Hunter wasn't even his name; it was his *rank*.

She held up her wrist, marked by two pink scars circling it down low, close to her hand. As he watched, fascinated and horrified, a bright scarlet earthworm burrowed under her skin until it circled her wrist like a bracelet, then solidified into a third ring of weird scar tissue. His eyes must've been playing tricks, because he thought he could see something moving inside the scars, like an eel in a mud puddle. And her eyes – her eyes glazed so deeply red they were almost purple.

'Got you,' she said, and kissed him, lapping at his lips and cheeks. She sat up and closed her eyes as though tuning out to a song only she could hear, and her forehead creased with concentration, little bubbles of rose-coloured sweat glistening. On her blouse, a circle of blood blossomed over her heart, and some kind of pattern grew inside it, rapidly blotching but looking vaguely star-shaped. She smiled at him then, like a prefect who'd just come head of the class, and said, 'But you – you do not have me.' The childish glee vanished. Her eyes snapped to green and then back to deep brown, almost black. Mira gripped his chin, forcing him to look at her. Her fingernails were long, glinting, sharp at the edge of his vision.

'If you tell Taipan what we've just done, you and me, he'll kill you. Do you understand? He will kill you and your mother and your girlfriend. All of you.'

He glared at her, wishing both she and Hunter were dead.

'If he tastes so much as a drop of your blood, you are a dead man. Understand?' She made him nod, his jaw aching from her pincered hold. 'Good boy.' She patted his cheek. 'You play your cards right, we might get to party later. Do you like the sound of that?' She crushed his balls once more, making him sob.

'Time, Mira.' Hunter had moved to the back door where he could look over the rear paddocks.

Mira uncurled, like a cat stretching, rising to her feet in one graceful movement. Kevin half expected her to raise her hands over her head, stand on her toes like a ballet dancer.

'The women?' Hunter asked.

'Let nature take its course,' Mira said. 'A boy has to eat.'

'Shit, Mira.' Hunter turned away as Mira rested the toe of her boot on Kevin's chin, making sure she had his attention.

'You tell your women, Grease Monkey. You make them understand.' She held up a warning finger. 'If one word of this gets out – just one little word – the Night Riders will come for your women. They will kill them all. And if they don't, I will. You want to survive this you keep your mouth shut and your veins to yourself. *Verstehen?*'

Did he understand? Loud and clear.

The two-way fuzzed. 'One coming in, from the back,' Hunter reported. 'We are out of time.'

'Let's go. Oh, Grease Monkey – we'll be just outside. Watching. Listening.' She held up her finger to her lips, then opened her hand to blow him a kiss.

And then she and Hunter were gone, leaving Kevin with the awareness that he was very lucky to still be alive. They all were. The room smelled of burnt meat but the alarm had quit, sometime. Then, as his mother ran toward him, and Meg stood in the hall with her knuckles to her mouth, he realised he wasn't actually alive at all.

It replays as though he's on a carousel ride:

His mother picking up the rifle and working the bolt – clack, clack, like bony jaws slamming shut – and running to the front door. Meg, there, right *there*, where only an eye blink ago Mira was crouching, licking his face. Meg, cradling his face and staring into his eyes; asking him if he's all right and what has happened. Her eyes are so very wide and glistening with tears, and the concern he sees there is acid in his heart. He pulls her to him and he bites into her shoulder, that point where her neck joins, and the skin is soft and steaming and opens like freshly baked bread and the rush of blood is simply the most intense – he comes explosively and she groans, her fist beating moth-like against his chest…

Screaming. Stereo, surround sound. It vibrates through him,

into his chest, into his blood; his heart races, trying to match that tune. He's screaming, too, down deep where the red flood doesn't reach…

Meg, torn away. Her flesh tears under his teeth. Her shirt rips as he claws to hold her. She sprawls on her arse and screams as she sees her blood for the first time. The scarlet leaches through her ragged T-shirt…

A girl, young, his age maybe, skin the colour of strong coffee, an unnerving glimmer of red in her eyes exactly the same as he saw in Hunter's, reefing him to his feet… He's drunk on his feet and his muscles are dough…

His mother, shouting, crying his name, over and over again, and his arm around the stranger, his feet dragging, and he realises, distantly through the crimson haze, that the girl's a lot stronger than she appears…

From the back door, looking over his shoulder and seeing Meg, horrified and staring as she holds her bloodied hands in front of her, and he's mumbling her name and thinking she won't want to stay with him now. His mother shrieks at him, 'Kevin', a long wailing siren that turns into an animal's anguished howl…

Stumbling across the yard and over the fence and across a paddock that feels as wide as the Simpson fucking desert, and it's hot underfoot, the earth still radiating daytime heat though the sun's well down…

A rubber bat dangling from the rear-vision mirror, and Deep Purple's *Black Night* blasting the cabin, the girl winking at him, her eyes the colour of red-gold honey in the dashboard glow and he thinks she doesn't look that dangerous…

The girl, asking, 'How are we?' and it takes a moment to realise she isn't talking to him, but a walkie-talkie. 'Lucky,' she says, and Kevin wants to scream 'bullshit', and she says, 'Thanks Hippie, see you back at the ranch', and then tells Kevin it looks as if they've made a clean getaway, but he doesn't feel clean, not at all…

Him asking, pushing the word out through the fog, 'Who...?' She says her name is Kala and tells him that everything is going to be all right and he laughs, a bitter choking sound, and closes his eyes as they speed away into the night because it's easier to swallow lies with your eyes shut...

The ride goes round, and round, and round.

SEVEN

The grain elevator sat like a rusting rocket ship next to the train tracks, the towering silos spotted black with missing panels, a skeletal gantry tacked to one side, broken windows staring out from the long cabin capping the tubes. There was nothing but dirt and mallee trees for miles; the lights of Barlow's Siding made a faint corona on the horizon. The site had been abandoned back before Kevin had left school, relegated to being a place to sink booze and get laid and drag race. The council had erected a mesh fence, as if none of the country kids could use wire cutters, and the sheds and silos were covered in graffiti and littered with the remains of camp fires, beer bottles and used condoms. It was a Thursday night, school had just started for the year, and he hoped to Christ that no-one was out here half cut and with their pants down. No-one other than him, anyway.

Kala circled the building and parked where they couldn't be seen from the road. She killed the motor and the headlights and the night came down, still and quiet under the cloudy highway of the Milky Way, the half moon riding high. She sat, hands on the wheel, as though catching her breath. She wore frayed jeans and a checked shirt open over an Iron Maiden singlet. At least she had good taste in music. A silver crucifix dangled from her ear where her spiky short-back-and-sides failed to reach. Her eyes were dark brown except at times when they caught the light in a funny way; they got a sheen over them, a kind of icy red glaze that made Kevin think of an eagle or a leopard maybe. That made him think of Hunter.

'Did you see anyone other than those women at your house; some suits, maybe?' she asked. 'Cops?'

He couldn't swallow. His heart shuddered; his lungs ached, airless. All he could see was Mira on top of him. God, it was as if he was right back there again, pushing against her weight, hearing her voice slicing into him like a harpoon:

You want to survive this, then you keep your mouth shut.

'No, nobody; just my family.'

'Lucky,' she said. 'Lucky your friends were there or you might have had a real unpleasant visit. You'd be dead now, probably. Your mum too, maybe. They don't like loose ends.'

'I'm a loose end?'

'Don't worry. Your mum will be okay as long as she plays the game. It's you they would've wanted.'

'What game? Who's *they*?'

'We should go. Taipan will wanna tell you what's what.'

She took the key. A glint of silver; a Mexican key ring, one half sun, the other moon. It disappeared into her palm, then into her jeans, her groin thrusting up toward the wheel as she manoeuvred to slide the keys away. She gave a slight moan, the kind that comes from sitting in one place too long, of muscles strained and joints locked.

That tiny sound electrified him from ear to crotch.

'Nice wheels,' he mumbled, for the sake of saying something, anything; afraid of the loaded silence; afraid of the unintended sexuality of her action, of the constriction in his chest, of the sudden and unexpected surge of lust stiffening his cock; ashamed that he could even notice something like the tight cut of her jeans at a time like this, let alone get a hard-on because of it.

'It might not be the most sensible car to drive out here, but I just love it,' she said, patting the vintage coupe's steering wheel with an affection that made him instantly jealous.

'Yours?'

'Black girl can't own a Monaro?' There was an edge to her voice.

'It's a classic,' he said. 'They don't make 'em like this any more.'

'No, no they don't.' Then, more gently, 'How are you doing?'

He cleared his throat. 'How do you think?' He rubbed his eyes and his face, crouched forward with the weight of the confusion filling his skull.

'Take your time,' Kala said. 'You're safe here.' The light came on as she opened her door. 'I'll go find Tai.'

Kevin could smell the abandonment; it drifted around him like smoke, filled the cabin, pressing him down into the seat. Kevin sat for a moment trying to make sense of it all as the last of the adrenalin drained from his muscles, leaving him exhausted. He fumbled for the door handle, then lurched out onto the ground and retched. When he was empty, his stomach a tight, collapsed hollow, he wiped the drool on his sleeve and pulled himself to his feet.

A whistle pierced the still, cold air. He pulled himself back to the now, to the fact he was alone with people he didn't know but who apparently knew something about what had happened to him and his family. He might, he knew with a rousing hit of realisation, die here.

'Whitefella,' a male voice called. 'Up here.'

Two figures perched like crows on a beam high above. Kala, and the biker who had... The biker from yesterday. *Today.* Only this morning. Taipan.

A rickety iron staircase led to a shattered remnant of landing near the couple. He made his way up slowly, aware of the tremble in the structure, the blotches of graffiti. He'd come here from time to time, to drink beer and make out around a campfire. This was the first time he'd been scared. He reached the beam and hesitated. The ground was a head-spinningly long way down, even if the beam was wide enough to sit on.

'C'mon,' Taipan said. 'Wotcha 'fraid of?'

Kevin gritted his teeth and inched his way along. The ground twirled. His guts tightened, hungry or nervous or both, making him dizzy.

Taipan sniffed as Kevin sat down beside Kala.

'You burn ya dinner, Kay?' Taipan asked. 'Stop for a sausage sizzle?'

'Bit of a mess at the house, but I got there in time. Just.'

'That blood part of the mess?'

'A girl got bit. But she's still kickin'.'

Taipan sniffed, patted his stomach. 'Makes a man peckish.'

'Shut up: you've been fed.'

His hand brushed her cheek and she pulled away.

It made Kevin nervous. The bar wasn't *that* wide. He wished they'd just sit still, damn it.

'VS was watching the joint,' Kala said.

'Them Hunters who picked me up at that old bitch's place?'

'Hippie didn't think so. A woman, he thought.'

'And no sign of them Hunters?'

'There was a four-wheel-drive; it followed the wrong car.'

Taipan gave a malicious chuckle. 'That Hunter, he ain't bin havin' a good day, has he?'

'You gonna tell me what this is all about?' Kevin asked.

Taipan took a packet of tobacco from his pocket and set about rolling a cigarette. Kevin watched with increasing frustration as the biker licked the paper to seal the cylinder, then tamped the end with his lighter before lighting up. Taipan offered the cigarette to him. Kevin waved it away. The biker's nose twitched. He asked Kala, 'This fella smell funny to you?'

'All I can smell is that stink you're so fond of.'

A curlew called, the high-pitched cry sending a shiver up

Kevin's spine. The iron felt cold through his jeans, the air fresh but thin as he fought for breath.

'Kala, why am I here?' Kevin asked. It was as if the biker could tell what Mira had done to him. Like he was just trying to decide the easiest way to kill him. He gripped the beam. 'What, what are you guys talking about?'

She turned to Taipan, but he just stared straight ahead through another noxious cloud of smoke.

'One of you, please – tell me what's going on!'

'You're a vampire,' the biker said finally.

'Piss off,' Kevin said.

'You're a vampire and nothin' can kill you,' Taipan told him. 'Nothin' much, anyways.'

'Yeah, right. And pigs can fly.'

'Pigs maybe. Not you.' Taipan reached behind Kala and shoved Kevin between the shoulder blades.

Kevin pitched forward, screaming all the way to the ground. He landed on his back. The impact knocked the wind from him, left his head ringing and his vision hazy. He could still hear, though, over the buzzing in his ears.

'Good one, Tai,' Kala said. 'What if he'd landed on something?'

'Like what? A wooden stake? That whitefella has to learn and learn quick if he's gonna make it. Not that I'm convinced that he should.'

'You can be such an arsehole.'

'You teach him, then. Maybe there's a bit more of the whitefella in you than the blackfella, eh?'

'That's not fair.'

'No, it ain't. You shoulda learned by now that nothin' is. Let me know when you've made up your mind.'

Kevin drew a deep, pain-filled breath and opened his eyes. Abstract shapes flitted across his vision like speeding clouds crossing the stars. He made out Kala and Taipan, standing on the beam.

'Take that whitefella to the farmhouse,' Taipan said. 'I gotta go pick up some gear, then we'll head for the coast. Somewhere with a bit'a cover till we shake VS off our tail.'

Kala's voice dropped, so low Kevin could only just hear. 'What about Willa?'

'She made her point.' Taipan rubbed his chest.

'Tai, be serious. After all of this, you're just gonna walk away?'

'Just leave it be.' He pointed at Kevin with his glowing cigarette. 'It's bad enough we got excess baggage.' He jumped and landed easily, on both feet, near Kevin. 'How you feelin' there?'

Kevin tested his vocal cords, the words coming out hoarse but gaining strength. The pain in his back and chest had subsided, making it easier to breathe. 'I'm okay. I'm alive.' Amazement burst into anger. He struggled to get to his feet. 'What the bloody hell did you think you were–'

Taipan pulled a pistol and shot Kevin in the chest.

Kevin slammed back into the ground, his hearing reverberating with the blast. He lay there, chest burning, gasping for air like a beached yellowbelly.

'Yeah, you're alive,' Taipan said, still pointing the pistol at Kevin. 'Lucky you.'

'Tai,' Kala yelled. 'That's enough!'

Taipan flicked the safety and returned the weapon to its place against the small of his back. 'That girl there, she'll look after you, eh. She plenny good at that.' Taipan shouted at Kala, 'Keep your eyes peeled, they'll be lookin' for us,' then walked around the corner of the building. A motorcycle shattered the quiet.

Kevin lay helpless, seething with impotent rage as the tail lights vanished. Kala arrived. She must have taken the stairs. He ignored her and finally was able to sit up. He felt his chest, and his fingers came away sticky and dark with blood. The sight made his throat constrict, his gut lurch. Jesus, it burnt, inside, like needles being stuck in his heart. A heart that had just had a bullet put through it at point-blank range.

'Was he for real?' he asked.

'What do you think?'

He eyed the blood on his palm, then wiped his hands on the ground, on his jeans, but he couldn't get them clean. The pain in his chest was fading. It didn't hurt so much to breathe.

'I guess,' he whispered.

She offered her hand and he let her pull him up.

Kevin eyed the beam overhead, the roughly Kevin-shaped depression in the dirt. 'Where'd he go?'

'Who knows? We're on our own for now.'

'I want to go home,' he said.

'It's not safe for you. Not for your folks, either.' She walked toward the Monaro. 'C'mon, you're gonna need somewhere to spend the day.'

'So the sun part's true, eh?'

'Yeah,' she said. 'Kind of.'

EIGHT

Kala nosed the Monaro into a rickety timber garage and cut the engine. The silence seemed almost solid, as though the world had changed with the turn of the ignition key. They had driven an hour or more, off the highway and along dirt tracks, until they'd idled over a grid and down to a farm house. Motes glittered in the headlights. A Sandman was parked in the bay beside them, a covered surfboard amongst the baggage strapped to the roof racks.

'Nice,' Kevin said. The panel van was fully tricked out with dolphins diving through sunset surf. The bright paint job seemed incongruous against the rough timber walls lined with cobwebbed hoes and rakes, coils of rusted wire, tin cans hanging on nails.

The headlights flicked off, plunging the garage into darkness. His eyes responded quickly, moonlight turning the doorway into a grey rectangle behind him. 'I know this farm,' he said. Kala sat quietly. Her breathing seemed loud in the quiet; fragile. 'The Crawfords'. You friends of theirs?'

'Never met them.' She opened her door, the cabin light making him flinch. 'We should get inside. It'll be more comfortable there.' She touched his hand. 'You'll be fine. I'll be with you.'

He pulled away. 'Like you were back at the house? At the silo?'

'We didn't have to save you, y'know.'

'Save me from what?'

'It was an accident, okay? None of this was meant to happen.' She stepped out and bent to look at him. 'You need something to eat, that's all.'

'That's all?'

She shut the door, leaving him in darkness again. He reluctantly levered himself from the car, then waited outside as she pulled the garage door shut. Timber slammed on timber, making Kevin jump. 'Taipan?'

'Nope, he'll be gone till tomorrow night at least, I'd say.' Kala kept her voice low. 'Don't worry. They know you're with me.'

The house loomed, dark and silent. Kala led Kevin up the few steps to the veranda. He paused at the top step as a bald, solid man stepped into the moonlight. He held a shotgun and wore a knife in a long, curved scabbard on his belt.

'This the bloke from the garage?' the man asked.

'Yep. Taipan made him.'

'Poor bastard.'

'Kevin, this is Budgie.'

The man answered with a nod.

'Who else is home?' she asked.

'Acacia, Hippie. Nigel. They might still be sleepin'.'

'We'll be quiet.'

'Reg and them went to keep the boss company. The others have already headed back to the nest.'

He opened the door for them. The back of his leather jacket bore the Night Riders' logo – a red-eyed skull with bat wings for ears. They went inside and down a central hall, passing several closed doors. There were pictures on the walls, a cabinet, but Kevin's focus was on Kala and whoever else might be here. The house smelled of dust and detergents and there was an undercurrent of something stale, something rancid – morning breath or mouldy cheese. Something else registered on Kevin's nose. 'Pizza?'

'Probably. Hippie's a pizza junkie.'

'I didn't think, you know–'

'We're not all vampires, Kevin.'

'Oh.' The word 'vampires' jarred. Despite Taipan's demonstration, Kevin still couldn't relate to it. The silos, Meg, Mira, his father: it was like a nightmare, no more real than a movie. Yet here he was, talking about pizza with these weirdos rather than sitting down to dinner at home. Tears burned in his eyes but he refused to let them fall.

'You can have some, if you want,' Kala said. 'It's not like you can't eat.'

'I'm not hungry.'

'Really?'

He shrugged. He was starving, but damned if he was going to admit it.

'I'm gonna get you something, anyway,' Kala said. 'You want a shower?' Her gaze lingered over his clothes, her nose wrinkling.

'Yeah, a shower'd be good.'

Male voices came from the kitchen, one whining, the other older, the drone of a hovering bee.

Whiny said, 'I'm tellin' ya, dude, we should be on the road. VS will be comin' hard after this.'

'No argument from me, man, but Taipan's the boss.'

'He should be bringin' us in, makin' us full blood. We aren't gonna be much use if the big kahuna sends his Gespensten-goons.'

'Hey man, I ain't in no rush to give up the sun. This fuckin' wolfbite's about all I can handle.'

A guillotine of silence fell as Kala and Kevin entered a large room with a lounge suite and dining table. Ammo boxes and guns – a motley tumble of assault rifles, sub-machineguns, handguns, sawn-off shotguns – cluttered the table; the area stank of gunpowder and gun oil. Leather jackets with the Night Rider logo hung from the chairs.

'This is Hippie, feeding his hairy face, as usual.' Kala pointed out a twenty-something bloke with long hair pulled back in a ponytail and a tattered shirt hanging almost to his knees.

The man waved a peace sign as the microwave dinged. 'Ah, McCain,' he said, and popped the door. The smell of freshly nuked pizza was overpowering.

'And Nigel,' Kala said. 'You might've noticed his board out the front on the shaggin' wagon.'

Nigel wore baggy three-quarter pants and a faded T-shirt. A headband kept his mop of sun-blond hair off his tanned forehead. Both men stank of cigarettes, and a sweeter fragrance, one Kevin had come across only rarely: marijuana. He half-heartedly held out his hand. Nigel kept his wrapped around a stubby of beer. Kevin put his hand in his pocket, feeling his face flush with the snub.

Both Hippie and Nigel had rashes on their faces, fanning out from their noses. Now that he could see Kala in the light, he realised she had it, too.

'Are you blokes–'

'Red-eyes, like Kala,' Nigel answered. '*Myxos*. You soon learn to tell the difference between master and servant.'

'Bathroom's there,' Kala said, a hand on Kevin's shoulder directing him to a door at the other end of the kitchen. 'I'll find you a spare set of clothes.'

He shut the door and flipped a wire hook through a loop on the jamb to lock it.

'Jesus,' he heard Nigel say, 'how strung out is he?'

'The boss back soon?' Hippie asked.

'Clear out if you want,' Kala told them. 'I'll handle it.'

'Watch yourself,' one of the men said, Hippie maybe, the voice muffled.

Kevin had no idea what they were on about, though he could almost smell their anxiety. He stripped, noting the crusty smears on his torso, a tan pucker where Taipan had shot him. Memories of Meg, scared and bleeding, made him nauseated. *You're a vampire.* Taipan's words haunted him, so unbelievable he found himself doubting anything was real. Yet the throbbing ache in his chest couldn't be denied. The mineral scent of bore water clouded around him with the steam as he luxuriated under the hot shower, scrubbing himself clean, letting the water spill from his mouth. He lathered himself again and again.

A knock at the door. 'I've made you breakfast,' Kala shouted, 'and I've got you some new clothes.'

'Give me a minute.' Kevin reluctantly stepped out and dried off with the nearest towel from the rack. He opened the door and took the bundle she handed him. He dressed quickly in the jeans and flannelette shirt – not a bad fit, well-worn, the jeans spotted with faint stains. He removed a towel covering the mirror and inspected himself in the spotty, steam-dappled surface. He ran a finger across his teeth. Everything appeared normal. He tried to convince himself the events of the past hours had actually happened, that he had been turned into something other than human. Something simply unbelievable. He felt normal. Totally normal. He pinched his arm. It hurt. Touched the wound on his chest. Felt the smooth, unblemished skin of his throat where that woman, Mira, had ripped into him. She was a ghost in the back of his mind, her thighs around him; her blood in his mouth.

And what about Meg? What had he done to her? She'd been so scared; so scared and so confused. Betrayed. Staring at his reflection, he wondered just who was staring back at him. Fury gripped him. All because of Taipan. 'You sonofabitch,' he yelled, relishing the release as he pounded the mirror to fragments. He clung to the edge of the basin, panting, fighting back sobs, watching uncomprehendingly as the cuts on his knuckles slowly closed.

The door shook as Kala hit it, shouting, 'Kevin? What's going on?'

He took deep breaths, swallowing down the panic and the rage as though they were razorblades. 'It's okay, just an accident.' He clenched and unclenched his fist, willing himself to relax. The sudden violence had helped release the pressure. Hold on, he told himself. Just hold on, and this will all make sense.

But my father will still be dead.

Kevin let out a deep breath, then used his towel to sweep the pieces of glass against the wall.

He opened the door. 'Sorry. I, um, broke the mirror.'

'It happens.' She brushed past. 'Drop your dirties out the back. Brekkie's on the bench.' She gathered his clothes from the corner where he'd kicked them, handed them to him and shut the door.

He heard the plastic crack as the toilet seat was dropped, followed by the echo of tumbling water. He walked away quickly, found no sign of Hippie or Nigel, so threw his dirty clothes onto the back veranda. On the bench, he found a slice of pizza, a mug smelling of coffee and another next to it containing a dark, steaming liquid. He gobbled down the pizza, relishing the bite of pepperoni. His stomach made a gurgle of disagreement. He reached for the coffee but somehow picked up the other mug; sniffed it, and cautiously probed the liquid with his tongue. It made his stomach growl, the saliva flow.

He almost dropped the mug as a woman spoke up behind him. 'Newborn, eh?'

He turned, embarrassment warming his face. It didn't help that the stranger was gorgeous, her skin shiny black, her face framed in dreads.

'I didn't hear you,' he stammered. 'I'm Kev. Kevin. I'm with Kala.'

'Good for her.' The woman leaned back against the fridge, dislodging a magnet shaped like a pineapple. She caught it in one hand and put it back in a fluid move so quick Kevin barely tracked it. There was a finger painting on the fridge: four stick figures besides a house under a yellow sun with long rays. 'The mechanic from the garage, eh?' the woman asked, as though nothing had happened.

'Yeah, that's me.'

She looked him up, down, up again. 'I'm Acacia.' She stood as tall as Kevin and was as wide in the shoulder. The sleeves had been torn from her denim shirt, revealing muscled arms. Several necklaces of beads circled her neck. She smiled broadly, her teeth white, eyes lit with humour, as she pointed to the mug in his hand. 'Don't let me put you off, mate. Most important meal of the day 'n' that.'

'You guys keep calling this breakfast but–'

'We work the night shift,' she said with a wink.

He nodded, and turned away from her to hunch over the mug of blood. It looked like tomato juice gone wrong. His gut churned. With his eyes closed, willing himself to stop smelling it, he sipped. Sipped and groaned in delight. It warmed him all the way to his toes. Numbed his forehead like a generous shot of OP rum. Before he knew it, he was lapping the last traces from the lip of the mug. An uneasy peace wrapped around him, as though he had just finished a huge meal and was ready for a nap. But he couldn't imagine sleeping any time soon. Not after all the weird shit he'd just been through.

'That all right?' Kala asked, a hand on his shoulder. Her fingers smelled of soap.

'Yeah, thanks.' He licked his lips and put the mug down on the sink, pushed it away from him.

'Rinse it,' she said. 'It stains.'

He felt his face flush again. He washed the mug and tipped it upside down on the draining rack. Vampires still had to wash up – bloody typical.

'Quite the neat freak, our Kala,' Acacia said.

Kala hugged Acacia and apologised for waking her. Acacia

brushed it away with a wave of her hand, then yawned. 'I was awake. Just wanted to see what was on the stove. He'll need more. A lot more.'

Kala nodded. 'There's not a lot left. I'm hoping Tai will–'

'He shoulda fed him already. The boy's barely standing.'

'He was in a mood.'

'Really?' She rolled her eyes, then added, 'I guess getting staked out by your own sister will do that.' She sighed. 'I'm sure he'll get around to feeding the pup. Anyway, I'm gonna stretch my legs. See if that storm's still building. Shout if you need anything.' She glanced at Kevin with what he took to be either suspicion or amusement, maybe both, then added, serious, 'Budgie's out the front.'

'Why don't I just jump in the car and leave? Get out of your hair?' Kevin asked.

'I don't think that's a good idea,' Kala said. 'Remember the girl at the house – your girlfriend?'

He stared at her, fuming, helpless, confused. Was surprised to see sympathy in her face.

'Stay till tomorrow night,' Kala said. 'When Tai comes back and everyone's, well, calmed down, then he can give you what you need.'

'And what's that? Another bullet?'

'More blood.'

He collapsed into the sofa. 'Was that what I just drank?' he asked, wiping his mouth.

'Decant. Stored blood. It'll keep the hunger at bay. For now.' She sat near him in a stuffed armchair.

'What the hell has happened? Who is Taipan, and why were those guys after him?'

'Until Tai gives the word, I can't say too much. It wouldn't be safe for you, and it wouldn't be safe for us. But basically, Tai found out his sister was out here, so he came looking, but there was a problem and she, well, I guess you could say she called the authorities, invoked a kind of restraining order. They were gonna put him away, but we stopped them. You just kind of got caught in the middle.'

'None of that makes any sense.'

'Sorry, it's the best I can do.'

'And my dad?'

'Unlucky, I guess.'

'Unlucky? So when can I go home?'

'Not now. Trust me, you're better off with us. We can look after you, teach you; and maybe later–'

'I hurt Meg tonight. Really hurt her.'

'She'll be fine. Takes more than a little love bite to turn someone.'

'To *turn* them?'

'She won't change, if that's what you're worried about.'

'Jesus Christ! I was worried I'd hurt her, not if I'd made her into something – something else.'

'Just be glad I got to you and not VS.' Kala walked to the kitchen and put the electric jug on. 'God knows what they would've done.'

If you tell Taipan what we've just done, you and me, he'll kill you.

He fought the memory, was amazed Kala couldn't see the guilt on his face. 'You guys keep mentioning them,' he said, looking for distraction. 'Who are they, this Vee–Ess mob?'

'Von Schiller. Kind of like, I dunno, BP or some other bunch of arseholes. They're based in Brissie, mainly, and try to lord it over the rest of us, tell us how to behave 'n' that. Real bastards. Anyway, they had a spy watching the house. We were lucky they didn't see us slip out the back.'

'Yeah,' he said, picking his words carefully. 'Lucky.'

Kala poured milk into her cup, as though making coffee and talking about vampires were the most ordinary things in the world.

She hadn't noticed Kevin's nervousness, the way he looked over his shoulder as though expecting to see Taipan there with an axe or a gun.

'VS has a lot of clout in Queensland,' she said. 'They got their hooks in the government and the cops and, well, pretty much everyone who's anyone.'

'My dad died today,' Kevin said quietly. The words seemed shallow; should he write them out fifty times? 'And no-one knows the truth of it.'

'There's no-one to tell,' she said. 'There's no-one you can trust. No-one who can make a difference, anyway.'

'There has to be *someone*. Dad's gone, the servo's gone – what are we going to do?'

'Your days of pumping petrol are over, Kev. Unless you want to run an all-night servo.'

He stared at the wall, trying to see past it to a future he couldn't even begin to fathom. The present was still far too slippery.

'Come on,' she said. 'It's getting late and I think we both could use a rest. Even you creatures of the night can use some kip, especially when you're still in the change. I'll show you where you can crash. We can talk more tomorrow.' Kala pointed toward the hall. 'This way.'

He followed. House dust tickled his nostrils, along with perfume and sweat, grease, nicotine, beer. And under all of that, the distinctive odour of blood. Damn, but he was still so hungry.

'This one,' she said, opening a door.

The room was about as big as his own bedroom. Black plastic had been taped across the window, a blanket draped across the mirror on the dresser. There was a single bed with a Star Wars doona, a small table and chairs, a box of toys. A khaki backpack sat on the table, showing a can of deodorant and a black bra through its open zip.

He hesitated at the door, reluctant to enter. 'Whose room is this, anyway?'

'Mine, now.' Kala yawned. 'We keep the mirrors covered as a courtesy.'

'Hey?'

'It takes a while, sometimes, to get used to the new *you*. Some never do, really.'

He flexed his hand, the cuts healed, the pain gone. 'Sure.' He sat down on the bed, making the springs squeak.

She grabbed the backpack.

'You're leaving?'

'I'll crash next door. You need your space, but shout if you need anything.'

He lay back, arms behind his head, eyes fixed on the ceiling spotted with stick-on stars and moons. It struck him that the false sky was possibly the most honest thing in his life right now. He was, apparently, a monster, one of many, and out there somewhere, out there in the world that he thought he'd understood but was clearly false, other monsters were hunting him. What in the hell could he do about that?

NINE

Reece leaned against the bonnet of the rental, feeling every minute of his 70-odd years. Not that he looked that old, of course. The past 40 hadn't left any marks – not on the outside, at least. Maybe he should just leave, find a beach somewhere and grow old disgracefully. Give young Felicity her chance to step up from Gespenstenstaffel to Hunter, to be Mira's new favourite. *Favourite* – he hated that word. Made him sound like a flavour of ice-cream. Maybe it was a little too close to the truth. He rubbed his face, wishing for a cigarette, but the Strigoi hated it when he smoked – the smell, the taste, *do you squander my gift?*

This was risky. The three of them out here like shags on a rock. He'd blown his cover with Diana Matheson, but Mira seemed happy with how things had gone. She'd had her tongue down Felicity's throat since they'd got back to the car; gasps and a metallic scent told him Mira was enjoying a celebratory drink. To hell with them.

He lit a cigarette, his hand trembling, and kept his focus on the forlorn house in the distance, its outline uncertain against the cloud-dark night. They'd done a drive-by when they'd arrived, then parked well down Barlow's Siding Road. And they'd got lucky: Taipan's red-eye had come in from the highway. If she'd noticed Felicity keeping watch, she hadn't given any sign. Any moment now…

Screams.

He straightened, hand on his pistol as he peered into the dark. Who knew how many Night Riders could be stalking them. The red-eye might've been a decoy or a lure.

'Our boy's up and about, then,' Mira said, her voice husky.

'Christ,' Felicity said, and he saw, from the corner of his eye, her brace against the car with one hand as she stumbled, her collar open, her throat smeared darkly. 'Is he killing them?'

Mira lifted a set of night-vision glasses while Reece fought the compulsion to run back to the house and jam his HeartStopper against the boy's ribs and put him down. *A boy has to eat*, Mira had said. Reece's stomach turned. This was wrong. So very wrong.

'There, across the paddock,' Mira said. 'The boy and a new friend. The Riders have collected their waif.'

The front door opened, a flash of light, and Reece could just discern the figures stumbling down the stairs: Diana and the young woman. What had Kevin called her? Meg. She had a patch of white – a towel, maybe – on her throat, and wasn't walking very well. Diana left her propped against the stairs and went underneath the house. She drove out in an old Falcon and helped the girl in, then sped off, heading Charleville way.

'Let's follow them,' Mira said. 'We'll have to make sure the girl gets treated properly at the hospital. Felicity: get an alert issued for the grease monkey. The Riders will think it strange if we don't throw up a few roadblocks.'

'You don't want to follow the boy?' Reece asked.

'Let them think they've got away.' She held up her hand; the blood bracelets crawled sluggishly around her wrists. 'The bloodlink's working. Once our reinforcements arrive, we can reel them in.'

Reece drove; letting pale, excited Felicity make the calls

from the passenger seat while Mira sat, silent and expectant and scheming, in the back. Felicity eyed him cheekily, the cat that had taken the canary, as though being munched made her special.

At the hospital, he made sure Diana saw him, and her look of pure hatred wasn't something he'd forget any time soon. But she and Meg played along and Mira had a word with the attending physician and was satisfied he'd take the money and keep his mouth shut. A nasty bite, she reported; the grease monkey had taken a good slurp before doing a runner with Taipan's red-eye.

On the drive back to Barlow's Siding, a call came in on Felicity's phone. It was a very satisfied Mira who handed the phone back after a short conversation.

'It looks as if our play with the grease monkey was wasted after all,' she said. 'One of Taipan's little playmates just offered a deal. The Night Riders are as good as ours.'

Great. Reece gripped the wheel tighter. *All of this fucking around for nothing.*

At the hotel, they found Constable Smith waiting for them. Mira and Felicity left Reece to handle it. Smith had gone out to the house and found scenes of a scuffle, some blood, and Reece fed him the official line about the gang having come back and the girl being hurt and Kevin being missing; an all-points had been issued. It was a federal matter, now.

Smith might not have bought it but he let it slide. The constable would bear watching.

Back in the room, Mira and Felicity were already naked and he made his verbal report as they watched him strip.

'Our men will be here by daybreak,' Mira said. 'Which gives us the rest of the night to paint the town red.'

He hesitated, one leg on the bed.

'Metaphorically,' she said as she pulled him down, then breathed out an exasperated, 'Gods, Reece: *metaphorically*.'

Much later, Reece sat on the rumpled, stained bed, feeling rumpled and stained himself from Mira's game of lick, sip, suck. His body was covered in bruises, gradually fading; the Strigoi did like to bite.

Usually, drinking would invigorate him, but now he was filled with lassitude and a thousand aches. All he wanted was to sleep. He lit a cigarette and wondered what Taipan would do with the newborn Kevin Matheson; if they found Mira's blood in his, it wouldn't be pretty.

Mira came in from the bathroom, her muscled body beaded with water, her short hair lank around the hard lines of her cheeks. There was no sign of the wounds from which he and Felicity had drunk, but the ruddiness in her face was proof enough of the blood she'd taken from them.

'You and your cigarettes.' She turned her back on him to open the veranda door and stand there, uncaring of whoever might see.

His eyes drank her in, the wide shoulders and the deep cleft in her spine still dewed and rosy from the shower, the shapely arse and toned legs. She had the body and features of a woman in her twenties, but he'd been around long enough to recognise the years of bloodlust that had sucked the excess flesh from her bones, that had pinched her face into a mask of cunning and avarice; to recognise the enormous age lurking in her eyes.

Mira was old enough to be bored but not old enough to give up, and that made her the most dangerous of the breed. And now she had a target – Taipan and his Night Riders.

She paced over to him and took the cigarette from his fingers, squashed it out in her hand, looked him deep in the eyes and asked, 'Why can't you overcome your nasty little addictions?'

'Been asking myself that for 40 years.'

'You look tired.' The way she said it, the way she looked at him: she knew. Forty years, and the blood was losing its kick.

Her Favourite was losing his flavour. Age was catching up with him.

The shower turned off.

'Felicity and I will be in the room next door. Get some sleep, Reece. Tomorrow's forecast is for cloud and rain. We'll take the Riders as soon as our men arrive, catch them in their pyjamas. They'll never know what hit them.'

TEN

The room closed in, the moons and stars glowing sickly green, cats eyes in the night. A Dalek glinted on a shelf. Books. A game console. A poster of a football team. A cricket bat, pads and stumps, sticking out of a plastic bin.

Where the bloody hell were the Crawfords?

Kevin sat on the edge of the bed, head in his hands, his guts clenching like a fist, his gorge rising. The door stood shut; he felt a pressure building on the other side. A pressure that bore down, bowing the timber, reaching for him, wanting to crush the breath from his lungs, the life from his body. He sprang to his feet, expecting the door to open, to find a grinning, bloody Taipan there with his mother's head in his hand, or maybe Meg, dead and bloodless. Gasping, he worked the window catch and forced it open. The night air rushed in, carrying the scent of dust and cow shit. He opened the window as far as it would go. Winced as the damn thing gave an almighty squeak. No footsteps. But no time to lose. Up and out, landing lightly on the balls of his feet, surprising himself with his balance.

He ran for the creek, that dark line of trees at the bottom of the slope the only decent cover in miles. Which way to town, to home? Right, he thought, with the moon behind him; his shadow a soft uncertain thing, preceding him over the stubble and the dirt as he sprinted, waiting for the gunfire, for the racing steps, for the motors. But there was nothing, just his footfalls, and he realised he could see well – very well – as he dodged the bumps and hollows, the stray logs. His breath came shorter and shorter; his vision narrowed. The ground tilted. He tripped, fell. He scrabbled to the windmill, clutched the rust-spotted frame for support and stared back at the house. No pursuit, no nothing. He lurched away, stumbling down the slope where water glittered dully in a pool surrounded by shrubs and trees, and farther down there was a crossing, the barest of trickles across the packed earth, the cutting indented with tyre tracks and hoof prints. He knelt by a pool, the scent of mud and rotting vegetation closing over him, but he splashed his face anyway, aware of the grittiness of the muddy water but relishing the cool shock. His stomach heaved with contractions. His vision blurred, the moon a wavering silver fingernail in the ripples he'd caused, the world shimmering till he could barely tell if he was looking at the moon in the pond or in the sky.

Reality slipped through his fingers like water; he held onto one thought – he had to get home. *The charcoal ruins.* He had to find his mother and Meg. *Screaming.* Had to know they were safe. *Bleeding.* Had to hold them. *Bleeding!* Had to.

He ran, sobbing, gasping, trying to stay beneath the level of the bank. Christ, he was hot. Burning up. He felt so empty, his guts wrapping around his spine. A bird called, the shrill, sharp cry of a curlew like a child crying for its mother, and somewhere a cow lowed, sounding scared. He staggered along, tripping over rocks and branches, skidding in mud holes, splashing through stagnant puddles. Then he smelled it – a new staleness, a cloying fragrance that belonged to abattoirs. Carcasses swinging on hooks, the concrete awash with red, the patter of it falling, the pungent scent of raw meat and fresh blood, the stench of shit and fear, fearful eyes bulging white in the crush.

Ahead, a twin cab four-wheel-drive lay crumpled nose-down

in the creek bed. A broken tree and flattened grass and churned earth showed where it had rolled over the bank. He recognised the vehicle. He'd replaced its shock absorbers not that long ago, the victims of too many miles of corrugation and stock grids. He crept toward it. A smear on the rear door. Mud? He knew better than that. He knew, deep down. And yet he reached, flesh and shadow joining across the white paint to rest on that silver handle. He heaved the door open. The cab light, strikingly stark, threw crazy shadows from overhead. A midnight raid on the fridge, light spilling out. He stared at the heaped pile of arms and legs, heads, naked flesh like candle wax. One child gazing sightlessly at him, his head bent backward over someone's thigh, his throat torn into pale shreds and hollow blackness. Mrs Crawford, stripped to bra and knickers, half covered in the middle of the tangle, long hair matted, lips torn, a frown on her face as though appalled to be seen in her underwear. Rusty streaks on her chest, staining the white of her bra. One nipple stuck out over the rim of the cup. He resisted the urge to tuck it back. Her husband, bare back arched toward him at the bottom of the pile, head and shoulder hidden in the foot recess.

Kevin stepped closer and closer, breath frozen, vision locked on the nest of flesh, the vacant eyes, the road maps of dried blood. He lifted a dangling child's hand, cold and soft. The smell of rot and blood and shit filled him. The smell of death. He sniffed, rolled that bony wrist between his fingers. Lowered his face, eyesight angling down, filling with a layer of crusted brown smears caking the tanned flesh, knobs of bone stretching the skin. Cold against his lips, so very cold. Raw chicken against his tongue.

Movement – an arm falling, a roll of head. He dropped the hand, jerked back, fell, barely registered the impact of stone on his palm, the other finding a splash of water and mud. He crawled away, eyes transfixed on the open door and the bodies within. He hit the bank and stayed still, cowering under an eroded overhang, roots like cobweb in his hair, the smell of earth wrapping around him; earth and mud and blood. He drew his knees up and stared and stared but the carnage remained. He sat there, too scared, too hungry, to move.

'Kevin?'

He blinked. *Meg?*

Shapes in the creek, approaching. Their shadows reached long and inhuman toward him. Reality crashed down as his senses returned, bright and clear and knife-sharp. He'd been biting his own hand. The dimpled flesh looked as if it had been pounded with a meat tenderiser.

'It's all right, Kevin.'

Fear in Kala's voice. Suspicion, too. Acacia followed her; the whiny surfer dude, Nigel, brought up the rear. He carried a military-looking rifle, like someone had shrunk an M-16 in a microwave.

'Taipan's gonna freak if he hears the pup saw this,' Nigel said.

'*If* he hears,' Kala snapped.

'Hey, that's not my worry. Taipan wants to go makin' any bit of trash he comes across–'

'Damn right it's no concern of yours,' Kala said. They walked spread out, as though through a minefield, converging on Kevin's hiding spot. 'Go and bring the van down, close as you can.'

'You want this?' Nigel held out the rifle.

'Take it, we won't need it,' Kala said, but Acacia grabbed the gun and sent him on his way with a jerk of her head.

Rocks and dirt cascaded where Nigel dug his way up the bank, but Kevin's concentration was on Kala, reaching out toward him as though he was a frightened kitten, even as Acacia said, 'Careful, girl, he's off his tree.'

'Kevin, come with us. We can help you. Honest. No-one's gonna hurt you.'

She was over-heating. An engine block boiling with oil. He could smell her, all coppery, rich like freshly ploughed soil.

He moved and she stepped back. 'That's right. Come with me. We can get you cleaned up. Get you sorted.'

'Jesus,' Acacia said, and her voice sounded so distant, as though she was speaking through a long tube. 'He's got the tremors, got 'em bad.'

'Let's get him back to the house,' Kala said.

'Hold this,' Acacia said, passing the rifle to Kala.

Acacia stepped up, a blur of motion.

He was on the ground, staring at the night sky, and then her face was over him, filling his vision. Something slammed into his chest, sank in, choking him from the inside out, and when she pulled away, so he could see again, he realised there was a length of round, smooth timber in his chest – a cricket stump.

Well and truly stumped. He wanted to laugh at the absurdity, to share the joke, to stand and grab Kala and kiss her and kiss her, but he couldn't move. Not so much as a twitch of a finger. He screamed but the sound was only inside his head, over and over, louder and louder, until the night came slamming down on him, starless and moonless and as silent as the grave.

ELEVEN

Confused, he wishes for wakefulness, but sleep has him fixed to the trail of dreams, and dreaming is remembering, even if the memories are not all his own.

Making love to Meg on a blanket beside the river

His father swearing under the bonnet of a truck

His mother stretching her back after an evening spent puzzling over the accounts at the kitchen table, and smiling as he places a cup of tea by her hand

Mira grabbing his cock and licking her blood-smeared lips

A woman with purple eyes, whose name is Mother, tells him to take care. She's afraid for what's waiting for him at Whitby Downs; she doesn't approve but she understands, and he's thankful for that, it's all he hopes for from her; and outside a dingo howls and dogs whine and his bike is waiting

The woman who is Mother tells him to take care. She's afraid of what he has become, what he might yet become; and he is a she, which is confusing but only after, when he thinks about it; and the words, spoken in farewell as a city door closes, spark such rage, such loss

*Khaki-clad police bundle a crying Aboriginal girl into a
cage on the back of a ute as though she is no more than a
stray dog and he screams at them to let her go and when
they come for him, he's happy, because at least they'll be
together*

There is much he does not remember, much that does not belong
to him. He does not recognise the abducted girl, yet, as the
incident whirrs by, all red-washed and hazy like a scene from
a horror movie, he knows it is intrinsically part of him. She
has been taken from him, and he wants her back. Wants her
back so badly he's prepared to not only die for her, but to kill.
The killing never ends. This, he realises, is what the woman
with purple eyes feared most, for these strange, anonymous
ghosts inside Kevin's bloodstream, who are part of him, but
not.

Kevin gasped awake, limbs and neck jerking. A door slammed.

Take care...

The sound so very far away; dream or real? Both? The scene
resolved. He was back at the house. The Dalek guarded him
from the shelf.

Exterminate.

He closed his eyes against the memory of bodies, jumbled
and lifeless.

When he opened them again, he realised he was naked and
clean with an ache in his chest. Then the hunger hit him, hit
him like a road train. He doubled over, groaning with need.
His senses surfaced, tentative, disrupted. Daylight pressed
down on the house, a fat man trying to choke him with thick,
sweaty hands.

A knock on the door. Kala – he smelled Kala.

He yanked the door open and stood staring, his muscles
taut. Saliva flooded his mouth as Kala, arm at full stretch,

handed him a mug redolent of heady blood scent. Kevin snatched the mug, unmindful as Kala pulled the door shut. He skolled the brew and lapped drops of scarlet from his hands. He ran a finger around the rim of the mug and sucked it clean. He was still starving, the sensation fighting against his own revulsion and fear.

Was he going to be added to the pile of bodies in the creek? Then why feed him? Why tell him these things, show him these things, if all they were going to do was kill him? Surely Taipan could've done it the other night at the silo. Or simply left him to Mira and this VS bunch. Only the faintest trace of a wound showed where Taipan had shot him the night before but there was a new wound, puckered and angry red over his heart. Out, caught behind. But the game wasn't over.

He dressed in clothes he found piled at the foot of the bed, trying not to think of their last owner. He took a deep breath, then stepped out. Time for the next innings. Voices carried down the hall and he paused, surprised at how clear the conversation was.

Kala: That was the last of the decant.

Acacia's gravelled bass: Taipan didn't give him enough. He needs to feed properly. He's caught in the change.

Kala: We need more blood. You want to go milking?

Acacia: Cow's blood isn't enough, not for a pup in the change.

Hippie: Ain't much in the way of livestock around, anyway.

Nigel: Just put him on ice and let Taipan deal.

Hippie: He's dryin' out, man. Got the DTs real bad. It's gonna screw up his change if he don't get fed.

Kala: Hippie's right, he needs fresh blood.

Silence.

Acacia: Don't look at me. He's already got Taipan's juice running through him. He doesn't need mine to confuse things even further.

Another silence, then Nigel: Sorry, I won't bleed for Taipan's new pet.

Kala: We could make a brew, each of us.

Acacia: From the vein, girl. It's not just the go-juice he needs, but the *connection*.

Kala: Watch my back, 'Cacia?

Acacia: Sure.

Kevin couldn't stand it any longer. He walked into the living room. Four sets of eyes greeted him, all scanning, curious, nervous. Nigel and Kala sat opposite each other across the coffee table, a plate of sandwiches between them. Acacia leaned against the kitchen counter, arms folded.

'Sleeping beauty awakes,' Nigel mumbled.

'How you feeling?' Kala asked.

'Confused,' he said.

Kala's hair hung loose and curling, her blouse knotted at the waist. Under it she wore a white bra, bright against her dark skin. She smelled of musk, of earth; a current passed through his body. 'Still hungry?'

'What's happening to me?'

'You're changing, still,' Kala said. 'You need to feed.'

'I guess bacon and eggs is out of the question.' The joke came out flat and bitter.

'No longer a basic food group.' Kala gestured to the sofa. 'Sit with me.'

When Kevin didn't move, she walked over and took his hand, led him across and pulled him down next to her. She undid her shirt. He felt the radiance of her flesh, dark and toned, and redolent in the aromas he had come to recognise as distinctively *Kala*.

Her hand caressed his face, the heat intense as her pink palm and fingers brushed his feverish skin. Her fingers caught at the back of his neck, pulling him down.

'Take your time. Be gentle. Acacia will watch over us, so don't be afraid.'

Acacia snorted behind him. 'Yeah, I love to watch.'

'It's okay.' Kala's voice quavered, her hand shook. The pulse in her neck beat like a bass drum.

Kevin shelved his shyness and buried his face in the crook of Kala's shoulder. He pushed the bra strap aside. She held him against her, her breath catching. Her flesh radiated body heat; carried the vibration of her speeding heart.

'Madness,' Nigel said, and stomped off, taking Hippie with him.

'What's his problem?' Kevin asked.

'Exactly that,' Kala said. 'His. He'll have to work it out himself. Forget him. I'm here, I'll look after you.'

He felt Acacia step up behind him, but she and the room quickly faded as his senses submerged into Kala, only Kala. His hands tightened on her firm body, desperate to feel her against him. His tongue lapped her skin and he tasted salt and soap; he smelled coffee and Vegemite and a rising musk that brought saliva gushing to his mouth. He kissed her tight flesh, burning against his lips. She gasped. He licked the pulsing artery, felt her windpipe bobbing with her ragged breath. Blood rushed through her carotid, thrust in a high-pressure stream from the heart. It thundered past like a coal train, then ran back along the jugular. His kiss became more desperate, making her whimper as his lips and tongue probed her skin. His teeth teased, drew a fold of flesh, squeezed, found the artery and held its delicate rush. Squeezed harder. Her back arched, thrusting herself into him, her hand a claw on his neck. There was a sudden throb of gum and tooth. She cried out under him. The gush filled his mouth with salty life. He sucked and sucked, deluged in a scarlet flood that swept away all reason, all awareness, sent him plunging into a whirlpool of desperate, crimson need. Buried in Kala, taking her into himself, Kevin fell into her kaleidoscope of memories, living each moment as though he was her, as they shuttered past, snap-snap-snap, dreamlike but all too real.

Everything is white except her and the road accident victim lying in the bed. Her uniform, the walls, floor, sheets: white. The patient is surrounded by machines, tubes, stands of dangling plastic bags.

Kevin's hand – the dark-skinned fingers long and thin, nails trimmed and neat, but yet undeniably *his* – reaches down to close the patient's staring eyes. The man blinks.

Snap

Taipan looms over him, thrusting, stoking the rising orgasm to the point where his body is just one, long scream. Taipan's face leans close, fangs glistening with drool, and the pain and pleasure take him higher than he ever thought possible.

Snap

The night is cold against his face, the bike vibrating between his legs, his hands clinging to the solid mass of leather in front as they ride under a full moon.

Snap

The bike stands nearby in a pine forest, the needles spiky and cold under his bare flesh as Taipan dribbles blood from his wrist into Kevin's hungry mouth. Two fingers of Taipan's other hand work between Kevin's legs, igniting a second fire. His strength grows with every scarlet drop he imbibes.

Snap

Taipan looks up, chin streaked with blood, eyes bloodshot, skin glowing. 'What did you just say?'

'I've had enough.' Kevin's voice is strangely yet familiarly feminine. 'I can't go on like this.'

Taipan answers, 'I need what they got.'

'I should be enough for you.'

Taipan stares and the accusation is plain enough to see.

Despair, fear, loneliness rise like bile. Without Taipan, what will he do? What will he be?

And then he gets the call – Taipan's call. And here he is.

Snap

TWELVE

Kevin stared up at the plastic light shade in the centre of the ceiling. He was on the floor, pain in the back of his head fading quickly. Acacia stood nearby with a broken cricket stump in one hand. She still had the pointy end, he noticed.

'Welcome back,' she said as she took a seat on the sofa.

Another piece of stump lay on the floor near him.

'Kala?' he asked, his voice thick, tongue heavy with blood aftertaste. His body was flushed, excited, eager. Yet he felt ashamed; Kala's lifestream still eddied through him, the emotions raw and powerful, making him feel like a trespasser. A trespasser or worse.

'She's okay. I had to let you know when you'd had enough, was all. Just a little whack. No permanent damage done. To either of you.'

Kevin sat up, dizzy with the sudden movement.

'You might like to change.' Acacia pointed at his crotch with the stump.

Splashes of blood spotted his chest; the front of his jeans showed a moist stain. He felt the cold stickiness followed by the burn of embarrassment in his cheeks.

'It happens, but it won't, not as often. After a while, it's all about the blood. Just the blood.' She sounded sorrowful.

Kevin stood, grateful no-one else was around, and went to the bathroom. His nose twitched at the assault of smells – disinfectant, soap, a touch of wood rot, urine. He rinsed his pants, his groin, his face, aware of red cheeks and lips all crazed in the mirror shards on the wall, the whites of his eyes showing bloodshot and pink. He returned to the lounge room where Acacia gave him the once over, then nodded her approval as he headed for the veranda. He hesitated at the door when he saw Kala leaning against the railing. Low, grey clouds promised rain. Storm birds called, answered by the harsh scream of a white cockatoo. It should have been just a normal day, an exciting day with the chance of a break in the long dry, but given what had just happened – the clammy wetness between his legs – it felt untrustworthy. You couldn't drink – feast – on someone's blood and then walk out to an ordinary world.

Kala smiled at him, then turned away. 'You can get away with a bit of sunlight when you're green, but the longer you go, the harder it gets. Just watch out that the sunburn doesn't creep up on you.'

'What happens then?'

'You've seen the movies, eh? Kaboom!' She clapped her hands and he flinched.

'You're kidding, right?'

'Yeah, I am. It's just slow and painful and messy. No fireworks.'

He walked over to stand beside her, his hands on the rail. Eyeing the thick clouds, he imagined the sun on the other side, straining to reach through to fry him. His skin crawled, but it was more the swelter of an open oven rather than the blow torch of impending incineration. The discomfort eased as he took in the view, each detail so clear, the line of trees marking the creek as sharp as a cut-out, the breeze cool and refreshing and smelling of rain. Kala's scent rose to tease him, musky and spiced with fresh blood. She'd put her shirt back on, her bare arms pimpled by the chill. A thick patch of sticking plaster covered the left side of her throat. Her skin was pallid, her eyes dark-rimmed.

Kevin swallowed, tore his eyes from the plaster. 'Did I hurt you?'

'I'm used to it,' she said, gaze fixed ahead. 'A couple of big steaks and I'll be fine.'

'I guess I need to thank you.'

'Feeling better?'

'The best.' He gave a nervous laugh.

She turned, grinning, her teeth so white. 'I'm good.'

He looked away, but she kept staring at him until he chuckled. 'Yeah, you're good.'

She asked in a low voice, 'What did you see, you know, inside me?'

'I saw Taipan give you his blood.'

'The secret to my youthful complexion.' She laughed, a touch of bitterness at the fringe, and then grew serious, moving to put her arm around him, her breast pressing against his bicep, her fingers cold. 'Sharing blood's as close as you can get to another person. It's an act of trust.'

If you tell Taipan what we've just done, you and me,
he'll kill you

'You okay?' she asked.

'Flashback,' he said. 'Whew. Just between you and me.' His stomach turned with the poison of deceit, even if he didn't fully understand it. 'I promise.'

Nigel leaned through the doorway. 'Sorry to crash the party, but Acacia wants us out the front. Someone's coming.'

THIRTEEN

They stood on the verandah, watching a stain of dust worm closer across the flats, a brown smudge against the grey of the storm-laden horizon. It was as if the vehicle was running from the storm, as well it might – the western sky was thick with dark, roiling clouds; lightning flashed in their innards and a chill breeze carried the smell of wet earth. Acacia and Kala looked apprehensive, biting lips, exchanging glances.

Nigel and Hippie stood next to the panel van, parked with its nose inside the garage with its bonnet raised. Both men clutched sub-machine guns in grease-stained hands. Motorcycle chrome glinted in the depths of the garage; Kala's Monaro was still tucked away in the second bay.

'Car trouble?' Kevin asked.

'Maybe,' Acacia muttered. She'd picked up a stubby assault rifle. Until he'd arrived here, he'd only ever seen those weapons on television. It explained the mess the gang had made of Hunter's four-wheel-drive. Hunter's four-wheel-drive and the servo; he couldn't afford to forget that. 'How's the van?'

'Good as long as you don't wanna go farther than the creek,' Nigel answered, without taking his eyes off the horizon. Silver-rimmed bullet holes spotted the purple paint. Cracks cobwebbed a window.

'Then we'd better hope that's Taipan coming.' She checked the sky, as though he might be parachuting in.

'Well, it won't be the Crawfords, will it?' Kevin snapped.

'No,' she said. 'No, it won't.'

'You just gonna leave them there, like that?'

'We'll burn them when we go. Can't risk the smoke till then.'

'Jesus! Just another "rural tragedy"?'

She shrugged.

'And what happens to me?'

She nodded at the approaching vehicle. 'I guess we're about to find out. It's a Rover, with bikes.' She relaxed her grip on the rifle.

'I'm gonna go wash off,' Nigel said, wiggling his grimy fingers.

'Dig Budgie out of bed, just to be on the safe side.'

Nigel stalked inside.

'Gets nervous, that boy,' Acacia said. 'Stinks like a wet dog. But don't you worry, young Kevin: no one's going to hurt you. You're Taipan's pup; we take care of our own. Nigel's been pestering Tai to come over ever since he joined up. Having you here – it's salt in the wounds.'

'He knows I didn't ask for this, right?'

She nodded and he felt Kala's fleeting touch on his shoulder, a sparrow landing and then taking off again.

'He doesn't see that,' Acacia said. 'Which is probably why Taipan hasn't done it. Ah, speak of the devil.'

They watched the ancient Land Rover beetle along the farm road, escorted by four motorcycles. A squeal of brakes; an urgent squeeze of his hand before Kala wrenched free and Acacia stepped to the stairs, leaving him abandoned at the rail. The vehicles pulled up and a half-dozen Night Riders scrambled from under the Rover's canvas. Kevin gripped the rail, bracing. Taipan dropped lightly from the tailgate.

'You all packed?' he asked Acacia.

'Sandman's still dicey.'

'No other trouble?'

'Just bringing your boy up to speed.'

'And how's that bin workin' out?'

'He's a quick learner.'

'Is that right?' He rubbed his chin. 'Is that right, Kala?'

She shrugged, a movement at the corner of Kevin's vision, and he felt as if he was meeting a date's father the morning after. Her father or her boyfriend. He kept his eyes averted from the weaponry as dread washed over him.

Taipan walked up to them. 'You taste him?' he asked Acacia, his voice a murmur.

'Hell no. He's your pup.'

He snorted, then rounded on Kala. 'How you bin, Kay?' Kala turned her face away to avoid his kiss. He gripped her chin so he could look her in the eyes. 'You're lookin' a bit pale.' He prodded the bandage at her neck.

'You told me to handle it,' she said.

'Not quite what I had in mind, eh.'

'Then you should've taken care of him back at the silo.'

'Had stuff to do, people to meet.' He pointed to the Rover. 'I knew you'd cope.'

'Then make up your fucking mind.'

Kevin bridled, his lethargy gone, his heart pounding. What was she saying? What was she saying about him? That he was just a job to her? Some kind of *trick*?

Taipan ran his hand down Kala's neck and pulled her into him. He stared at Kevin over the top of her head, his nose wrinkling as though he'd stepped in dog shit. 'So, our Kala's bin lookin' after you all right, eh, fella?'

'She's been very kind,' Kevin said.

'I know.' Taipan tapped his forehead. 'You bin havin' some of them dreams, fella?'

'A few,' Kevin said.

'Me too.'

'You know, I didn't ask for this.' Kevin squared his shoulders and faced Taipan full-on.

'Life's like that, ain't it?'

'I just don't understand why you seem to be blaming me for something you did.'

The other gang members stirred, all eyes fixed on him and Taipan. Worse than opening the batting or bowling the first ball. At a cricket match, the audience wasn't armed to the teeth. He focused on Taipan and the way the man was holding Kala against him.

'I'm not blamin' you for nothin',' Taipan said. 'I just got more on me plate than nursin' some whelp, that's all.'

'So why'd you do it?' Kevin asked.

'You mean you don't know?'

'The only thing I know for sure is that you're a cunt.'

Taipan pushed Kala to one side. 'Think you can take me, fella?' His eyes locked on Kevin's, his brown irises huge and tinted olive-grey in the muted storm light. 'Got a gut full of fresh juice and shit on the liver, eh?'

Kevin's heart hammered. His hands fisted. All he could see was Taipan's mocking expression.

'You can have first swipe,' Taipan said.

'Tai,' Acacia said, but didn't move.

Kevin took a step, fist back.

Fuck!

Taipan had him against the wall, pinned by the throat.

Just the way Mira had.

He clamped down on the thought, fear squeezing him harder than Taipan's grip ever could.

'Maybe I should take a taste, eh,' the biker said. 'See just how much bedside manner little Florence Nightingale there has been givin' you.'

Kevin flailed at Taipan, punching his face, arm, nuts. Like hitting a dozer.

Kala pulled on Taipan's shoulder. 'Tai, let him go!'

'This fella needs to learn his place. He's an accident, nothin' more. I thought he might be useful, but he ain't; just somethin' else for us to worry 'bout.'

Taipan's grip was so tight, Kevin couldn't even swear.

'Tai,' Kala shouted, half-plea, half-protest.

Taipan released Kevin, sending him stumbling against the rail.

'Why can't you just let me go?' Kevin said, a hand to his bruised throat.

'You think you can cut it out there, fella?'

'I can try.'

'Nah,' Taipan said. 'There's not a lot of me in you, but there's enough.' He rubbed his chest, an abstract motion. 'You better stick with us so we can keep an eye on you.'

Kevin and Taipan stood, stares locked, with Kala between them.

Light rain pinged on the iron roof. A misty curtain dropped around the house. Thunder rolled across the flats. Hippie stepped back into the garage, retrieved his jacket where it lay hanging on one of the motorcycles and shrugged it on. The new arrivals scattered for shelter. One woman pushed onto the verandah, complaining under her breath about 'wolfbite one minute, drowning the next'.

Acacia manoeuvred Kala out of the way. 'If you boys can put your pissing contest on hold for a moment, you might care to know that we've got company.'

FOURTEEN

The downpour reduced visibility to maybe the length of an oval. Kevin stared, trying to see through the rain, to detect whatever had spooked Acacia. Nothing. Just his anger turning to confusion and frustration. Lightning cracked and a peal of thunder shook the veranda. Someone rammed a magazine home with a metallic click, sounding insignificant after the storm's roar.

Acacia looked around, her nose twitching as though she could smell something rotten. 'They're out there, all right. Someone go fetch Nigel. And where the fuck's Budgie?'

'Here they come,' Taipan said with a nod.

The rain fell heavier and louder; thunder rolled over them like army tanks. And now Kevin could hear vehicles, low and rumbling.

Taipan sprawled doll-like on the ground, arms and legs spread wide as the report of a rifle shot echoed over the flat. Kevin reached for Kala but Acacia was ahead of him, throwing the girl to the ground as a ragged volley broke out. Kevin dropped to the floor. Muzzle flashes sparkled through the rain. Timber shards erupted from the walls. Bullets whizzed overhead. Taipan's gang returned fire, filling the air with man-made thunder and lightning.

'They're coming up from the gully,' a panicked voice shouted.

'Sneaky bastards,' Budgie said as he appeared on the veranda, unloading short bursts toward the creek. 'Usin' that storm to come at us in the daytime.'

'Inside,' someone yelled. 'Take cover!'

'No,' Acacia shouted. 'That's the fucking Strigoi standing up there. We have to get out of here.'

Taipan hauled himself to his knees, his chest bloody, and shook his head like a groggy boxer. 'That bloodhag? Here? I'd love to get me hands 'round her scrawny neck. But Acacia's right. They got us by the balls.' He grabbed a biker by the sleeve. 'Bring the Rover 'round. We can't lose that gear. The rest of youse, hit the bikes – meet up at the shearing shed.'

'You got it, Tai.' The biker pulled keys from his pocket and took a step. There was a sound like a fist hitting a punching bag and he dropped in mid-step and lay still. The keys shone dimly in his outstretched hand.

Kevin grabbed the keys. It was pretty obvious he was just as much a target as anyone.

He heard his father shout, *Son, wait.*

He stayed low.

Bullets whipped around him, thudding into the farmhouse and garage, clanging against the panel van, ripping holes in the Rover's canvas cover. He slithered eel-like down the stairs and across the ground till he could haul himself into the Rover. Soldiers approached from the creek, a line of camouflaged uniforms dashing in short spurts up the gentle slope. Others were advancing in quick dashes from the west, wraiths in rain, with vehicles following behind.

Mira, unmistakable in her coat, stood beside a vehicle identical to Hunter's custom BMW, with Hunter by her side. They wore body armour under their coats, and swords.

Swords! What the fuck? Bullets smacked into the Rover. Kevin hit the starter. A quick reverse and turn and he pulled the Rover up beside the veranda, its nose pointed toward the creek. 'Kala, get in!'

Men ripped the canopy aside and jumped aboard. Revving motorcycles added to the cacophony.

'Go,' Acacia urged. 'Go!'

The Rover filled with the clamour of automatic fire. Kevin winced, his ear drums shredding. Gunpowder wafted around him. He planted his foot. The Rover lurched off with a scrawl of gravel and mud. Bullets whipped through the canvas, rang on the body, shattered the windshield. Something punched Kevin in the back, stole his breath. He bent over the wheel, relying on body weight to steer as he fought to stay conscious.

'Straight through them,' Acacia told him.

The Rover ploughed over a scraggly lemon tree and tore down the slope. Someone stood behind Kevin, firing. Shells bounced around Kevin, stinging his skin, rattling on the floor. A man in a uniform appeared beside them. A gun barked and Kevin had the impression of the man doing a star jump, his weapon flying from his hand before he fell. Kevin wrenched the wheel to the right as they reached the creek, the vehicle jolting along the rough ground.

'Head toward the main road, best way you can,' Acacia said.

He nodded, heard someone say there were cars up at the house, some pursuing, and someone else asked if the rest had got away, if the bikes had been able to slip through the net. Wind shook the vehicle and rain pelted down. Kevin could barely see the ground ahead. But he managed to find a crossing and they nosed across the creek and up the other side and no-one, as far as he could tell, followed them through the downpour.

Taipan settled into the seat beside him, an assault rifle in his grip.

'Nice job, fella. Don't make us mates, but.'

'Suits me,' Kevin said. 'Is Kala all right?'

Taipan checked behind them. 'Yeah, we're in the clear. Keep drivin', that mob might be comin' still.'

'Who are they?'

'VS. The enemy.'

'They were trying to kill us!'

'Yeah, they do that a lot.'

Kevin stared at Taipan.

'Still wanna go it alone?'

He had no answer for that.

Taipan pointed past the bonnet. 'Watch the road, eh. We're not outta the woods yet.'

FIFTEEN

They drove south and east, using secondary roads and avoiding towns, refuelling from jerry cans when they needed to. Two bikes travelled with them. Once they were clear, Hippie replaced Kevin behind the wheel. It was a welcome relief. His arms felt heavy, as though he was carrying spare tyres in each; he could barely keep his eyes open. A result of his injuries, he wondered, or the daylight, reaching through the clouds to knock him around? Kala's slow kaboom. He crawled into the dimness of the tray with Taipan and Acacia to sleep away the rest of the daytime. Water sloshed in the floor though the rain had stopped. Half a dozen khaki crates stamped with yellow stencils vibrated noisily in the back; the sight made Kevin nervous. There were enough munitions to start a small war. He tried not to think about what would've happened if a bullet had hit the wrong spot.

'From a friend of a friend down south,' Taipan told him, and patted a nearby box marked SAM with all the affection of a man for his favourite dog. 'Even got us a splinter to stick in their eye in the sky.'

'Lucky that bird wasn't up today,' Acacia said.

'Mighta lost more if it hadda bin,' Taipan said, his tone bitter.

'Probably the storm,' Acacia said. 'Or maybe we weren't important enough.'

'Oh, we're important, all right. Important enough for that bloodhag to risk sunburn. We got lucky, is all.'

''Bout time we had some of the good variety,' Acacia said. 'Nigel, you figure?'

'I reckon.' He made a face, as though he'd bitten into something rotten. 'Wish I could get me hands on that surfer-boy.' Taipan bundled his jacket for a pillow and closed his eyes.

'Wish I could get my hands on that chopper,' Acacia said dreamily, her voice already heavy with sleep.

'You can fly?' Kevin asked her.

'I was a shit-hot stick bitch back in my day. Ha, my actual day, that is. Had to break a few heads to convince those white bastards that a black sheila could fly as good as they could, but I got there. Musterin', mostly. They called me "the black cockatoo".'

'Because you could fly,' Kevin said.

'No,' she replied. 'Because I had more balls than most of them rotor jockeys.'

He looked at her blankly.

'They reckoned I had a cock or two, geddit? Anyway, I had to give that up when I got bit. Not much call for night musterin', eh?'

'How about the black cockatoo and the white galah keep it down, eh?' Taipan growled.

'Needs his beauty sleep,' Acacia whispered. '*Lots* of it.'

'Shuddup if you don't wanna try flyin' again – without them wings.'

'So when was the last time you flew?' Kevin whispered.

Acacia went very quiet, the humour fading to melancholy, maybe; hard to tell what was behind those eyes when they were glazed with that opaque jade. She gestured to him and he stumbled over crates and people to sit next to her.

'I was flying Bells on a property in the Centre. Sweet machine. Reliable, great visibility. This one time, there I am in Alice, taking a break with my girl. We had to play it pretty straight back then. The boys didn't like it, seeing women off the market. Hardly a target-rich environment, you know what I'm saying? Good way to get yourself a beating or worse. So, we're in this bar, a bit quiet, off the main strip, eh, and this bloke comes in just after dark looking like he's walked barefoot and backward all the way from Darwin. Bad news written all over him. But he wants a pilot. He wants a pilot to fly him, overnight, to Adelaide. He has a briefcase full of cash. Thousands of pounds.

'I say yes. Cassie's against it. The bloke smells wrong, smells like trouble; but the money, that's different. I tell her, I'll be straight back, and with that kind of cash behind us, we can get out of the Centre, go anywhere we want. Somewhere we can hold hands in public without gettin' bashed. It doesn't sound like too much to ask, does it?

'So we skedaddle, right there and then. We hire a chopper from a contractor I know and fly to Adelaide. No sooner are we on the ground than the bastard jumps me. I've landed well out of town, there's no-one around for miles – I'm toast, right? But he gets a case of the guilts and brings me back. You know what he says to me? Last thing I hear before he bolts and leaves me to it, sun comin' up and that? He says sorry. Hunters got him not long after, so I found out later. Pity. I would've liked to have caught up with him myself to find out just how sorry he was.

'Anyway, by some miracle, I don't get sprung, and that night I fly back to the Alice and get my girl. Not as easy as it sounds when you don't know what the fuck's just happened to you and you've got a serious case of the tremors, eh, and we shoot through. We make a bit of a mess of it till Mother tracks us down and gives us some how-to.' She fixed her eyes on him, owl-like, staring into him, blinking like a camera shutter, her eyes flicking between brown and that luminous green. 'And we've stayed with her since, helpin' others like you to get their shit together. Not all of them stay. That's their choice. But we tell them what's what and how to go about things, give them their chance to stay ahead of the Hunters.'

'The Hunters. That's who just shot the shit out of us, right? Gespensten-something or another. Nigel mentioned them back at the house.'

'Same thing, different clothes.'

She told him to get some sleep, then, and he dozed, his body flushing fire and ice. The throbbing bullet wound in his back kept jerking him awake. Memories of the shootout teased him.

'Shit!'

'What now, fella?' Taipan grumbled.

'The bastards got Kala's Monaro.'

'One thing you whitefellas gotta learn,' Taipan said, 'takin' somethin' and keepin' it are two different things.'

SIXTEEN

Reece looked past his reflection in the window to peer inside the Monaro's cabin. 'You find any keys for this?' he asked Felicity, standing behind him.

She shook her head. It was still raining; like pebbles being thrown on the garage's unsealed tin roof. At least the thunder had moved on.

'Impound this. And see if the judas knows who used to drive it.'

'Didn't figure you for a car man, Reece.'

'I have hidden depths.'

'Yeah, real deep. Middle-aged crisis, much?' She pulled up the hood on her anorak and squelched back to the house. She still limped, having taken a bullet during the charge on the farmhouse. He'd told her to hang back, to let the troopers go in first, but she hadn't listened. Maybe if she'd seen Dave lying on the stretcher with a fistful of face missing, she'd have been a little more cautious.

Reece had stuck close to Mira; hadn't shot anyone nor been shot by them. Should've been more enthusiastic, he supposed, his career being in the balance, as it were, but he couldn't shake that expression on Diana Matheson's face: the fear, the loathing. You'd think a copper would be used to being despised, but there you go. And just for once, he'd earned the enmity. He ran his hand over the car's roof – nice, real nice, though the bullbar kind of ruined the shape – and paused on the way out to check the Sandman once more. He'd seen it before, too; yesterday morning, blocking the road and then chasing him and Dave. He stepped out into the soaking rain, relishing the cold hit on his face and neck, washing away the urge to take the surfie and drown him in a pothole. The arsehole had been one of those who'd hounded them into the roadhouse, who'd killed Dave and, inadvertently, left a woman a widow and her son doomed.

'They're heading east,' Mira shouted from the veranda.

He splashed across to join her.

'He tell you that?' Reece asked, indicating the surfie. He was handcuffed to a veranda post and Felicity had him up against the rail so his back was getting saturated. The judas looked miserable. Perhaps he was starting to realise just what a bed of nails he'd made for himself.

'The blood,' Mira said, lifting her left hand to show her bracelets of scars. 'Vague but good enough till I decide to pay the grease monkey a dream visit. Young Nigel hasn't told us anything we didn't already know. Wish I'd brought a toothbrush; traitors always leave an unpleasant taste in the mouth.'

Reece checked the surfie again and noticed the russet dribble crusted on the man's neck. She hadn't healed the wound, just left it to close up naturally. He was a red-eye; it wouldn't take long.

'We've turned this place inside out. Call it a day?'

Mira shook her head. There was a reddish sheen on her forehead and cheeks, a flush on the throat where her hood didn't quite cover it. 'Not till I know there's no clue to the location of the Riders' nest.'

'Nothing at all from the surfie?'

'Useless. I get the idea that Taipan never trusted him.'

'And you do?'

'Don't be stupid. But the blood doesn't lie. Not to me.'

'A girl drives the Monaro,' Felicity reported, standing away from Nigel as though treachery was contagious. 'Half-breed called Kala. Got a soft spot for the mechanic, apparently.'

'Taipan's moll,' Nigel added, as eager as a puppy to please. 'Real stuck-up little slut. Opened a vein for the pup as quick as you please.'

'Jealousy's a curse, isn't it?' Mira said to Reece.

'Speak when you're spoken to,' Felicity told Nigel, emphasising the point with a slap on the head.

'So's avarice,' Reece said to Mira, then asked Felicity, 'Got a final count?'

'Four cold even, all red-eyes; no prisoners.'

'Eight dead, no vampires. Not exactly a runaway success.'

'Taipan's proving as slippery as his namesake,' Mira said. 'Damn it.'

He thought she was going to take another shot at him for having let Taipan escape in the first place, but a four-wheel-drive pulled up. Felicity excused herself to talk to the driver. 'They've found something down in the gully,' she reported.

'I didn't do it,' Nigel said, and Reece felt like slapping him, too. Had Mira promised him immunity for his crimes? Justice sometimes really was blind.

'It's the family who own this place,' Felicity relayed. 'They're all dead.' She hesitated.

'Yes?' Mira demanded.

'They bled the two children. Decant, by the looks, but they did bleed them.'

Mira snarled. 'I want that bastard, Reece. I want him on ice.'

'Why him, Strigoi?'

'We are a self-policing society, Reece. It's how we keep the herd off our back. We take care of our own business.'

'But if you weren't chasing the Night Riders, they wouldn't

be running. They wouldn't need to do the things you don't want them to.'

'I'm starting not to like you.'

'I was a cop for twenty years. It's all about motive.'

'Motive and opportunity, *detective*. Am I right?'

He nodded.

'Well, right now, I have the opportunity. The motive is none of your business. Be satisfied that I'm trying to take a pack of killers off the streets, and know that the rewards for those who help me will be substantial.'

Felicity joined them on the veranda. Maybe the word 'rewards' had carried. Red-eyes' hearing was exceptional, especially when the subject interested them.

'What will we do with the judas?' she asked.

'We had a deal. We'll honour it. In our own time. Take him back to Jasmine's and see if he can't make himself useful. I want you to keep an eye on things there.'

Reece said, 'Turner won't like that. She'll see it as interference.'

'Whitby Downs, her own side project notwithstanding, presents a sizeable investment on our part. She's stepping up as a serious part of our bovine food chain. She'll fall into line, or just fall. Her choice.'

'I'll tread lightly,' Felicity said. Her tone soured, though, as she asked, 'May I ask where you and Hunter Reece will be, Strigoi?'

'Back in 'Bane. Hunter Reece will be kicking aircraft mechanics in the balls until they fix my helicopter. And I will be paying a visit to another mechanic. With what I've got in mind, a kick in the balls will be mild by comparison. Now, let's get the hell out of this daylight before we all lose another layer of skin.'

SEVENTEEN

Commotion woke Kevin, but by the time he'd clawed his way to alertness, he was alone in the back of the Rover. He felt like shit, that was a fact. Cold and very thirsty, he pulled himself upright on one of the crates and scanned his whereabouts. Flat plain dotted with Mitchell grass like a mangy dog's coat, distant trees blending into the darkening sky. The remnants of storm clouds stretched like threadbare rags, dyed pink and purple by the last rays of sunset.

'We're here, sleepyhead.' Kala peeked in over the tailgate. The tattered canvas looked like a tent flap. 'Give us a hand to unload, eh?'

He pulled himself to his feet, feeling groggy. 'Where's "here"?'

'The Shed.'

He folded the canvas back and they dropped the tailgate. The Rover had been parked close to one wall of a long, tin building. There were gaps where sheets of corrugated iron had come loose. The yards, not a straight post or rail to be seen, were being reclaimed by scrubby trees, and a fig was prying at the far wall with its tentacle roots.

Kala introduced a bloke called Reg – he sported an impressive blond mullet – and a red-eye, Penny, a sparrow of a woman dressed in jeans and a matching leather vest, her skin the light brown of weak tea. Reg pocketed a set of wraparound sunglasses, highlighting the raw oval of sunburn around his green-glowing eyes as he gave Kevin the once-over. Penny's narrow, almond-shaped eyes measured him from under her black fringe like a crow assessing road kill. A faint butterfly rash dotted her face; her eyes flashed red. The rash showed on her throat, too, highlighting a set of four dark dots, pimples or a tattoo maybe, just above her collar.

Reg was round like a grain-fed bull, the kind of body Kevin equated with men who blocked the doors of back-alley strip clubs and tattoo conventions. Most of the Night Riders had physiques that brought to mind folk who had grown old in the saddle with skin parched from too much sun. Was Reg just not as old yet for the vampire inside to have sucked him dry, or was he just better fed? Penny, on the other hand, looked as if the only thing holding her up was piss and bad manners. She had an energy about her, a jumpiness, that his mother would probably have politely described as being highly strung.

'You gonna pass me that Esky or stand there starin' at me tits all night?' she asked.

He slid the Esky down to her.

'That's light, anything in it?' he asked.

Kala laughed. 'You wanna watch what you're throwing around, Kevvie. You're stronger, now. Stronger, faster – a regular Six Million Dollar Man, eh?'

Penny hoisted the Esky. 'You better learn it quick before you go shakin' hands with anyone.'

Kevin grabbed a crate of camping gear. Nowhere near as heavy as he'd have expected. The extra muscle could've come in handy around the garage. The thought turned sour and he shoved the crate down to Kala, followed by another.

'You right with that, sport?' Reg asked. 'I'm gonna wheel the bikes round into one of the pens, get 'em out of the weather.'

Kevin nodded.

'I'd get a move on. It's smoko time, eh.'

Kevin jumped down from the Rover, grabbed the last crate and followed the women inside.

The gang had made camp along the shearing board, a timber platform butting up to the pens. Kevin waited inside the door for his eyes to adjust; grey twilight drifted in on the dust through the open hopper window. Someone had propped the swinging shutter open with a stick, but the room remained heavy with the smell of lanolin, dirt and ancient shit. He was probably breathing it in; the powdered leavings of thousands of sheep who'd passed through this place. Webs clustered thick in the corners and some of the posts were smeared with bird shit. Snakes must love it, he thought.

One road bike was already parked in the nearest enclosure; Reg wheeled the second one in as Kevin looked for a place to land his cargo.

Hippie, smoke dangling from his lips, took Kevin's load. 'Siddown, mate, before you fall down,' and Kevin leaned back on a handy rail.

Reg dumped a full-face helmet and long Driza-Bone and eased down onto the floor. 'Got some serious wolfbite, man. Bloody clouds thinnin' out like that. I'm red all over, I reckon.'

Taipan pointed at Kala. 'That myxo could've taken the Beamer.'

'Nah, it wasn't like I couldn't handle it.'

'No-one rides *the Beamer*, eh,' Penny said.

'Just glad we got here when we did, that's all I'm sayin'. Could use a drink, though.'

Penny slipped away from his reaching hands and busied herself helping Hippie open tinned fish and beans. Kala boiled a billy of water on a small gas stove. The air became spiced with canned sardines and tuna, sweet tea, strong instant coffee...

He hates the espresso machine. He hates having to serve at the counter and he hates having to use the

register for anything other than fuel, but most of all he
hates that bastard espresso machine. 'You can fix an
18-wheeler but you can't steam milk' his mother
laughs, and his father adds, 'I'll have a tea,' sharing
the joke, time and time again, never growing tired.

Kevin swayed under the power of the memory, had to grab at the rail to steady himself.

'I'd kill for a steak right now,' Penny said, dribbling beans back into the can off her spoon.

'Wouldn't we all,' Taipan said, eyes locked on Kala.

'You say scotch fillet, I say O-negative,' said Reg, and Taipan laughed.

Kala carried a mug over to Kevin. 'How are you travellin'?'

'Just,' he said.

She held out the coffee; their fingers touched as she passed the mug to him. 'Hope you like it black.'

'I don't mind it,' he answered, and smiled.

She smiled back, coyly, then asked quietly, 'You want something harder?' She tapped two fingers against her inner elbow. 'You don't look so flash.'

'I'm okay,' he mumbled, and licked his desert-dry lips. He tasted the coffee, winced – like sour creek water.

'How's that back? I saw you took a hit.'

'Sore.'

'And the rest of you?'

'Like I might be coming down with something.'

'You sure are.'

'Like a fever. Kind of hallucinating or something, you know?'

'You're in the DTs,' she said, taking his hand, removing the shaking cup, tugging on his arm. 'I can help you. C'mon, we can go down the wool floor if you don't want that mob to see.'

'Kala!' Taipan pointed to the Esky. Its lid had a cross scrawled on it in red marking pen. 'A blood bag'll do him.'

'But Tai–'

'Give him his feed than get your skinny arse over here.'

The building was very still, very quiet. Everyone was looking at Kevin. What did they expect him to do?

'Smoko,' Taipan announced.

'All right!' Reg slapped his leg and yanked Penny to her feet, squashing her against his chest.

'You go easy on that girl,' Taipan told him. 'You bin tappin' her hard by the looks.'

'Fuck, Tai, a man's not a camel.'

'Still, we got a way to go yet.'

'I been shot up good, Tai.'

'If she can handle it. Otherwise, you tap Hippie there.'

'I hate the taste of his weed, man.'

Penny pulled against his grip, but he held firm.

'Reg,' Acacia said.

'C'mon, Penny,' he pleaded. 'Just a dram to keep me going.'

'When do I get mine?' she asked, and there was bitterness there, a hardness that pulled at her lips and turned her eyes to neon glass.

'Once I got some fresh stuff under my belt,' Reg said. 'When I can spare it.'

She rolled her eyes, mouth set tight, but pushed her sleeve up.

Penny murmured, 'bastard', and then her features went slack, the anger draining away; she slumped into Reg, moaned, swayed, whimpered. In that moment, she looked tender, soft; vulnerable. Kevin looked away, his guts churning, telling himself he was revolted.

'Hippie,' Acacia said with a toss of her head. 'I don't mind the taste of your weed. If you can spare a drop.'

'Always got a drop for you, Acacia.' Hippie walked over to her, complaining good-naturedly that he hadn't had time for a decent smoke in days. He reefed off his T-shirt and allowed her to drink from his throat.

'There'll be brew at The Farm,' Taipan said. 'You myxos will just have to put up till then. C'mon, Kala, get a move on. You know I don't like waitin'.'

Kala came to Kevin with a coffee jar. It was about two thirds full, the sides splashed with a viscous red stain that made him think of transmission fluid. Groans, the wet smack of lips on skin; the aroma of fresh blood. The pain in Kevin's back intensified. His eyesight cleared, but dark edges irised in until all he could see was the jar and the hands that held it. The lid unscrewed and he had it, like a cat on a mouse, and he gulped it down. He slid to the floor, cradling the empty jar like a dero nurses a bottle. His back blazed. He gave a little cry, jerked forward. A nail? A splinter sticking out of the wall? A metallic clunk. Kala knelt and took his hand and dropped something into his open palm. A mushroom-shaped piece of metal. He'd seen the like before, from shooting targets. A squished bullet.

'Souvenir,' she said.

'Kala,' Taipan shouted again. 'That fella ain't the only one sufferin' from lead poisoning.'

Kevin watched her walk away, across to Taipan, and he felt the blood boiling in his system, and he knew, as Penny slumped and Hippie shuddered, that he needed more. Lots more.

Kala stood in front of Taipan and reached up her arm.

Two fingers tapping against her dark brown arm, the veins standing purple under the skin

But Taipan, watching Kevin over her shoulder, tore off her shirt and pulled her singlet and then her bra down around her waist. She stood there like a soldier at attention, arms pinned by her clothes, as, eyes locked on Kevin's till the very last, Taipan bit into the side of her neck. Slowly, ever so slowly, then in a last rush, her hands came up to grasp him to her as her knees buckled.

Kevin stumbled out of the shed, finding his way through the pens and down the ramp and out into the falling night, the night of tortured clouds and distant stars and a curlew's girlish call. Kala's moans followed him like ghosts sitting on his shoulders. He walked out into the paddock until he couldn't hear anything but the night, and he clenched the bullet tight in his fist, as though he needed any further proof that this was all too real.

EIGHTEEN

Kevin stood, amazed at how well he could see, how well he could hear, how he could almost measure the millimetres his feet were sinking into the saturated ground. How he could sift the scents of the earth and the trees; the lanolin and sweat and shit soaked into the shed's timbers. He thrust the misshapen bullet into his pocket and pulled his hand back as something jabbed him. His house keys. He pulled them out, ran his thumb across the teeth of the front door key, pushing it down hard against a sky-big yearning to just run. The key to a home he wasn't even sure he could go back to without being arrested. Without having to face questions he couldn't answer. He wished with a strength that made his heart ache that he could ring his mother, just to know for sure she and Meg were okay. To say sorry.

'Always nice after rain,' Acacia said, scaring the hell out of him. She hadn't made a sound.

'Just a quick bite, then?' he asked, and she winced. Damn it, but he'd thought she was different to the rest. To Taipan. He pushed the keys back into his pocket.

'Those myxos are runnin' low; I only took what I needed to stay sharp. But I'm concerned about how you're goin'. That baggy wouldn't have gone far, not with a bullet in your back. Not when you're still in the change.'

'Like you said, those myxos are runnin' low.'

'Don't go cuttin' off your nose to spite your face, Kev. They give and we take, and then we give back. They're the ones who are here coz they want to be.'

'They want to be?'

She stayed quiet, letting him process, letting him try to work it through.

'She wants to be,' he mumbled.

'Not what you expected?' Acacia asked.

'None of it. I didn't expect none of it. Didn't know about it, didn't want to know about it. Don't want it.'

'Some of us don't get the choice. That's life, isn't it? It serves it up and you just deal, best you can.' Acacia touched his shoulder. 'The rules are different for us. It's not all bad, you know.'

'No?'

She looked around, as though cataloguing: moon, trees, earth. 'It's nice after the rain, isn't it?' she said again.

'Yeah, it is,' he conceded, and then the frustration boiled out again. 'I still can't believe all this shit. A couple of days ago I was looking at nothing more than working the servo, hoping that Meg and I had some kind of future out here. Now I'm wondering how I'm gonna find enough blood to drink and keep from getting shot.'

'It's a rough ride, I know, and Taipan isn't the most caring father, is he? If it's any consolation, he's not exactly over the moon about havin' a whitefella in his blood.'

'That bastard is *not* my father.'

Taipan's rough voice interrupted them. 'Talkin' 'bout me?'

'Yeah,' Acacia said. 'I was tellin' the lad here what an arsehole you are, but guess what? He'd already figured it out for himself.'

'You said he was a quick learner, eh. I need to talk to the fella.'

'Sure. Play nice, now.'

Acacia melted into the night with the silent grace of a deer, leaving Kevin and Taipan alone. Kevin wished she'd come back.

'I got somethin' I gotta give you,' Taipan said. 'Not the best, me bein' hurt, but I gotta do it now before you get too far along.'

'What's that?'

'The change. You got one foot in, one foot out. Bit like us blackfellas, not belongin' nowhere proper. I gotta give you some more, finish it off.'

'I feel better,' Kevin said. 'After that – drink.'

'Not as good as you will. Trust me. It's a real buzz, fella.'

'What if I say no?'

'Then you stay what you are now: piss-weak man, piss-weak vampire.'

'Fine. What do I have to do?'

Taipan held out an arm. 'Just drink.'

'You got a cup?'

'I am the cup.' Taipan raised his other hand, knife glinting in the wan light. 'You need to get yourself one a these. Cleaner, eh.'

Kevin stared, his body running cold.

Taipan slowly drew the blade across his wrist. The blood glistened darkly in the moonlight as it welled, then dripped to the ground. The scent invaded the air.

Kevin hesitated.

Taipan thrust his arm forward.

Kevin tasted, just a lick.

'Better than that bottled shit, eh? Fresh is best, fella: remember that.'

Kevin moaned as the world submerged under a red tide. He dived in. Taipan surged into him with every desperate swallow.

Kevin lost himself.

He was no longer Kevin.

He was Taipan.

The ache is intense. A constant, corrosive emptiness that not all the blood and brawling in the world can fill. There is a house, a two-storey homestead, distinctively Queensland with its corrugated iron roof and white weatherboards and curved iron awnings. A separate building at the back houses seasonal workers. Massive sheds cover harvesters and tractors. A railway line cuts through the surrounding cane fields, used only during harvesting season when the diesel locos pull long trains of steel cages heaped with freshly cut stalks off to the mill.

This is the house of sorrow; a white house for white pain. A winnowy girl dresses in white and serves tea. She is barely pubescent, her breasts budding. Her hair is worn in a bob cut under a white cap; her long, thin legs are clad in white stockings, her slender arms covered by long sleeves. Her face is round and radiant, her brown eyes alert with humour. She likes serving tea. It is all she has known, serving tea and being taught to play piano and cross-stitch, to cook and to mend and pronounce her 'ings'. She loves swimming in the creek and running in the moonlit fields when they are bare and furrowed, waiting for replanting. She loves visiting the nearby beaches at Hervey Bay; loves licking ice-creams on the esplanade and riding the dodgem cars and shooting pool.

Taipan hates it. He refuses to pronounce his 'ings'. He hates the starched clothes, he hates the tea, he hates the white boys making jokes about his sister, the vile hunger in their eyes feeding on every patch of skin she shows, the way they whisper too loud the words of hate – boong, Abo, coon. She is his sister and he hates everything about her. Yet he loves her so intensely it burns. His mind and heart rage. He remembers when the coppers came and herded the children like dogs into the paddy wagon. Being slapped for speaking his tongue, learning to say the Lord's Prayer under the nuns' hawkish gaze. Being inspected by the good Christian folk looking to save his soul. Hitting the man who would have taken his sister and left him. Remembers sensing something different about the woman with her hair in a bun, her tiny glasses, her elegant stature, the billowing skirt and cameo at her neck-high collar as she picked his sister and him from the dorm one night. Jasmine calls them Christopher and Heather but he refuses to use those names. She is Willa, only Willa.

He finds Jasmine with his sister one night, all blood and fangs and licking tongue and thrusting, caressing fingers. She uses his love of his sister, his now monstrous sister, to keep him prisoner. When he is at what she calls his manly peak, Jasmine comes for him, too, seeking to quell his rebellious nature with her own bloody power. But it works the other way, the blood fuelling his resolve, giving him the strength to break free, plumbing depths of strength as old as the earth itself. He manages to wound Jasmine before jumping from an upper storey window. With a vow to free his sister, he flees into the night. An owl watches him leap the perimeter fence and push through the green cane. He takes the bird as a good omen; his sister will be protected in his absence.

He becomes Taipan but she remains Willa, always Willa. She is the ache that won't dull, the emptiness that can't be filled, the shame that can't be washed clean.

NINETEEN

It was fully dark when Kevin came to his senses. He stood and brushed at the mud caked to him. The half moon had dropped in the sky, but it was brighter than he remembered; much, much brighter. The stars felt close enough to touch. The softest of breezes caressed the hairs on his arms. The scent of fresh exhaust. Voices. The Night Riders had guests. He walked back to the shed, noting the bikes parked near the Rover.

Hippie shouted to him from where he sat puffing on a sickly sweet cigarette. The scent triggered a memory of Derek and Hippie in the farmhouse, of that aroma draped around them like a feather boa.

'Back from walkabout, eh? Budgie and his boys arrived just a jiffy ago. G'arn inside outta the cold.'

'You coming in?'

'Nah, I'm on guard duty, man.' He blew a cloud of smoke and chuckled. 'I'm the high in the sky.'

Kevin headed for the door. He'd never seen much in the way of drugs. Some of the lads on the cricket team had had grass, but that was about it. He'd never got the point, never understood the trade-off. Never wanted it bad enough to get a boot up the arse from his old man.

He paused at the door, feeling like a gatecrasher as the

hubbub filled the room on the other side. *Never had any time for drugs, and look at me now.* He pushed through the noise barrier, stepped onto the shearing platform and damn near tripped over Penny. She was sitting with her back to a wall and a steaming mug of soup clutched in her hands. She looked ashen.

His mother, when she'd been sick when he was young, real sick, all grey with sunken eyes and knobbly bones and thin, tight, yellowed skin.

He stumbled, regained his balance, blinked the afterimages of the memory away, to find Reg sitting beside Penny. She leaned on his shoulder, her eyes filled with a staring weariness.

'Hey,' he said, forcing himself to focus. He was back in the shed, but the sorrow and fear were taking longer to drain away.

The rest of the gang were crowded around the Esky where Taipan and Acacia kneeled over a map by the light of a hissing gas lamp. Budgie gave Kevin a nod from the midst of the gathering, their subdued chatter making him think of a swarm of midges.

The Night Riders, caught somewhere between the thrill and guilt of survival.

Kevin felt like the kid who'd turned up to a party in fancy dress when it wasn't. Unnerving crimson and green eyes studied him, as if the gang could see inside his head, as though they knew Taipan had come to him in the night, had fed from Kala and then gone to Kevin and given him his blood memories. But he couldn't see Kala – where was she? What had happened to her?

'Taipan?' Concern pushed him forward.

The biker was talking to Budgie, who bent to point something out on the map.

Closer. Louder: 'Chris?'

Taipan leapt to his feet, forged through the gangers toward him. Before Kevin knew what was happening, Taipan's fists were bunched at his collar, pushing him hard up against a pole. It was like being squashed against a crush by a wild bull. Taipan's eyes blazed with ice-green fury.

'You don't say that name. No-one says that name.'

'I saw; I heard–'

'You saw – you heard – *nothin'*.'

Kevin nodded, embarrassingly aware of everyone watching.

'You don't mention *him*, you don't mention *her*. Not to me. Not to anyone. You got it?'

'Sure, sure.'

Taipan let him drop and stepped back. 'All right, you mob, listen up – party's over. We can't afford to stay here for a day. We need to lay down some mileage, keep some daylight between us and that VS mob. So start packin'.'

Kala appeared out of the scrum and came to Kevin where he sagged against the post. 'You okay?'

He pulled away, feeling guilty but not sure why. Taipan had fed from her and then fed him; it all felt wrong somehow. Dirty.

'Remember what I told you back at the house,' she said. 'We keep it to ourselves.'

He nodded. A few of the gang had smirked when Taipan had torn him a new one, but most just looked anxious. There were, he realised, a lot of guns.

Kala reached again and this time he let her touch him. She brushed at the dirt. 'I guess we all look pretty scruffy, eh? Sleepin' rough.'

'You don't look so bad,' he said.

'You're well enough to flirt, you're well enough to help pack the gear.' Her lips lifted at the corners in a smile that made his chest tighten. He hadn't been lying about her looking good. Had to shut down the flash memory of feeding from her. From her and Meg; God, Meg.

'Hey,' he asked. 'What was that thing?' He jerked his head at Reg, standing, helping Penny to her feet.

For a moment, he didn't think Kala was going to answer, but then she admitted, 'We need it. Like a drug. But from just one. It gets too confusing, otherwise, two or more in your head at once, pulling you in different ways.'

'So if you drank my blood, what would happen?'

'If I drank enough, absorbed enough, we'd forge a link.'

'But you're already linked to Taipan.'

'His blood is stronger, so his link would be stronger.' She bit her lip, then added, 'He's my fix.'

'What about Nigel, then? Who was his fix? Why didn't they know he was gonna dob you all in?'

'Nigel didn't have a fix. He got fed a brew – different vampires mixing their blood. None of them strong enough to make a link, but enough to give him all the benefits – healing, strength, sharper senses.'

'But–'

Taipan forced his way between them. 'Does this look like a QCWA meetin' to you? You still waitin' for ya tea and pikelets? I said get packin'. Now say goodbye to Budgie there and let's get to it.'

'Where's Budgie going?' Kevin asked, but Taipan was hauling Kala away to help Penny.

'Takin' a few of the lads inland,' the bald biker said from where he crouched nearby over his saddlebag. 'Gonna raise some hell, run some distraction.'

'Good luck, I guess,' Kevin mumbled.

Budgie gave him a wink. 'You keep your arse out of the daylight, and we'll catch up with you at The Farm in a coupla days.'

'The Farm?' Kevin asked, but everyone was in motion, Taipan herding them.

Before he knew it, he was scrambling into the back of the Rover with the three red-eyes. Penny was already asleep; Kala looked exhausted, nodding off where she lay on bedrolls next to Penny. Hippie sat at the back, rolling a smoke. Taipan took the driver's seat and dug out his tobacco pouch. 'Hop over here,' he told Kevin. 'You're ridin' shotgun.'

Kevin scrambled into the cabin to find a submachine gun, its bare steel stock extended, on the seat.

'You can shoot, eh,' Taipan said. 'You bein' a country boy 'n' all.'

'Sure,' Kevin said, though the automatic was a bit more advanced than the guns he was used to.

'Just don't shoot ya dick off. Or mine.' Taipan gave him a cheeky look, as though he knew just what temptation he'd presented Kevin with.

'Kala looked pretty wiped,' Kevin said as he made a point of keeping the barrel pointed out the window.

'Don't mind 'bout that myxo. That girl needs her rest, that's all. Don't go botherin' her. She might hafta drive, once the sun comes up.'

'What about the bikes?'

'Hippie and Penny can handle 'em.'

Hippie threw a victory salute of acknowledgement of his bike-riding prowess.

Taipan clashed the gears and the Rover lurched forward, the bikes swarming around it. Budgie's group split off at the bitumen with a beeping of horns. Budgie threw a long mono of farewell.

They drove, and the night was vivid, the stars bright, the Rover a miasma of diesel and dust and gun oil, the sound of engine and tyres subsiding into a drowsy background hum. Kevin fought to stay awake. He didn't want to go back into that dreamscape where everything was, he presumed, real. Where snippets of his life would rise and goad with forgotten details, where bits and pieces of Taipan's life and Kala's, too, would bob up through the stream, throwing him off-kilter, each so very personal, threatening to make him forget who he was. And for all that, none of them would reveal the one truth he most wanted to know.

'What happened to my father?' Kevin asked.

'You didn't see it?' Taipan asked, tapping his forehead.

'No,' Kevin said. 'I saw your sister, and you, at a cane farm. Is that where we're going?'

'That place is gone, long time ago,' Taipan said. 'And like I told you already – you don't talk to me 'bout Willa. You don't talk to no-one 'bout her.'

'Okay then. What about my dad?'

'I won't talk to no-one about him, either.'

The compulsion to push the man out of the Rover was so strong it made Kevin quiver. But all he did was say, 'Fuck you. Fuck the lot of you.' He sat and watched the sign posts to familiar places flash by in the night. It reminded him he was going farther and farther away from home. He wondered about his mother and Meg. Did Taipan dream of them? He hoped not. Finally he succumbed to his exhaustion, slept, and it all happened again, but this time – this time – he saw everything.

He uses the wall for support as he scrambles to his feet, his ankles still bound by wire. The mechanic has the shotgun pointed at him. The son's blood is in his mouth; his lifestream's pulsing through his mind.

'This first-aid gig is startin' to become a habit.'

'What's wrong?' the father asks. 'Did it work?'

'Lost too much. You don't wanna donate a pint, eh, Thomas?'

'Did it work?'

'It takes time. But yeah, it's worked, all right.' The hunger is in the kid, wormin' through him. He can feel it in his blood.'

'This cop was healing while I watched.' Thomas nods at the Hunter on the floor near his son.

'Scratches for the likes of him. This is heavier kadaicha. All the way to the soul.'

'When I know my boy's alive, then I'll help you out of here.'

'Might not have that much time, fella.'

'Then you're in trouble, aren't you.'

'One of us is, that's for sure.'

'Fine, I believe you.' Thomas hands him the pliers, then puts a set of keys on the corner of the desk and steps away. 'For the truck. In the garage.'

'Keep ya truck.' He gestures at the office door, blocked by a filin' cabinet. 'You get me outside, my gang'll take care of the rest.'

'And you'll let us all go?'

He squats, back to the wall, awkwardly cuts the wire away from his ankles. 'We couldn't give a shit about you. Don't know about them other blokes though.'

'I'll take my chances.'

'There's more to that Hunter than meets the eye, eh.'

'I figured.'

'I don't reckon you have. They don't send just anyone to pick up my kind. Maybe you should just use that.'

The father considers his shotgun. 'I'm not a murderer.'

'He is. So am I.'

Thomas walks to the cabinet, puts the shotgun down. 'Then let's go, before he wonders where I've got to.'

'Actually, I was already wondering that,' the Hunter says from the doorway. Fuck. The barrel of his pistol covers them. 'Letting him go isn't the best idea.'

'My son's dying. My wife's up at that house. We're surrounded by gunmen. You tell me what you'd do.'

'I'll tell you what you should do – ice that bastard and then help me keep them out.'

'I can't do that,' Thomas says.

And then it all goes to hell. Petrol bombs explodin', the buildin' shakin' and burnin'; the air turnin' to smoke. He grabs for the Hunter's weapon. The gun goes off, once, twice; the second shot gives him his chance as the Hunter jerks back in time to save his own face. He thumps the Hunter and then kicks him to the shithouse. Runs for the door. The place is blazin', crashin' down, and outside the sun is a furnace and *he hopes his people can catch him in time coz he doesn't wanna have to go to ground here, not with all the attention that's gonna descend on this joint like Ashton's fuckin' circus. He spares a glance for the kid on the floor and thinks, it's a waste, but it's for the best, given the risk, and spares a moment's thought for the poor bastard lyin' on the floor with a hole in his chest who simply had no idea, they never do, and thinks good riddance for that Hunter Dave, doin' all right on my blood, the cunt.*

Another blast shakes the joint and he sees the Hunter, wreathed in smoke, comin' for him again, and he's outta time. He hurls the filin' cabinet to the side and tears open the office door and runs outside and hopes his people have a brolly handy coz it's plenny hot out here, but not as hot as the barbie he leaves behind.

And later, in the back seat of Kala's Monaro with her blood pumpin' through his veins, he realises the kid's survival instinct has come through. He'll have to send someone back to nab their new mechanic after all.

TWENTY

The sky was still dark, the moon low, when they pulled into a lonely service station. A sickly yellow corona beyond the darkly swaying fields marked the nearest town. They refuelled and shortly after turned off the highway. The Night Riders extinguished their headlights, relying on moonlight as they followed a narrow road, passing paddocks and occasional gateways, darkened homesteads sitting at the ends of long, dirt drives. Eventually, they reached a sign post that warned of 'no through road' and cut the engines.

Taipan pointed at a house, barely visible through a stand of eucalyptus trees. It was brick, one-storey, with a double-door garage to one side. 'Whaddya think?'

'Is this The Farm?' Kevin asked.

An anonymous snort was all the answer he got.

'Looks good,' Penny said. 'Only the one neighbour, fair distance away.'

'Can't hear no dogs, either,' Reg added.

'Why are we doing this?' Acacia asked.

'Coz we need to rest up outta the sun,' Taipan said. 'Coz we need tucker, the good stuff.'

'Not like this, Tai. Not this close to a town. Not with VS at our heels.'

'We're doin' it. You don't like it, the highway's over there.'

They stared at each other. Fear iced Kevin's skin. Acacia turned away.

'Any of you other fellas got a problem?' Taipan asked, sweeping the gang with his gaze.

Kala stared at the ground.

'We're with you, Tai,' said Reg, flexing his fingers to make the knuckles crack.

'Rightio, let's walk 'em up, eh. Kala – you, Hippie and 'Cacia mind the Rover.' Taipan motioned to Kevin. 'You keep an eye on the bikes. Not a sound from none of youse till we give you the nod.'

Kevin stood between Reg's BMW and Penny's Kawasaki, watching powerlessly as Reg, Penny and Taipan crept up the gravel drive. He tried to catch Acacia's eye, or Kala's, but they both ignored him. 'Whose place is this?' he whispered.

'Dunno,' Acacia answered. 'Shut up now, eh.'

The three bikers approached the manicured lawn, the grass brown, a line of rose bushes resisting the drought. A couple of polythene tanks squatted by the garage. A swimming-pool sized lagoon glimmered down the paddock, cracked grey banks making it look like an ulcer. Taipan and Penny kept watch while Reg picked the lock. A dog yapped as the door swung open. The three bikers darted inside. The barking stopped mid-yelp. Kevin winced.

After a nerve-wracking wait, Penny re-appeared and waved them up. They tucked the bikes in next to two vehicles – a sedan and a four-wheel-drive – and parked the Rover where they felt it would be least conspicuous. 'I'll do a shuffle later,' Hippie said. 'Get it under cover before sun-up.'

They stepped around the dead dog as they followed Penny through the laundry into the living room.

Kevin balked at the sight of the heeler lying in a pool of blood. 'What the hell are we doing here?'

Acacia gave a look that said dumb questions didn't deserve answers.

The lights were on in the kitchen and adjacent living/dining areas, the curtains pulled tightly closed. A middle-aged couple sat gagged and bound in their nightclothes on the sofa. Their daughter, fourteen or fifteen maybe, hugged her younger brother where they huddled in their pyjamas on the floor. Taipan and Reg leant against the kitchen counter, arms crossed with the air of stockmen taking in a cattle sale.

'It's a smorgasbord,' Reg said by way of greeting. He grinned like a great Dane.

Kevin felt the dread descend with all the surety of nightfall.

Kala, Hippie and Penny helped themselves to food and drink in the kitchen. A kettle boiling, crockery clanking, sounded over-loud and disconcertingly normal as the tension in the living room rose. Sweat broke out, clammy under Kevin's arms. His body froze, muscles locked as he waited for the storm to break.

Reg and Taipan began to strip, piling their clothes on an armchair.

'Got a case'a the shy, 'Cacia?' Taipan asked. 'Want us to turn our backs?'

'Now we're here, you should feed,' she told Kevin as she began to undress.

'You heard 'Cacia,' Taipan said. 'You want a bib or somethin'? Get ya gear off if you don't wanna make a mess.'

Reg shouted for Penny. In the background, meat sizzled in a pan, releasing its charred aroma. She came in, a glass of beer in one hand. 'You bellowed?'

He tore the boy from his sister's grip. The girl clawed at Reg and he knocked her down, then thrust the terrified boy at Penny. 'Keep an eye on dessert here for a bit, won'tcha?'

'Do I look like a nanny to you?'

'Just do it.'

She drained her glass and held it out to him.

'Don't get pushy,' he told her. She thrust the boy back at him, so Reg pulled a knife and cut his arm and bled into the glass till it was half-full.

'Nice head.' Pink foam coated her lips as she drank the blood in eager mouthfuls.

'Now piss off while I have dinner,' he told her. 'We can play swapsies later.' He slapped her arse.

'Steak's almost done anyway.' Penny threw the empty glass. It smashed into a family portrait on the wall, fracturing the glass and leaving the photograph hanging askew. She grabbed the sobbing boy and led him into the kitchen. 'You are a plump little dumpling, aren't you?'

The daughter screamed her brother's name and the brother screamed back till something muffled him.

Kevin stood, paralysed.

The father tried to stand but Acacia pushed him to the floor. She sliced his shirt away in pieces, cutting his chest, then began to lap, savouring each mouthful.

Taipan tore the mother's nightgown open and buried himself in her throat. Her panicked features burnt into Kevin's vision as his frozen mind tried to work out what to do. Pinned under Taipan, the woman stared down at her daughter, her mouth moving soundlessly in some futile prayer, some final words.

Reg leaned over the squirming girl, pinned her arms above her head and used his fangs to rip open her throat.

Kevin shouted at them to stop. He grabbed Reg's shoulder and tugged him away. The girl stared up at him. Blood spilled down her chest, darkening her nightie with lurid scarlet.

Reg's crimson-smeared lips curled in a sneer. 'Feed or fuck off.'

Blood scent clouded the air. The father swore and swore, his bound legs bucking. Acacia bit down on his inner elbow. The man's helpless rage quickly turned to terror. His eyes bulged as his vitality bled away.

Kevin shook his head. 'I can't do this.'

'Your loss,' Reg said.

'You have to stay strong,' Acacia said, slurring slightly. 'Try the girl. A short life won't crowd you too much. Just make sure you stop before the end. You won't want her hanging around, not till you can handle the lifestream.'

'I don't even want to know what you're talking about,' Kevin said, stumbling backward, his vision so very bright and clear, his body trembling.

Taipan smirked at him, his white teeth outlined in crimson. 'Fresh from the vein, fella.'

'I can't!'

Kevin ran. He reached the laundry. A shape loomed behind him. A tap on his ankle sent him careening into the side of the washing machine, then to the floor. When he got to his feet, he found Reg blocking the door to the garage. Kevin tried to push past, his mind a black wall of desperation. But Reg held him fast, and then a pain in his back robbed him of all strength. He choked; coughed up a gout of blood. Reg lowered him to his knees, then pushed him over.

Taipan stood over him. 'Whaddya think you're doin', fella?'

Kevin couldn't say a word, couldn't even lift a finger. The fury of being once again helpless threatened to burst his skin. He seethed as he was carted back into the living room like a bale of hay and dumped on the floor next to the family. He landed on whatever Taipan had jabbed into him, sending a sharp pain slicing into his back. His head lolled to the side, revealing the young girl next to him, whimpering, her arms pulling her legs tight against her bloodstained chest. He wished with all his might that the stake would send him into oblivion, but his body fought, the blood fought. He stayed painfully awake, life and death fighting a tug-of-war for his heart; he stayed awake and powerless as Reg approached the girl again. She offered the barest of resistance as Reg pushed her down. He forced her legs apart and buried his fangs in her groin.

'Man, this is awesome shit,' he said, teeth outlined in gore. 'There's horse riding, swimming, tennis. And a boyfriend – a girlfriend, too! I *love* this women's tennis.' He punched Kevin's arm. 'Can't believe you don't want some of this. It's not like you can just go do this shit for yourself. Not anymore. Here, have a taste.'

He bent over Kevin, pried his jaws open and dribbled a fresh mouthful of blood into his throat. Kevin choked, but even staked out, he felt the blood being absorbed by his system; by his very cells. Sluggish, though; not like the lightning he'd felt when he'd fed from Kala. He experienced none of the lifestream that Reg was bragging about; nothing but the torpid warmth and the horrible sensation of drowning.

Acacia lifted her face from the father's femoral. 'Reggie, you fuckwit. That fella's not gonna get nothin' out of that. Not with that spike in his pump.'

'Fuck,' Reg said, sitting up and wiping his mouth. 'I should just piss on him. That's all this gutless pup is worth. I gotta take a leak.'

He walked out and Kevin heard the waterfall.

'Shut the door at least,' Acacia shouted. 'Fucking yob.'

'That fella's on the money, but,' Taipan said, rolling off the mother, her throat one tattered gash. 'I ain't tasted sunshine like this in a long time. Bin livin' too quiet in the nest.' He crawled over to the girl and bit into her arm, then went to the father and whispered something to Acacia before he drank from him, too.

Reg came back and went for the girl again. 'Shit, she's done. Oh, well, still got room for some boy juice.'

He called Penny to bring in the son.

'You must have hollow legs,' Taipan said. He hoisted himself up against the sofa, licking blood from his fingers. The mother sat silent and still above him.

'I'm a growing lad, what can I say? Penny!'

She brought the boy in, hands on his shoulders. The lad stumbled along as though he was sleepwalking. Welts on his face showed where a hand had been clamped over his mouth.

'Bleed that young'un,' Taipan told Reg. 'Bleed him and wait for it to settle.'

'What's it matter? Blood is blood.'

'You don't want that kid stuff in ya head, I'm tellin' you.'

'I don't get it.'

'And you don't wanna. The little buggers feel everythin' so intense-like. It'll do ya head in. Penny, see if you can't find some bottles or jugs or somethin'. We'll bag what Reggie can't finish off, eh.'

The snivelling boy – he couldn't have been much more than ten – stood in Reggie's light grip like a calf in the crush while Penny fetched a couple of plastic jugs. Reg slit the boy's throat and held him over the containers.

Kevin couldn't even close his eyes. Couldn't even scream.

Finally, it was over. Reg rolled the body onto the floor and picked up the smallest of the containers, the first to have filled, and tasted the blood. He screwed up his face. 'Might as well be that hospital shit. It's not much better than moo juice.'

'It's the right way to do it,' Taipan said. 'Bag 'em,' he told Penny, and she took the containers away.

The vampires lolled around the room, faces turned beetroot, eyes bloodshot.

'I need to piss something fierce,' Reg said, dragging himself to his feet and waddling for the loo again.

'You keep an eye on 'em while we water the horse, eh?' Taipan said to Kevin as he stepped over him. The biker walked slowly, his skin an oily, bruised black. Kevin heard him open an outside door. Acacia leaned against the wall near the toilet door, swearing at Reg to hurry up.

The three of them had only just returned, vague presences outside Kevin's vision, when he heard Kala swear. She crouched over him.

'What have you done?' she asked Taipan, and then shouted over her shoulder, 'Jesus, Penny, why didn't you tell me?'

Penny stood behind the sofa, Hippie behind her. 'Didn't seem important,' she said, and wiped her mouth with the back of her hand.

'Think I'll go move those cars around, maybe have a smoke,' Hippie said. 'Call me if there's brew.'

'It's okay, Kala,' Taipan said. 'The whitefella just needed to calm down a bit. He ain't no good to no-one if he don't eat.'

'You're a pig, you know that?'

'Oink,' he said, and dug around in his clothes for his tobacco pouch.

Kala rolled Kevin over and withdrew the object that had stilled his heart. He gasped as his body shuddered back into action.

She rolled him gently onto his back, then wiped off the knife and skidded it across the floor out of the way. 'Take it easy, Kevvie. You're fine.'

He shook his head, unable to talk. The smell of blood, piss and shit surrounded him. He inched away from Kala; the scent of her cut through the miasma, made him want to hold her hard and fast.

Meg, the blood streaming from her neck, her face twisted into a mask of horror

'It takes some getting used to. There's plenty of normal tucker in the pantry if you wanna fill up on something.'

'There's baggies in the fridge,' Penny said. She crouched beside Reg, where he slumped in an armchair. 'You got something for me, baby? You can spare a drop or three, right?'

He pushed her away. 'Later, Penny; I'm digestin'.'

She stood quickly and stalked out. A door slammed.

'I'm gonna go rinse off,' Acacia said, and padded off down the hallway.

Kevin lay very still amid the carnage, staring at the ceiling, anywhere but at those bodies. Tears pricked his eyes, ran warm down his cheeks.

Kala wiped the tears away. The back of her fingers were smeared with red. 'Kev. Can I get you something?'

He shook his head violently. His gut was a tight ball, caught somewhere between ravenous hunger and the urgent need to throw up.

'Hippie reckons we're, like, the planet's defenders or something,' Reg said as Taipan passed him a cigarette. 'The people, they're the disease, and we're like those anti-thingies that attack it.'

'Antibodies?' Kala suggested.

'Yeah, that's the things. *Anti*-bodies. That's us.'

'No,' Kevin said, sitting up so he could see the biker properly. 'You're – we're – more like a cancer.'

'What are you on about?' Reg asked. 'You don't know nothin'.'

'I know about cancer. They cut a great chunk of it out of my mum.'

His father, an arm around his shoulders, the smell of the hospital all around, the walls so bright it was like they were in a spotlight, just the two of them. It's in her womb, son. They're gonna have to take it out. *And then the tears, tracking down those leathered cheeks, the grip on his shoulders so tight, suffocatingly tight, and for no reason he could name, Kevin was crying, too.*

'Antibodies attack the invading cells,' he said, pushing past the memory, the moment, so fresh, so *now* he felt the tears budding. 'But you guys are attacking the healthy ones.'

'Let's get this straight,' Taipan said. 'That lot you're losin' blood over, they was all gonna die anyway. Cancer, maybe, like you say. Or a car wreck. Old age. Us mob, we don't hafta worry 'bout that stuff. All we done here is speed things up a bit. So maybe you should be countin' ya blessin's, eh?'

'Blessings? So how do you know that kid or his sister wouldn't have grown up to cure cancer? Who are you to judge who should die and who shouldn't?'

'We're nature, fella. That's who we are. Nature don't care

135

which town it knocks down with a cyclone, which town it floods. We're nature, and God help them who get in our way.'

'You're wrong,' Kevin said.

'Killing is a last resort,' Kala said, her gaze darting from Taipan to Kevin.

'You can always go veggo,' Reg said.

'That's what Bhagwan'd say,' Taipan said.

'Who's Bhagwan?' Kevin asked.

'The guru of veggo,' Reg said with a snort.

'You'll meet him at The Farm,' Taipan said. 'Him and his little myxo pets.'

'Bhagwan doesn't kill humans,' Kala said.

'But he still needs what they got,' Taipan said, tapping his forehead. 'There ain't no gettin' around that.'

'But he doesn't kill,' Kala repeated.

Kevin wanted to ask more – who was Bhagwan and what was this veggo business and what did people have that the vampires needed – but exhaustion claimed him. It was all too much. He needed silence. He needed to get away.

Outside, magpies warbled and crows called, plovers gave their staccato cry. The dawn chorus was tuning up.

Kala grabbed Kevin's arm. 'You *don't* have to kill.'

'Get some sleep,' Taipan ordered. The heat of a new day teased at the horizon outside the walls. 'We got a long drive tonight if we're gonna make The Farm.'

'You're wrong,' Kevin repeated, but no-one was listening, too busy arguing over who was going to sleep where and who was going to have the next wash. 'We're not natural,' Kevin murmured to himself. 'We're *not* nature.' *Nature doesn't cry.*

'C'mon, let's go lie down.' Kala led him down a hall into what he guessed had been the son's room. He tried to ignore the model airplanes hanging from the ceiling. Kala sat on the bed and gestured for him to sit with her. Her eyes were dark-rimmed, her shoulders slumped. She pushed him down gently, then lay beside him.

'Won't he be angry if you're in here with me?'

'With a bellyful? Nah.' She stroked his cheek. 'I'm so sorry. You believe that, don't you?'

'Not your fault,' he said.

'That's not how it should be done. Not when you're so raw. God, I hate him so much sometimes.'

'Me too,' he said, his hunger stalking him. It would be so easy to open her arm. To feed.

'You'll have to do it eventually,' she said, her voice soft.

It jarred him, took him a moment to realise she hadn't been reading his mind, just continuing her conversation.

'But I'll do what I can to help you through. Till you're ready. Variety really is the spice of life, I'm afraid.'

He clasped her hand, well away from his face. She couldn't carry him; not with Taipan feeding from her as well. Eventually, if she was telling him true, he'd need more than she could give him. *Variety.*

'They use us up,' she murmured. 'Our lives become ordinary, y'know. Can you imagine what it's like to share your blood with a person, to be that close to them, and to know as you're doing it exactly what they really think of you?'

'How do you–?'

She pulled her hand free and held it to his lips. He froze, afraid to even draw breath. Her flesh…

'No more questions. There's plenty of time for that tomorrow. We all need to sleep now.' She rested her head against his shoulder. Her breathing deepened.

Kevin stared at the ceiling as Kala slept, waves of anguish rolling through him – anguish and disgust. Voices filtered through the walls. Sometimes they laughed, even after what they had done. It was a mercy when the voices finally subsided and silence settled over the house. But her words haunted him. What made him think that, in the long run, he would turn out to be any different?

TWENTY-ONE

''Bane,' she said, spitting out the word. Mira always called
Brisbane that. She hated the city, hated every sun-drenched
square inch of the place. Reece didn't mind it so much. Brissie
was home, after all. He was used to the humidity and the long,
boiling summers with their long, boiling days. But then, he
was only a red-eye, a serf, a leech. He could still swim between
the flags if he wanted to cool off.

The chartered helicopter arrowed in across the sprawling
city, the lights below spread out like a glittering melanoma
fading to black in the forested western ranges. They approached
the centre of the corruption, where light-chequered towers of
silvered glass winked red warnings from their rooftops and
the meandering river flowed oily and striped with reflected
lights.

Mira had been quiet for most of the flight, staring out into
the dark, the reflected glimmer of her eyes like purplish nebulae
on the glass. Contemplating what she'd tell her boss when they
landed? Or how she'd punish Reece for having dropped the
ball in the first place? Long memories, vampires; they knew
how to hold a grudge.

Mostly, though, she looked as tired as he felt, and just a
little haunted.

'Strigoi?'

Nothing. Just that stare, down at the city lights, as though she could burn the place down with her gaze.

'Mira?'

'Tell them to be quiet, Reece; I'm thinking.'

'Hey?' They were alone in the cabin, the crew sealed off in the cockpit.

She looked around then, eyes wide, lips quivering, and a hand moved to her temple as though to exorcise a headache. The red glimmer faded from her eyes, replaced by a flash of pale green as they caught the uncertain light. Then the concrete curtain descended and she snapped, 'What is it, Reece?'

'The Big V didn't know about any of this, did he? Not till that roadhouse went up.'

'I'm sure I don't know what you mean, Hunter Reece.'

'How pissed is Maximilian that you used Turner as bait?'

'I am Strigoi. I do what I please. And I do not explain it to red-eyes.'

'And yet you've allowed Taipan and the newborn to ride away into the sunset.'

'Allowed?'

He indicated her wrist, and she stilled the subconscious act of twisting at her scarred bracelets.

'What are you waiting for? *Who* are you waiting for?'

'You're a clever boy, Reece. You work it out.'

In for a penny, in for a pound. 'You're going for Dee, aren't you.' Which was as close to her name as anyone was game to get, such was the scandal around Danica's defection. Humiliating for Maximilian, devastating for Mira.

Danica, she of the purple eyes. The reason he'd stumbled onto Mira's nightmare world. Danica, running, and Mira, with his bullet in her chest, getting up off the floor.

He wondered if Mira, too, was revisiting that incident that had brought the two of them together. That had, in some ways, kept them together.

An encouraging half smile turned cold as she said, 'The Night Riders call her *Mother*. Did you know that?'

'You expect Kevin Matheson to lead you to Taipan, and Taipan to lead you to her.'

'That's method. What about motive, my clever detective?'

'Political favour. Revenge. Both.'

'You think I've gone behind my master's back to pursue some kind of personal agenda that the eradication of the Night Riders would more than justify.'

'Something like that.'

'With deductive reasoning like that, it's amazing she's managed to elude you for all these years.'

The pilot announced their imminent arrival, saving Reece the effort of trying to find a riposte. He'd nailed it, though; Mira was up to something and she'd been caught out. Now they were all in the dog house.

'So what do you think of Felicity?' Mira asked without looking at him.

'Nice freckles.'

She rolled the comment around, as though savouring the girl's blood once more, and turned to him. 'Given any thought to retirement, Reece?'

'Have you, Strigoi?'

She chuckled. 'Yours or mine?'

The chopper landed on the roof of the Von Schiller Industries tower, a combined business and residential building not quite managing to gets its head above the crowd. A full squad of the elite Gespenstenstaffel formed an escort into the building as Reece and Mira alighted.

'Boss has rolled out the red carpet for you, Strigoi.' Reece's words were all but lost in the downdraft and howl of the departing chopper.

'Subtle, as ever,' she answered.

They stepped into the antechamber and waited for the door

to seal behind the guards before hitting the elevator button. The doors opened instantly.

'We're going to Two, then we'll report in,' Mira told the escort, and the leader said no problems, they'd take the next one. So she wasn't in that much trouble; one benefit of working for your old man. But the warning was clear.

'Boss can wait till I've got my face on,' Mira said – to the escort, or to Reece, or herself, as the doors slid shut.

'No sign of our bird,' Reece said, changing the topic. He didn't want to be the meat in that particular shit sandwich. Not if the two most powerful vampires in the city – in the state, maybe even the whole country – were going to lock horns.

'Working on it out at Caboolture,' she said. 'More privacy there.'

Her thumbprint and keycard took them to the second floor. Not even Reece had clearance to access that floor – not the second, nor several others in the basement levels. Few vampires trusted the vulnerability of altitude, but Mira preferred a room with a view – not too high, mind.

The elevator's voice sounded bored as it announced their arrival.

'Strigoi?'

'You're off the hook for tonight, Reece. Report to the maintenance shed. If his highness wants to question you personally about the Rogue's escape, I'll call you. Otherwise, get me my helicopter. I need that chopper the instant they make contact with – with *her*.'

Reece rode the elevator up one floor – Mira liked her Favourite to be close by – and made his way to his quarters. The apartment was best described as cosy, furnished with all the hotel-like charm the corporation could muster. At least it had a balcony – if he craned the right way, he could see the winking warning lights on the aerials stuck like acupuncture needles into the spine of Mt Coot-tha. He hadn't bothered with personal touches: no memorabilia of the life before had been allowed, and the life of now offered little worth remembering. Certainly not lately. His presence was marked chiefly by a shelf of paperbacks – thrillers and crime, mostly – and a handful of CDs he rarely listened to. Never had quite come to grips with the digital stuff; it was probably the copper in him, but he liked things that he could touch.

He showered, changed into a fresh suit, poured two fingers of Bundy and lit a cigarette. He tried to shrug off the memories of the fire fight on the road, of trying to drive and look after Dave, of pushing vials of go-juice into his mouth and achieving nothing. Even if they'd had back-up, they would never have got away clean. That's what he told himself. Dave would still be dead. He'd dozed on the flight but he needed more, a hell of a lot more. But that would have to wait until he had this helicopter sorted out. Otherwise, he might be the one left out in Whoop Whoop carrying the shit can while some ambitious bitch with cute freckles was riding Mira's elevator to the second floor.

TWENTY-TWO

Kevin must've fallen asleep, because it was uncomfortably light in the room, sunshine leaking in around the edges of the spaceship-decorated curtains, and Kala was gone. Hunger gurgled in his stomach. He crept down the hall. The scent of blood and human waste hung heavy in the air, so thick it made him gag. The bodies lay lined up on the floor. He stepped over to pull the hem of the girl's torn nightdress down to hide her wounds. Stiff and grey, she stared up at the ceiling, unseeing but still looking scared.

He washed his face, poured a glass of water but could barely drink it. His stomach heaved at the first touch. He was shaking, from his hands to his feet, and his back pained from his 'icing'. The fridge opened and it took a moment to realise it was his hand on the handle. Bloody memories swam in front of him, gauzy and horrible; blood and screams and gore, and...

It's a smorgasbord

I love this women's tennis

Bleed that boy

The container on the bench – how did that get there? And hands, his hands, opening the top, and that scent floating out like invisible tentacles drawing him down into the blood. The hint of vinegar reminded him of the poached eggs at the café in town.

He sobbed, and the plastic rim was against his lips.

The blood, cold and thick, slid past his teeth, coated his tongue.

He spat into the sink; the scarlet stain stared back.

He wiped the residue from his lips.

Maybe if he microwaved it.

You are a plump little dumpling

He heaved, bringing up bile, and washed the whole mess down the sink.

Kala came to him, standing with her hip against his, an arm around his shoulders. Her neck was marked with red blotches. Her hair, her breath, smelled of Taipan. 'Hey, early bird.'

He slammed the container's lid shut. 'Hey. I was just–'

He was caught in the act; shame choked off his explanation.

'You don't really want to drink that, do you?'

'No,' he said.

She took it from his hand and put it back in the fridge. 'Here.' She offered her wrist. 'Better than decant.'

'I can't. Not from you.'

'If not me, then who?'

Blood pumped through the purple veins in Kala's wrist, dark tributaries under dusky skin. He could smell it, hear it, taste it. Hunger seized him with the sudden ferocity of a shark. His fangs emerged unbidden, his mouth flowed with saliva. She smelled of the earth and blood; she smelled of life, and not even Taipan's stench could quench his thirst.

His fangs sliced into her flesh. Severed the veins. Blood squirted into his mouth. He sealed his lips around the cuts and gulped her down until she moaned for him to stop; until she pushed him away. He sagged to the floor, carried under by

Kala's lifestream. The hammer of her heartbeat pounded in his ears. Her life whirled through his veins.

He wiped his mouth, licked his lips, the back of his hand.

She'd bound the wound with a tea towel, had slid down beside him while he zoned out.

'Will you be all right?' he asked.

'Sure. Once the wound closes.'

'How long will that take?'

She unfurled the bloody towel. A series of cuts still oozed blood, making his hunger stir anew.

'Dribble some of your blood on this.'

'What?'

'Use a knife if you're shy. Or let me do it.'

He held out his hand and she sliced his palm with a dagger from her boot. He jumped at the sudden pain. 'Chicken,' she chided, then closed his bleeding hand over the wound on her wrist.

'What now?' he asked.

'Voila,' she said, and slowly removed his hand. The skin of her wrist was unbroken, just a few pale dimples showing where he'd bitten her.

He held up his own hand. There was no sign she had ever cut him, just a smear of blood, which he licked off as though it was chicken grease. 'You heal like us?'

'Faster than normal. Vampire saliva makes wounds bleed. Your blood cancels it out.'

'All this blood–'

'You don't need to worry. There isn't a disease yet that can overcome your systems.'

'Wow, what a comfort.' He jerked a thumb at the living room. 'Is it always this way?'

'Not always.'

'I can't stay with him. These people.' A surge of emotion, the hot burn of tears, stole his voice.

'I know,' she said. 'It was the main reason I left him.' She passed him a tea towel. 'You should know that Tai finished them, all of them except the boy.'

'I'm happy for him,' he said as he wiped his eyes, his cheeks. The material came away smeared with the slightest touch of pink; his body had all but absorbed the tears, unwilling to even let that much sustenance escape its pores.

'Don't be. He's got them in here, now.' She touched her forehead. 'Maybe here as well.' She pointed to her heart. 'Every time he shuts his eyes, he'll see them – what he did to them, what he took from them. They live in him, now.'

'I don't think that's much comfort to them,' Kevin said.

'It's more than most get. He could've just let them bleed out, or used a knife. He didn't have to take them with him, but he always does, despite the risk. His way of thanking them, I guess.'

'You know how sick that sounds?'

'I guess it's all how you look at it. But what else can you do, Kevvie? Von Schiller is on your arse and we're the only friends you've got.'

With the sun on the other side of the house, Kevin found a spot on the veranda shaded by a screen of bougainvillea vine. Kala had gone back to bed, but he couldn't sleep; not in there.

Hippie regarded him from the other end where he kept a yawning look-out. 'You aren't thinking of running off, are you, man?'

'In this heat?'

Hippie laughed, then said, matter-of-factly, 'He'd find you quick smart.'

'I gathered. Nah, thought maybe I could give you a break if you wanted to rest up.'

'He'll have my hide if you piss off on my watch.'

'He's got the car keys and taken care of the phones. What can I do?'

'You checked, though.'

Kevin sat on the veranda all afternoon, preferring the discomfort of the slow boil of ambient daylight to the fetid atmosphere of the house. He fought off sleep, tried to keep the dreams at bay. Taipan's life, Kala's, so many others: secrets he didn't want to know, revealed in red-washed snippets, nonsensical and confusing, invariably horrifying. He clung to the day. He welcomed the prickling pain of daylight, of wolfbite, as a distraction to the alternating disbelief and panic he'd felt as he considered his options.

Shadows deepened. Twilight fell, chill on his skin. The Night Riders would be stirring. His time was up.

TWENTY-THREE

Kevin rode on the back of Reg's bike, following Kala as pinion with Taipan. Penny took point. Acacia and Hippie had left in the Rover, headed for a place called Mother's Nest that he'd never heard of and no-one was inclined to tell him about. Hippie's last act had been to torch the house; the poisonous reek of burning hair and petrol clung to him.

They pulled up after an hour or so to refuel at a rundown servo that reminded Kevin of his family's. He stayed quiet when the girls went in to buy snacks, standing out of the waft zone as Taipan and Reg lit up.

'You been pretty quiet, boss. What's the go?' Reg asked.

Taipan stared out at the road. 'Where are the VS, Reggie? They had me twice and lost me twice, and we bin leavin' a trail a noseless Alsatian could follow. It's not like that mob to give up so easy.'

'Hasslin' Budgie, maybe? Or Acacia – VS got a good look at the Rover. They might be on her tail.'

'They might,' Taipan agreed, 'but don't go knockin' the Landy. It ain't the fastest, but it'll go where those modern jobs won't. Plus, a half-decent mechanic like our pup here can keep it on the road with nothin' more than a ball of string and some sticky tape. Ain't that right, fella?'

'They're good vehicles, all right,' Kevin said.

'Nah, I reckon they ain't chasin' coz they already know where we're goin'.'

'You reckon Bhaggy set us up?' Reg said.

'Maybe. He's the one that told us 'bout Jasmine headin' west to be a cattle grower, eh.'

The women returned bearing plastic bags. Kevin smelled meat pie kept too long on the rack. Both Kala and Penny looked weary.

'Okay to drive?' Kevin asked Penny as she slipped her shopping into a backpack.

'I had a coffee; that mud would keep an elephant awake.'

'Straight to The Farm, Penny,' Taipan told her. 'Over the range and up the guts. Keep your eyes peeled, eh?'

She frizzed her hair, then slipped her helmet on. 'I hope Bhaggy's got breakfast ready. I could eat a horse.' The skin around her eyes looked sallow where it showed through the slit in her helmet. Her eyes were lit with a red-eye glow, feral, hunted. A dog expecting kicks, not pats. She kicked her bike into gear, didn't bother to check with the others before she laid down rubber and sped off, leaving them swallowing her smoke.

'Meals on wheels,' Reg said with a whoop. He revved up and took off after her, jarring Kevin into a tighter hold.

They slid over the range and down onto the coastal hinterland. They stopped only to refuel, and there was no conversation other than about the time of night and pushing on. There was no feeding, the vampires apparently still sated from the butchery at the farmhouse.

Kevin envied them; hunger plagued him like ticks on a bullock. Coke and a few mouthfuls of chocolate bar just didn't cut it. They drove all night, carving north through fields of small crops, brown-grassed hills spotted with cattle, eye-blink villages locked up and dark for the night, small towns with only a few cars parked in front of the pub.

They drove all night and no blood was spilled. That was something.

They were winding through hills somewhere near Mt Morgan, the eastern sky still securely dark, when Penny slowed, then pulled up sharply near a simple T-shaped timber sign. 'Brahman stud', it said, with only a couple of rusty nails to show where it had once had more to its name.

'Bloody near missed it,' she said as they stopped next to her.

'Off,' Taipan told Kala. 'Hold the bike while I suss things out.'

He closed his eyes and slumped in the saddle. After a few minutes, he woke up again. It reminded Kevin of the way his dad would take power naps in the afternoon, just ten or fifteen minutes. A cup of tea or two and he'd be good for the rest of the day.

'Looks all right, but I'm not takin' any chances. Kay, you double up with Penny. I'm goin' up on me lonesome. I'll flash the headlight if it's safe to come on up. If I don't, split, ring the hotline and tell Mother what's goin' on. Okay?'

'You really think Bhaggy sold us out?' Reg asked as he drew a gun from his saddle bag.

'Dunno, but let's play it smart. You get so much as a sniff of VS, you hit the road.'

Kala stood beside Penny's bike, looking like a schoolgirl whose mother hadn't arrived to pick her up. Kevin wanted to throw her on a bike and take off. Why couldn't they? What was to stop them, if this was a trap and Taipan didn't come back? That'd be some kind of justice, wouldn't it? Some kind of compensation for everything Kevin had lost?

He tried to do the mathematics as Taipan rode up the hill, slow and careful. By the time Taipan arrived at the homestead, its windows lit and now its veranda light shining, he still hadn't arrived at a solution. How did you balance the loss of your father and your livelihood, your whole life? What would it take to make that right?

'Thank Christ for that,' Reg said, and Kevin realised a light was winking at them from the house. Reg holstered his weapon and kicked the bike into gear. 'Smoko.'

The withered remains of an orchard lined the driveway; the rows of bare trees gave the impression of a graveyard as they climbed the hill and parked next to Taipan's bike. Kevin dismounted, stretching his stiff legs and sore shoulders. The homestead had seen better days. Paint peeled from the timber walls; its peaked corrugated iron roof was stained with rust. A Moreton bay fig towered over one side of the building. A frayed rope dangled from one of its thick, gnarled branches, probably where a swing had once hung but looking too much like a broken hangman's rope for Kevin's liking. Outbuildings were scattered farther up the hill.

Taipan stood at the top of the front stairs with two men and a woman. One of the men wore a loose, collarless shirt hanging to his knees over his strides; the other two strangers wore jeans, long-sleeve shirts and Blundstone boots: farmers' uniforms. As Kevin followed the Night Riders up the stairs, he realised he was looking at a vampire and a red-eye couple, and any sense of normality took a swerve to the left.

Budgie appeared behind them, beer in hand, smiling broadly. 'What took you so long? We're down to the last carton.'

They crowded inside, the Night Riders and their three hosts.

'Any word from that cockatoo of ours?' Taipan asked.

Acacia's old nickname jagged Kevin's attention like a parrot's squawk, and he was relieved to hear she'd been in touch to say that she and Hippie had arrived safely.

There was greeting and talking, hugs and thumps on backs, then showers and a change of clothes, and while cattle lowed in the background, they were ushered into the dining room and served cups of warm, pink-foamed blood that stilled the hunger but failed to ease a deeper-seated need; it was water where beer was called for.

Kevin sat alone, a stranger slumped over his schooner at a

local bar, surrounded by the Night Riders but not talked to. The red-eyes, Kala included, had retreated to the kitchen. Delicious scents of meat and pasta wafted through along with a burble of voices. Staff in the kitchen, Kevin thought, while the masters sat at the table.

Bhagwan had long hair, a full beard, sharp teeth protruding over his lips, a quick, ferret-like expression. Kevin had expected a man with that nickname to be more relaxed. The guy got more nervous when Taipan suggested Kevin should stay.

'What?' Kevin said. 'You're gonna dump me here?'

'How long?' Bhagwan asked Taipan.

'I bin keepin' him lean. A week at most.'

'Hot?'

Taipan shook his head. 'Lukewarm at best. I'm the hot property 'round here.'

'I don't know if I have the resources for that,' Bhagwan said, flashing an apologetic grimace in Kevin's direction.

'You mean you don't wanna share ya myxos,' Taipan said. 'I thought you was weaning yourself.'

Bhagwan rubbed his forearms, first one, then the other. 'Of course, but still, it's a delicate balance. This one is – no offence, young man – still so raw. So passionate.'

'And you're so very serene here in Shangri La. Beef prices getting you down?'

'I don't want to kill,' Kevin said.

'Admirable,' Bhagwan said. 'We do kill the occasional cow – fresh meat, for the help.'

'Gotta keep the help healthy, eh, Bhaggy,' said Taipan.

'We don't kill here. We take as little as we must. We give them only what they need. This is not some decadent sty.'

'That'd be the royal *we*,' Taipan said with a wink to Kevin. 'The hermit, some call him; probably why VS tolerates him. Just a lonely little bloodmuncher keepin' his own little stud – as long as he supplies all the cow juice the master wants. Go on, Bhaggy: show the young fella ya trophies.'

The man hesitated, then pushed a sleeve up to show a pattern of thin scars making a ladder on his forearm.

Kevin frowned.

'Mementoes,' Bhagwan said, 'reminders of my weakness.' He tugged the sleeve back down.

Kevin felt his undamaged chest. 'I thought we healed as good as new.'

'Silver nitrate.' Bhagwan's voice was low, as though offering a kernel of forbidden knowledge. 'Laced into the wound. Keeps it from going smooth. One for every time I succumb.'

Taipan snorted. 'As if carryin' their ghosts in your noggin' ain't enough.'

'I know a guy in Brisbane,' Bhagwan said, ignoring the biker, 'who does it for a living – scars, tattoos. Mixes blood and other stuff to make the ink. Does great work. Just ask my red-eyes, they'll show you.'

'I bet they will,' Taipan said. 'You'd think a bloke that good could make himself look prettier, wouldn'tcha? Ugly bugger, that Needle. Cunnin' but.'

Anger flashed in Bhagwan's eyes, quickly fading as Taipan stood. 'Some wear their memories, their failures, on the outside.'

'So when was you in the big smoke, Bhagwan?'

'Years ago,' he said as the biker loomed over him. 'I haven't seen the Needle in years.'

'Still, good of him to let you know about Jasmine's settin' up shop out west, eh?' Taipan sat next to Bhagwan, an arm around his shoulder. The man shrank away. 'So how is business, Bhaggy? VS still payin' top dollar for ya moo juice? Maybe lookin' for some spilt beans on the side?'

'Jasmine's move into primary production is no threat to me.'

'No? Sure you didn't think that maybe I'd dust her for you, to get at me sister? Or maybe that if you gave VS me head on a plate, they'd let you keep ya little farm goin'?'

'You know I don't operate that way, Taipan.' He gestured at the others at the table. 'Your people, Budgie and Co., they've been here for a day already. There's been no Gespenstenstaffel busting down doors, has there? We've been nothing if not accommodating.'

'I'll drink to that,' Budgie said, raising a glass, but there was a nasty edge to his voice.

'So why stop now?' Taipan continued as though Budgie hadn't spoken, as though he didn't have an entire pack gathered around the table. 'This young fella wouldn't eat much, wouldya fella?'

Bhagwan's face tightened, his words coming out like a tyre losing air. 'I don't take sides, you know that. I give VS their blood, I give it to you. You all leave me alone. That's the deal.'

'And all I'm askin' is that you share ya even-handedness with this young fella here, till his system's had a good flushin' and he's ready to hit the road. Never to be seen by you, or me, again.'

'And you're leaving–'

'Sunset. First thing.'

Bhagwan darted a look at Kevin, then back at Taipan as the biker disengaged and picked up his glass. 'Maybe.' He glanced toward the kitchen as a woman's laugh cut the air.

'I like ya myxo,' Taipan said. 'She smells like, like golden syrup. 'Member that stuff? Come in tins, eh. Usedta eat it by the gallon.'

Bhagwan crumpled. 'Sure, sure, the pup can stay. But you're going, right? Sundown. No tearing up the town, no going into Rocky to raise merry hell.'

'Glad to hear it,' Taipan said. 'A week, Bhaggy, just till he's clean.'

'You made him – how clean can he possibly get?'

'Cleanish, then. He's got a hard-on to go back west, set up a business, have some kids. White picket fence, all'a that.'

Bhagwan smiled weakly.

Reg, setting down a fresh jug of cows' blood, laughed. 'The great Aussie dream.' He clanged his glass against Kevin's empty mug.

Kevin extricated himself from the gathering. His fate appeared to have been decided; he had no interest in what further mayhem Taipan was planning. He walked into the kitchen to tell Kala the good news, but his presence immediately shut down the conversation where a gaggle of red-eyes sat eating and drinking around a Formica table. The scents rushed around him – food, wine, beer.

'Did you want more?' Bhagwan's woman asked, and the man added cheekily, 'Light or heavy?'

'Just returning my glass.'

'Sink's there, knock yourself out,' the woman said. The man stared at him, calculating.

'Okay, Kevvie?' Kala asked over a half-demolished plate of T-bone and vegies.

Taipan loomed in the doorway behind him. 'Bedtime, kids. And whitefella,' he said, looking at Kala, 'Bhagwan says you can stay. He'll get you a set of wheels when it's time to go. All right?'

As if he had a choice.

Kala's face was a blank mask as she rose. Penny slouched up after her, looking exhausted still.

'C'mon,' Taipan said. 'We're campin' in the quarters, there. Bhaggy don't want us upsettin' his "ambience".'

They marched onto the veranda, Taipan's hand on Kala's neck, guiding her, and Reg – his face as red as a stoplight – with his arm around Penny's shoulders.

'I'll be down in a minute,' Kevin said.

'Suit yourself,' Taipan said, 'but don't stay up too late. Wouldn't wanna get Bhaggy's nose outta joint.'

Eventually, with pink staining the sky, the male red-eye fetched Kevin. The man looked weary and dark-eyed; he smelled of sex and fresh blood. Kevin thought he detected Reg's scent on him, but maybe that was a holdover from having had his helmeted nose pushed into the biker's back for hours. The man's shirt was open almost to the navel. A tattoo showed over his heart – one of those loopy Egyptian crosses in tarnished silver.

'Hear you'll be staying with us for a time,' the man said, reaching out his hand. The red-eye had a firm grip, a work-rough palm and fingers. A touch of wolfbite coloured his cheeks; a four-dot pattern like Penny's decorated his throat above his collar. Kevin followed him to one of two ramshackle quarters sitting side by side near a set of stockyards. A horseshoe hung over the door of one.

'Budgie's bunch is in that one,' the man said, pointing to the hut without the shoe. 'Your boss wants you in this one. With him.'

'About your boss,' Kevin said, 'everyone says Bhagwan's a veggo, but he drinks your – human – blood.'

'It's a renewable resource, y'know.'

'But he cuts himself when he does it. As though it's wrong.'

'It's hard for him to admit he needs it.' The man shrugged, as though they were talking about an eccentric aunt rather than a creature existing on the blood of others. 'I don't mind.'

'Is it worth it?'

'I get this.' He pulled his shirt open to show the curvy cross etched into his skin.

'You got a tattoo?' Kevin asked, suspecting he was being toyed with.

'You are a little virgin, aren't you?' The man stood close to Kevin, a hand cupping his cheek. His eyes were red spots, hypnotising. 'How old do you think I am?' His hips pushed against Kevin, backing him up against the veranda rail. Beer, musky sex, his steak dinner, his blood, Reg and his road-stained leather. The man's blood, his desire, rising to the surface. His hand, rough on Kevin's cheek. His eyes, huge, twin bloody moons filling Kevin's vision. His voice, husky, saying, 'He drinks, I drink. It's a win-win situation.'

But, Kevin thought, *variety is the spice of life.*

The door thumped open behind them. The man started, dropped his hand, but didn't move back. He looked over Kevin's shoulder toward the door, from where the stench of Taipan's freshly lit cigarette rolled down.

'Givin' me boy a lesson there, myxo?'

'He did ask,' the man said, hands on his hips.

'Well, you can give him all the answers he can handle after we've gone,' Taipan said. 'Now piss off.'

The man gave a surly smile and stalked off toward the main house.

'Get inside before you make Kala jealous,' Taipan told Kevin. 'Last night together and all'a that.'

Kevin shook his head, groggy with confusion. Normally, if a bloke had bailed him up like that, he'd have given him a thrashing. But all he'd wanted to do to this fella was – taste him. He rubbed his forearms as they crawled with the thought of Bhagwan's scars. He'd have to watch himself around Bhagwan and his pair of misfits. Still, they couldn't be worse than Taipan's bloody gang. Could they?

TWENTY-FOUR

Oh-four-hundred on Saturday morning. Not even twelve hours since the men with the clipboards had given Mira's helicopter the thumbs up. Which meant he'd been released from the veritable banishment of hanging around the workshop getting in people's way, a brooding symbol of their mistress's displeasure. On the plus side, he had caught up on some much-needed sleep, reading and drinking, interrupted only by calls for updates from the Strigoi and invitations from smart-arse technicians to look at pieces of incomprehensible machinery. The guns, though: those had been cool.

The alarm buzzed again and Reece slammed the clock, only to realise, finally, that it was his intercom making the racket.

Up. Yawning, fur-tongued, he hit the answer button. Yes? Shit.

Yes, Strigoi. Right away, Strigoi. Three bags full, Strigoi.

And my, wasn't she excited. Someone was in for a bollocking.

Unshaved and clad in full kit, he made his way to the helipad, pronto. There, squatting on its skids like a malignant beetle, the matt black machine looked even deadlier than it had under lights in the workshop. The waxing half moon hung low over the hills in the west, weak in comparison to the city's wattage.

There were few stars, not like that amazing starscape he'd seen out west. A view like that, you could almost understand the attraction of living in the middle of nowhere. Almost.

Mira met him on the roof. The hilts of her swords poked out of the gap where she held her cape-like Driza-Bone shut against the downdraft of the rotor blades. A squad of Gespenstenstaffel already huddled inside, armed with automatic weapons and standard issue broadswords.

'Bit early for a test flight, isn't it?' he asked, shouting over the engine noise, squinting into the wind. 'First light's less than an hour.'

'I've had a most pleasant dream,' she told him. 'I'm fairly certain I know where Taipan and the grease monkey are holed up. Problem is, Taipan's getting ready to ditch the boy, which means–'

'Not very fatherly,' Reece said.

'Which means,' she continued, her irritation clear, but quickly passing as she ushered him to the door and her excitement took over again, shining green and bright in her eyes, 'this is my last chance to catch that slimy little biker. Now stop annoying me and get on board. I have to get back into that grease monkey's head and make sure he doesn't go anywhere before we get there. Daylight or not, Reece, we are going to kill more than a few birds with this stone.'

TWENTY-FIVE

The wooden walls pulsate with a dark violet glow; it's as though the cabin has been enfolded within a heart, purplish light streaming through its membranes as the beat makes the floor reverberate. As Kevin's eyes adjust, he sees Mira standing behind Meg, slowly peeling off the girl's blouse to reveal her lacy bra, the generous swell of breast. Meg bites her lip as Mira's hands strip back the cloth to show her stomach, navel, knickers.

'Jesus, Meg,' Kevin says. 'Where are your strides?'

Meg smiles. 'Where are yours, Kev?' She kisses Mira as her blouse folds like a sleeping dove around her naked ankles.

Kevin looks down. Naked. He's naked in the dorm, but none of Taipan's gang are around. It's just the three of them. The three of them and a white shape propped on a sofa.

'That's right, *Liebchen*,' Mira says. 'Just us. Don't worry about that silly slut. She died happy.'

The white shape comes into focus – a sheet covering someone sitting on the old sofa. It slips down, revealing the head and torso of the girl the Night Riders killed, still in her bloodstained nightdress. She looks at Kevin, her mouth open silently. He smells again the burning hair and wants to vomit. The girl dissolves into ash.

'I said not to worry about her,' Mira says, her voice crackling with command. 'Watch us. Stay with us.'

A gash appears on Kevin's arm and bleeds silver. He grabs the wound, but then another appears, and another, climbing up his arm. Then they vanish.

'Pay attention,' Mira says.

Her lips run down Meg's throat, across her shoulder. She eases the bra strap off, leaving a depression. Licks it. Meg sighs, holds her bra to her chest as the strap slides down her bicep. Mira slips the other strap down and pulls Meg's hands away to let the garment fall. Meg's nipples are hard points. Mira cups the girl's breasts, making her lean back, eyes closed, lips parted and glistening. Mira bites down and Meg cries out. Blood washes from her shoulder, across her breasts. A line of crimson wriggles across her stomach, slowly staining her knickers.

Kevin shouts Meg's name. Her eyes flicker open. 'What?' she asks dreamily.

'What the hell are you doing? With her?'

'What you asking me for? It's your dick she's sucking.'

He looks down, aware of his nakedness, of his aching erection and the touch of lips and tongue, wet warmth sliding down the shaft, fingernails stroking his thighs and balls.

Mira laughs up at him. 'Got something for me, Grease Monkey?' Her fingers pump his shaft, nails bright scarlet against his flesh. Before he can protest, he comes, spraying red with the pressure of a burst fire hose. Mira laughs again, lapping up the flow as it splashes across her face and breasts.

'Come for me, *Liebchen*, that's the way,' she cackles. 'Give me all you've got.'

Kevin hauls her to her feet, her skin slippery under the bloody shower, and throws her face-first against the wall of the dorm so hard it shakes. He parts her legs as blood streams down her back and across her buttocks. Above their heads, a red neon horseshoe rattles against the timber. It winks on and off like a cheap 'Open' sign.

He shoves himself into her. He wants to hear her scream, but all she does is laugh.

Kevin woke, breathless. A heavy bass beat filled his ears. He stared around the darkened room, his eyes picking out the glow of sunlight through the cracked weatherboards, the floating dust, the bodies of his companions sprawled in the one main room of the cottage.

He stared, surprised not to see bloody handprints on the wall where he'd fucked Mira in his dream. He swallowed hard. Just a nightmare, a terrible bloody nightmare. The bass rhythm faded.

Kala stared at him, her eyes a feral red. 'What is it?'

'Bad dream,' he said. 'That's all.'

'A dream? Or something in your lifestream – a memory?'

'A nightmare, actually.'

She crawled across to where he lay. She was wearing just a singlet and knickers. 'What did you see?'

He blushed. 'My girlfriend.'

'And what was happening?'

'I'd rather not say.'

'Was she the only person in it? This is important, Kevvie. You need to be straight with me.'

'No,' he conceded, 'Mira was there, too.'

'Tai: you hear that?' Kala nudged the biker, then shook his shoulder until he stopped batting at her and actually opened his eyes. 'I think the bloodhag's been sending to Kev.'

'What?' Taipan looked at Kevin, bleary-eyed.

'Kevin dreamed about Mira.'

'Now that's some kinda wet dream. So where you seen that bitch before, fella?'

'Just at the farm. The Crawfords' farm. During the attack.'

Taipan got up, and faster than fast, a knife appeared in his hand, broad bladed and curved to a point. A gutting knife. 'We all saw her there, fella, but you're the only one gettin' hot and sweaty 'bout her.'

'It was a nightmare, that's all.'

'We don't dream, fella. All you got in ya head is what you put there. Well, you and me, right? And I sure as shit ain't had that bitch's fangs in me. So tell me again, how come you've got her in ya noggin'?'

'How would I know?' Kevin looked around: the door? A window? Would he last longer outside in the sun than he would in here? The myxos would hunt him down, hunt him down and drag him back to Taipan and that'd be that.

Kala stood between Kevin and Taipan. 'Leave it alone, Tai. He's only a pup. He could see anything in the blood and not even know what it is.'

'I'm askin' the fella some questions here, Kay. Keep ya nose out of it.'

'What's important isn't how he came to see it, but what he saw. If Mira knows where we are. So Kevvie, what was it like? Did the dream seem real?'

'Pretty fuckin' real.'

'And you're sure it was a dream? Not just a memory from before?'

'No, it was definitely a dream.'

Kala grabbed Kevin's shoulders, her voice urgent. 'What did Mira say? What happened?'

'I don't remember, really.'

Taipan pointed his knife at Kevin. 'What did you tell that bitch 'bout us?'

'Nothin'. Nothin' at all.'

'Where were ya – in ya dream?'

'Here, I think. There was–'

Taipan swore, started kicking the people around him. 'Get

up. We gotta get movin'.' He stared at Kala. 'I reckon they know we're here, all right.'

'Fuck, Tai,' she said. 'It's daylight.'

'Don't matter, we gotta run.'

'It's broad fucking daylight.' She began to pull her jeans on.

Taipan grabbed her by the arm and shook her so hard she let her pants go. They bunched around her knees. She screamed at him and he released her. Swearing, she reefed her jeans back up. The stud clicked.

'We hafta get outta here, Kay. You and Penny get up to the house and find us some wheels. Give Budgie's mob a shout on the way past, too.'

The women left and, shortly after, Budgie's mob crammed in with them.

Time was measured in heart beats, trickling sweat, the shuffle of boots and squeak of floorboards. Reg clicked the safety of his submachine gun on and off, on and off. 'You wanna send the myxos off, Tai?'

'Let's give them girls a few more minutes.'

'What about him?' Reg asked, pointing the gun at Kevin.

'I'm thinkin' 'bout that.'

The Night Riders kept watch, the silence painful, the tension claustrophobic as they waited. And waited.

Kevin, unarmed and ostracised, shrank back against one wall and wished for it to be over.

Finally:

'Car coming,' Budgie said, his voice a whip crack.

'Kala,' Taipan said. 'About bloody time.'

'There's something else,' Reg said, looking toward the ceiling.

Kevin concentrated, heard the rhythm from his dream, low and deep. Looked up, as though he could see the helicopter through the weatherboards and iron.

'This is gonna be close,' Taipan muttered as he opened the front door and stepped away from the scorching ray of sunshine that splashed on the floor.

A truck chugged up. Wide timber rails made a cage of the back with a loosely tied canvas tarpaulin for a roof. It stank of cow shit. Penny opened the rear gate. It banged against the sides as the truck started to reverse. Beep, beep, beep. Like an alarm clock going off.

'Go,' Taipan shouted, and the gang crowded around the door. The truck stopped and Penny lowered a plank as a make-shift ramp.

Reg, swearing, wheeled his bike past Kevin.

A shadow passed over them, and it sounded as if they were being run over by a slasher, the helicopter's noise battering the cottage as it turned to face them.

'Down,' Taipan yelled.

A whoosh. The world exploded.

TWENTY-SIX

Deaf. Blind. Confused. Kevin tried to stand and couldn't, lurching across the floor like a drunk lizard. Heat washed over him. He rolled, crawled, not even sure what direction he was going. Hands hauled him up and he couldn't resist; just stared around at the blurred, smoke-screened world, his hearing filled with the crackle of flames, the mechanical clatter of automatic weapons.

'Hang on!' someone shouted. He reflexively closed his hands into fists, grasping leather in his hands. The reek of ash and blood filled his nostrils. Sunshine blazed. He shrank away, insecure on the saddle, and the rider swore at him.

The bike jerked into motion, dust flying around them, the thumping of the chopper like being in a tin drum being beaten with sticks. There was another long burst of automatic fire, deeper than the high-pitched stutter of the Night Riders' weapons. The gun sounded as if it could chew through concrete.

The bike bucked through scrub, shaking Kevin as though he was a sack of potatoes. Sunlight strobed through leaves. The helicopter moved off behind them, trailing gunfire. Kevin clung like a koala to its mother in the midst of a cyclone. The path smoothed out, the trees gave way to blue sky. The sun cooked him inside his clothes. He shut his eyes against the heat and the pain, let the world shudder by, a strange and deadly thing. Darkness finally closed around them. It was still daytime, but they were out of the sun. Someone prised Kevin's grip loose. He fell helplessly, rocking the bike and making the rider curse. His eyes stung painfully, as though they'd been sprayed with pepper.

'Fuck,' he croaked.

Something moved nearby. Taipan, blurry through tears, carrying something. Hot flesh hit Kevin's face. He grabbed it with both hands. Didn't think. No time for thinking. Just bit down and drank and drank. Something mewed like a kitten. Just one soft cry. He knew, then, but that part of him was submerged under desperate red need. He would cry later. Now, he could only feed.

'See, fella,' Taipan said, sitting back against the wall of the garage, his voice coming from a million years away, 'you ain't that different.'

Late afternoon sun was probing at the curtains when Kevin came to. He lay on a leather couch, the room lit by the blue-grey flicker of a television with the volume turned down to a murmur. Taipan drank beer and smoked. The biker had showered and changed clothes, but still wore his tattered jacket. His helmet sat on a nearby table, a silver dent showing where a bullet had scored one side.

The memories of the young girl Kevin had fed on – had *consumed* – followed him out of sleep.

Nicola, stirred by the noise of a motorcycle, is on her way to the bathroom; no Saturday morning sleep-in for a farm girl, not even a teenager who needs her beauty sleep, not when there are horses to feed and groom, chores to be done, assignments to get started, even this early in the term. Her life totally sucks. She's on her way to the bathroom, just like any other day except she's pissed at her father for leaving her behind, when she hears a sound from the kitchen where her mother's preparing round two of breakfast. There's a noise from the kitchen that doesn't sound right. Nicola, bleary and rubbing at her eyes, walks down the hall and asks her mum if everything's okay but quickly realises it isn't, because an Abo is fucking her mother on the table. Fucking her, but why is there so much blood? He drags Nicola, screeching and clawing, through the house and throws her down beside a dead white guy and the dead guy wakes up and...

Nicola. Age 15, turning legal in two months and three days, not that she was counting. Liked cats and horses, was extremely good at Geography and English but was bitter that her Maths and Science weren't good enough to study as a veterinarian. A bit whiney, Nicola: Why do I need chemistry to look after animals, Mum? I don't understand.

Kevin fought free of the lifestream's last tentacle, like dragging himself out of a vat of molasses. 'Where are we?' he asked, summoning the energy to sit up.

'You know as good as me,' Taipan said, not even bothering to look at him.

And he did. A horse stud on the fringe of Mt Morgan. Nicola was dating one of the hands, a local boy. He was as thick as two planks but knew all about handling horses – horses and Nicola.

'What did you do with her?' Kevin asked.

'Put her in with her mother. Dad's away in Rocky lookin' at nags. Be home late tonight or tomorra, but us fellas'll be long gone by then. Still, don't go answerin' no phones, eh.'

'The girl was upset that she couldn't go, too,' Kevin mumbled to himself as the emotions resurfaced. Tears pricked his eyes. 'She had an assignment to do. On Iraq.'

'You look like Baghdad, fella,' Taipan said.

'I feel like it. Fuck, my leg's sore.' Kevin looked down and gasped. 'Fuck – me leg!'

His left leg was missing from a couple of inches just below the knee. Nothing but a stump, the pink flesh mottled and lumpy. His left hand was a mess, too, black and red and filled with needles, and now his leg was throbbing – his leg, his hand, his ribs.

'Don't panic,' Taipan said. 'It'll grow back. Like them geckoes, us mob.'

'Jesus fucking Christ, Tai– I've lost my leg!'

Taipan stared at the television. 'You're lucky that's all it was.'

They were alone, Kevin realised. 'Where are the others?'

Taipan shook his head, swigged his beer, kept his eyes on the screen. 'I dunno where none of them are. That Kala, she maybe all right. I feel her sometimes. But maybe it's just a ghost, like that missin' foot of yours.'

'Kala. So it's just us?'

'Great, eh.' Taipan sipped on his beer. 'You shoulda told us about Mira's little fuck fest.'

'I couldn't–'

'My fault. I get it. Too busy on the warpath to see what's in fronta me face.'

'How do you know about Mira and me?'

'I had a taste while you was sleepin' it off. Seen a bunch of stuff. Young Nic there. The bloodhag. Ya dad. Ya girl. It ain't easy, eh – havin' to give it all up for life on the road.'

'You make it sound like it was a choice. Hang on, you had a what?'

'Till we get to Mother's, you need to stick close to me. Or at least, close to this. Okay?' Taipan pulled his necklace out from his shirt, a disc with what looked like canine teeth on either side. The battered medallion had a misshapen silver oval set in the centre of a five-pointed star inscribed on the disc.

'Lucky for us, that farmer has a good workshop. I already took some of ya juice to muddy the water a bit. I jigged this

169

best I could to keep you off their radar. Course, I mighta just stuffed it up for both'a us, me not bein' up with Mother's kadaicha and all that. But I figure your trace will be weaker, seein' as how it's so old and the hag only got the one good tumble with you. This should fritz her bloodlink good enough till we can get to the nest and Mother can knock you up somethin' better.'

'So how close is *close*?'

'This is good. Touchin' is better. But there'll be enough'a that on the bike.' Taipan drained his stubby and stood.

'And you did all that while I sleeping? Had a good swallow, took a gander through my life, stole some blood.'

Taipan over him in the servo.

Furious, Kevin lashed out.

Taipan dodged easily. 'Settle down, fella. I did what I had to. I shoulda tasted you at the silo, even if it ain't right, drinkin' from ya own. But who'd've thought that bloodhag would get to you so quick, eh? Me pack has paid the price so you just be glad I don't try 'n' make up for it now.'

'You black bastard.'

'I love the way when you white pricks get upset, the first thing you find to accuse us of is bein' black.'

'You– you did this to me.'

'And you lot did this to me. So let's call it even, eh? I gave you the curse coz ya old man wanted me to. You wanna blame someone, blame him.'

'And he made you bite me while I was unconscious, did he? Made you take me – my life, my memories – without even asking.'

'I had to know the truth. That's it. Jesus, fella, it ain't like I fucked you.'

'What's the fucking difference?'

'Ya arse ain't sore, is it? Listen, we're in this together, all right? I coulda left you there, but I didn't.'

'And why didn't you? Why did you choose me over Reg, or Penny, or Kala?'

'You was nearest. I didn't know who I had till we was on our way.'

'Sorry.'

Taipan snorted. 'Luck'a the draw. What'd you want – flowers?'

'You are such an arsehole.'

'I've heard that. Guess I'm one of them "acquired tastes". Anyway, this is the way it is: we're stuck here till sundown. They got that chopper up in the air still. They prob'ly got the cops in as well, doin' searches.' He stared at the empty stubby, then threw it at the wall. It shattered. 'You want a beer?'

'Fine.' Kevin lay back and closed his eyes, seething, trying to process everything Taipan had told him. He wanted a long shower. He wanted to know if Kala was alive or not. He wanted his life – his leg! – back. He wanted to sleep forever and wake up at home to find all this was just some horrible, shitty nightmare.

They spent the rest of the day in uneasy silence, listening for trouble, drinking beer and watching nonsensical television from, it seemed, another planet: cars, hamburgers, home theatre; holidays in Fiji.

Why do I need chemistry to look after animals, Mum? I don't understand

They'd made the headlines, but the story on the television didn't seem to be the same incident they'd survived. Charred ruins and body bags, no sign of anyone they recognised – VS being camera shy. Road blocks in place, the stern reporter said, the survivors armed and dangerous but no descriptions.

Kevin thought, 'Beware of strangers bearing guns', but he didn't say it out loud in case he spewed.

Cheap T-shirts, clubs with pokies and $15 steak nights.

Taipan kept watch in case the police came doorknocking

and Kevin struggled to stay awake, afraid of re-entering Nicola's short life while his injured body cried out for more.

Celebrity marriage, celebrity divorce, celebrity tits.

They sat in silence, waiting for the day to end.

TWENTY-EIGHT

They lost time going through the bush to get clear of the town, and then rejoined the road going west. Kevin sat behind Taipan, his mind blank, mostly healed hand holding on tight, his wounded leg itching like a dog with mange. He didn't realise anything was wrong – anything new, at least – until Taipan pulled the bike up at the end of a long straight. Kevin raised his head for the first time since they'd hit the bitumen. Moonlight painted the barren paddocks in shades of grey. A creek cut across the flat in front of them. A road sign indicated a bridge ahead. Two police cars blocked it.

'I can see four of them coppers,' Taipan said.

'Can we go round?'

'We don't have time for that. I wanna be a long way aways from this place come sun-up. Nup, we gotta go through.'

'Jesus, Taipan, they're cops.'

'They're workin' with VS. That makes 'em the enemy. Reckon you can ride this?'

'With one foot? I can't work the shifter.'

'I'll leave it in first. Can you do it or not?'

'Sure, I guess. What are we gonna do?'

'Just drive on up to them mob and keep ya head down. Wouldn't wanna lose that other foot, eh. Gimme a few minutes, then act all distractin-like.'

Taipan ran off and was quickly lost in the scrub. A light showed in the distance – a homestead, perhaps. Kevin counted the time but lost his way when images of Nicola's wrist watch surfaced.

Happy birthday, sweetheart.

His leg was in constant pain, but his ribs had eased to being merely annoying. Having to hold the clutch in wasn't doing his injured hand any favours. Damn, but he was hungry.

Taipan appeared next to him, shocking him so much he almost stalled the bike.

'What're you waitin' for?' Taipan demanded.

'Where–'

But Taipan was gone, as instantly as he'd popped up.

Kevin took a breath. He'd had a gutful of Taipan. If he could've, he'd have turned the bike around and left the biker to make his own way to – to wherever. But that was hardly an option, not now; especially when he couldn't even get out of first gear. The Kawasaki jerked forward as he released the clutch, the bike revving under his inexperienced hand on the throttle; it felt as if the machine wanted to throw him off, resenting such ungainly treatment. When he got closer, he turned on the headlight, keeping it on high beam to try to dazzle the cops. One waved a fluoro baton, indicating he should pull over, and then the cop dropped it and ran to crouch with his mates behind their vehicles, the glint of barrels unmistakable. The thought of being shot made Kevin's skin itch. His leg throbbed as though it had caught fire. He crouched low over the tank and concentrated on keeping the bike upright.

The police car lights rotated blue. A cop with a megaphone commanded him to stop. Kevin weaved his way toward the roadblock at a crawl.

'If you don't stop now, we will shoot,' the cop shouted, anxiety clearly audible through the electronic buzz.

Taipan appeared amongst the cops. He sliced the throat of

one, kicked a second into next week. He ran at the other two. One fired a shot, a dying reflex as Taipan felled him with a blow to the neck. The fourth he pinned from behind and drained.

Somewhere nearby, a dog barked.

Kevin wheeled over and shut the bike down, using his good leg to hold the machine up. It wasn't as if he could kick the stand down. He concentrated on the machine, anything to distract him from the bodies.

'You need a refill?' Taipan asked.

'Nope.' His body protested, but he was having enough trouble filtering out Nicola's life. Just how much blood could he possibly drink?

'Could be your last chance before we get where we're goin'. You need the fresh stuff, keep that leg gettin' better.'

'I can't,' Kevin said, 'not like this.'

'That Kala, she's a bit of all right, eh? It ain't always like that, fella. Gotta take it where you can.'

Kevin choked on the stink of urine, blood, gunpowder. 'I can't.'

Taipan turned his back and pissed a stream.

'So what was that trick – popping up and then doing the vanishing act? You got some kind of teleporter or something? Like in *Star Trek*?'

'Get real, fella. That shit ain't real.'

Taipan zipped himself up, then threw a collection of pistols and spare magazines into a saddlebag.

'Well, how did you do that?' Kevin asked.

'Black magic,' Taipan said, tapping his nose. 'Shove over. I'm drivin'.'

Kevin bit back a curse. What he wouldn't give for a straight answer. He made room on the saddle, dodged Taipan's boot as the biker mounted.

'What about these blokes? You gonna just leave them here – like this?'

'VS can clean 'em up. They woulda radioed in for sure. We

gotta make miles. A lotta towns to go round between us and where we gotta get to.'

Taipan revved the bike into life, cancelling any further conversation.

Kevin sat back, preferring to use the sissy bar on the back of the seat than hold on to Taipan. After a while his thighs ached from gripping the bike. He felt giddy with the pain in his leg and the memories of Nicola.

Iraq is a country in the Middle East. It has been a fucked-up mess ever since the overthrow of Saddam Hussein

She had thrown the textbook against the wall in disgust, wishing she could be in Rockhampton with her father. Kevin knew just how she felt.

TWENTY-NINE

Taipan had, whether by good fortune or good planning, grabbed Penny's rugged road bike to make their escape. The Kawasaki was a sleek blue-and-silver hybrid with a generous fuel tank and top suspension. Its off-road capabilities were put to the test when they had to dodge more roadblocks and town centres, cutting across paddocks and negotiating scrub, taking to dirt roads and cattle tracks where necessary. Fuel was their major worry, Taipan leaving Kevin in the dark while he bought or siphoned petrol. Between towns, Taipan kept the bike red-lining, relying on his superior reflexes and pure skill to keep them on the road and out of the way of stray livestock and potholes.

No matter how far they went or how fast, the disaster at The Farm rode with them. They didn't speak any more than necessary. Kevin couldn't blame Taipan for hating him – it had been Kevin who had led the gunship to their hideout and he felt terrible about that, very aware he was sitting on Penny's bike, that Kala might be dead or a prisoner, that all those people he knew might be dead, too. But Kevin hadn't asked for this and hadn't known any better. Taipan had to share the responsibility and he'd admitted as much. Maybe the biker was considering that, too. Maybe that was the real reason he had the throttle open, the engine whining. Guilt wasn't so easy to leave behind.

Rolling, brown hills became increasingly flat; dusty-green trees increasingly sparse. Sagging barbed-wire fences lined the road, somehow containing the grey Brahman and red Droughtmaster cattle that dotted the paddocks like headstones. Fallow fields lay scratchy with stubble. The details of the inland landscape emerged from the pre-dawn darkness as the eastern sky started to lighten. The fuel gauge was showing fumes and there didn't seem to be a town within coo-ee. Kevin's nervousness grew. They were dangerously close to being out of petrol and out of night. Not a good combination.

They passed a set of stockyards, the loading ramp leaning and overgrown, and Taipan changed down until they were at an idle. He ran the Kawasaki off the bitumen onto a barely visible gravel road.

'Hold on,' he warned, the first words he had uttered since the last fuel stop. The bike juddered over an overgrown grid of steel rails. It was all Kevin could do to keep his seat.

Taipan steered the bike along the winding track. On the other side of a rise they came across the ruin of a homestead, its iron roof splotched with rust and holes, its walls bowed after years of neglect. They drove toward a shed tucked away amid a thin stand of timber. Its warped wooden walls looked as though they would have fallen years ago were it not for the net of lantana holding them up.

Taipan leaned out and opened the rickety paling door just enough to wheel the bike inside. He turned off the engine. The sudden silence was deafening after hours with the motor, the road and the wind.

'We'll spend the day and see if we get any visitors, eh,' Taipan said, glancing toward the sky.

Kevin slid off, hopped to the door and pushed it shut. He was in a shed big enough to house a tractor. Hessian bags hung across the gaps in the walls. He stayed at the door, propping himself against its flimsy support, waiting to see what Taipan was up to, the darkness lit only by the dusty beam of the bike's headlight.

The biker stepped off and stretched. Kevin held his breath. A distance of perhaps three steps separated them. If Taipan wanted to get rid of Kevin or simply take out his frustrations, then this was a good place to do it, here in this dilapidated, anonymous building. No-one would ever know. Taipan moved. Kevin steeled himself, but the biker stepped away to an obscure pile of stuff covered by a tarp. Kevin scanned for a weapon. A loft hung low at a crazy angle at the back, likely to collapse with the next dust cloud under its load of cobwebbed, nondescript machinery. Under the loft were a few musty hay bales, some drums and crates. Even if there was something Kevin could use, he had no hope of dodging the biker to get to it.

'Gimme a hand, eh,' Taipan said. 'We gotta shift these drums here.'

Kevin paused, waiting for a trick. Then said, 'sure', and hopped over to where Taipan manoeuvred drums. Kevin did his best to help, using the drums for support as he heaved them along.

'They're full,' he said, bemused yet again at his own strength. 'Fuel?' He didn't really need to ask. The smell was obvious, raw against the hay and dust.

'Yeah. One of me stashes.'

Kevin didn't reply, feeling stupid.

'Stop ya worryin'.' Taipan groped around on the floor, unconcerned about exposing his back. 'Things've gone to shit, that's for sure, but it ain't ya fault. I'm not sayin' I like you any more than I done before, and I think you're too soft most of the time, but I ain't gonna kill you, if that's what you're afraid'a. Now, get some rest. I don't think VS will foller us out here, but this is as far as we go till we know for sure.'

'Why wouldn't they?'

'We're goin' bush. That mob don't last too good out here.'

'Aren't you scared that Mira will trace me? Even with that necklace – can it stop her from getting inside my head? Sending that chopper after us again?'

'They ain't hit us yet. Nah, I figure we slipped the noose. Can you sense her, anythin' at all?'

Kevin shrugged. All he felt was pain in his foot and a general cloud of despair.

'That bloodhag might have some idea – prob'ly why it took'em so long to find us, eh. Maybe had to fly right over the top to know for sure. Maybe even then, they just let that rocket off on spec, out of frustration-like. Maybe they was fed up with Bhaggy – who knows how that mob thinks?' The biker pulled up a trapdoor, causing a wave of choking dust to roll across the floor. 'You can sleep in here, fella.'

'You're kidding.' About four men could fit in the hole, lying side by side.

'It's plenny safe. Bin used lotsa times.'

'Where are you gonna sleep?'

'I got me own place.' He must have sensed Kevin's flaring suspicion because he pointed to the dirt. 'A safe place. Nowhere near you.' He stood, brushed off his clothes and walked to the door.

'I thought we had to stay close.'

'We got some good miles behind us. A few more feet of earth ain't gonna hurt. 'Less you want me in there with you.'

'So you can take another slurp? I'll take my chances with Mira's pornos, thanks.'

'Thought so.' He turned back to the door.

Kevin glanced at the slice of lightening sky he could see through the doorway. Dawn's approach teasing his skin, like ants creeping under the surface. 'You're going outside?'

'Goin' to ground,' he said with a wink, then added, 'Not too far.' A hand pressed against the medallion under his shirt. 'If I'm not here when you get up, you can have the bike.'

Kevin laughed bitterly. 'Fat lot of good that's gonna do me.' He hopped to the trapdoor.

'Don't worry, fella,' Taipan said. 'A coupla days, you'll be just like new. Won't even hafta think about it too hard. The body remembers, better'n we do.'

'What do you mean?'

'Ya foot. Unless you wanna pretty it up. Grow a sixth toe or somethin'.'

'Wait. You mean I can control what happens to my body?'

'Sure. Mind over matter.' He tapped his forehead.

'But Bhagwan said you had to use silver-somethin'.'

'I like Bhagwan – I hope the mad bastard made it – but for a bloke who reckons he's some kind of guru, he can be as thick as a post sometimes. He just uses the silver nitrate to help him focus on what he wants. But he don't *need* it.'

'So my foot is gonna grow back, whether I think about it or not. Like my chest did when you shot me. And when you staked me.'

'That'd be about it.'

Kevin rubbed the stump below his knee, gently prodding it to prove to himself it was real. It was already longer, down almost to the ankle. He tried to keep his mind completely blank; tried not to think of chicken feet. Just how much concentration would he need to make something happen?

'Rest up, now,' Taipan said. 'Got a bitova drive tomorra before we get to the nest. Mother can show you some stuff to help keep that head on ya shoulders. Then you can do what you wanna. Me, I aim to get even.'

'And who is "Mother"?'

Taipan yawned. 'I'm goin' outside for a bit. Tuck yourself in.'

Kevin fumed as he watched Taipan walk out. What was the big deal about this Mother person? He could just make out Taipan's shape, sitting cross-legged on the bare ground not far from the shed, an orange glow and pungent odour indicating he was smoking a final cigarette before bunking down. If he feared the imminent dawn, he gave no sign.

Kevin eyed the hole in the floor, swore, then hobbled over and awkwardly lowered himself. He fought back a moment's claustrophobia, then pulled the door shut above himself and was trapped in the cold, dark space. Panic scratched at his insides when he thought of Taipan standing above him, pouring fuel over the door and setting it alight. Then he felt dawn pressing down outside the walls of the shelter and grudgingly embraced the oblivion that sleep brought. The dreams, though – the memories – he could do without them...

THIRTY

Naked, the night air so cool on his flesh, he owns the world as he falls into an effortless lope. He throws the stake he's made and a gym bag over the fence, then takes a run-up and jumps, thrilling with his athleticism as he springs to a post, sticks, then uses it to vault without touching the wire. But the impact is enough to trigger a motion sensor running with the strands of barbed wire across the top of the mesh. Spotlights beam out.

He hits the ground, hurls the bag out of sight onto a shed roof, then grabs the wooden stake and – sinks. Earth closes in, warm, welcoming, safe. Footsteps and voices vibrate through the soil and then fade. He waits, letting his senses range, and only when he's absolutely sure no-one's around, he surfaces, the dirt falling from him like water from a Driza-Bone. A shake, heeler-style, a puff of dust, and he claws up to reclaim his bag. Is a little surprised to find it still there. Dressed, he tucks the stake, as long as his arm, uncomfortably into his belt and begins his search. He creeps through the dark toward the house where lights show through cracks in curtains. No dogs – this mob don't like them, and the feeling is mutual, he suspects. Best friend to man but choosy about the monsters.

He's a shadow, he's a mote of dust, he's the breeze. He wafts on to the verandah, ears sweeping for danger, nose sniffing for that familiar scent. Jasmine Turner, all blood and stale air and mustiness, and there, his sister, ti-tree and creek water, the earth after rain. His heart beats faster as he creeps to a door and cracks it open. Kitchen smells drift from the rear of the house, but he's looking at a dining room lit by candles – no, electric bulbs shaped like candles, though he does smell wax, wax and violets, cooked beef, wine: too many to count, too many to sift, these scents that belong to another him, a younger him, back before that world ended and this new, night-clad one began.

A piano plunks a distracted scale, and the stillness adds an element of threat to those half-hearted notes, a soundtrack for something not quite right. The notes range higher as he creeps, almost in time, and he wonders how they can possibly know he's here and, conversely, how they can let him penetrate this far.

But she's here, just on the other side of that screen: a set of collapsible doors that divide this dining area from the space beyond. He can smell her. Feel her. Beams of light show through the vertical slats and he detects slight changes of movement as the pianist shifts on the stool. He reaches the edge of the divider, left open to form a narrow doorway, and he sees her in her white dress with its high collar and sleeves to the wrists, skirts to the ankles and the dainty shoes with bows, another bow in her hair tying back that luxurious midnight mane.

She hits a final, jarring note and turns her face to him, and his heart breaks open. Time has not healed this wound, merely scabbed it over; seeing her rips it raw again and he reels, grips that timber slider for support as he sways under the impact of an avalanche of moments, each one a bleeding ulcer on his soul.

He fights through to her, to the here and now, and her name is an ember on his tongue.

'Willa?'

'Chris? What the hell are you doing here?'

'Don't call me that,' he begs.

'You prefer "Taipan"? Is that who you are now?'

'It's what they've made me.'

'No, Chris, you've made that all by yourself.'

'Come with me. We can talk about it out there, on the road, where we belong.'

'Why can't you understand, Christopher; I don't belong out there. That's not what I want.'

'And this is? Bloodsack for that bitch?'

She seems almost amused, sitting there, hands in fingerless lace gloves in her lap. 'I do hope this isn't a lesbian thing.'

'I don't give a shit about that and you know it. Blood's blood, pure and simple; I don't care if it comes in a tube or a jar. It's what she's done to you that I can't stomach. Made you inta a little white doll, just like her, and now she's feedin' off'a you.'

'You don't think that maybe I made myself like this? That I actually care for her? That we share each other's blood because we like it?' *Anger in her voice, for the first time, real anger, and the situation is slipping out of his control.*

'It's her blood in you. She's all but feedin' off herself.'

'Familiarity can just as easily breed security as contempt, Chris. I made my choice and you made yours. Why can't you just let it be?'

Words won't come. Because, he wants to say. Because. The love wells up, the love and the loss, and it's as big as the sky and it feels as if his skin will burst with the attempt to contain it.

'Oh Chris.' *Her hand lifts, then falls, the distance between them uncrossed. She stands, and her voice takes on a quiet, urgent tone.* 'Did you bring that for me?'

He fingers the stake, a foot of mulga sharpened to a point.
'Never.'

'Kind of old school.'

'Some places, only the natural stuff can go, eh.'

'We don't have metal detectors here; not yet. May I see it?'
He hesitates.

'They know you're here. They've probably rung Brisbane
already.'

'I couldn't believe it when I heard she'd left the coast.' He
hands it over. He'd hardened the tip over a fire, imagining the
whole time ramming it into Jasmine's heart. 'I had to see you.'

'If they catch you–'

'It'll be worth it.'

'Chris–'

A door eases open, a footstep sounds, and he knows, down
in that place where his senses prowl ceaselessly, that they've
been out there for a while now, waiting for whatever signal.

'They'll kill you, Chris.'

'They can try.' He turns, putting himself between her and
the door.

'They will. Unless I stop them.'

She's quicker than he realised – must be all that old girl's
blood in her, he thinks, but he doesn't dodge, doesn't defend;
is too startled, maybe too resigned. Hell, he's too slow, plain
and simple. He didn't really think she'd come away with him,
but he didn't think she'd betray him, either. So he stands, mouth
open, surprised, as she rams the crude stake into his back, all
her uncanny strength driving it into his heart. For a moment
he stands, and then the heart gives up, skewered and useless,
and the power is cut and he falls, dead but not dead, and he
looks up at her and takes one small glimmer of hope with him
– in her eye, quickly wiped as the men rush into the room, a
single crimson tear.

Something tugs at his insides.

He isn't Taipan anymore.

He's Kevin, and he's lying still, pinned down. Bruise-purple daylight pushes through cracks in the wall. Dirt. He's in the dirt. Petrol. Petrol and dirt. The servo? He remembers being buried, but not scared. And now he's buried again, but he's scared. Scared of–

'Hey.' *Mira sits astride him, her skirt up around her thighs, her scarlet nails tapping on his naked chest.* 'What are you doing down there, Grease Monkey?'

He pushes against her presence, not just on his body, but in his mind, too. This isn't right. This isn't how he remembers – how he knows – it happened.

'Where are you?' *she asks.* 'It looks nice.'

But he doesn't rightly know and he clamps down on the road signs, on the vague idea he's got. Instead, he thinks of home. Mira seems distant, as though she's leaning through a gauzy curtain, and it's tightening, thickening, as he becomes more aware of her, aware of the fact that this is not a memory. This is not real. He imagines the curtain wrapping around her, tighter and tighter, as tight as a cocoon, as tight as a mummy's bandages.

'Now Kevvie, is that anyway to treat an old flame? I thought you'd be happy to see me, me and your little friend here.'

The body in the curtain is Kala, the material tight around her naked body, and blood seeps out, expanding stains from her eyes and throat, arms, groin.

The curtain tears away and Mira, in a blood-red body suit, steps out like some kind of glossy butterfly leaving a cocoon. Kala stands behind her, strapped to a vertical X.

'She's quite upset that you left without saying goodbye. She's not the only thing you left behind, is she?'

Mira dangles a foot, the ankle a torn and bloody stub, like a lost sock.

'Don't worry, Kevin, we'll look after your little friend for you.' *She runs a claw down Kala's chest, making the girl squirm.* 'Yes, we'll look after her.'

'Don't you hurt her,' he cries.

She laughs. 'Hurt her? Of course I'm going to hurt her. But that's all right. You run off home now, see if your family, if your girlfriend, will take you back.'

He's naked in a chair in his kitchen and Meg's sitting in his lap, straddling him. He pushes her skirt up and she's naked and huge and he slides into her, his cock as hard as a crowbar, and she frowns.

'Kevin,' she says, and then the consternation turns to horror as his cock expands, a real fucking Pinocchio's nose, and he shouts, 'Lie to me, lie to me, bitch!' And his cock is a sharpened stake hardened with flame and hate and he rams it into her, a timber missile looking for her heart. A purple-black light the colour of grape skin bursts from her eyes.

Taipan looms over him, biting, bleeding, and he screams then...

He bursts awake with his chest heaving, his mind roiling, and he thinks, just before he smacks into the trap door above him, that he hears Mira scream, too. It's some consolation.

THIRTY-ONE

Reece sat on the penthouse's balcony, the remains of a greasy breakfast pushed to the far side of the table so he could spread out the morning paper and enjoy his second cigarette of the day. Morning heat was already wrapping its clammy hands around him, dragging sweat from his armpits and down his back, the air barely disturbed by the gentlest of breezes drifting in off the sluggish brown river. Traffic hummed, a constant flow across the city's two bridges; life going on, unaware of the secret battles being fought to maintain its blissfully ignorant security.

He smiled at the sight of the keys to the Monaro on the table, then turned his attention to the paper. He raised it to block out the glare and that uninspiring vista of tin roofs and thirsty gum trees on the other side of the river, that singular, aerial-studded hump of drought-brown mountain in the distance.

Yesterday's attack on The Farm had been more exciting than any drug raid from his policing days. The chopper had taken out a few soft targets – Mira had been certain that her bloodwalk had given her enough information to pinpoint Kevin and Taipan well enough to make an entrance without endangering them. His plan would've been to drop the jackals first and let them go in under cover of daylight, use the chopper for fire support, but Mira did like her toys. Only after it had strafed the fuck out of the Farm had it deployed the troops, and then they'd had to work fast before law enforcement and media arrived. Mira was getting lazy, perhaps even careless, in her old age; her pursuit of Taipan was verging on reckless.

The front page, and yesterday's television and radio coverage, showed they'd got away with it. But it was getting harder to paper over the cracks. Hiding behind his false IDs, calling in favours from their plants in the media and the cops and the government; all the bullshit made him long for the good old days of kicking in doors and breaking heads and leaving the explaining to someone else. Where was Felicity when he needed her?

Still, this gig had its rewards.

Mira called.

Reece took a last inhale of his ciggie, a slurp of coffee, scooped the Monaro's keys into his pocket and headed inside.

He checked the second bedroom. The Night Rider moll lay cuffed to the soiled bed. Mira had spent two long sessions with Kala since they'd brought her in. The second time, after it was clear that Taipan and Kevin Matheson were not among the dead, he was fairly certain the torture had involved some of Mira's hoodoo. The red-eye was barely conscious, but her body was mostly healed. A bath and a decent feed, maybe a transfusion, and she'd be good to go. He picked up his pace, arriving at the master bedroom as Mira called him again. Taipan's escape had infuriated her; sure, she'd found compensation, but he didn't want to risk aggravating her further.

Clothing littered the carpet like oddly shaped stepping stones. The curtains were closed. The bedside lamplight revealed a wine bottle and glasses, the remnants of room service he'd ordered after midnight. Green eyes regarded him from the gloom. Mira lay, propped up on pillows on the rumpled king size in a white silk robe, remarkably clean amid the splatter. Bhagwan's two red-eyes lolled naked and listless at her side.

'Think I might've found a suck-up present for Jasmine,' Mira said, her voice languid from her all-nighter. 'These two cow pokes are both very good in the saddle.'

She slapped the male on the arse and told them both to leave the room.

Reece waited patiently by the door till they'd slunk out, looking like the survivors from a natural disaster. Chests scratched, skin blotched and pale. Their matching ankh tattoos struck him as being too cute.

Mira gestured him over. She was surprisingly chipper. The upside of a night of blood drinking, he supposed, her frustrations drowned for the time being.

'We made the front,' he said, waving the paper as he walked to her side.

'All you'd have to do is run down the main street naked to do that. Assuming there was anyone around to notice.'

'Nothing the television didn't have last night. Amphetamines on a commercial scale, tied into an outlaw motorcycle club. Rival gang or a falling out in the ranks. Yada yada. Bhagwan would have a purple fit.' If he wasn't on ice in a wardrobe, waiting for Mira to decide whether to let him keep his head.

'Then he'd be a hypocrite. He was one of the biggest drug suppliers in the state.'

Past tense: didn't bode well for the veggo. 'I'm not sure cow's blood counts as a controlled substance.'

'A substance of addiction, nonetheless. Did you enjoy your cigarette?'

'Very much, thanks for asking.'

'It ruins your tastebuds and your sense of smell.'

A small price to pay for the irritation it caused her. 'It's good for my nerves.'

'Jackals aren't supposed to have nerves.'

'Us Hunters do. Keeps us alive.'

'If the smoking doesn't kill you first.'

'We both know that's not likely.' Although, the way he'd been feeling lately; what would happen if her blood lost its power to maintain his body in this strange almost-stasis? Would all those years come rushing back at him like a rubber band stretched tight and released, or would he just pick up where he'd left off, going sedately into old age with only memories of when he'd been damn near indestructible?

Mira studied him, detecting his mood, he supposed; the blood didn't lie, not to her. She had to know he was tiring. That he was approaching a T-junction of mortality and immortality. No, a cross-roads: 'involuntary retirement' was also an option.

'No further word of our Taipan, I take it?' she asked.

'Not since he took out the roadblock last night, heading west. Coppers aren't happy.' Two dead, two in hospital. No, there was nothing to be happy about there. Poor bastards never stood a chance.

Mira didn't acknowledge his disapproval. The cops were just pieces on the board to her; so was he, for that matter, especially now that he was entering what some called red-eye menopause.

'Taipan and the boy have gone to ground,' she said. 'The grease monkey is shutting me out. Resisting me.'

'He can do that?'

'Oh yes, especially at this distance. He was still in the change when I bled into him, and not even I can predict what effect that will have had. I suspect he's got a little of me in him.'

'Can he back-trace you?'

'No.' She took his hand and laid it on her left breast, directly above where the nipple pushed through the silk of her robe. The top curve and point of her pentagram tattoo peeked out from under the rim of the shiny material. 'I took the requisite precautions. I've always been a big believer in practising safe sex. You can never quite tell just what kind of monster a child will grow up to be.'

She kissed his hand and released him.

'Besides, despite the anchor,' she waved her left wrist with its fleshy bracelets at him, 'bloodlinks lose potency with time and distance. Even without his active resistance, I doubt I'd be able to trace him back to the nest, not with the bloodbitch throwing up interference.'

'So they've escaped.'

'We've destroyed the body, now we have only to take the head. I have a new plan to draw them out.' She gave a mischievous chuckle. 'Jasmine is not going to like it.'

'Back to the Siding, then?' He kept his voice neutral, hiding his weariness. Maybe it was the tropical heat, wearing him down, but he had seriously hoped that this raid would be the end of it.

'Back to the Siding. Tell Felicity to expect us. But first,' she propped a leg up; her robe fell open to the groin, 'I think you've earned a drink, Hunter Reece.'

Mira drew a nail down that tender skin, opening a beaded line across her upper thigh.

He kneeled, and as he went to it, she cracked the paper open.

'Mm, nice pictures. We did make a mess of Bhagwan's spread, didn't we?'

He lifted his head, his tongue coated with her blood. 'Was all that firepower really necessary?' he asked. They'd heard the explosions and gunfire in Mt Morgan, so the paper reported. Like a war, one resident had been quoted as saying. *What's the world coming to?*

'Well, I did consider hanging you out the door on a piece of rope with a crossbow, but I have grown fond of your insubordination.'

She pushed her thigh at him, and he traced the wound again with his tongue, hungry for the rush.

'Nice job on the chopper,' he murmured. 'Having all the toys tucked away like that.'

'Worth the delay.' She popped her head around the paper to smile at him. 'We can't fly around with cannons and rocket pods hanging off us, can we? People would talk.'

'They'd all want one.' And finally, the blood rush hit, sweeping him away. He buried himself in her blood, loving it and hating himself at the same time.

'Exactly. When you're done, find some clothes for Taipan's red-eye and dump her. Let's see which way our courier pigeon flies. Oh, and Reece – you'd better give her back her little knife. I need her to arrive in one piece and the roads, they just aren't safe these days.'

THIRTY-TWO

Kevin lay panting in his shallow grave, letting the memories of the night before, the nightmares of the day, subside. Mira had come to him, and he'd fought her off, kind of, and he'd fallen back into his torpor. Now, exhausted and hungry, he struggled to orientate himself once more. Earthen walls, his healing foot paining as if it'd been wrapped in broken glass, and the rising fear – his old friend Fear. Had Mira worked out where they were? Did she really have Kala prisoner? And where was Taipan?

He pushed the lid up a fraction. A trickle of dust came in, threatening to make him sneeze. Warm twilight air carried the aromas of stale hay and petrol. He opened the lid higher. No ambush, no enemies, no Taipan. But the bike was still there. Kevin sat on the lip of the hole, then used a nearby drum to pull himself upright. He shook himself free of the dust he'd collected overnight, then tested his half-formed foot. The blob of flesh wouldn't take his weight. The bones had yet to harden inside the gelatinous lump; toes were mere suggestions of bumps along the front. Dirt stuck to the soft meat.

'You wake up early, that's good. It'll keep you alive. Must be a bit'a blackfella in you, eh.'

Kevin jumped at Taipan's voice, muffled from outside.

Kevin lurched to the door, wincing as his new-born foot felt every pebble, and stood, crane-like, the sore foot off the ground as he used the lopsided jamb for support. Taipan sat just outside the door, bare-chested and cross-legged, as though he hadn't moved since they'd arrived.

'I didn't know if you'd still be here,' Kevin said, his voice harsher than he intended. Crows called, reminding Kevin death sat within a few paces.

'You mean you ain't happy to see me?' Taipan's tone was as dry as the dust in Kevin's hair. 'Or just that you didn't know if you'd wake up alive?'

Kevin limped around so he could see the biker's face. 'Both, maybe.'

'Well, like I told you, you can stop ya worryin'. Fact is, I made you; I ain't gonna put you down, not unless you give me reason, and then it'll be to ya face, not in ya sleep.'

He looked away, through his latest breath of smoke to the descending night.

'We both got fucked up by that Von Schiller mob, okay? There'll be a reckonin', don't you worry 'bout that. Then, if me and you reckon we still got business, we can sort it out.'

'Still–'

'Later. It's the best deal ya gonna get, so take it, fella.' Taipan rose slowly to his feet, seeming reluctant to stand, dusted off his pants.

'I had another dream,' Kevin told him. 'A Mira dream.'

'What did that bitch have to say for herself?'

'She,' he hesitated, not sure how much he should tell – but if Kala was in trouble – 'she's got Kala.'

'How did it feel?'

'Bad, of course.'

'Did it feel like truth?'

'How should I know?'

'Don't matter. You tell her where we was?'

'I don't think so.'

'That's somethin', then.' Taipan grabbed a T-shirt – a faded and holey Midnight Oil – from where it was draped over a nearby bush. Taipan juggled his cigarette as he shrugged into the shirt. 'We'll make a mile, eh.'

'What about Kala?'

'What about her?'

'If Mira's got her–'

'Myxo's ain't like us, fella; the blood's just Botox and a good time to them. Kala ain't bin to the new nest. All she knows about Mother is a phone number. Mira can ring it till her finger bleeds, it ain't gonna give her shit.'

'Still, if Kala's a prisoner, shouldn't we go get her?'

'And walk right into their trap? Nah. I had all the stakin' I need jus' lately.'

'Can't you tell where Kala is – just so we know for sure?'

Taipan shook his head. 'That girl's alive, I reckon, but she's weak and far away. Listen: if Mira's got her, then there ain't nothin' we can do. If Mira ain't got her, then that girl can get her own arse to Mother's nest.'

'God, I hope she's all right. I hope all of them are.'

'Yeah.' Taipan crushed his cigarette butt into the ground. 'Hungry? I'll rustle us up somethin' to eat.'

'Out here?'

'Ain't you ever heard'a bush tucker?' Grinning, Taipan let his head fall back as though he was stargazing, but his eyes were shut. He extended his hands, fingers wide, as though enjoying a breeze Kevin couldn't feel.

Stars had started sprinkling through the descending night, unmarred by city lights, just the moonlight for competition. Kevin breathed deeply, luxuriating in the sense of space, of belonging. It took him back to his childhood; another life ago. Anger kindled – the biker shared that memory, now; Taipan had not only stolen his future, but his past as well.

Kevin heard the rhythmic thuds of approaching cattle. Two grey shapes appeared out of the dark, their ears flopping on either side of their coffin-shaped heads. Brahman-cross steers. They padded up to Taipan, nuzzled his hands with their moist noses, their shoulders the same height as his. The biker moved slowly, ran a hand over their necks and humps. The steers flapped their ears; one brushed its tail up over its hindquarters.

Taipan drew his knife. Sweat glistened on his face.

'Hard work?' Kevin asked softly, afraid of upsetting whatever spell Taipan had cast.

'Yeah, but a fella's gotta eat. You wanna get us a mug from them saddlebags there?'

Kevin found a dented metal mug. His face must have shown his hesitation.

'Don't worry, fella, I ain't gonna kill'em. No point shittin' in our nest. Just takin' enough to put back some of what we lost.'

He pointed to Kevin's new foot. 'Might have a spare pair'a boots lyin' 'round here, too. We can take a look when we fuel that bike up. Tucker first.'

He brushed his hand down the neck of one steer, speaking in low, soothing tones. He found what he was looking for, pinched a handful of skin.

'Hold that mug here.' He cut through the vein. The steer twitched as the blood spurted out, boiling and black in the faint light, until a grey froth covered the top of the cup. The smell soon overpowered any squeamishness. Taipan pinched off the vein as Kevin skolled the brew.

'It's good,' Kevin said, wiping his mouth and putting the gory mug back into position. 'Not *as* good, but good enough.'

Taipan chuckled, but focused on the steers. The one he'd cut was shivering, its tail lashing. It stared back from the corner of its wide eye.

Kevin drank again and again, until Taipan rubbed a handful of dirt into the wound and let the steer go. The steer wandered off a little way before folding down to rest. Taipan drank from the other, not as much. The second steer walked over to its mate and licked its nose before settling beside it.

'So, how do you do it?' Kevin asked.

'Jus' do,' Taipan said.

'I can't.'

'Ever tried?'

'No,' Kevin conceded. 'I never thought to. I've seen, you know, in movies, rats and bats and stuff.'

'You'd rather eat a rat?' Taipan shook his head.

'I've got a lot to learn.'

'Yeah, you ain't wrong 'bout that.' And then he relented. 'C'mon, time to go home.'

THIRTY-THREE

They sped through the night, hour after hour, meeting only a few road trains. The long double-decked trailers reeked of cow shit and diesel. People out west tended to avoid driving at night, and when they did, they liked to have a tonne of bullbar and serious spotlight wattage out front. The roadsides were littered with dead kangaroos, the occasional bullock and even one emu, and more modern road kill – vehicles, burned out or stripped, victims of distance and too little maintenance. Signposts urged drivers to beware of livestock and other silhouetted animals, to 'revive and survive', and warned of fatigue zones and accident black spots, but Taipan was having none of that. Kevin found the drive nerve-wracking, and he was glad of some small reprieve when Taipan pulled up at a service station.

'Keep an eye out, I gotta make a call,' Taipan said as he dismounted. 'Then we'll fuel up and be on our way, eh.'

'You got a mobile? Can I call home?'

'You can't use this one. Wait over there.' He waved toward a wall. 'And keep ya face covered if you go near them bowsers.' He pointed to a security camera.

Kevin swore under his breath, but went. He watched, increasingly dumbfounded, as Taipan sat at a picnic table, rested his head on his forearms and, apparently, took a nap.

'Fuck this,' Kevin muttered and went to the loo, pissed a pathetic, pinkish dribble and washed his face. A rank urinal was one of those times he wished he could dial down his sense of smell. He hobbled out in his new sneakers. They'd found a reasonable fit among Taipan's stash of spare clothing; he could imagine that fleshy jelly filling out inside the shoe like a mould. He hoped his body knew how to make toes.

A young man in a service station uniform approached Taipan, still slumped at the table.

'Shit.' Kevin limped over.

The attendant gingerly reached out to shake Taipan's shoulder. The biker didn't stir.

'Hey,' Kevin shouted.

The attendant looked around. 'Is he pissed? I could report him, you know.'

'He's just tired. Long drive.'

'You his mate, are ya?'

'Yeah, I guess.'

He snorted. 'Well, he can't sleep here.'

'Haven't you ever heard of a driver reviver?'

Taipan sat up, wiped his face, blinked. 'Problem?'

The young man stared at him, opened his mouth to say something. Taipan stared back. The attendant closed his mouth, mumbled 'Fine' and slouched away.

'You got the bike filled?' Taipan asked.

'You said to watch your back.'

'Good job you did'a that. Pull up a pew, Hoppy. I'll look after it, eh.'

Kevin was too frustrated to sit down. He hadn't seen Taipan use a phone at all – had the biker waited for him to take a leak? What kind of bullshit was this? He walked over to where he could see inside the servo. There was a pay phone just inside the door. It struck him that he'd lost a chance; he could've reverse charged. Damn Taipan, keeping him rattled. The biker went in – he was actually going to pay. Probably wanted to put the wind up the attendant again. Kevin turned away as money changed hands. He didn't want Taipan to think he was spying.

When Taipan returned, Kevin was studying a faded road map painted on a signboard. Peeling pink lines stretched out from the arrow saying, 'You are here'. West to Longreach, east back to Rockhampton, Barlow's Siding unmarked but far to the south-west.

'Find yourself yet, fella?' Taipan asked, and Kevin wasn't entirely sure he meant geographically.

'Why did you do it, really? Why did you do this to me if it's all so dangerous?'

Taipan started to roll a cigarette. 'I told you, didn't I?'

'Tell me again.'

'I cut a deal with ya old man.'

'And you really don't know who killed him.'

'Not even in me blood. You shoulda seen that much.'

'I see all sorts of stuff, but I've got no control over it. It just hits me–' he slammed a fist into his hand. 'Christ, I can hardly tell who's who; whether I'm them or they're me.'

'Ghosts,' Taipan said. 'We all get 'em. They live in the blood, eh. Not alla them. Most don't stick. But some, because you took a lot, because there's some connection maybe, they stay.'

'How do you deal with it? These other lives, popping up all the time.'

'My mob are kinda used to that. Time don't always work the same way for them.'

'Huh?'

He tapped his nose.

'So if I've got your blood, I should have that power, too.'

'Maybe. I don't have no country. No people, either.' The words fell, bitter, like juice gone off. 'I thought this, that bein' like this would open that to me. Would reveal it outta me blood. But it didn't work like that. That bitch flooded me. There's more'a her in me than there is'a me.'

'Big gamble.'

'She made me sister. Only way I could save Willa was to become like them.'

'*Big* gamble,' Kevin repeated.

'Never been much of a gambler.' He rubbed his chest, that reflex drawing his hand – but now Kevin wondered if it was the recent stab wound Taipan still felt, or if it was something deeper, the type of wound to the heart that not all the vampire blood in the world could heal. Not without leaving a scar, anyway. 'Mother'll help you deal with alla that. She knows about this stuff, eh.'

'So, this Mother – is she the one who, you know, the one who turned you into – you know?'

Taipan laughed. 'Nah. You woulda seen the bitch that did.' He put a finger to his forehead. 'Jasmine Turner, her name is. I'll be seein' her 'bout that one day.

'Mother, she ain't like that. She's plenny old, older than Jasmine even. Mother is jus' what we call her, eh. When I seen her for the first time, I was plenny fucked up. As fucked up as a bloodsucker can get. But she set me right. Helped me control me anger. Helped me make up for alla bad shit I done.' He exhaled a cloud of smoke. 'Well, maybe not alla it.'

'So how much longer until we get there?'

Taipan shrugged. 'Can't tell you that till we get there. If that VS mob finds out where she is, they'll come after her with all guns blazin'. I ain't gonna let that happen.'

'Wouldn't Mira have sucked that info out of Nigel?'

'Nah, that surfie didn't know shit. Never did trust him.'

'And Kala doesn't know either?'

Taipan studied his cigarette. 'Prob'ly not. Still, another reason for us to get where we're goin'.'

'Jesus,' Kevin said, leaning against the sign and looking out where the road vanished into night. 'Don't you get tired of never trusting anyone, of always looking over your shoulder?'

'Sometimes. You get used to it, eh. Best idea is to keep movin', I reckon.'

'So that's your home, is it? The road.'

Taipan gestured toward the bitumen. 'Yep, that's me: always happiest on walkabout.' He grinned.

'You're full of shit, aren't ya.'

'You figured that out, eh?'

'How long have you been doing this – been, y'know?'

Taipan shrugged again. 'You lose count, after a bit. It's all just one day after another.'

'How do you keep going then? Every day, just more of the same?'

Taipan laughed. 'Tell me this, fella – who don't? Who don't just live every day, more'a the same?'

'Where's the point?' Kevin hit the map, making the tin wobble.

'All I know is somethin' me father told me when I was a young fella, before they came and took me to the mission school. Me old man said to me, you can't go back, you gotta look ahead. If you're lookin' over ya shoulder, you're bound to run into somethin' in front of you.'

Taipan chuckled and took a drag, making the cigarette glow all the way down almost to his lips. 'He was talkin' 'bout drivin', but it still makes plenny good sense, eh.'

'Yeah, I spose it does. Where is he now?'

'Died in a car smash,' Taipan said, tossing his cigarette. 'C'mon, we're burnin' night time.'

They were a few kilometres down the track before Kevin realised that Taipan had never known his father. He really was full of shit.

THIRTY-FOUR

Taipan pulled up opposite the airport on the eastern side of Longreach. They were facing the tail end of a jumbo, part of the Qantas museum. The facility seemed to be throwing up as much light as the rest of the town combined. It was about nine o'clock; there was barely any traffic. The airport's car park appeared empty, though at that distance it was hard to tell due to intervening trees.

'Whaddya think?' Taipan asked.

'They still got flights this time of night?'

'Like we was gonna fly. We might play it safe and take the scenic route, eh. Don't wanna fuck it up when we're this close.' He turned off the headlight and took a left off the main drag. They passed the hangar-shaped roofs of the Stockman's Hall of Fame, the oversized jackeroo sculpture out front the only witness to their passing, and then ran out of road, but Taipan didn't stop, just slowed down as they steered onto a gravel track that became little more than wheel ruts in a paddock. They crossed a gully and followed a westerly track till they reconnected with the main road running south out of Longreach. Once out of sight of the town's feeble glow, Taipan turned on the lights and gunned the bike.

An hour and a half later, just when Kevin thought his arse

had been permanently spot welded to the bike seat, a faded, flaking sign loomed near a turn-off and Taipan slowed. The sign's metal surface was peppered with bullet holes. Stonehenge, it announced, population a hundred and a bit. A dangling piece of timber advertised last year's annual rodeo, back in November, and another mentioned the township's other claim to fame – home to a piece of Australia's famed Jindalee over-the-horizon radar. Some disgruntled wag had sprayed the words 'fly in fuck off' over it.

'Livin' under the radar,' Taipan said with a laugh, and he drove farther south a short way before again slowing, to turn onto a dirt track.

A timber sign at the fork, the crossbar askew like a rotting gallows, bore the words 'emu farm' in barely legible black paint. They nosed past bare paddocks, the bike bouncing over corrugation, sliding in bulldust. They topped a rise and slowed some more as they approached a farm. The old homestead, with a peaked iron roof that curved over the veranda, sat inside a perimeter of mesh fencing twice as tall as Kevin. Sheds dotted the compound. There was no sign of emus.

They pulled up outside a wire gate. Two squat dogs trailed dust and sharp yaps as they charged across the yard, stopping only to avoid hitting the fence. Taipan waved a hand and the dogs went quiet.

Bit of heeler in them, Kevin thought, heeler or kelpie, one a speckled grey and the other black, and both of them all teeth and curiosity. Their eyes glinted blood-red as they switched their attention between Kevin to Taipan, alternately yipping and whining, caught between the want of a pat on the head and the need to rip the stranger's throat out.

Two guards appeared from a nearby feed shed – a couple of sheets of tin nailed to a simple timber frame – and walked over, guns held loosely by their sides, their eyes flashing crystal green in the bike headlight's dusty glare.

'It's me,' Taipan said. 'Tell Mother we're here.'

The men greeted him. 'She's takin' the rays down at the rock pools but shouldn't be too long,' one volunteered. He wore a maroon and gold football T-shirt with a lion on it. His mate sported a Mohawk, possibly dyed in the same team's colours. Both wore loose leather vests. Kevin didn't need to see the logo to know they were Night Riders.

Mohawk spoke into a two-way radio. 'Taipan's here with a whitefella. I'm openin' up.'

He grabbed a pole that leaned against the gatepost, and for the first time Kevin noticed the grisly additions – the pole and each fence post was topped by a skull. Cows, dogs, a sheep with curved horns. Mohawk lowered the skull – a bullock with horns draped in feathers, a smear of what had to be old blood on its forehead between the vacant eye sockets. As soon as the skull touched the earth, Kevin felt something in the air – some kind of current or vibration – break. The guy in the Lions jersey unlocked the gate and ushered them through. As he relocked the chain, Mohawk sliced his hand on a knife and swiped blood onto the skull, then lifted it once more.

'Good to have you back, cuz,' the Lions supporter said, more obviously relaxed, his rifle slung over one shoulder. He clasped hands with Taipan, a kind of high-five with thumbs on top. 'Mother said you had some trouble, eh.'

'Plenny.' Taipan paused. When he continued, his voice was low. 'Any of me mob make it back?'

'That Acacia, she came in a coupla nights ago. Surprised you didn't hear Cassie squealing from wherever you were. Kept the rest of us up, that's for sure.'

'Too right,' Mohawk said. 'So who's that fella there?'

'A fella I ran into. A mechanic. One of us mob, now.'

The guards exchanged a glance. 'Go on down, she'll know you're here,' said Mohawk.

Kevin felt their stares like laser sights on his back as Taipan steered down the slight slope to the main building. The dogs, tails wagging, yapping intermittently, ran beside the bike.

Acacia, in jeans and singlet, appeared in the doorway of one of the largest sheds. Her face caught between a relieved smile and a mighty yawn, she gestured Taipan over and shooed the dogs away.

Taipan ran the bike in, finding space between the Rover and a Jeep with its bonnet up; a lamp hung from a hook overhead.

The bike burbled to silence. Kevin stepped off, gingerly testing his regenerated foot for support. Better. Not a hundred per cent, but at least it could take his weight. No crutch required.

'We were starting to think that maybe you weren't coming,' Acacia said.

'Me, too.' Taipan stepped from the bike and stretched. 'Good to see you, 'Cacia.'

They embraced and Kevin thought he saw tears in her eyes. 'Just you?'

Taipan nodded, hugged her again.

She stared at Kevin over Taipan's shoulder. He couldn't read her expression, didn't know if that was good or bad.

'So who did you kill to get this place?' he asked.

She flinched.

'No one yet,' Taipan said, the threat obvious.

'You don't have to be afraid,' Acacia said. 'We didn't bring you all this way just to murder you.'

Way to go, he congratulated himself. How to lose the closest thing to a friend he had, just because he was scared shitless. Would the Night Riders really help the man who'd led to the slaughter of so many?

A flash of light behind her caught Kevin's eye – a door opening and shutting at the house. A girl walked toward them – late teens with shoulder-length corn-blonde hair, wearing cut-off shorts and a tight T-shirt. A little chubby, definitely cute. She ran the last few steps to give Taipan a rib-cracking hug. 'Cuz, you made it!'

'Cassie.' Taipan stepped back and the girl stood by Acacia,

an arm around the woman's waist. Acacia draped an arm across Cassie's shoulders.

'This is the new fella.' Taipan indicated Kevin with a jerk of his thumb.

'Kevin, isn't it?' Cassie said. 'You two look totally knackered. I'll take you up to the house, hey. Get you something to eat.'

'I'll finish off here.' Acacia gave Cassie a peck on the cheek. 'Be up soon.'

'You betta get that truck sorted out,' Taipan said. 'We might need to move in a hurry.'

Acacia swore, and the sound of metal on metal followed them as they left.

Cassie led them up the few stairs onto the veranda. They took off their boots, Kevin favouring his healing foot. The two heelers lay on either side of the door, reminding Kevin of the lion statues that some fancy folks put on either side of their front gate. The dogs raised their muzzles from their forepaws in tandem, sniffed, then resettled.

'Good boy, Byely,' Taipan said, kneeling to pat the white dog, and then having to reach over to do the same for its whimpering companion. 'You too, Cherny.'

Cassie ushered them inside. 'C'mon, I got a brew on.'

They went down a hallway, the walls marked with bright rectangles of paint. Music played softly behind a closed door, a radio announcer blared behind another.

Cassie heated mugs in the kitchen. 'The good stuff.'

Kevin took one gratefully and let the decanted human blood calm his nerves. It went down way too fast; he swayed as the infusion flowed through him, setting his foot to tingling and leaving him craving more.

Dogs barked, answered by a whinny outside the kitchen. Cassie went outside, closing the back door behind her. Kevin glimpsed a caravan, dented and dusty, and someone leading a horse, the two heelers panting at its hoofs.

'Mother's back,' Taipan said, and finished his drink. 'You better show some manners. She don't hafta take you in, y'know.'

'Do I get a say in that?'

'You said plenny already. Just shut up and maybe learn somethin', eh.'

Cassie returned soon after. 'I'll take you to the study. Mother's on her way.'

Kevin rinsed his mug – Kala would've approved, he thought with a twinge – and followed the girl and Taipan up the hallway. He felt like a duckling flopping around at the end of the queue. Tail-end Charlie was always the first one to go, right?

THIRTY-FIVE

The study felt cooler than the rest of the house, snug, the walls draped in dark cloth and smelling of incense. Soft carpet. The only furniture was a crammed bookshelf along one wall and a large wooden chest against another. Kevin glimpsed words like *The Final Solution*, *World War* and *Supernatural*. Cassie lit candles around the room, then gestured for them to sit on the square cushions on the floor. They sat, facing the wall and its shuttered window. Crystals hanging from the ceiling caught the light like a broken mirror ball. A shadow passed across the doorway. Kevin turned. A middle-aged woman entered, hugged Cassie, then shut the door after Cassie left with a promise to be close by if she needed anything. The newcomer stank of horse; under that, some kind of herb, thyme perhaps.

The spice rack in the kitchen, his mother sorting through, lamenting her latest failure to grow cardamom from a seed; his father saying a bit of salt 'n' pepper was all it needed; and his mother saying, 'You aren't that spicy, Mr Matheson'; and the bolognaise being so bloody good, flecks of mince and sauce splattering the table where the spaghetti got out of control; and him muttering and his mother shaking her head, that gentle, gentle smile.

'Mother,' Taipan began, but he fell silent as the woman stood next to him and nursed his head against her thigh. Her hair hung in two dark braids, as dark and glossy as a crow's wing, her features somewhere between Russia and China, the eyes slightly almond shaped, the brows heavy, cheeks severe. But her expression was pure compassion as she said, 'I heard; felt. A sad day.' She sighed. 'I wish you could let her go.'

'She's my sister.'

'Willa hasn't been your sister since Turner sank his fangs into her.'

'And what about me? She did me, too.'

A hand in his hair. 'That she did. And yet, here you are.' She glanced at Kevin. 'And this one?'

'Somewhere between makin' and wakin', Mira got her fangs into him. I thought maybe we could use him to track her down. Get even.'

Did her face harden, just then, when Taipan said Mira's name? Kevin couldn't be sure. But clearly Mira was not in the woman's good books. Or perhaps scared her.

What chance did Kevin have if the Night Riders' grand guru was afraid?

'And still you think of revenge,' Mother continued.

'What else is there?'

'Survival.'

'What makes you think they're different?'

'Ask Penny and the rest.'

Taipan pulled away, and the woman hugged herself as though suddenly cold.

'Sorry,' she offered. 'That was petty of me. "I told you so" won't bring them back.'

Taipan rubbed his face with both hands as though waking from a nightmare. 'But you're right. I made this fella and somehow that bloodhag got her hooks in him.' He hit his leg in frustration. 'I shoulda checked. I shoulda bin more careful;

maybe I shouldn't'a gone at all. It's my fault so many have bit the dust.'

'It was their choice to follow you. Be careful you don't weigh yourself down with guilt that isn't yours to bear.'

She studied Kevin, appraising but sympathetic, a vet diagnosing a sick pet.

'Now, what's this about Mira riding this boy?' she asked Taipan.

'His old man and me, we done a deal. Only, this fella ain't sleepin' so good.'

'Bad dreams?' She squinted, as though she could see through Kevin's clothes, and Kevin fidgeted, not knowing what he should say, if anything. Her expression softened. 'My name is Danica, though most of this bunch of miscreants call me Mother.'

Dan-ee-tza: the way she drew out that ee, twirled her tongue around the last syllable, sounded far too exotic to be out here in this isolated dust bowl. She should've been a pole dancer or a circus performer – trapeze maybe, with her slender, tightly muscled build.

'Kevin,' he replied finally, his name sounding brutally common and sadly insufficient.

The scuffed toes of riding boots poked out from the bell-bottomed hems of her trousers. The front laces of her puffy shirt hung loose as though to show off the numerous pendants she wore. She reminded Kevin of a sideshow fortune-teller with her big hooped earrings and wrists jingling with bracelets. What the hell was she going to do – read some tea leaves? They'd come all this way for this?

She kneeled beside Kevin. 'Yours has been a difficult journey and I fear it's far from over.'

He wanted to say 'no shit', but the woman's presence didn't encourage rudeness. He winced when his addled mind came up with, 'Um, Taipan's told me all about you.'

'Really?' She settled in a cushion facing them, then lit a small brazier; the flame cast an orange glow on her dusky skin. Her dark eyes caught the light. Pungent incense wafted into the room. She smiled, full lips parting to reveal perfect white teeth. Such dainty hands, flashing with rings.

'There,' she said. 'That's nicer, isn't it. Now, let's have a look at you.' She held out her hand.

Kevin didn't move, confused.

'Give it over,' Taipan told him, pointing, and Kevin belatedly extended a hand.

Danica sliced his wrist with a fingernail, her grip holding him firm as he jerked under the sudden pain, and bent to draw a mouthful of his blood from the wound. She sat back, eyes closed, and began to rock ever so slightly.

Kevin glanced at Taipan but the biker's gaze was fixed on Danica's face, his features set in a mask of adoration. The wound on his wrist throbbed but the bleeding had stopped; he held it in his lap as Danica zoned out. The beginning of a headache beat behind his temples. The room heated up, closed in around him. His heart pounded. What the hell was she doing to him?

Then the sensations ceased as though someone had snapped their fingers.

Danica opened her eyes, revealing irises of liquid violet.

Her voice sounded husky, almost echoing, as she told him, 'You've been marked, Kevin. Marked with blood.'

'What does that mean?'

'It means Mira has traded blood with you. She uses the link to invade your dreams and possibly even your waking thoughts. The risk is real.' She frowned, causing a sense of unaccountable unease to sweep over him. 'But we're a long way from her and the power fades with distance.'

Her brow smoothed as she nodded to herself, licked her lip as though tasting the last of his blood. She held his gaze. 'You will never be truly free from her while she possesses a sample of your blood.'

'I don't think she took any,' Kevin said. 'Not like in a bottle or something.'

Got you. But you, you do not have me.

'She has her ways,' Danica said, staring at him; *into* him.

'I did what I could to keep her out,' Taipan said, fingering his pendant.

'You did well,' Danica said. 'And this place has its own protections. From what I can see, the immediate threat to us is small.'

'Still, they might'a captured one of me pack. Kala, maybe, or one of them others. We oughta do somethin'.'

'What would you suggest?'

He paused, then said in a rush, 'We got the firepower. Let's take 'em out, once and for all.'

She shook her head. 'You know that's not my way.'

'Damn it, Mother, all this slinkin' and runnin'–'

'How much more do you want to lose?'

He looked away, ran a hand through his hair. 'Nothin'. I don't wanna lose nothin' more.'

'We knew this haven wouldn't last forever. They never do. But I don't think we need to panic. That's probably what they want. No, I doubt Maximilian will risk making more waves, not without proof of our exact location. We'll move on, but in the meantime, I can give Kevin a talisman of his own to protect him from Mira's sight until he either destroys the source of the spell or Mira uses up her supply of his blood.'

'Are you saying that I should kill Mira?' Kevin said.

'You need to destroy the blood she has,' Danica answered. 'Or wait for her to exhaust it.'

'Or I could simply stay right the hell away from her.'

'She would infest your dreams. But if you offered no

215

advantage to her, with time she would probably grow bored and leave you alone.'

'So, what do you want from me?' Kevin asked.

Danica patted Kevin's hand. 'For now, you can stay here, rest, regain your strength. We can teach you how to protect your mind from intruders and how to cope with the blood rush.'

'I could use some help, for sure.' Kevin rubbed his forehead, trying to silence the voices...

Iraq is a fucked-up mess in the Middle-East

You're only young, Kevin. You've got time

No longer a basic food group

'What I really need is to talk to my mum.'

'That can be arranged.'

He glared at Taipan. 'And I need to know what happened to my dad.'

'We bin over this, fella. Whaddya want me to say?'

'I want you to tell me the truth!'

'I could say the Hunter. It was his gun. I could say me. I kinda brought the Hunter there, eh? But I reckon most of all it was jus' dumb fuckin' luck what did ya old man in. You wanna take it further, you jus' say the word.'

'That will be enough,' Danica said. 'Bad things happen. We cope the best we can. There is nothing to be gained by taking anything "further". Not in my camp. Do I make myself clear?'

Both men nodded, with all the acceptance of chastened schoolchildren making a silent vow to finish it outside the fence after the final bell.

She sighed. 'It's late and you've both suffered far too much. You need rest.' Kevin went to stand up, but she took his hand. 'Before you go, I need you to help me prepare a talisman, Kevin. Something to help you sleep uninterrupted.' She opened what looked like a wooden pencil case and retrieved a glass vial as long as his little finger. She passed him a small knife and had him cut his finger and fill the vial with blood.

'Good. It's going to take me a little while. Cassie will show you to your room. I'll send the talisman when it's ready.'

Cassie stood behind him. He hadn't heard her come in. Kevin got up; his sore foot failed him and she grabbed his arm to steady him. Taipan didn't move.

'It's okay, Kevin,' Danica said. 'You're safe now.'

So she kept saying, and yet, all he could smell was fear.

THIRTY-SIX

Kevin leaned against a wall and pulled on his sneakers while Cassie waited to guide him to his bunk. Byely and Cherny sniffed at him. In the near distance, a dingo howled, and the dogs turned as though searching for the source.

'Who are you people?' he asked.

'Your friends, if you let us be,' Cassie said, patting his shoulder. 'Mother will be able to help you sort things out. Rest now. You've earned it.'

The dogs flanked them as they started out across the yard. Kevin eyed her as they walked. Smooth stride, a glimmer of red in her eyes, a mark there on her neck where the collar of her shirt hung open. She caught him looking, and he said, 'So you're a red-eye?'

Cassie stopped to face him. The dogs pulled up, too, regarding him curiously, ears perked. 'So?'

'Just checkin'. Learning to tell people apart, that's all.'

'Top of the class, then,' she said, and resumed walking. 'You can ask if you want. I don't mind.'

'Ask?'

'You were staring at my brand, right?' She touched the mark on her neck, four dots making a square, two finger widths apart.

'I've seen something like it before.'

'Brand is just what we call it. Four, usually; sometimes just two. On the neck or over the heart. Lets other fangers know you're spoken for.'

'"Brand" makes it sound like slavery.'

'I think of it more as a wedding ring.'

'Kala didn't have one.' At least, he didn't think she had. He would've noticed, surely.

'Tai never marked her. Not overly expressive, that fella.'

'So, you and Acacia, eh.'

'Yeah, even before she got the change. She was flyin' choppers in the Centre back then, really cool. But then, well, we had to get out of Dodge.'

'Hard to leave home?' he asked, feeling the sudden swell of loss.

'She *is* my home,' Cassie said. 'My country is wherever her feet are touchin'. This is you.' They'd reached a demountable cabin, naked aluminium walls and flat roof, three steps up to the tiny porch that ran down one side. 'You'll find everything you need inside: clothes and stuff. Gimme a shout if they don't fit.'

'Sure,' Kevin said. The door had no lock but when he opened it, he found a bar that could be slid across from inside. 'Is there a phone?'

'If Mother says it's okay, I can bring you one. You won't have long, though. Tracing, you know; we can't be too careful. You mustn't tell anyone where you are, not even a hint. Oh, by the way – probably best if you stay in tonight. Not everyone knows who you are. Wouldn't want any misunderstandings, eh.'

'Thanks.' He shut the door and threw the bolt. The cabin consisted of two rooms – the kitchen/lounge/bedroom and the toilet/bathroom. Metal louvres covered the windows; the walls and cupboards were timber veneer. Anything not veneer was white, except the orange bedspread and the grey lino. Simple, featureless, but more comfortable than a hole in the ground.

Kevin sniffed a carafe of blood on the table. Still warm, smelling unmistakably of cow. He hesitated, wondering if he'd be able to smell if anything had been added, knockout drugs or something, then decided if they'd wanted him out of the way, they could've done it easily enough already. The drink hardly touched the sides. When he'd drained the last, he headed for the shower where the steaming water inspired his mind to wander from one absurd thought to another, ending with the notion of creating a vampire cow. Fearing for his own sanity but strangely tickled by the idea, he towelled off and changed into the clothes Cassie had provided. She'd guessed the size well.

He slouched on the bed, restless after days of motion, enjoying being clean, licking his lips as though he might find a trace of dinner he hadn't already absorbed. He stared at his foot, marvelling at how flesh and bone had grown back, and how much it still itched, on the inside, where he couldn't scratch it. He tried to wriggle the stubby toes, hoping they wouldn't turn out webbed or hoofed or something equally weird. He was concentrating on imagining his foot with five normal toes when a knock at the door made him jump. He pulled the bolt back cautiously.

'You decent?' Cassie asked.

'The clothes fitted fine, thanks,' he said. 'Though I could, um, use another drink.' He pointed to the empty carafe, its insides dripping with the sticky remains of his meal.

'I'll see what I can do. Here, swap you.' She held out a mobile phone. 'Three minutes. No mention of where we are, okay?'

'Cool. Tell Mo– Danica, that I appreciate it. My family...' his voice tailed off as a surge of emotion cramped his cheeks and jaw. Heat rose behind his eyes. He shut himself in the en suite, sat on the loo and stared at the phone as he summoned his courage, tried to find the words. Tears blurred his vision. What the hell could he tell her? Better to ring Meg. Meg could pass a message on. He dialled. The phone clicked like a Geiger counter before he heard it starting to ring at the other end. Seven chirps in, it was answered.

'Hello?'

Words stuck in his throat like chicken bones.

'Hello?' she asked. 'Who is this?'

Tears rolled down his cheeks. Very slowly, he cancelled the call and leaned against the wall, hand on the phone trying to hold on to that connection to Meg.

The dingo howled and Kevin straightened, wiped his eyes, sniffed. It sounded as though vehicles had pulled up in the compound. There was a burble of voices, broken by shouts and calls. Kevin returned to the bedroom.

'That was quick,' Cassie said, taking the phone.

'No answer,' he told her. 'What's going on?'

'Mother's called a powwow.'

'What about?'

She shrugged and headed for the door.

'Can I come?'

'Probably best you stay here.'

Kevin was sick of being told to rest, to relax, to take it easy. He opened the metal louvre, but Cassie was out of sight, and all he could see was the glow of headlights, not the source. Dogs barked and whined. He smelled wood smoke, wafting in with the sound of sticks being tapped together. There was a guitar; the eerie wail of a didgeridoo; people crying.

Taipan had brought him this far because he thought Kevin might be useful, but Danica had said he wasn't. Which left Kevin where? At worst, a threat; at best, an annoyance. If decisions were being made about his future, then he wanted to be there. He slipped out the door. Using the cover of trees and sheds, he crept toward the slight dip that hid the gathering from sight.

A couple of four-wheel-drives were parked facing it, their headlights aglow, and he crouched, the better to slink across the open ground to that hump of ant nest there, about waist high, but if he crawled–

The world shifted, the darkness shimmering like curtains overlaid by phantom places and times, linked by one overriding sensation: don't get caught. Taipan, creeping through his supernatural life, decades of reflex and skill rising up through Kevin's mind and muscles. One moment wrapped around him and pulled him under...

He's in a street he knows – just knows – is in Brisbane's Fortitude Valley and there's a club that is identified only by a shut door and a naked bulb above it illuminating the street number, and outside there's a man in a suit, and they get to talking. They end up in a nearby alley with a mesh gate and overflowing bins, and the smell of decaying garbage and stale piss and a blocked gutter rises around them. The man has his slug out and Kevin's on his knees in the muck of the sidewalk, sinking his fangs into the man's femoral.

As hot blood gushes, the man comes across his shoulder. And he knows then, from the blood, that the man's a dentist who takes a little too much pleasure when patients – young patients – are under the gas, that the man's wife wouldn't approve of him doing that nor of him being here, they have children of their own for Christ's sake, and he thinks then that maybe those nuns back out in the bush were on to something after all.

Maybe no one is innocent. Maybe they will all be judged and found wanting when they die. But he won't die. He's been judged already. In a world without innocence, he can fit right in. But there's his sister. Willa is not evil. She did not deserve this; she is not this. He will set her free. He will save her. Even if he has to damn himself to do it–

Someone shook his shoulder and he jumped. Had someone discovered him, there with that body on the pavement and the blood on his mouth and the sprog on his shoulder?

He whirled, ready to strike, ready to flee.

Acacia stood beside him, and he wasn't in the alley. He was in the paddock, vulnerable, lost.

'This isn't the best place for bloodwalking, Kevin.'

'Yeah, no.' He wiped his face, surprised to find it clean; hunger surged through him, fuelled by the memory, his body trembling. He stepped away from her, quickly, but quietly, Taipan's stealth clinging.

She held his arm. 'You might as well come with me. See what's what.'

'Sure.'

'It's good that you can ride it,' she said as she led him toward the gathering. 'Use that lifestream stuff when you need it. You just gotta make sure it doesn't take you over, eh.'

'It's intense.'

'Makes it harder to keep it under control, but you have to if you don't want to get lost in bedlam. Here, sit with Cassie and me.'

The headlights had been killed. More than a dozen people sat in a circle around a bonfire, as many showing red eyes as green. They formed clumps of twos and threes, except for Taipan who sat more or less by himself, and nearby, Danica, cross-legged, with her two dogs sprawled on either side.

'That fella shouldn't be here,' Taipan said. 'He's tainted.'

'No moreso than I am,' Danica said. 'We will pass the blood.'

'He's a threat.'

Murmuring followed Taipan's assertion and Kevin squirmed under the attention, wishing he'd followed Cassie's advice and stayed away.

'That didn't stop you bringin' him here,' Acacia said.

'It was worth it to get a shot at Max's bloodhag.'

'Enough,' Danica told them, and the group fell to silence, the crackle of the flames replacing the muttering and whispers. 'The chalice.'

Hippie took a silver cup to her and she used her knife to open her arm. She bled into the cup and then Hippie took it around the circle.

'Peace be with you,' he said as each vampire drank from it. Acacia drank, her eyes shut; she swayed slightly as Hippie took it back. He paused in front of Kevin.

'Him too,' Danica said. 'Taipan made him; he's one of us.'

Kevin sipped the blood; numbness spread through him. The vestiges of Taipan's experiences drifted away. He saw the hollow with sudden clarity, his senses as sharp as the twinkle of stars, the snap of timber in the fire.

Hippie handed the chalice back to Danica. She stood and spilled a little into the fire, saying, 'This is for our lost souls, may they travel in peace,' and someone sobbed, a single cry as brutal as a rifle shot.

Danica set the chalice down so the dogs could lick it clean. 'And now, we of the long night will bleed for our brothers and sisters who still share the day.'

Hippie handed her another chalice, larger than the first, and this time he took the knife for each vampire to slice and bleed. By the time the cup reached Kevin at the end of the line, it was almost full.

'Not you,' Danica said.

Taipan snorted, and Kevin sat, feeling dirty and alone, as the chalice went to each red-eye. Some groaned as they drank, reminding him of Penny as she sucked down Reg's blood; others, like Cassie, might've been drinking milk for all the reaction they showed, little more than a swipe of the tongue across the lips.

'The blood makes us one,' Danica said, again letting the dogs clean the cup. 'Before we discuss our current situation, Acacia has an item of business.'

Acacia held Cassie's hand. 'I would like to offer Cassie the long night.'

'I respectfully decline,' Cassie said.

'Please, Cassie; the blood isn't holding. You're in the tremors.'

'I'm okay. I can go another month. And another one after that.'

'Jesus, girl, is the sun so important to you?'

'No, but you are. You need someone to watch your back. Now more than ever.'

'We could watch each other's.'

Danica interrupted. 'It's her decision, Acacia.'

'It's the wrong one.'

'Not when it's made from love.'

Taipan said, 'Acacia's right, though. We need new blood. Untainted.'

'The dreamwalks are gettin' stale, it's true,' said someone else, Lions maybe.

'We're hardly in a position for a recruitment drive,' Danica said.

'But we'll need more if we're to hold off Max's mob,' Taipan argued.

'Not when we're on the road. The only plus from this whole tragedy is that with less of us, our mobility is increased.'

'So where are we runnin' to next?' Taipan asked.

'West, I'm thinking. Maybe into the NT. I'm open to suggestions.'

'Jesus,' Acacia said, 'I've spent my whole life tryin' to get away from the Territory.'

'We're gonna run outta places to hide,' Taipan said. 'We should use that fella's taint to track Mira and take her out.'

'I don't want to hear this,' Danica said.

'And *he* probably shouldn't. Just in case that bloodhag is smarter than you think. She might have some new tricks, eh.'

'Fine. Cassie can walk him back while we talk this out.'

Kevin stood, but paused as Cassie gestured for him to walk with her. He looked around the circle, acutely aware of the animosity and curiosity directed at him. 'For the record, I want out. I'll learn whatever it is you think I need to know, but then I'm gone.'

'Don't let the door hit you in the arse,' Taipan said.

'We'll talk tomorrow, Kevin,' Danica said. 'Once you're trained, well, then you decide what path is best.'

He followed Cassie. When they were out of earshot, he said, 'Taipan and the boss got a difference of opinion, eh.'

'I guess.'

'So why is it that the vampires drink her blood only, while you red-eyes get a brew? I'd've thought the vamps would get your juice to suck on.'

'They do. Ours, cattle, whatever. But vampires, usually, won't drink each other's, not even as brew. Too many lives in there. Too much confusion.'

'Like me seeing all of Taipan's shit in his blood.'

'If you say so.'

'So by drinking Danica's, they get only her shit.'

'Not even. Mother's got the knack. She can keep the noise down; she can still the cacophony in others.'

'The cock-what?'

'The ghosts. Bedlam. When you've swallowed too many, when you carry too many, all those lifestreams can send you loopy. You get crazy, and then you fall into a kind of coma. Kind of like Alzheimer's, except, instead of remembering nothing, you remember everything. Everything from everyone you've ever drained. Anyway, Mother can make it go away. There's something in her blood.'

'Who makes it go away for her?'

'No one. Taipan says she's losing touch, that she needs fresh blood, fresh lives. The funny thing is, of all of them, she's the one who doesn't need to worry. She's kind of immune to bedlam. She can control the ghosts really well. By drinking from her, the rest of them get a little bit of it, too. Enough to keep them sane. It's not a licence to slaughter, but. She's got her limits.'

'Well, that's comforting.'

They reached his cabin and she said, 'Home again. You'd better stay put this time. Tai has got them thinking you're some kind of spy. No one will go against Danica, but still, accidents happen. Just keep your head down. No creeping around. She's gonna help you, you'll see.'

'Is all this bullshit why you don't want to be like us?'

'Seriously, as much as I love Acacia and want to be with her, I'm more use as a red-eye than a full blood. Maybe later, when I've got no choice.'

'Is that why Kala never said yes?'

'You'd have to ask her.'

'I wish I could.'

'Look, I'd better get back. But I'll drop in on you before morning, okay?'

Inside the cabin, the silence felt oppressive. He liked Cassie. He envied her relationship with Acacia. He acknowledged, and it made him feel like a piece of shit but the fact was undeniable, that after all that blood, all that fear, her simple companionship meant he really wanted to taste her. Danica's blood had stilled the voices but stoked his hunger. He prowled, restless; decisions were being made without him – he'd failed, yet again, to take control of his own life. He paused occasionally to look toward the powwow, unable to see anyone, thinking that this was how a circus animal must feel, waiting for its chance to perform, aggravated by some sense that this was not where it belonged.

It was close to sunrise when there was a knock at the door. He slammed the louvre shut and pulled the heavy curtains, feeling as though he'd been caught looking at something he shouldn't.

Cassie was outside. No lynch mob. That was something.

'They done? What's the plan?' he asked. *Do I live? Do I get to leave?*

'Jury's out, but we're definitely moving on. Here, more food.' Cassie hoisted a carafe topped with pink foam in one hand while retrieving a velvet bag from a pocket with the other. 'And Mother wants you to have this.'

Kevin thanked her and she said good night. He drained the carafe, then emptied the contents of the little bag on to the bedspread. The talisman was a round metal disc, much the same as the one Taipan wore. It was etched with a five-pointed star. Embedded in the centre was an egg-shaped locket, about the size of a five-cent piece, soldered shut. The metal felt warm. He wasn't used to wearing jewellery and wasn't comfortable about trying to sleep with it on, but there was something about Danica's calm assurance. Probably her eyes, he thought. You don't mess with people with weird eyes. With the pendant looped around his neck on its leather cord, he slid under the sheets, suddenly aware of just how tired he was. Eventually, he slept. He didn't feel the pendant, and he did not dream.

THIRTY-SEVEN

The chopper carved through the night like a shark through sea water. Riding with Mira and a squad of jackals in the light-proofed cabin, Reece could barely merit they were moving. But moving they were, back to Barlow's Siding, back to where this particular wheel had begun to turn. He fingered the Monaro's keys in his pocket; tried not to think of Dave and all the bloody mess since.

Mira jerked back to awareness in the seat next to him, the purplish glimmer in her eyes fading fast; there was a flash of typical vampire chartreuse before she looked at him directly, revealing the deep brown irises a Labrador would be jealous of. Her fingers reflexively traced the fourth blood bracelet on her left wrist.

'No dice?' he asked.

'What?'

'You were trying to trace Matheson, weren't you?'

'Yes. Yes, of course. But no, nothing.'

'And the girl, Kala?'

She shook her head. 'Not unexpected. She's awake, distrustful. All I got, apart from a bucket of angst, was a vague impression of a tall man with a saddle, a cowboy perhaps–'

'A jackeroo maybe?'

'And standing stones.'

'Standing stones?'

'You don't have an Australian word for that?'

'We're not big on them here. The Devil's Marbles? But that's miles away, over in the NT.'

'She might have some Celt in her, how would I know? You'd expect cave paintings from someone like her, wouldn't you? Maybe a dance around a campfire.'

Reece pulled his mobile and hit the map.

'Here,' he said, blowing up a portion of Queensland with swipes of his fingertips. 'Is this what she might've meant?'

'Stonehenge? Really? What next, an Eiffel Tower?'

'No stone monuments but, you know, if the name fits. Shall we check it out?'

'Ask the pilot where we are.'

Reece hit the mic to talk to the flight deck. They were twenty minutes from Whitby Downs, slightly farther from Stonehenge, but, the pilot said, there was a no-fly zone in the area due to the Jindalee radar installation.

'I don't think it's worth the hassle,' Reece told Mira. 'There's a lot of country out there and we'd be relying on you being able to get a hit from Kala. For all we know, they've taken her out by now.'

'No, I'd know if she was dead. It is only natural the Night Riders will be suspicious of her. They will expect me to have tried a bloodlink and they will be satisfied when they find it. All I need is for her to survive long enough to deliver the message.'

'And if she doesn't?'

'Then, Reece, we are well and truly up, what do you Australians say? Shit creek.'

'With or without the paddle?'

'That's why I like to keep you around. You have so many quaint expressions.'

What slang did Felicity have up her sleeve? He imagined

she'd be excited at their return and another chance to impress. 'We could send in the troops to sweep the area. After the ruckus back in Rocky, it wouldn't be hard to explain a ground search for Taipan.'

'We hardly have the manpower for that. No, we'll let the plan run its course. They'll come to us.'

'And you're sure we can trust Turner? That it wasn't her who set Dave and me up?'

'Bhagwan tipped off Taipan early.' She jerked her head toward the rear of the cabin, where a body bag lay on the floor between Bhagwan's two red-eyes. 'I don't know how he heard that Jasmine was setting up out here – for a veggo, he had a very good grip on his mind – but the word reached the Night Riders before we were ready.'

'Home ground advantage, I suppose.'

Her hand fisted. 'We should have sent more men with you. Should've known Taipan wouldn't be out there by himself, regardless of Jasmine's assurances.'

Which was, he suspected, as much of an apology as he'd get. 'Hindsight, eh.'

'It'll wear you down, especially when you've got as much of it as we have.'

'And Dee?'

'One domino at a time, Reece. Kevin Matheson first, then Taipan, then the bloodbitch.' She snatched his wrist, so hard it hurt, her face tight with desperation. 'And no more mistakes. We – I – can't afford to waste any more time. We roll them up, and then we all get to go home to live happily ever after.'

Reece's headset crackled with the news they were close to Whitby Downs. Mira released him.

'Happily *ever* after,' she repeated.

He clenched the car keys in his pocket. He'd been hoping to claim the Monaro as a spoil of war, once the dust had settled, but Mira was offering a lot more than that. A lot more. Now all he had to do was work out how he felt about that.

THIRTY-EIGHT

Under a swirling purple sky, Taipan bears down on him, all dirt and blood and maleness. Like being buried under iron flesh. Kevin pushes and punches. Futile. He screams as fangs tear into him and his life – his essence – is snatched away in great, greedy gulps. When he is spent, his body drained, there remains the humiliation of hot, slick flesh pushed against him. The blood flows. He swallows it down, his turn to feast, his need overcoming all else and driving him into the red bliss. But this is not the unrestrained torrent; this is the measured dose – this much and no more, regardless of how much more he wants. He could drink a lake, feels as though his legs are hollow and endless, running all the way to the core of the planet, maybe spilling out the other side, two long streamers of liquid crimson floating into space. He drinks until the tap is turned off, the tit withdrawn. He lies, fuming, starving, as the images come; the memories made of tastes and smells and hidden emotions. They come with the rush of a cyclone, spinning, brutalising, howling. Lives upon lives, carried like flotsam in the scarlet cascade. He is lashed to the mast in a heaving sea of lives cut short. Death swamps him, fills his lungs, stings his eyes and flesh, saturates his very cells.

And then comes peace.

He lies on the shore, warmed by the gaze of velvet eyes

like twin suns in a lavender sky. The eye of the storm. The sea stilled, the banshee howl subsided; the dead returned to their graves, uneasy, but still. He basks in the soft light.

Danica is a phantom at his side. She urges him to stand. There is something yet to do. He rises, reluctant to leave his rest, and follows her gentle instructions.

Slowly, surely, he builds a wall across the frozen sea. In the wall he makes doors, and behind each he locks the voices and the faces and the deathly pallor; the laughter, anger and tears.

'Leave plenty of space for more,' Danica advises.

The words drift by, seagulls wheeling against a lilac sky. The wall stretches on forever.

Nicola falls on the ground at his feet. She's in her nightshirt and knickers, hair mussed, face tear-stricken, lips twisted with panic and glistening with drool. Her heartbeat fills the world; her body is hotter than the sun. The flow of her blood sounds like a waterfall. She screams as he tries to pick her up.

Danica points and he pushes the girl in that direction. She stumbles through the door.

Iraq is...

The door swings shut with an echoing click, and then there's silence.

'And now: Mira.'

The name shakes the world.

Seagulls turn to steel, wings sharp as they dive about him. He crouches under the onslaught, skin opening with a hundred beaks and claws and razor wingtips. His blood pools. The birds dive into the puddle, flapping and squawking, melting and melding together. A shape forms, head then shoulders, chest, hips; her skin bubbling with

233

wings and beaks as the birds mould into place. She stands, curves dripping blood like strawberry sauce. Great wings, as thin as a bat's, flap out behind her and then transform into her unmistakable cape.

A vase shatters, the sound of the world ending. Blood traces jagged slow-motion lightning bolts across the sky. Mira's fingers stretch like roots and wrap around him, penetrating like thorns into his flesh. Her fangs are those of a sabre tooth, dripping ichor. Her nipples stare at him, silvered seagulls' eyes. Her cunt is a clam-like beak, clacking open and shut as she reels him in.

He darts forward, latches his fangs around her left tit and sucks hard. Her other nipple pours with blood in sympathy; he grips it hard, fingertips sinking into the flesh, as she tries to dislodge him. She writhes, jaws snapping on air above his head, but the ground is rock, trapping her feet, and his hold is unshakeable as he guzzles her down. Seagulls covered in afterbirth push out of her left wrist and fall dead to the ground. She shrinks, tendril grips shrivelling.

Kevin sucks her blood furiously. Mira gets smaller and smaller till he's draining the very last of the juice from a desiccated baby doll, arms and legs as spindly as bird legs; skin cracked like a clay pan; hair like spinifex cropped short above those blazing red eyes. He ignores her furious stare and carries the weightless husk to the nearest door and throws it inside. The last thing he sees before swinging the door shut is those eyes, burning in the dark–

Kevin surfaced from the meditation. They'd started the sessions in the late afternoon, and now it was night. This latest trip had seemed to last years, rather than scant hours.

Danica sat before him, legs crossed, hands clasping his. Breathing three beats in, three beats out. A curl of incense smoke writhed past her elbow. Her eyes opened, fading from purple to green to brown. 'How do you feel?'

'Exhausted. But good. Better.'

She studied his eyes, looking into him. Kevin felt a prickle in his forehead, nothing more. She smiled. 'Good, very good. You have an aptitude.' She unfolded from her sitting position like a flower opening, only letting go his hands when they stood face to face. 'That's enough for now. Keep practising; it'll become automatic with time.'

'I appreciate what you've done. I can't hear any of them.'

Iraq is...

He shut the door softly.

'If you avoid killing, the rooms will remain empty. The memories will be like visitors, rather than tenants, and will leave in time.'

'Works for me.' Kevin pulled on his boots as Danica packed away her gear. 'So what–'

She held up a hand and stared off into space, a sign he had come to recognise that her mind was otherwise engaged. The yapping of dogs, like Morse code, carried through the walls. Danica blinked, smiled. 'You were asking?'

'Was that a message? Anything about Kala? My family?'

'Come. We have visitors.'

Danica sent him out the front while she went to the kitchen to put the kettle on. The cool night slowly penetrated his skin as he basked in the crisp air, the stars beaming, pregnant moon reassuringly bright and serene. A battered ute – bullbar, row of spotties across the top of the cab – wormed its way down from the front gate as Kevin stepped onto the veranda. Byely and Cherny trotted alongside the vehicle. He squinted in the headlight glare, eyes adjusting quickly, and then again as the ute pulled up near the stairs and the lights were killed, leaving him in the dimness of the moon and the hallway light beaming through the open door behind him.

Taipan and Acacia emerged from the garage. Taipan was stripped to the waist, Acacia shrugging a jacket on over a singlet. They reeked of oil and grease, familiar smells from a lifetime ago. The dogs sniffed around the ute.

Hippie emerged from the driver's side, hands busy patting the dogs. 'Wow, a reception committee. But where's the grog, you dumb mutts, eh?'

The passenger door opened and Kala stepped out. She looked exhausted, hunched inside a heavy ex-army coat. She wore a grey tracksuit under it. Her hair was a matted nest, her face streaked with the muddy tracks of tears.

'Hey,' she said.

Kevin moved to hug her, stopped, aware of people watching; of Taipan looming between them like a thundercloud.

'So you made it, eh?' the biker said.

'No thanks to you.'

'Couldn't stay,' Taipan said. 'The place was too hot. Plus that Mira had her hooks in the boy, eh. Had to get him out of her reach; it was either Mother or the choppin' block.'

'Yeah, right, you were so concerned about Kevin's welfare, I'm sure.' She brushed his hand away. 'I need a shower and a pee. Thanks for the lift, Hippie.' She handed him back his jacket and stalked off, brushing past Kevin with barely a look.

'How did you find her?' Kevin asked.

'She rang the hotline,' Hippie said. 'Mother set up a rendezvous in Longreach and sent me to pick her up.'

Taipan rounded on Hippie: 'Didn't think to tell me, eh?'

'Mother said go. I went.'

'Did the girl say how she got away?'

'Kept her head down and hitched, I gather. Didn't say much, just that it had been pretty tight.'

'I gotta talk to that girl,' Taipan said, and stalked off.

'Tai,' Acacia called, but he didn't look back. 'You sure you weren't followed?' she asked Hippie as he lit a cigarette.

'Nah, I would've noticed.'

A shout – a scream! – came from inside the house.

Byely, leg cocked on the front wheel, yapped like a car alarm.

Kevin raced into the living room.

Taipan held Kala from behind, his teeth in her neck. Furious and weeping, she kicked futilely at his ankles, raked his forearms with her nails.

'Let her go, arsehole,' Kevin yelled, and charged. Taipan looked up in surprise. Kevin fired a punch past Kala's face that connected squarely with Taipan's gory jaw. The biker staggered backward, dragging Kala off balance. Kevin closed in but Acacia grabbed him from behind, pinning his arms to his side. He swore at her to let him go.

Taipan threw Kala to the floor and advanced on Kevin.

A carafe of blood shattered against the wall, leaving a massive stain, slowly dripping as though the wall itself were bleeding. Everyone stopped.

Danica stood in the doorway, her face dark with fury. 'What the hell is going on here?'

Outside, the dogs were going ballistic, claws scrabbling at the front door. Acacia released Kevin and he knelt beside Kala, but she pulled away. He looked to the others for help, but no-one moved. Cassie appeared behind Danica, then hurried away.

'There better be a damn good reason for this,' Danica said, crossing her arms. 'I was fond of that jug.'

She waved a hand and the dogs fell silent, the air in the room turning thick and ominous in the sudden quiet.

Taipan pointed at Kala where she slumped on the floor, one hand pressed to the gash in her neck. 'Tell 'em where ya earring is, Kay. The one ya white mum gave you.'

Kala covered her ear with one hand. Kevin hadn't noticed the little silver cross was missing. He should've, though; Taipan had. But then, he hadn't known her mother had given it to her, either. Despite what he'd seen in her blood, he realised he didn't know her very well at all. And clearly, not as well as Taipan.

Cassie entered the room and handed Kevin a tea towel; he held it to Kala's wound. He felt her blood on his skin; felt the smell invade his nose, his throat, his lungs. She wouldn't meet his eyes but she pulled the towel in tight, trapping his hand under hers.

'No way did she sneak past VS and the cops,' Taipan declared, his voice vibrating with disgust. 'She had to cut herself a deal.'

'Bullshit.' Kevin held onto Kala, willing her to say something to prove Taipan wrong. 'Kala would never sell us out. She's human – it would've been easy for her to get through, easier than for us. *She* wouldn't have had to kill anyone.'

Danica stepped in front of Kala and faced the crowd. 'Tai and Kevin can stay. Everyone else – out.'

'Are they coming for us?' Acacia asked, reaching out to hold Cassie's hand.

'How would I know?' Kala said bitterly. 'I'm a sender, not a receiver.'

'I said out,' Danica ordered.

When the door had closed behind them, she asked tenderly, 'Kala?'

Kala stared at the floor, and when she spoke, her voice was a low monotone, rimmed with shame. 'I was to contact Mira when I knew for a fact that you were here. But I wouldn't have. They couldn't have programmed me that well, not with Tai's blood in me.'

'You got no idea what that bloodhag can do once she's got her fangs in you,' Taipan said.

'Tai, that's enough!' Danica glared at him. 'Should I send you out, too?'

He looked not so much chastened by Danica's outburst, as restrained. His muscles were tight as he spoke, the words driving out like steam, 'They could be on their way now, ridin' a trace, just like they did with the boy.'

'While she's awake? Here? It's most unlikely. But I should've gone with Hippie to collect her. I should've checked her out there without endangering the camp.'

'No,' Taipan said. 'That woulda been too big a risk. Coulda

bin Hunters or anythin' trackin' that girl. No, she shoulda stayed the hell away.'

Kala rubbed at her arms, her throat. 'How can I stay away? After 40 years, how the fuck can I stay away?'

'Leave her alone.' Kevin lifted Kala to her feet and wrapped her in his arms. 'You've hurt her enough.'

'Gods, enough, the lot of you,' Danica said. 'The horse has bolted. But they can't have seen this place, Tai. My wards are stronger than that.'

'Close enough is good enough.'

'Jesus,' Kevin said. 'Doesn't anyone even care what they did to her? You're talking as if Kala doesn't even matter.'

'It's our lives, fella.' Taipan pointed at Kala. 'She knows it. We can't allow VS to get their hands on Mother. She's the only thing holdin' us together.'

Danica laid a hand on his shoulder. 'None of us is more important than any other.' She took Kala's face in her hands. Kevin squeezed Kala's arm so she knew she wasn't alone. That not everyone was ready to feed her to the wolves.

'What happened?' Danica asked.

'Mira – she got me.' Kala collapsed like a balloon deflating, her admission the last puff of air.

'And how did you escape?'

Kala looked away, down at her feet, her answer a mere mumble. 'She let me go.'

'I need to see. May I?'

Kala pulled back, shaking.

'It's all right, Kala. I'm not going to hurt you. I just need to see what happened.'

'What are you gonna do?' Kevin asked.

'Nothing I haven't done with you,' Danica said.

'It's okay, Kevvie,' Kala told him, breaking away from his touch to face Danica square on. 'I don't mind.'

'Let me see,' Danica said.

A bite. A blood rush.

Kevin sensed the connection form between the two women.

Danica emerged, blinking. She bit her own forearm and smeared blood on Kala's wounds. Then she told her, 'Taste me. Take me into you.'

Kala licked Danica's forearm, then began to suckle.

Danica gave a single, sharp, 'ah'. Her eyes showed purple through slit lids. Then she murmured, 'There's something more – locked; *blood*locked.' Her gaze found Kevin, her brow furrowed, then she slowly disengaged from Kala.

'Hold her,' she told him as Kala sagged into his arms.

'Did you see?' Danica asked Taipan. She looked at Kevin, then back to Taipan.

'Did you see what?' Kevin asked. 'What'd they do to her?'

Taipan ignored him, his focus on Danica. 'I saw her with Mira, nothin' more.'

'It *was* Mira,' Danica said. 'She forged a link; she's very good.' There was measure of respect in her voice, of admiration. 'I've dampened it. I doubt it would've penetrated my wards; but still, they've probably got some idea where we are. We move out tonight as planned.'

'Where we gonna go, eh?' Taipan stalked to a window and looked out, as though expecting – hoping – that VS storm troopers would come crashing into the compound at any moment. 'All this runnin' and hidin', I'm plenny sick of it. When we gonna hit back?'

'When we can win. For now, the road is our only sanctuary.'

'We should hunt Mira. We know she's in Rocky. We know she's only got a few men with her. We could take her by surprise. That'd be a big loss for Maximilian von Shitter.'

'No.'

'Sooner or later, it has to come to this. My money's on sooner.'

'And I say later.'

'I want out,' Kevin said. 'Out for me and Kala. You lot can do what you want, but I want no part of it.'

Taipan ignored him, his focus on Danica. 'Like I said, what's important is keepin' you out of their claws. Nothin' else. And the best way of doin' that is smashin' 'em.' He drove his fist into his palm. 'If this fella has any balls at all, he'll help. Otherwise, he can just piss off, and take anyone who can't stomach a fight with him.'

Danica held out a hand, palm up, to hush Taipan as she asked Kevin, 'You don't want to avenge your father?'

Kevin resisted her gentle goading. 'I got family who need me to look after them. I've seen what the VS guys can do and I've seen what you can do, and I'm not gonna join some suicide mission and leave my mum with another grave to cry over.'

'So what you gonna do, fella?' Taipan asked. 'Throw that girl there on the back of a bike and see the world? How far will you get with that bloodhag on your tail?'

'A damn sight further than if I go with you, that's for sure. They've got a gunship, for Christ's sake!'

'Don't worry 'bout that bird. I got a little surprise for it down there in the garage.'

'Sure you have. It worked great at The Farm.'

Taipan's eyes narrowed, and for a moment Kevin thought he was going to attack. The man trembled, his hands fisted. 'Never figured you for a coward, fella.'

'Ain't nothin' cowardly about looking after your own.'

'Yeah? Just who do you think ya own is these days, eh? Take it from me – there ain't no goin' back.'

'I'll take my chances.'

'Enough,' Danica said. 'Kevin, take Kala out, let her rest. I need to think about this. Tai, let's find Acacia and work out our next move.'

The hallway was crowded: Acacia, Cassie, Hippie, a bunch of others, all clustered around the door. They looked at Kevin and Kala with naked curiosity, perhaps pity.

'What're you two doin' here?' Taipan snapped, singling Mohawk and Lions out of the crush. 'Get out to that fence.

You want that VS mob to catch us with our pants down?'

'We heard the dogs,' Mohawk said, but Lions hit him in the arm and they shouldered their way out.

'We're in it up to our necks,' Taipan told them. 'Can't afford to be slackin' off.'

Danica stepped out by his side, looking pensive.

'We need more troops,' he told her, then swept his gaze around the assembled Night Riders. 'Reinforcements. Full-blooded.'

'Don't look at me, man,' Hippie said, backing away till he hit the wall, a stubby of beer clutched protectively against his stomach. 'I like my dreams just the way they are.'

Taipan snorted. 'Didn't think you'd have the spine for it, Hippie. Too fond of ya pizza.' He mimed having a cigarette, then shoved Kevin and Kala. 'Make yourself useful and take these two to the demountables. Separate, eh? And keep an eye on 'em.'

'You want me to–'

'Just do it! We're in deep shit here.'

Acacia pushed to the front to drape her arm around Cassie's shoulder. 'What's goin' on?'

'Come into the kitchen,' Danica said. 'The rest of you, keep packing.'

'C'mon, Hippie,' Kevin said. 'You want to show us where Kala can bunk down?'

'Yeah, sure man. Looks like you're outta the house, eh, Kay?' He glanced at Taipan.

'Looks like it,' she muttered.

He waved a half-empty stubby down the hall. 'This way.' He opened the front door and had to dodge as the two dogs bolted inside. 'Everyone's in a rush tonight.' On the veranda, he rested the stubby on the rail and pulled out a cigarette packet and thumbed his lighter. Cigarette in mouth, he mumbled, 'So what's the story?'

'Those your wheels?' Kevin asked, indicating the ute.

'In a communal kinda way.'

'You got the keys?'

'Hey, man, I don't want any trouble.'

'Then give me the keys.'

'Kevvie?' Kala asked.

'You heard Tai. We're prisoners here. If we don't go now, we might not be able to.'

'I don't–'

'You'd rather stay here – with him?'

A long silence, and then, 'No.'

'Gimme the keys, Hippie. I can belt you if it makes it easier.'

'Nah, it's cool.' He handed them over. 'Um, good luck, I guess.'

'Keep it. You'll need all you can get if Taipan has his way and you all go on the warpath.'

Hippie looked back at the house, his face a mask of anguish. He puffed furiously on his cigarette.

He was still standing there, a picture of indecision, when Kevin floored the ute. Mohawk and Lions raised their hands, but Kevin accelerated, aware of them unslinging their rifles, and behind him, Byely and Cherny barking where they raced in the ute's dust. He gritted his teeth and locked his hands on the wheel and kept the pedal pressed to the floor. Kala cried out and ducked down, arms over her head. The engine howled, threatening to blow its guts out.

They hit the gate.

There was a shriek and the crunch of impact. Metal sliced over the ute like massive bird claws. One panel of mesh slid from the bonnet with a clatter and they were on their way, skidding and rattling out to the highway, headlights blazing their way south.

'Made it,' Kevin said.

'Yeah,' Kala said, but she wasn't looking at him. She had her feet up on the dash, her arms around her knees, her face turned toward the door. 'Yeah,' she said again. 'We made it.'

THIRTY-NINE

Kevin checked the mirrors, expecting to see cops or VS or Night Riders appear at any moment. But the road remained empty.

'I think we'll have enough fuel to make Barlow's Siding,' he said as the gauge hit the one-quarter mark. His voice sounded loud inside their headlight-and-bitumen cocoon.

'And what then?' Kala asked.

'I reckon we head back to my place. Check on my mum. Meg. Everyone.'

'And then?'

'Open to suggestions.'

She shrugged. After a few more kilometres of silence, she said, 'I probably would've stayed, you know, if they'd let me.'

'Loyal to a fault, you are.' He looked at her, but she was staring out the windscreen, and he wondered if she saw the past or the future there. 'Want me to turn back? Drop you off?'

'No, us leaving was the best thing we could've done. If Mira is tracking us both, we might buy Mother some time. Taipan was right, Kevvie: I was a risk. And I can't blame him for what he did. The nest is home for all of them, probably the only one they've ever known. Even if Taipan and I could dredge up the knowledge of our families – who our mobs were, where they were from – we still couldn't go back. Well, he couldn't, anyway. They think vampires are a white man's disease.'

'Didn't the Aborigines have vampires before us lot came? I mean, it's not just Dracula and that fella from New Orleans? Y'know, Tom Cruise, is it?'

Kala laughed. 'Lestat? Wow, that's an old one. But no, it's not just them. Pretty much every culture's got some kind of blood drinker in it – no sparkly ones, though, I don't know where they came from. But Taipan's variety is all Euro. Any blackfella with even one foot still in their country can smell it a mile away. They know he doesn't belong, no matter how much he wants to.'

'Will people know I'm not the same?'

'You'll be all okay as long as you keep your head down,' Kala said. 'White folks are pretty good at not noticing things that make them uncomfortable.'

'I guess. Cross that bridge when we come to it.'

What if Taipan was right and he couldn't go back – couldn't fit in? And maybe Danica was right, too – maybe he did want revenge. But against who? He knew next to nothing and he was driving farther away from the only people who could teach him. At least he had Kala. Kala knew stuff. She might not be able to get inside his head like Taipan and Danica, but she could fill him in on the theory. That, and keep him fed. His gut twisted at the thought. Is that all Kala would come to mean to him – a meal ticket? Is that all anyone would come to mean to him?

'So what are the Aboriginal vampires like?' he asked.

'Dunno, never seen one.'

Kevin checked the moon-washed, flat nothingness unrolling beyond the windscreen. Not exactly the big city; he could see why the VS mob wouldn't be relaxed out here. No shops, no shade; no veins. 'Yeah, well, I don't think anyone has the right to blame you for what happened. It's not as though you went with Mira willingly.'

'They caught me, they – she took my blood, and made me drink hers. I knew – well, hoped – she wouldn't be able to track me out west. Not outside of my dreams, anyway. Damn it; it's all gone to hell, Kevvie.'

'It's just as well we're getting out, then, eh?'

'Are we?'

'There must be some place where VS doesn't have all the power. Somewhere we can just be ourselves.'

'Maybe Perth? I honestly don't know. I think you'll find any place with a lot of people will have someone – some *thing* – preying on them.'

'We can worry about that once I've got Mum and Meg out of danger.'

She paused, then asked, 'Are you thinking of bringing them?'

'I can't leave them trapped between your lot and Mira.'

'You don't think that's a good enough reason to try to bring VS down?'

'I don't want to kill anyone,' he said. 'Not ever again.'

'Again?'

He swore under his breath as he felt Nicola knocking at the door in his mind.

'I was totally out of it,' he confessed. 'After the Farm, y'know. It was horrible. I kept seeing her, feeling her; I can't do that again. I can't be like *him*.'

'So what will you do? Go veggo, like Bhagwan?'

'Maybe. With the insurance from the servo, maybe we can start over. I could even work daytime, out of the sun. No-one would notice. Plenty of animals out west, too.'

'You know why they call people who live off animal blood "veggos"? It's because if all you drink is animal blood, you end up a vegetable. You need human blood; you need their lives, their dreams. Their souls, maybe.'

'That's why Bhagwan had those myx– those red-eyes.'

'Bingo.'

He licked his lips, so dry, and he eased off on the accelerator, seized by vertigo, as if he was on the roof of a house, right near the gutter, and the slope was steep and it felt as if the iron was lifting under his feet, sliding him closer and closer to the edge.

'Would you – do you think – stay with me?' he asked.

'I'm here, aren't I?'

A corner, a road sign; he slowed down for the rattle and bump of a cattle grid, and then accelerated again.

'So what would *you* do?' he asked.

'Try to leave – again. Go to Melbourne or Cairns or Darwin, just be a normal, ageing person again. Get a job, pay my taxes, grow old. Die.'

'Is that why you didn't get Taipan to make you one of us?'

Her red-brown eyes bored into him. 'I don't regret anything, except for getting caught. I was just lucky Mira thought I was more use to her alive than dead.'

'So what *did* happen?'

'We pulled up in the truck, Penny and me, right? Outside that hut where you lot were waiting. Then the chopper came in and there was dust everywhere, it was very loud, made my teeth rattle. It kind of circled up and around, so it was facing us, and then there was this sound, like an oxy rig lighting up, and there was this puff of smoke from the chopper, and for a minute, I actually thought something had hit it, that Tai had shot it down, y'know. Then the truck just exploded.

'I don't remember much at all, just lying on the ground wondering what the fuck had happened. That was when they grabbed me. I was a bit banged up, but I was okay. They took me into Rocky, to a hotel. Mira was there; I really don't want to go into it.'

'It sure got Taipan and Danica excited.'

'Fine. The bitch took my blood, she made me drink hers. Okay? We were bloodlinked so she could spy on me. She told me to dob you all in but she knew I wouldn't. She was just using the link to find us, but Mother is too smart for that. That's it. Okay?'

'I'm not sure what they thought they'd gain from doing that, if they knew they couldn't force you to give us up and that the link wouldn't work.'

'Desperate, maybe. Maybe because I'm only a *myxo*, they didn't care. Or maybe they just didn't find anything in my blood worth keeping me for.'

'It sounds pretty desperate, all right. Once we knew you'd been captured, no-one would trust you. I mean, once you were here, how could Mira possibly force you to go through with it? Did she threaten you?'

'No, it was just the bloodlink.'

'It doesn't make sense. There must be more to it. Danica mentioned something. What was it – a bloodlock? What's that?'

'Hocus pocus. I'm not a bloodhag; how would I know?'

'And you're sure–'

'Jesus Christ. Fine. Pull over.'

'What?'

'Just do it!'

'What are you going to do? We're in the middle of nowhere; you can't hitch from here.'

'Just pull over!'

He stopped the ute.

She unzipped her tracksuit jacket. She wasn't wearing anything underneath. 'Help yourself.'

'What?'

'You heard me. You want to see what's in my blood – here, help yourself.'

'That's not what I was saying at all.'

'How else will you know what Mira did to me? What she wanted me to do? How else will you know you can trust me?'

'Sorry. Sure. Okay. But not from there. Give me your arm.'

'Shy?'

Kevin shrugged.

Kala zipped her top closed and rolled up her sleeve. He tested her veins, decided on the elbow. She sighed, then gasped as his fangs opened her flesh. Kevin dived into her lifestream and became Kala.

The explosion sweeps the world out from under his feet. There's blue sky and black smoke and distant, muffled noises that don't make any sense. His body is pain and he crawls away from the heat and flames. Men pick him up – he has no control over his limbs, is slung like a sack of chaff into the back of a car, with cold, tight restraints on his wrists. Slapped for bleeding on the seat. Threatened with a good hard fucking, but the second man in the car warns his friend that 'she' will know, and her orders not to damage the merchandise were explicit.

He has an impression of flat plains and a wide road and distant hills and forcing himself to defy the pain wracking his body to sit up and focus. A life-sized statue of a grey, hunchbacked bull on the median strip. One of the guards tells him to lie down, but he ignores the thug's command and watches the city slide by. It's hot, the kind of summer day that sucks the moisture out of you and leaves you feeling like a husk, like a cicada shell, empty and split and ready to crumble and drift away on the wind. He's about ready to drift away. Wishes he could. He wants to ask them to turn up the air con but he has no spit, can make no words. He is a shell filled with pain and fear and he knows the worst is yet to come.

A wide brown river with muddy banks is spanned by two bridges. A handful of boats – half-cabins and tinnies, another with sails – bob on the water. It all looks so peaceful and mundane. Hard to believe he's about to die. His bladder is painfully full.

The car turns upstream and parks in an alley. His captors haul him out, none too gently, and he finds the air to give a cry. They're wearing suits, with identical haircuts that suggest they're cops or soldiers. Wide shoulders, cold eyes. Gespenstenstaffel for sure.

They drag him through a rear entrance choked with plastic crates and crumpled boxes and an overflowing steel bin. He glimpses stainless steel benches, hanging pots and a seriously large refrigerator.

They enter an elevator, the guards filling it with their mass. One presses against him and he hopes it's the guard's pistol digging into this hip. Still got a sense of humour. You go, girl. One holds him against the wall as the elevator slows and the door opens. A rough hand gropes his breast. His gut heaves and he tells himself to be still: these two are myxos and he can't take them. They march him to the end of the corridor. One knocks on a door and is told immediately to enter.

The penthouse is spacious, cool and dark, the curtains closed, the air conditioning cranked up. Goosebumps rise on his arms. He wants to sink into the plush carpet and disappear.

Mira turns, a glass in hand. She wears a silk robe over black sports underwear. She has amazing calves, the bitch. Another cop looks up from a table of radios, hand at his shoulder holster–

Hunter!

Kevin's knowledge jerks him inside Kala's experience; he almost misses Mira ask: *'What have we here?'*

'One of the sluts hanging out with the Night Riders,' a guard tells her. 'She had these on her.' He dumps a bunch of stuff on the table and pulls a dagger from the collection: 'Had this pig sticker in her boot.'

'A girl can't be too careful these days.' Mira shakes her head in mock disappointment. 'Put her on the couch and keep searching. Taipan can't have gone far.'

The guards seat him none too gently, then leave.

Hunter walks over to sift the items on the table. He pushes the dagger to one side, then dangles a set of keys. 'The Monaro? It's your ride, isn't it?'

He says nothing, but his heart contracts at the sight of the Mexican key ring in the hands of Mira's red-eye. Thinks about snatching the dagger and driving it into the man's eye, but the distance is too great, his legs too weak.

And now Mira leans in close enough for him to smell the wine on her breath. 'I do hope we didn't kill Taipan. Did we?'

He shrugs.

'You're the one who rescued the grease monkey, aren't you? After he'd taken a chunk out of his pretty little girlfriend. How's he getting along? Made friends with Taipan?'

He seals his lips, forces his teeth together. He really needs to pee.

'I'm told the grease monkey has taken a shine to you. That you've been suckling him. How does Taipan like sharing his squeeze with a white boy?'

'I'm no-one's squeeze,' he says, the anger – the fear – bursting forth despite himself.

Kevin suffers a moment of odd confusion, hearing the words, experiencing the attraction – the affection – Kala has for him.

'No?' Mira seizes his arm so fast, so hard it makes him squeal. She grabs the dagger from the table. A deft slash opens his skin – he flinches, but she holds him firm as she dribbles blood into her empty glass, then sips.

'Mm, I taste – let me see – a little bit of black, a little bit of white. The grease monkey's fed from you, but you haven't tasted him. Not yet. You think he likes you but you aren't getting your hopes up because you know he's got a girlfriend and he is a bit of a mummy's boy. Is that about right? You wish you could get away from your boyfriend but you're afraid to, because you don't want to get old. Not yet, anyway.

'Stupid girl. Why do you choose to stay one of the herd when Taipan has offered you immortality? When you could be so much more than they?'

'Fuck you, bitch.' The words come out slow and thin and resigned, but at least they come out.

'What a splendid idea.' Mira's hand is on his throat, pinning him despite his desperate, feeble punches and kicks. Mira's other hand slashes and rips away his ragged clothing, heedless of how much damage is done to the skin underneath. Mira seizes the silver cross and tears it from his ear. 'Nice,' she says, and throws it on the table before lapping at the wound. Hunter takes a two-way radio out on to the balcony.

The door snicks shut, leaving him alone with the woman. Mira forces him down into the sofa and kisses him hard–

Kevin suffers double visions as seeing – enduring – Kala's rape recalls:

Taipan over him. Blood on his mouth. Teeth in his flesh. And then, black skin under his lips. Rich, rich blood
Mira pinning him, her teeth in his throat, her blood in his mouth reaching all the way into his soul like liquid cancer –

His heart thuds in his chest, his stomach heaves, his skin crawls with a million filthy roaches

Mira drinks and then forces her blood into Kala's mouth and Kevin again tastes Mira's life, that incredible array of death and disaster, pleasure and pain. And something more. Something insidious.

She has paid a second visit to Kala's lifestream and she has left something behind. Something for him.

The bloodlock snaps open.

Kevin is jolted out of Kala's lifestream into something else altogether:

A vision. A nightmare. It's so strong he can smell Mira; he can taste her.

He tries to slam the door on her, send her back to that room in his head. She's too strong, her blood entwined in Kala's and his in hers:

Contact.

A purple sunset tints a square timber arch lilac. Kevin knows the gateway – he's driven past it plenty of times. Whitby Downs.

The gateway shrinks, grows a middle cricket stump to become a wicket, the lintel becoming rough bails. Kevin is bowling. At the striker's end, Taipan waits, incongruous in whites, tapping the pitch with his bat in preparation. Kala waits at the non-striker's end. Meg is wicket-keeper; his mother is at gully. There are no other fielders. The stands are empty.

Kevin checks the scoreboard: Night Riders are nine batsmen down and need four runs to snatch the win from Von Schiller. There are three balls remaining. Kevin pushes off from his mark, striding out into his full pace.

The umpire's white coat flutters around his ankles and Kevin notices the umpie is wearing leather boots. Shit. He can't see her face, but he knows who the umpire is. Hardly impartial.

He steams in, jams his front foot down just inside the crease and rolls his shoulder, fires the delivery down. Nasty little bouncer, a bold move; if Taipan gets under that, he could send it all the way, a four or a six, game over. But the ball jags a crack in the pitch and hangs low. The willow sails over the top and the ball smacks Taipan on the ribs, right over the heart. He drops the bat. Falls to his knees. Blood stains his whites, pouring from the hole in his chest. The umpire's finger comes up: he's out.

Meg and his mother hoist Kevin on their shoulders for a victory lap. When he looks back as they leave the oval, he sees the umpire has used the stumps to stake Taipan and Kala out on the pitch, the sticks shoved through their ankles and wrists. Victory, with two balls remaining.

He doesn't need to hear the on-field commentary to understand the meaning of this bizarre cricket match. *Blood calls to blood.*

He's got three days to deliver Taipan to Whitby Downs, or his mother and Meg are dead.

FORTY

Rage sent Kevin hurtling out of Kala's blood memories, back to the surface of his own consciousness.

'What is it?' she asked. 'What did you see?'

The pendant Danica gave him had turned uncomfortably warm against his skin. 'Mira used you to send me a message, the bitch. She knew you'd find me. That I'd drink from you. She says she's got my mum, and Meg, too.' He groaned, hands to his forehead. 'She wants to trade them for Taipan.' He stumbled out of the ute and slammed the door, beat his hands on the roof, turned and leaned back, fighting for breath, fighting the claustrophobic fear. The night was huge, the plains stretching out, but he felt as if he was in a box. A coffin.

Kala laid a hand his shoulder. 'Are you sure she told the truth? That it wasn't just a warning? A dream?'

'It felt like truth.'

Kala startled, eyes wide, the red centres flaring and expanding, as she looked at something by the tailgate. He turned as she hunched into him.

Taipan.

'You mob didn't get too far. Run outta fuel or outta guts?'

'How did you catch up to us?' He hadn't heard a vehicle, a bike.

'I got me ways.'

Kala relaxed her grip, stood a little away. 'He's shadow walking.'

'He's what?'

'He's not really here.'

'Real enough,' Taipan said, stepping closer, his boots silent on the bitumen.

'What do you want?' Kevin asked. He studied the man, looking for signs that he was just some kind of projection or hologram. Nothing.

'We're movin' on. But Mother says it's safe for Kala to come back. You too, if you want. Train you up proper. Give you a chance out here, with or without us.'

'I can't,' Kevin said. His voice broke. 'They've got my mum, and my girlfriend.'

'Now why would they do that? What makes you so important, eh?'

'They're offering a trade.'

'Ah,' Taipan said. 'Mother?'

'You.'

'Same thing. Either way, no deal.'

'I didn't expect so.'

'You could help him,' Kala told Taipan.

'By walkin' into a trap again? Let me think about that. Nah.'

'Prick.'

'So what're you gonna do, fella?'

'I should hand you over.'

'Should you? I guess it might stop this happenin' to some other bastard, eh. You'd be doing the world a favour, maybe. Whaddya think, Kay?'

Kala looked away, chewing on her lip.

'You've thought about this, then,' Kevin said. 'That maybe you don't deserve to be here.'

'Not up to me to say who does and who don't. I ain't that clever. But I figger I got the same right as anyone else. Not many of us get a choice about whether we want to be here or not, but since I am here, I reckon I'll hang 'round for a bit. Guess I'm selfish that way.'

'I'm gonna go home and keep my family safe. From Mira and from you.'

'Sure you don't want me to come hold ya hand?'

Mira wanted Taipan – would it really be so bad to give him to her? Maybe she'd throw in some kind of vampire maintenance manual. Oil change every 10,000 kilometres or six months, whichever came first.

'Don't tempt me. You do what you have to, and I'll do the same. But I'm not giving anyone to Mira's mob. From what I saw of what they did to Kala, they're no better than you lot.'

'That's a compliment if ever I heard one. It's suicide, y'know.'

'They're my family.'

'Not any more.'

'They're going to die.'

'That's gonna happen anyway. The only question is how and when.'

'Well, my answer is, not now, and not at the hands of those cunts.'

'I tried to get my sister out of it and what did it get me? A stake in the heart.'

'I'm not expecting my mother will try to kill me.'

'Mothers have been known to give up their kids. Whether they wanted to or not.'

'My mind's made up.'

'Kay?'

'I'm not letting him go by himself.'

'Bravo.' Taipan clapped, a single impact of hand against hand, but no sound came from it. 'You got a new fix, eh.'

'You're the one runnin' away while Kev's gonna go up against Mira. Why don't you take responsibility for the mess you've made and help him?'

'Hey, they ain't my mob. Besides, I didn't ask for this curse, any more than the fella there did.'

'Jesus, let's play pass the parcel, why don't we.'

'Not like you to put yourself on the line, Kala. This fella must be gettin' to you, eh.'

'You are such a–'

'Nice guy, I know, I hear it alla time. I'll be at the gorge till the end of the week, in case you see sense.' He stepped backward, hesitated. 'And whitefella, just remember that the earth is your friend, eh?' He gave a knowing wink that left Kevin puzzled. Took another step and vanished as though he'd never been there at all.

'Nice trick,' Kevin said.

'He's the only one I know who can do it.'

'Doesn't look like he'll be teaching it to me.'

'You might already know, just, you know, you don't know that you know. Y'know?'

He laughed, and she laughed, and he said, 'All I know is that I know nothin'. That, and that you're drivin'.'

They ran out of night before they reached Barlow's Siding, so Kala pulled off the road and parked where a gully shielded them from the road. Kevin took refuge in the ute's cab under a tarp that Kala found in the large tool box in the tray.

'All our cars have something like this,' she told him. 'Kinda makes you wish for Nigel's Sandman, eh?'

'Or your Monaro.'

'Yeah, or my Monaro. I hope those bastards are looking after it. God, I hope that surfie's not driving it,' she said, and shut him in the cabin.

Kevin remembered all those warnings about locking pets and kids in cars, so wound down the window, even if he felt fairly certain that those warnings no longer applied to him. He lay there, constrained by the thick plastic, sunlight blasting down on his cage, locked in his own head with the memory of the dream sent to him, of his family and friends being held prisoner.

When the sun was low enough for him to risk emerging, he found Kala huddled on a patch of grass in the shade of a tree, a dusty water cooler nearby. She sat up as he approached, stretching, like a cat in a patch of sun. He had an urge to sit with her so she could lie with her head in his lap.

Meg's hair shines in the sunlight, golden against the denim of his jeans, and a magpie trills and she says they can go anywhere, with him being a mechanic and all, and he asks why they'd go anywhere when everything they need is here, and she asks, smiling, her teeth bright and eyes sparkling with tease, that hasn't he ever wanted more than this mosquito-plagued billabong and scrappy ghost gum, and he says that's fine, it'll rain sometime and then there'll be yellowbelly as well, and she says she isn't planning on going anywhere, they're young, there's no rush, but doesn't he sometimes wish that maybe there was more, and he says if there is he doesn't need it because all he needs is her, besides, he isn't going to leave his parents to run the servo by themselves, and she says that's all the more reason to see something of the world before they settle down and have babies.

He sat down, legs shaky, just out of easy reach of Kala.

'You sleep okay?' she asked.

'A little. You?'

'A little. You look distracted.'

'I won't ever have children, will I?'

'Where did that come from?'

'Just something I was wondering.'

'No, you can't have children. Not the regular way, anyway. You'd think the blood would make super sperm, wouldn't you, but I guess nature has some sense of justice.'

'What do you mean?'

'Can you imagine a vampire foetus? What it'd do to the mother?'

The baby, all teeth and claws, bursting out through its mother's – through Meg's – stomach. *Alien*, much? He shivered. 'A simple no would've done.'

'How about I drive?' Kala asked.

'Sure. I'll buy you dinner when we get there.'

'At the very least,' she said, offering a grin.

'It's not far. Another hour or so.'

'Good. I hope you're cashed up. I am very hungry, Kevvie.'

The way she said 'very hungry', with that look from under her lashes, it made his balls tighten, and he laughed. Laughing felt good, and he tried to cling to that joy of light flirtation, as though they were going on a date, but the closer they got to Barlow's Siding, the harder it got, and by the time they were approaching his home, laughter was the furthest thing from his mind.

'Kevin? Earth to Kevin – are you receiving me?'

'Hey? Sorry, I was miles way.'

'Ah-huh. So, what's the plan?'

'Check if Mira was telling the truth. That's the first thing. Then, well, I guess if she's got Mum or Meg or both, I'll have to get them out.'

'Just you?'

'You can drive.'

'Gee, thanks. But seriously. You're sure Jasmine has them?'

'That's what the dream said.'

'How much do you know about her?'

'Bits and pieces. I mean, before all this crazy shit happened, we just knew that someone had bought Whitby Downs. Some eccentric bird from the coast who swans around in a Jaguar, of all things. She turned it into some kind of fancy rehab joint, that's what people said. Got its own chopper pad and everything, so the rich and famously fucked-up don't have to be seen by us yokels. We called it the asylum. It still runs sheep, though, and cattle. They buy groceries and stuff in town. Hey, maybe I could sneak in that way and smuggle Mum out?'

'Have a lot of late night shopping in Upper Bum Fuck, do you? Sorry, I know it's your home. I mean, I'm from the sticks, too; I can't throw stones. But, it's like, y'know, how long do you want to wait for them to run out of eggs or whatever?'

'Fair enough. So what do you know about the joint?'

'Well, from the road, it's no different to any other station, but once you get in you'll see the difference – fences, lights, guards.'

'That's some rehab.'

'It is, kind of. Jasmine Turner is this kind of guru. She's run these places all over the state. Fangers fly out from the coast to relax and recuperate and enjoy the veins.'

'So who is she?'

'I only know what Tai has told me, which usually amounts to "fucking bitch", but she's definitely old blood. Among the first to come out here, looking for a clean start, or a clean getaway. I guess that VS mob would call it *lebensraum*.' She rolled her eyes.

'No idea how many goons she's got working for her? Any of those Gespensten-stuff-alls that you guys are so worried about?'

'Gespenstenstaffel. Almost all red-eyes and fangers. But no, she's unlikely to have them. Not that it matters.'

'Why's that?'

'We're here.' She steered off the road and pulled up on the verge.

His gut lurched. They'd turned the final corner and he could see the humped ruin of the servo and, farther back from the road, the iron roof of his house glinting in the moonlight.

They sat in the silent dark, waiting for their eyes to adjust, building up the courage. He could feel the presence of Jasmine's base, kilometres to the south, looming up on his horizon like some towering wreck of a castle on a mountain top. Its shadow stretched all the way to here. Was Mira sitting in that upmost turret with a telescope? Was his mother in the dungeon?

'Why doesn't it matter how many men Jasmine's got?' he asked again.

'Because she's old,' Kala answered, and her voice was flat with resignation. 'She's so old she can take you out with one hand and still serve tea and scones with the other.'

'Oh,' he said, and opened the door. 'At least I get scones, though, eh?'

FORTY-ONE

They crept through the scrub alongside the verge. The ruined service station didn't look as if it'd been touched – no signs of a clean-up. They crouched beside the fence, their backs to the ruins that still smelled of charcoal. The house sat silent and dark. Glass glimmered underneath – the windows of his Commodore most likely; his parking spot was nearest the servo, but it might've been the family sedan. There was no sign of his father's work truck. They scrambled over the fence and sneaked, crouching, to the bare Hill's Hoist, as though that slender pole could somehow hide them; could deflect the bullet or the net or whatever the expected ambush might offer.

Kevin sniffed for any scent out of place. His ears ached with the effort of listening for the betraying boot scuff, the creak of a leather sole or brush of cloth from a man moving against the stiffness of a long watch. Nothing. A plover's ratchet cry was the only sound to break the silence.

Kala hugged him, her hands firm and warm on his shoulders, sliding around his waist, the firm length of her body pressing against his back.

'It's cold and you owe me dinner,' she murmured in his ear, but her levity seemed forced and foreign.

An engine carried through the stillness. Miles away, but

his fear flared and he wished they'd hidden the ute farther off the road. The distance back to the vehicle felt massive, as though they'd parked it in Melbourne. The few spindly trees in the yard offered the only cover. Not enough.

Kala hung back as he dashed to the back stairs. He paused to again test the air with nose and ears. Still nothing. He gestured for her to join him, then, one slow footstep after another, he crept up the stairs and listened at the door. No television. No radio. Nothing that smelled like fresh cooking. The house felt empty, unlit windows staring out. He turned the door handle. Locked. Tried to get his keys from his jeans pocket without jingling them. His only memento, he realised: the keys to his house and his car. The metal rasped as he inserted it, sounding as loud as a hacksaw. The tumbler clicked like an axe falling. He paused, hand on the door knob, Kala waiting at the bottom of the stairs. A vehicle came down the main road from the south, slowed slightly as it approached the T-junction, but drove past.

Kala smiled gamely as the noise of the car faded. He motioned for her to get ready, then pushed the door open. The smell of detergent met him, a faint odour of old roses, eucalyptus that made him think of his mother and the oil she dabbed on her collar to help her breathing when she went to bed.

He stepped in, tensing as the floorboards creaked, but he could feel the emptiness. He waved Kala up. He pulled the door shut behind her but didn't lock it in case they had to leave in a hurry. Again. He turned on the light. The room was as he remembered it and that threw him; surely, after all that had happened, something should've changed? He felt as if he was breaking in rather than coming home.

They walked into the living room.

No notes for him. No 'back in five minutes', no 'gone to Meg's for dinner'. No welcome home banner and his friends jumping out: Surprise!

'She's not here,' he said.

'That doesn't mean Jasmine has her. Let's look around, maybe there's a message.'

'Why would she do that? It's not like she'd expect me to come back. I'm probably all over the news by now.'

'Why? What have you done?'

'Let me see. Attacked my girlfriend, helped kill two families and some cops. That's enough, surely?'

'Could you have stopped any of it? Did you honestly have a choice?'

'A man's always got a choice.'

'To live or to die, that's the only choice you've been given. Maybe you haven't noticed, but the normal rules don't apply to us.'

'They have to,' Kevin said. 'They're the only rules we've got. If I let them go, what have I got left?'

'You've got me,' she said, and hugged him fiercely. She pressed her lips to his.

For a long, long moment, he did nothing but stand there, his body warming with the heat of hers. She pulled back, eyes questioning, and his hands, seemingly of their own volition, moved to embrace her, pulling her hips hard against his. His face lowered to hers and he kissed her. Her lips opened to him instantly, beckoning his tongue. Hunger stirred.

'No teeth,' she whispered awkwardly, a hand pressed against his mouth.

He stood very still as he fought to rein in his emotions, his hunger, and was rewarded with the sensation of his fangs retracting into his gums. Kala's breath wafted warm across his face and then her hands slid under his shirt, clawing at his chest, rubbing his nipples. Her mouth opened to his again. He picked her up easily and took her into his room. He lowered Kala gently to the bed. She lay there, eyes shining in the gloom, open and trusting and yearning. He took off his shirt and then crouched over her, unzipped the tracksuit jacket slowly to reveal her naked chest. She sat up to shed the top – something heavy hit the floor, she told him to ignore it, it was nothing – and pulled him down on top of her. His lips found her throat. She tensed when he nibbled, but his fangs stayed sheathed as he concentrated on his lust. He found her nipples with his teeth and tongue, lapping sighs from her. Her back arched, her fingers twined in his hair.

He pulled her pants down, revealing a dark thatch. He probed her belly button and inhaled the musk of her awakened sex. His tongue found her, opened her, delved into her. Her pelvis rose to meet him. He teased her velvet lips with his teeth between greedy strokes of his tongue. He hit her clit and she gasped. She flowed, the chemical sex washing over him, drowning all thought and reason. He delicately thrust a finger, then two, into her and she pushed against the intrusion, taking him deeper. He heard, felt, smelled, tasted her orgasm.

He sat up and reefed open his pants, thrust them down. She guided his cock into her. Her heat closed around him. Her knees moved up, her thighs clenching around his hips.

'Fuck me,' she whispered, and he hurled himself into her, losing himself in the moment of abandon. Kala shuddered under him, her fingers digging into his shoulders and back, legs wrapped tightly around him. He came quickly in the wash of her second orgasm, submerged in the sensations of her body.

Their breathing slowed, finding a common tempo, and her muscles slowly released him. Kevin slid from her and lay beside her, sweat cooling between them. He heard another car approaching. He heard Kala's heart, the intake of her breath, the gentle squeak of the bed as she adjusted her position to better stroke his cheek.

'Was it all right, without the blood?' she asked.

'It was perfect.' In the moment he said it, it was true, but in the heartbeat after, he felt like a liar, because he remembered the intensity of feeding from her, of being totally immersed in her and how she had lingered afterward. All he had now to show for their time together was a sticky cock and a hunger that ran like a wire from his gums to his gut.

She kissed him and he said, 'I should get up.'

'You gonna cook that dinner now? I'm starving.'

'Once I've caught my breath. Must be a tin of something out there.' She slapped him playfully, then tracked a short, rough-nibbled nail down the veins of his forearm. 'Maybe something a little juicier?' That look, from under her long lashes, teeth biting her bottom lip.

His insides churned, stirred by lust and nerves: could he do it? Blade or teeth?

– You need to get yourself one'a these. Cleaner, eh –

The motor got louder. White light splashed across the window as the car approached, coming from the township.

'Better get dressed,' he said, quickly sliding from the bed to look for his jeans.

A flash of disappointment on her face, then she said, mischievous again, 'Your mum? That'd be embarrassing, eh?'

'I'd live with it, if it meant she was free.' He delved in the dark, hauled his jeans up, felt again the guilty stickiness between his legs. How long before even sex became obsolete? How long would it take for blood to become his only pleasure?

She rolled, her body painted in the wash of the headlights. He wished for a camera to record her dark curves outlined in that soft light. 'You're gorgeous, totally gorgeous.'

Kala smiled at him, teeth so white in the gloom. 'You better be careful. Keep saying things like that and I might get the idea you like me.'

'Nah,' he said and hauled on his shirt. The car pulled up out the front of the house. 'Shit! They've stopped here!'

Her smile vanished. The fear on her face drove a shard of ice into him.

'VS?' she asked.

'No idea. We'd better get out of here – fast.'

The front gate squeaked.

The snick of a pistol's slide being drawn back sliced through the suspense. Kala had a small pistol, as big as her hand, the kind of thing Sean Connery might've used in his 007 days.

'Where the hell did that come from?' he whispered.

'Tarps. Guns. We're regular Boy Scouts, eh? Can we get out the back?'

'No cover,' he said. 'Fuck – the light! We left the light on!'

'Could they have seen it from the road?'

'Hell, yes.'

Footsteps on the stairs. Cautious. Quiet. He could only just hear them over the drumbeat in his ears.

He ran to the living room and turned off the light.

The footsteps stopped.

Kala crouched in the hallway; pistol aimed at the front door.

Silence, then the clink of keys. His breath caught. The front door pushed open, cautiously, faintly bumping against the wall.

Meg's voice: 'Hello? Is anyone there? Kev, is it you?' And he heard the fear, the suspicion, the excitement. 'Kevin?'

'I'm here,' he said, aware of Kala standing straight and tucking the pistol away.

Meg appeared in the entry. He raised an arm against the sudden brightness when she hit the switch by the door. Her gaze found him, her face a beaming smile, and then it froze and slowly faded as Kala walked across the room to stand beside him while he hastily did up the last of his shirt buttons. Kala's hand touched the small of his back, the softest of endearing touches.

'What are you doing here, Kev? Everyone's been looking for you, you know.'

'I just wanted to know if you and Mum were okay.'

'Oh, we're fine,' she said, a hand going to the bandage on her neck. 'Thanks for asking. How are you?' Her gaze wandered over Kala, no doubt noting the girl zipping the jacket up all the way to the neck.

'I'm okay.'

'So it seems.' Her eyes grew hard, her jaw setting firm. 'And just where the fuck have you been? Didn't they have phones? We've been worried sick.'

'It's hard to explain.'

'I'm listening.'

He noticed the carry bag she'd dropped at her feet. 'Where's Mum?'

'She was at our place for a few nights, but day before last she moved out to the asylum.'

His last, faint hope was crushed out. 'The asylum–'

'Sorry, I shouldn't have called it that. She's at Whitby Downs.'

Kala gave a sharp intake of breath as she took his hand.

'What's she doing there?' Kevin asked.

'Kind of came out of the blue. She rang earlier, asked me to fetch some fresh clothes for her. I guess it's just as well she didn't come with me. I wonder what Di would've thought, seeing you here – with her.'

Kala spoke, her hand reaching around Kevin's waist. 'Seeing her son with a black girl, do you mean?'

'Seeing her son with a girl who isn't me.'

'Meg, it's um,' his voice failed.

'What is it, Kevin?'

He felt both women staring at him.

'It's complicated.'

Meg crossed her arms. 'Try me.'

'I – I'm different. Things have happened. Shit, I don't even know where to start.' He ran his hands through his hair, smelled Kala on his fingers. He crossed his arms, felt Kala step back.

'How about you begin with why you're sneaking around your own house in the dark – with her.'

Kala said, 'It's hard for them to understand. They have to experience it, to see it for themselves. Even then they find it hard to believe. They'll make up any number of stories rather than accept the truth.'

'Why is she talking about me like I'm not even here?' Meg asked.

'Jesus,' Kevin said. 'Look, I can't do this, not now. Shit's happening. I need to get to Mum. Meg, you need to leave. Get out of the Siding, at least for a little while.'

'You're kidding, right? A week ago you were begging me not to go.'

'Things have changed.'

'No kidding.' She fired a laser stare at Kala. 'I don't know where you've been this past week or so, but I've been here, looking after your mother. Once they let me out of the hospital.'

She pointed to the bandage on her throat. 'They said I almost died, Kevin.' She paused, then rammed it home: 'The police aren't looking for *me*. No, I'm not going anywhere until you've told me what's going on; why you attacked us.' She pointed again to her bandaged neck. 'Left a wound like a mad dog, the doctor said. Then this *woman* turned up and ran off with you. Not a word. Not a phone call. Your mum's sick to death with worry.'

He sat down on the arm of nearby chair, his face in his hands. Kala stood behind him, at the corner of his vision, embracing herself as though the room had turned very, very cold. Her scent folded around him like a cloak.

Tears glistened in Meg's eyes. She walked over to him, her gaze holding his. She stood in front of him, her hands cupping his face.

'I love you, Kevin Matheson. I love you and I'm telling you now that there's nothing we can't work out. You say it's complicated, so let's go down to the cop shop and sort it out. Right now. Turn yourself in. Get it cleaned up. Because I know you, and I know if you've done things, bad things, wrong things, that you've done them for a bloody good reason. That you had no choice. All we have to do is tell Smithy and he can clear it all up. How about it, Kev?'

The tears came in a gush and his jaw quivered so much he

couldn't speak. He held her hand, tried to keep his gaze from the bandage. 'Meg, I–'

She pulled her hand from his and wiped his cheek and held the fingers up in the light. 'Oh my God, Kevin, what's happened to you? You're bleeding.'

He wiped his cheeks and saw the smear of crimson on his fingers. 'Like I said, Meg. It's complicated.'

She poked a finger at Kala. 'What has this bitch done to you?'

'It's not her fault.'

'We really should go,' Kala said. 'We've been here too long as it is.'

'Are you going to go, Kevin? Just run away again?'

He stood, pushing Meg back with gentle pressure on her arms. 'I do have to go. I have to. To keep you safe.'

'I'm sorry – but can you please explain how running around the countryside with this black slut is keeping me safe?'

'Don't call her that.'

'So you're defending her now? You're pathetic. Both of you.' She snatched up the bag. 'I'm getting your mother her clothes. Unless you want to take them to her and explain yourself? How would you like that?'

'Jesus, Meg.' Kevin jumped to his feet and grabbed her by the wrists. 'Promise you won't go out there. You have to stay away from Whitby Downs, do you hear me?'

'Why?'

'They're bad people, Meg. Really bad.'

'They're looking after your mother.'

'She's a prisoner, a hostage.'

'Let go of me!'

He released her, stepped back while she massaged her forearms, one at a time.

'Are you hearing yourself? I can't stand any more of this. Not tonight. I'll come back for the clothes once you two have finished – whatever it is you're doing.'

They moved quickly once Meg had driven off. Kevin packed while Kala washed off two days' worth of road dirt and blood. He sifted the kitchen for food, then scoured the other rooms for a few possessions he might need. Clothes, his mobile phone, wallet, his father's .243 and a box of ammo from the gun safe. Almost felt himself again, no longer a man without cash and licence. But the rifle, well, that was the sinister element, the fact of his new reality. It wasn't kangaroo and wild pig he'd be hunting. He left his house keys.

Kala dressed in a combination of his mother's and his clothes. A marked improvement over the tracksuit Mira had turfed her out of Rockhampton with.

'I still need the camping gear,' he told her as she went over his inventory.

'Want me to bring the ute around while you finish up?'

'Nah, we're taking the Commodore.'

'You don't think it's too hot?'

'The ute can barely hit 100 going downhill.'

'Fair call,' she conceded.

'Besides, we'll have tunes.' He held up his mp3 player. 'You like Acca Dacca, don'tcha?'

'Oh dear.'

He winked, but he was painfully aware that the odds were against him, that they might never even get to use half the stuff he'd just collected. Not if he failed to save his mother. He couldn't wait to get behind the wheel of the Commodore and crank the stereo to high heaven. He had a desperate craving to hear *Highway to Hell*.

FORTY-TWO

Jasmine Turner had kept her last name. Not many did. It usually was the first thing to be shed, a farewell to the past and a hello to the new, incomprehensible future. Most would give up their mortal names – their mortal lives – entirely as they reinvented themselves; some would do it over and over again. Ziggy Stardust had nothing on them. But not Turner and not Maximilian von Schiller, who used the past as an anchor, grasping its stability but sacrificing flexibility and, with it, the capacity for forgiveness. Old vampires bore old grudges and, standing again in the living room of Whitby Downs, Reece found himself eager to get the hell out of there before a whole flock of pigeons came home to roost. Despite Mira's assurances that Turner would not dare upset Maximilian's apple cart, he just couldn't bring himself to trust the old bitch.

She sat facing him, holding court from a high-backed chair near the empty fireplace. The heat of the day lingered in the room, though it had been cooling off outside when Reece had ducked out for his sundowner cigarette. Through the window behind Turner's shoulder, out past the machinery shed and the chopper pad and the boundary fence, the paddocks were fading into the darkness. He didn't like that hill out there. It provided too much cover for someone approaching the house. Not that anyone had yet. No, since they'd arrived two nights ago, there had been a whole lotta nothing out there, and the tension was starting to tell.

'How much longer are you people going to be here?' Turner asked as Nigel, looking sour in his black trousers and white shirt, did a circuit with a tray of drinks. Reece and Felicity, nominally guarding the door, waved him away. Heather, Turner's piece of crumpet, sat at the piano looking demure, also not drinking.

'You mean you don't like the guests I brought you?' Mira asked, taking a glass. She occupied an armchair as far from the windows, and Turner, as she could.

'That *veggo* was of no use to me.'

'Oh, Jasmine, I thought you two would've had notes on farming, and things, to compare. I do hope his offsiders are more to your taste.'

Turner wasn't a bloodhag but she was wily. It had taken a full night of sampling Bhagwan's red-eyes to decide Mira hadn't planted them to spy on her; Reece was surprised either had enough blood left to donate to this soiree. Turner had had no such qualms about the widow Matheson, the poor woman, and had been spending most of her spare time with her.

'We're trying to run a business here,' Turner said. 'Hard enough to do in an inbred town like this without your goon squad scaring the cattle and displacing my musterers.'

Reece could understand where she was coming from. The place was definitely overcrowded. An extra squad of Gespenstenstaffel and two of mundane VS Security goons had arrived by road from Brisbane, forcing Turner to send most of her workers away until the situation was resolved. The tower must've been feeling pretty empty; no wonder Maximilian was pushing Mira to wrap this up quickly.

'I would be only too happy to leave you to get back to

farming cow juice and peddling stolen lifestreams, if only you could've divined the location of the Night Riders' hidey hole from Bhagwan or his red-eyes.' Mira raised her glass. 'Tasty, by the way.'

'And now you have yet another body on her way here. Yet another one to account for when this *situation* has been *resolved*.'

'But I thought you and the widow were getting along well, Jasmine. A nice long lifestream for your customers – the whole outback experience for them to sink their fangs into. I'm sure young Meg will also have a certain flavour. She did say she was coming, didn't she, Felicity?'

'Tonight, after work, once she's collected the widow's gear. Which would be any time now, I guess.'

'It doesn't matter how many you bring out here,' Turner said, making her point by getting to her feet. She stood behind Heather, her hands on the pianist's shoulders as though drawing self-control from her too-tense body. 'The mother, the girlfriend, the pet dog – it doesn't matter. The fact is, the boy isn't coming. Face it. Either your mole didn't deliver, or the boy was too smart to fall for such an obvious trap. He and his black tramp are long gone.'

'Oh, Kala delivered it, all right. I felt the connection last night. Faint, but I did feel it. The grease monkey still has two days' play remaining until I "call stumps". I don't mind sharing quarters with my Hunter, here, and I take it you don't mind having your *offsider* in the coffin with you? It's only for a couple of nights more, I assure you.'

'It's unseemly,' Turner said. 'An abuse of my arrangement with your *master*. I am a locutor, not some bailiwick for his lordship's empire.'

'If you'd delivered the biker on ice instead of insisting my men drive all the way out here, none of this would've happened.'

'If you'd been more efficient at setting me up as your honey trap, this wouldn't be happening,' Turner snapped.

Mira's mouth opened to retort, but she froze, distracted as though by something no one else could hear. A bee or a fly, maybe; there was no shortage of flies, though they usually buggered off after sundown.

Mira sprang to her feet. 'Felicity, Reece – let's take a reconnaissance flight, shall we? Give *Locutor* Turner her house back for a spell. She has so many guests to entertain, we shouldn't take up all her attention.'

'You and that infernal machine,' Turner said. 'Spooking the stock, making tongues wag in the town.'

Mira put her almost empty glass back on Nigel's tray. 'Get the pilot, Reece; I'll join you out there. This red-eye piss goes right through me.'

FORTY-THREE

Kevin drove south, AC/DC blaring fit to shake the car's doors. The repetitive beat pounded like a wrecking ball at the hard concrete of his fear. He sang along to *Jailbreak* and hoped he had better luck than the hapless escapee in that song. Tried to gee himself up with *Hell's Bells*, but stumbled over the line about dying young.

He was trying to convince himself that he was indeed *TNT* when he had to brake hard to avoid overshooting the turnoff to Whitby Downs. Penny; poor Penny. Would he avenge her, or join her?

Kala turned the music down. 'You okay there, Angus?'

He overlooked the fact that Angus didn't sing – maybe that was her point. 'More of a Bon man, myself.'

'Then don't drink too much.'

He huffed, wondering if there was a more serious message to her gag, and turned into the property.

Iron letters spelt out the station's name, dangling on chains from a new-looking plain grey-steel mailbox. Farther back from the road, insubstantial in the headlights, loomed a weather-worn timber arch with the almost illegible property name carved into it. A shiver passed through him as he recalled Mira's blood message.

'No guards,' Kevin said.

'Not out here.'

Kevin eyed the box. 'Maybe I could sneak in with whoever collects the mail.'

'Only if they wait till night time. C'mon, let's take a squiz. There's a good spot, a windmill–'

'How do you know that?'

'I've been here before, remember.'

'Of course you have. I never even thought of that until now. All of you – you came here to rescue Taipan, and then you shot the shit out of the servo. You killed my dad. You killed me. Jesus Christ, Kala, you lot even killed the dogs!' He turned off the engine and twisted in his seat to face her front-on. 'Which one were you, out there on the bikes while we were lying dead on the floor?'

'I was there. I did my share; I admit it. But we weren't after you and we weren't after your dad.'

'You threw fire bombs.'

'We have to cover our tracks; you know that.'

'You burnt the servo to the ground. With us in it.'

'We didn't know! The Hunters had Tai, and then Tai got away, so we gave them jackals something to worry about so they couldn't chase us. Honestly, if I could take it back, I would.'

He sat, staring, trying to reposition yet again his understanding of how his new world worked. For all he knew, Kala could've shot his father. She could've shot him.

'Bite me if it helps,' she said, offering her arm. 'Take a walk in my lifestream. See if the answer comes to you. See if we can still be friends.'

He'd seen it before, he realised, in her blood. Bits of it. Guns. Bikes. The Monaro parked way back, ready to swoop down with its boot open. The Sandman, peppered with bullets, already limping back to the Crawfords' place with a cargo of vampires forced from the hunt by the sun. Red-eyes versus red-eyes, and the Night Riders caught out in the open not knowing if Jasmine was sending help, if VS had their eye in the sky.

He'd tasted her doubt, the relief of having Taipan in the car, quickly replaced by the fear of pursuit jostling with the glee at having won. The Molotovs – she'd been driving, not shooting, not lighting the petrol-soaked fuses – had been thrown as much in elation and panic as in anger.

He knew all this and had been afraid to look any further, to risk losing the one person he felt he could – needed – to trust.

The bullet that had hit him had come through the wall or the window; it might have been aimed, more likely it was a random burst and he'd copped it unlucky.

As for his dad, well, someone's finger had been on the trigger – Taipan's or Hunter's. He was starting to wonder if it mattered which. It hadn't been Taipan's decision to go there, it hadn't been Hunter's to be sent to collect Taipan. The blame trail went back decades, at the very least, if anyone cared to pick at it, and Kevin didn't. It was too vast, too irrelevant. That massive depth of history, that cycle of wrongs and revenges that had somehow caught him up in its undertow – it was unfathomable. What mattered, what was keeping him afloat, was the simple fact that someone was threatening to hurt his family to force him to do something. His choice was simple: stop them.

'Kevin, are you going to ride my lifestream or not? Are we friends?'

'Friends. Definitely. I don't need a bloody tour to see that.'

'Good. I'm glad.'

Her hand came out of her jacket, and she gripped his in both of hers. Only now did he see the bulky outline in her pocket.

'Were you going to shoot me?'

'Only if I had to.'

'I'm glad we're friends, then.'

'Believe me, Kevvie. I'm on your side.'

She kissed him, and didn't stop till he kissed her back; he

clung to her with all the desperation of a drowning man grasping a life ring.

'Show you the windmill?' she asked.

He started the car. 'If you're my Girl Guide, shouldn't I get a cookie?'

'You've had your cookies for tonight, mister.'

Kevin nosed the Commodore through the gateway, taking it slow as they wobbled across a grid. He kept his headlights off, relying on moonlight to illuminate the dirt track winding across the paddock. The nervous silence was broken by the rumble of the motor, the crunch of pebbles under the tyres, the occasional ding of a stone against the chassis or the guard. He waited for the trap to spring, for the spotlights to come on and the soldiers to jump out. He remembered all too well the troops attacking the Crawfords' farmhouse, the pain of his bullet wound, the men on both sides who fell and didn't rise.

They crept along, and finally Kala gestured to a less-worn track branching off to one side. It wound around tree stumps and ant mounds onto a creek flat and finally reached a windmill, the daisy of its vanes unmoving in the still night air. A concrete water tank and trough sat at its base, the area churned bare by hoofs.

Turning off the engine, getting out of the car – his back itched, waiting for the nasty surprise. There was a rise on the other side of the gully in front of them with a light source glowing below the crest. He could imagine all too easily a line of soldiers up there taking aim. Could imagine a squad hunkered down behind the lip of the gully, like Anzacs in a trench waiting for the whistle to blow. They walked, and his senses roamed with the keenness of a blade, but all he smelled was earth and mud and wattle; all he heard was plover and curlew.

'I can't see the homestead,' he said to Kala, his voice sounding unnaturally loud.

'We have to go up,' she said, reaching for the frame of the windmill.

He climbed after her. The touch of the steel triggered a swarm of memories; he clung like a beetle, trying to maintain not just his grip on the tower but on reality.

Taipan had come this way, coasting his bike to a stop here before walking it out of sight into the gully and approaching the homestead on foot.

Kala had followed his trail, and perched up high, right there, watching the Hunters leave and signalling to her fellow Night Riders, vampires braving the encroaching dawn, red-eyes fearful of having to finish the job without them, of having to protect the night crawlers and themselves as well.

There had been only the one vehicle, the unsuspecting Hunters driving into the ambush, but their four-wheel-drive had proven tough and the men tougher, and they'd pushed through, had reached the highway, but the Night Riders had had it blocked and the Hunters had pulled a hard U-turn and ended up at the roadhouse, leaking water and blood and running out of time. This was where the events that had killed Kevin's father and changed Kevin's life – his very being – had begun. Now here he was, reliving those moments, the anxiety and the fear and the desire, the present and two versions of the past overlying uncomfortably through all his senses. He clutched the steel, fighting to focus his mind as Danica had taught him, to push through to the present.

Kala waited patiently like a kid hanging on a fence, arms and legs pushed through the structure right near the top where the faded Southern Cross wind vane stuck out from the centre of the iron flower.

'Slow poke,' she chided as he finally clambered to her side.

'Just checking out your arse.'

'Lucky I'm not wearing a skirt then, eh?'

From their perch, they could see over the gully and the intervening hill to Jasmine's base. Kevin felt, again, that strange overlap of Taipan's and Kala's experiences, the strangeness magnified by the sight of a commonplace farm given a deadly, uncommon air.

The single-storey timber house looked unremarkable with its tin roof and wrap-around verandah. It faced them from the northern side of the compound, surrounded by haphazard outbuildings. A split-rail fence divided the house from the various sheds and stockyards. The lawn was a drab dark olive; outside, the paddock was dirt and stubble.

A high fence, similar to the emu fence at Danica's nest, surrounded all the buildings. Spotlights made pools of light around each post – at least they weren't animal skulls. A long, tall machinery shed filled the south-west corner of the compound, big enough to hold the largest of farm tractors, but its doors faced the house across the wide expanse of yard and Kevin could see only the back wall from his vantage point. There was only one gate, a double panel of mesh in the southeast section of fence. Two men with guns slung over their shoulders guarded it, standing close together as though chatting.

'I'm open to suggestions,' Kevin said. 'Those stockyards give a little cover.' He thought that was where Taipan had gone across, but the fence hadn't been lit that night. They'd ramped up their security since that incursion. Then came the chilling thought: they'd turned the lights on for him.

'Maybe there's a better angle on the other side. Somewhere dark we can cut through the fence.'

– Wish I could get my hands on that chopper –

Four lights illuminated the corners of a concrete square he assumed was the landing pad for Jasmine's fly in-fly out celebrity operation, about midway between the machinery shed and the house.

'Fly by night,' he mumbled.

'Say what?'

'Takes on a whole new meaning, doesn't it? I wonder where that chopper is.'

FORTY-FOUR

Reece and Felicity waited by the door of the helicopter as the pilot went through his flight check.

'So how are you getting on out here in the sticks?' he asked her. They'd been working opposite shifts, she travelling between the homestead and Barlow's Siding to handle the public relations, him acting as punching bag for Mira night and day.

She shrugged.

'Bloody hot, isn't it? A real dry heat.'

'Let's get one thing straight, Hunter Reece.' She leaned toward him, looking up with mock coyness. 'Just because you've seen me naked, doesn't make us mates.'

'You're not my first *ménage a blood*, you know, sweetheart.'

She moved away, looking toward the homestead.

Reece lit a cigarette and was rewarded with a nose wrinkle, a shuffle. 'Just out of curiosity, how old are you?'

'What's it to you? Want to brag to your mates in the locker room?'

'I just like to know whose blood I've been sharing. Professional interest.'

'Six on twenty,' she said with a smirk.

He motioned toward the rank pin on her collar, the blade

centred through the stylised GS logo. He wore his, too, to help avoid accidents with all the bored, gun-toting grunts hanging around. 'And you've made Dagger already. Impressive.'

'I'm a quick study. You?'

'Plus four,' he said.

'Specifically?'

'Forty on thirty-six.'

'Getting past your prime, old man. She offered you the bite?'

'Age and experience,' he said with a shake of his head. 'I got a few miles left in me yet.'

Mira appeared on the veranda.

'How old's the boss do you reckon?' Felicity asked.

'Twenty, twenty-two, going on about 600.'

'About what I figured.' There was a touch of awe in her voice; awe and desire.

He made a point of checking her throat, the same place where his own bore the four dots arranged in a square showing he was claimed by a single vampire. Her skin was unmarked; not even a mild case of wolfbite. 'So you've got your dagger after only six years, but you haven't got your shield?'

'Not yet,' she said with a sly smile.

Mira arrived. 'No smoking near the bird, you know that, Reece.' She stepped up into the chopper and took one of the front seats.

Reece toed out the cigarette.

'She wasn't talking about the chopper,' Felicity jibed as she scrambled after Mira and took the seat next to her.

Bitch, he thought. *Just when we were getting on so good.*

The rotor started to turn and Reece slammed the door after him, prepared for an uneventful twenty minutes of flying and Felicity's latest no-news. Turner had refused to allow Felicity to stay at the homestead while Mira had been at the coast, and the girl had turned it to her advantage, forging a "close working relationship" with the copper, Smith, who Reece couldn't help but feel a little sorry for. The poor kid had no idea what he was letting himself in for; if he was lucky, only his heart would get broken.

Reece ached for another smoke. He hoped young Matheson wouldn't show his face. That he had the good sense to just run; to cut his losses and run. They'd taken out at least seven Night Riders in the Rockhampton raid, including two fangers; he doubted what was left of the gang would achieve much against three squads of VS muscle, a handful of narky vampires just itching to blow off some steam and – last, but not least – this very fine gunship.

Mira ignored the lack of news, her attention focused out the window, though her eyes were shut as much as they were open, as though fending off a migraine. The purple glimmer that indicated she was tapping the power of her blood showed through her lashes.

Felicity gave up in the face of Mira's silence, eventually whispering to Reece, 'Is something up?'

Reece shrugged.

'Too loud.' Mira shook her head, as though to dislodge a buzzing insect in her ear. 'But she's close, I think; awake, guarded, but the fear, the fear – blood calls to blood. Reece, we need to be on our guard. I think this could be it.'

'Another circuit?' he asked, heart rate rising.

Felicity turned to the window, scanning the murky landscape below.

'Home,' Mira said, rubbing her blood bracelets. 'I need peace and quiet to try to connect to Matheson's squeeze. Hard, when she's awake and guarded, but the fear – I'd recognise that anywhere. She can't hide it from me.'

They were on their return approach, coming in from the south, when the pilot asked, 'You got someone out by the windmill?'

'Have we?' Mira asked. 'A little night maintenance? They'd better not scare off the grease monkey. Unless–'

Felicity's hand went to her pistol. 'Nothing I know about.'

Reece said the same. He abandoned all thoughts of snatching a smoke when they landed. Damn it, why hadn't the kid run?

'I definitely saw a vehicle there,' the pilot said. 'You want me to come around for another look?'

'No.' Mira grabbed Felicity's wrist so tightly the girl gave a little cry. 'It's them. I can feel it. I can feel *her*. Get us down – now! Then hang back till I send the word to close in. No shooting. I need them alive and in one piece.' She turned to Reece. 'I want you, with me, in full kit, as soon as you can. Felicity, you rouse the troops, but quietly, and stay by the radio. Hunter Reece and I are going on a little foray.'

'Are you sure you should go, Strigoi? Just the two of you? It could be another ambush.'

'Which is why I want this bird in the air with its talons out, and you on the ground with every gun ready. But yes, I'm going. We've set them up, now it's time to knock them down.'

FORTY-FIVE

The hum of a distant vehicle teased at the edge of Kevin's hearing. Meg, following him, delivering his mother's clothes despite his warning? The idea made his pulse quicken. He glanced at Kala, but she was staring at the compound; she didn't seem to have heard the engine.

'Any idea on how to get in – without wings?' Kala asked.

'Taipan jumped the fence.'

'Yeah, well, we saw how well that worked for him, didn't we?'

'And he did something – sank into the ground, to avoid getting caught.'

'Another of his tricks.'

'I think I can do that one. In the servo, when it was on fire. I think I remember being down there.'

The earth is your friend

'I don't spose it's like swimming? You could kind of burrow under the wire.'

'I don't think it works like that. More like an elevator,' he said, moving his hand up and down.

'Ground floor or basement, huh? Pity.' Kala's head whipped around, peering skyward. 'Chopper's coming.'

The undulating beat got louder as the machine flew closer, coming in low. He felt horribly exposed clinging to the windmill; below, the Commodore seemed to glow like a neon sign. Why hadn't he bought a black car? The helicopter slowed as it approached the homestead, the sound beating at Kevin as the machine flew almost directly overhead, then wheeled a tight arc and landed on the pad. He tensed as the door opened. The rotor blades kept turning, slow and mesmerising, kicking up a border of dust around the pad. Hunter got out, followed by a young woman dressed like an accountant or something. Then Mira in her bitch suit. They ran for the house. The chopper lifted off again, heading away from them, to the north, toward Barlow's Siding.

'Where do you think that bird's going?' Kala said.

'Blow the shit out of some poor fool, maybe. Didn't see any guns on it, though.'

'I'm sure it's the same one. I guess they all look the same.'

'Who was that girl with them?'

'No idea. She wasn't at Rocky.'

'They looked like they were in a hurry, didn't they?'

'Maybe they just flew in from the coast. Prob'ly no loo on that machine.' She laughed.

'I don't like it. I think we should go and maybe have a look from the other side.'

They began to climb down, but Kevin stopped when he heard a car rev to life: a Jaguar driving out of the garage next to the homestead.

'The lady of the house is leaving,' he said.

'Could be our chance?'

'I dunno. Can you grab the rifle off the back seat?'

'What are you going to do?'

'I just want the scope.'

By the time she returned with the gun, handed it up to him and he'd climbed high enough to see the homestead again, the Jag was driving out the perimeter gate.

'What's Turner up to, I wonder.' He sighted on the car, the windshield dark, the lights of the homestead's fence casting a silhouette of two people in the front. 'If she's leaving, this could be our shot.'

'Is that the chopper I can hear?' Kala asked from the base of the windmill. 'Or is there another car coming?'

Not Meg, he pleaded silently. *Please, not Meg.*

'I think it's the chopper,' Kala said, answering her own question.

And finally the light hit the car so he could see clearly. It was Hunter driving. And in the passenger seat, looking right at him: Mira!

'It's a trick – Mira knows we're here!' Kevin dropped the rifle to Kala and scrambled, virtually fell, to the ground, and ran after her to the car.

He didn't worry about showing his lights as he pointed the Commodore toward the highway. The moon, fat and bright, was adequate, but he needed everything he could get, at least till he reached the highway.

'Oh shit, oh shit,' Kala said.

Kevin concentrated on driving. Lights flashed in his mirrors, spurring him to push the car as fast as he dared. Slightly faster. The arse swung in the gravel corners. The chassis crunched as they hit dips.

They reached the bitumen and he fishtailed, rubber screeching, as he steered for Barlow's Siding. He was already thinking of the road ahead, of where they might find shelter. An old garage at the back of the abandoned butcher shop, the bush fire brigade's shed on the other side of town; anywhere with a roof and walls to shield them from both the air and the road. But he couldn't think of anywhere on this side of town.

He coaxed more speed from the Commodore and trusted his knowledge of the road to help him make it.

A bridge came up, the dip and rise of Three Mile Creek. Not far now. Could they make the silo? Would VS expect him to head for home where he could hide the car under the house? Was that the first place or the last place that they'd look? Shit, he didn't even have his house keys.

They crossed the bridge and climbed out of the gully.

And drove into the sun, or so it felt.

The light blasted him, blinding all the way to the back of his head. Kala squealed, threw up her arm to shield her eyes. They skidded onto the verge, gravel clattering against the car's underside, steering wheel jerking spasmodically in Kevin's hands as he fought for control. They passed under the blazing light, the helicopter's thumping beat reverberating in the cabin as the downdraft shook them like dice in a cup. They pulled up in a choking drift of smoking brakes and dust.

'They're right on top of us,' Kala shouted.

'Get out,' Kevin told her. 'Run back to the creek. Hide!'

'I can't leave you.'

'I'll draw them away. Catch up at the silo, eh?'

'Damn it, Kev, this isn't the time for heroics.'

'So get out!'

She leaned across and kissed him, then bailed. She pulled her pistol and emptied the clip, two-handed, at the hovering machine. It wheeled away, chased by one, two, three sparks on its underbelly.

The darkness returned, leaving Kevin's vision splotched with bright splashes.

Kala slammed the door. The helicopter turned back toward him, but higher, he thought. Headlights appeared in the rear windshield.

Kala was away, lost in the dark. Now it was his turn.

He hit the pedal, spat gravel, rocketed back onto the bitumen.

The chopper pulled away, the spotlight lancing down behind him, off to the side of the road, scouring the area near the bridge.

The headlights grew large and bright in his rear window. A horn blasted. The vehicle was on his tail. He wished he could flip the side mirrors to get some of that glare out of his eyes, but he wasn't game to take his hands off the wheel. Not on this road with its uneven surface and rough-as-guts drop-offs.

The lights blazed on his right hand side as the car caught up to him. The bonnet inched forward, the silver Jaguar figure like an arrowhead, pulling level and then past until the two vehicles were neck and neck.

Kevin glanced sideways, aware of a corner looming ahead. The Jag's tinted window lowered. Dread gripped him in its freezing hand – a rifle? A grenade?

Mira!

Laughing.

She leaned out of the window, as though to kiss him.

Kevin swerved away, the tyres thudding into gravel. He lurched back at the Jaguar. It didn't give ground, but kept its place beside him.

They took the corner and Kevin, on the inside, managed to gain half a car length.

Ahead, Two Mile Creek loomed. The bridge – it wasn't wide enough for both cars. He had to get there first. Had to. That would make them fall back, maybe give him time to reach the Siding. That was all he needed. If only he could grab the rifle on the rear seat. If only he could use it and drive at the same time. No time for if onlys.

A yellow warning sign: Narrow bridge. No overtaking.

No overtaking.

He willed the Commodore to go faster. Its roaring engine and vibrating frame told him it had nothing left.

Almost there. The bridge; his chance. The rev counter clocked his panic as it speared as far into the red as the dial could go.

Rat-a-tat-tat on his window. Mira, her nails, bright, glistening, rapping on his window. Crazy fucking bitch!

The window bulged with a crack of glass. A second punch

penetrated the tint. Slivers stung his face. Her razor nails slashed at him like shears.

Kevin jerked the wheel. The Commodore shuddered as it slipped off the bitumen. Kevin stomped on the brake. The car slewed out of control. It ploughed across the drain, through a barbed wire fence, then careened into a barren paddock.

Dust boiled over the car as it slid to a halt, side-on to the creek, facing the road. Kevin sat, hands clenched on the wheel, foot jamming the brake pedal to the floor.

Silence. Then the hot-metal clicking of the bonnet. The Jag had pulled up on the bridge, brake lights glowing through a drifting cloud of blue smoke.

Fuck, he'd almost gone into the gully.

A shape appeared in the dusky illumination of the Commodore's single remaining headlight. Mira, cape billowing around her ankles. Grinning.

'Christ,' Kevin whispered.

She stopped in front of the bonnet, her eyes reflecting green. *Get out*, Kevin told himself, but his muscles refused to work. *Get the rifle! Do something!*

Mira stalked closer. Cracks in the windshield made her appear disjointed. The sound of scraping metal penetrated Kevin's daze as she ran a key, a rock – something – up the side of the car. She waggled her nails as she peered through the window at him. 'Hello, Grease Monkey. Miss me?'

Kevin made his hands leave the wheel, unclip the belt. He scrambled for the passenger side, desperate to get away.

'Allow me,' she said. There was a deafening tearing of metal, the car rocking, and the door was gone. She yanked him out, hurled him tumbling on the ground. Air rushed from his lungs.

Mira leaned back against the shattered side of the Commodore as though waiting for a lift. Her face was reduced to skull-like shadows by the harsh side light from the Jag, parked on the road to illuminate the Commodore. There was something feline about the way she moved, inspecting her nails as though the only damage she'd taken from smashing his car was chipped enamel.

A black cat suit sheathed her from ankle to wrist. Over it, she wore a sculpted Kevlar corset covering her chest, stomach and back; two ridged neck guards projected from the collar like the stubs of wings. A loose skirt almost covered her thick-soled knee-high boots. She'd accessorised with leather armbands covering her forearms and a wide, studded collar. A silver cross swung from her left ear. Two belts crossed her hips, holding sword, dagger and pistol. The Driza-Bone swept about her. She wasn't taking any chances, dressed to stay out all night and half the morning; clearly, she'd over-estimated. But he'd try to make her earn it.

Kevin staggered to his feet, clutching his stomach as pain sharpened across his chest, the side of his head, his shoulder. Air found his lungs and he gasped for it. He glanced at the road. A figure picked its way through the loose strands of wire fence.

Bright light blasted down on them, dust flying as the chopper hovered overhead. Mira shielded her eyes.

The man approached, his hand up to his forehead, the other clutching a walkie-talkie. Hunter, in his long coat and rough suit, tie hanging loose, handgun and a silver truncheon dangling from his belt. His clothes looked slept in. Kevin couldn't remember his real name. There'd been too much time gone by, too much blood under that particular bridge.

'No sign,' he shouted over the din.

Mira waved at the chopper, an angry cut of her hand. It seemed to nod, then arced away, spotlight doused, leaving Kevin dazed.

'So,' Mira said. 'Where's your little playmate gone? Not Taipan, I don't suppose.' She shook her head, considered her left wrist as though checking the time on a watch she didn't wear. 'The girl. I liked her. Tasted kind of earthy.'

Hunter stood to one side, looking tense as he pulled the truncheon from his belt.

Mira struck.

Kevin had time for one punch, a pointless air swing. Then the ground thumped Kevin on the back of the head, his shoulder blades. Pain speared through him. When the red flashes had cleared from his vision, he found Mira squatting on his chest, her legs on either side trapping his arms. He jerked his gaze to hers. Green eyes, scarlet lips, brilliant ivory teeth so sharp and white. Her nails dug into his temples, scratched down his cheeks so heavily he expected to see blood.

'Now this is familiar, isn't it?' she said.

Her tongue lapped at his jaw and cheek. Her breath gusted hot against his ear as she whispered, 'Where's my Taipan? Where's the one *he* calls Mother?' Kevin tried to reef his arms free; her knees ground the bones to the point of breaking. 'You like it rough, Grease Monkey? Is that it?'

She pushed his head back.

Her fangs tore into his neck.

All he could think was, *Not again.*

'No, no, no,' Mira muttered as she sat up. A thin trail of blood – his blood – trickled from her lip. Her tongue, bright pink, lapped it up like a lizard cleaning its chops. 'You're not telling me anything I don't already know. I'll have to go deeper if you're going to play hard to get. Tell me where Taipan is. Where *She* is.'

Kevin's mind screamed. He used the defence Danica had shown him, locking his mind up tight.

Mira spat blood, wiped her mouth. 'You can't hide in there forever, boy. We'll have to discuss this over a warm drink, what do you say? Reece, pass me that staker.'

A glint of silver, a tube as long as a ruler in her hand, raised up, a rocket against the sky, and then: re-entry. She punched the tube against his chest. There was a gush of air, a thump that left a sharp pain and a long, insistent ache. She stood, handed the baton back to Reece who twisted the handle, removed a capsule and pocketed it, then re-holstered the tube in his belt. Kevin couldn't move, pinned like a butterfly by that weight in his heart.

This was, he realised, another option for getting into the compound, but it certainly wasn't his first preference.

FORTY-SIX

The suit he'd seen with Hunter and Mira at the chopper – he felt sure that's who the young woman was – met them at the front door. From where Kevin slumped, drunk-limp between two SWAT gorillas in body armour and sub-machineguns strapped across their chests, he could make out a bullet-proof vest, hair pulled back in a ponytail, tight lips that'd probably make her look pretty if she smiled. Red eyes.

Mira, her back to Kevin, Hunter next to her, called the ponytail Felicity when she asked if there'd been any sight of the Night Riders, and Felicity said no, there hadn't, and the person who'd hared off from the Commodore remained on the run.

Go, Kala! If he could have flipped these bastards the bird, he would've, but he'd have to be content with the warm inner glow. It made a nice adjunct to the ripping pain in his chest that, instead of sending him into staked-out bliss, was keeping him infuriatingly awake.

Mira sounded a touch grumpy when she said, 'Get into town, find out if anyone's reported the noise, make sure the cop isn't concerned.'

'What will I tell him?'

'Tell him I lost an earring and everyone's been looking for it,' Mira snapped, and Kevin smiled on the inside.

'Pig shooting?' Hunter suggested.

'And get rid of the grease monkey's car.'

That dashed Kevin's amusement. The poor bloody Commodore. He'd done it up himself. Just a bit of body damage, he reckoned. Shocks, front axle maybe; she was far from written off.

The goons hefted him, changing their grip after the delay, and carted him inside as Mira led the way. He didn't see much more than the legs of the guys carrying him and the timber floor before he was dumped on something soft. A piano melody died away, and a woman said, 'take it out', and then Nigel was looking at him, blocking his view of the ceiling rose and the modest brass chandelier hanging from its centre. Good ol' Nigel, looking like a fish out of water in his understated penguin suit. He pulled on the stake in Kevin's chest with a set of pliers. Really tugged. Kevin lifted as the stake dragged him up, then finally came free. He gasped and fell back, swallowed the urge to vomit, then looked around at the place he'd seen only in his peripheral vision. He was on a sofa, one hand and foot dangling on the floor, almost touching a massive rug in nondescript emerald and cream. Boot prints – someone hadn't wiped their feet. He sat up and coughed, using the action to hide his search for a way out. Coffee table. Elegant chairs. A fireplace, photographs lining its mantel. A stake there, wooden and black-tipped.

Some places, only the natural stuff can go, eh

He grimaced in recognition – Taipan's stake. The one his sister had used to capture him, before the Hunters had arrived and replaced it with something more elegant.

The music resumed, something slow that made him think of mourners leaving a cemetery in the rain. The piano sat near a window draped in lace, with heavier drapes pulled back to reveal a verandah and the sterile glare of the lights lining the outer fence. Seated at the piano, fingers caressing the keys, was a teenage girl – Willa. Taipan's love flowed through him unbidden, so powerful it made him groan. Beside her stood a colonial matron in white – skirt to her ankles, long-sleeved blouse, hair in a bun. No makeup. Jasmine Turner, in the flesh.

Taipan's emotions and experiences rushed over him, tumbling him like a leaf in a river. Much of Taipan's life had faded from Kevin's veins, but the greatest love and the greatest hate remained. They sat, side by side, playing – Beethoven? *Someone* in Kevin's blood knew the music. Maybe it was even him.

'Welcome,' Jasmine said, her clipped English accent strangely familiar thanks to Taipan's lifestream – no doubt about the source of that information. 'Drink?'

He followed her gesture and saw for the first time Mira sitting on the other side of the room, holding a glass of red – blood, if his nose was telling him the truth – before her as though she was studying its contents against the light. Kevin turned to see who was behind him – Hunter, at the door, and Nigel, carrying a silver tray with the blood-smeared spike and a crystal carafe. Nigel filled a glass from the carafe and held it out to him.

'Before it's all gone,' Jasmine urged through a false smile as she wrenched her gaze from Mira back to him.

Kevin sat up, took the drink, sipped. A-grade cow. *Beggars can't be choosers*, he thought, and the throb in his chest agreed. Hunger scraped at his insides, teased saliva at the whiff of the drink.

'Where's my mother?' he asked.

'Where's my Taipan?' Mira answered without looking at him. She really was beautiful, he thought, but like a car – no amount of trim could disguise the fact that it was still a machine, cold and hard and uncaring. The piano missed a note, almost stopped, but Jasmine motioned for the girl to continue, and she did, ever so softly.

'Taipan isn't coming,' Kevin told them.

'That wasn't our deal,' Mira said.

'I didn't agree to any deal.'

She looked at him, then. 'Foolish you.'

Hunter took the unfinished drink from his hand.

'I am sorry, young man,' Jasmine said. 'It's not personal, I assure you, but I really cannot tolerate another home invasion. Our Christopher is quite out of control and must be made to see reason, before he does someone an injury.' Jasmine's gaze darted to the ugly stake on the mantel, then back to him. 'I had hoped you might be more forthcoming about his location.'

He stayed silent.

'I was going to talk with you further about the matter, but the lush is most insistent she gets first bite of this particular cherry. Perhaps we will get to have a chat before you go.' She patted Willa's shoulders, an action both affectionate and possessive. Willa looked at Kevin with something like an apology.

Mira sneered and put her glass down.

Hunter motioned Kevin to stand. 'You gonna behave or do I have to ice you?'

Kevin held out his hands. He was totally outgunned. The best he could do was wait and hope. Find out where his mother was being kept and then...

Hunter grabbed one arm, Nigel the other, and they walked him from the room.

'Introductions are over,' Hunter said. 'Now it's down to business, I'm afraid.'

Behind them, the music wound down to end on two singular notes, like the sound of a church bell ringing. He'd got it wrong, Kevin realised – the mourners hadn't been leaving the funeral, but arriving.

They took him through the house to the rear verandah and outside, and for a moment he thought about breaking loose, running, but that wasn't an option. Even if he could take the two *myxos*, he still had to free his mother and get out of the compound. No, they wouldn't have allowed him out here if they thought he could get away.

They walked across the patchy lawn. They were on the eastern side of the house. To the south was the machinery shed he'd seen from the windmill, but now he could see inside – Nigel's panel van, Kala's Monaro, a farm four-wheel-drive, a tractor. The chopper sat on its landing pad between the house and the shed.

They stopped at a square building, some kind of tool shed or storage room made from thick wooden planks. Iron bars covered the window facing them; the door was of solid timber bound in rusted iron.

'Here you go – the guest quarters.' Hunter opened the door. 'Bed's been made.'

An earth floor gave Kevin some hope for a disappearing act, if he could only follow Taipan's mystical lead, but regardless of whether he was locked in or locked under, the fact was he'd still be locked. Still, it was something, and he'd grasp at whatever straws he could. He squinted as his eyes adjusted. Moonlight slanted in through a barred window, striping the room with parallel shadows. A sturdy single bed with bare mattress, a wooden chair, and a tall table the kind you might put a telephone on.

'Strip, then lie down,' Hunter ordered, and now Kevin saw the manacles hanging at each leg of the bed.

'I'd rather stand.'

'Take off your clothes, or I'll cut them off.'

Kevin stripped, keeping his back to the men.

'Throw these rags outside,' Hunter told Nigel, then pointed Kevin at the bed. 'Make yourself comfortable.'

Kevin laid down, biting back bitter tears as Hunter locked the cold metal around his wrists and ankles.

'Could use some curtains,' Kevin said. 'Some pictures, maybe.'

Hunter, at the door, shook his head, then gestured to one window. 'Plenty of natural light, saves on electricity. Sun comes up through that one.' He checked his watch. 'About nine hours from now, give or take.' And then, softer, almost gentle, 'You might want to consider telling Mira what she wants to know before then.'

'One thing before you get your barbecue fork,' Kevin said.

'What's that?'

'At the servo, with my old man. What happened?'

'Huh?'

'Did you kill him?'

'Well, I can't really answer that, sport. I came in and your old man was helping Taipan to do a runner. There was a scuffle, the gun went off. Your old man went down and Taipan clobbered me a beauty and bolted. Then the fire came and I had to make a choice – you, him or Dave. I chose Dave.'

'I haven't seen him here.'

'He didn't make it.'

Kevin nodded. He was, perversely, almost sorry for Hunter. All that effort and his mate had died anyway. Another run on the losers' scoreboard.

Hunter paused at the door, waiting for Nigel. 'You coming?'

'I'll keep an eye on him till the main event.'

'Suit yourself.' He handed the surfie the keys and went out. 'I'm going for a smoke.'

Nigel stood close enough for Kevin to see him without lifting his head.

'So what happens now?' Kevin asked.

'One of three things, I'd think. One, they'll torture your mum. Second, they'll torture you. Or third, they'll do both.'

'How about four: you let me go? I take my mum and we never see each other again.'

Nigel dangled the keys. 'There's a fifth option, but.'

'I'm listening.'

'You tell me where the Night Riders are, them and their boss lady.'

'Why would I do that?'

'Because protecting them is a waste of time. Taipan is just using you, same as he used me. They'll just chew you up and spit you out. I saw it coming, I got out. You should do the same.'

'Join up with Mira's mob?'

'Could do a lot worse.'

'How do you figure that?'

'I'm going back to the coast. Gonna go surfing again. VS is letting me do that. One more good trip before I give up the sun for good.'

'Aren't you afraid of that wolfbite?' Kevin asked. 'Sounds pretty nasty.'

'So long as I can still hang five, it doesn't worry me.' He rubbed his face, as though feeling the pattern of redness there; Mira had been putting him to use outdoors, it seemed. 'A bit of ache and pain. It goes away soon enough, and it'll be worth it. Can't wait to hit the water.' He gave Kevin a wink. 'And the women. Can't wait to hit them, either. Nothing like a good fireside shag at the end of a day in the water. I love a woman in a bikini, don't you?'

Meg, white bikini against her brown skin, nipples pushing darkly through the saturated cloth, dew dotting her stomach, the shape of her through the knickers and his fierce, sudden erection. The taste of muddy water on her lips, the lumpy earth of the creek bank pushing through the towel, the sun blazing on his shoulder blades, then blinding him as they flip and she mounts him, the loose top flapping around her wobbling breasts as she rides him with her eyes shut and mouth open; and afterward, days after, over bacon and eggs in the café, she says with a cheeky smile, 'I had to throw those mud-stained togs out; I just couldn't get them back to white; never again, black from now on'.

I wonder what Di would've thought, seeing you here with her.

Nigel hadn't noticed his lapse, was still waxing lyrical. Some kind of confessional with the doomed man or something, just a chance to explain why he was a gutless cur, but that was really all the explanation Kevin needed.

'I was doing all right, getting up the ranks, my boss was a good sort, gave me plenty of time off to compete and I had time in the morning to catch some waves before clocking on. I was like you, a grease monkey, but it was all luxury stuff where we were, dude, the Surfers Paradise chardonnay set, you know what I mean? The "beautiful people", as Aussie Crawl would say. You probably never heard of them, eh? Old school, now. Doesn't even get played on the radio out here; it's all Slim Dusty and that boot-scootin' crap, right? I hate this backwater, man.'

Wanker, Kevin thought. Everyone knew Aussie Crawl, even if it was only *Reckless*; even if they couldn't understand the words. Why hadn't Hunter taken Nigel with him?

He was still talking. 'Up the coast, just chillin', this little beach where no-one goes, and there they are. You can't blame me, can you? I mean, that Penny's a right bitch but she's a hot little sort, and Kala, well, that half-caste skin…'

Kevin runs from the school bus into the garage because Dad's working on a vintage Chevy for the man up the road who has an old-time museum with a mail truck and a fire engine and a whole shop of bottles, all different shapes, white and green and even purple, but the Chevy, she's a real beaut, and he tells Dad as he's passing him

*ratchets about the new kid in class, from down south,
and how a kid said he was a half-caste, and his father
appears out of the Chevy's innards with a look that
freezes the smile on Kevin's face, and says, 'We don't use
that term, it's derogatory', and Kevin asks, 'What's
doggatory mean?', and his father says, 'It's what you
wish people wouldn't say to you if you was them', and
Kevin says, 'Well, what is he then?', and his father says,
'He's a young fella at a new school who'd probably like
a friend'*

'…a camper van, one of those old Vee Dubs that just never say die, and it's getting on to sundown and we're talking the talk and they're stoking the fire and I'm thinking I'm in backpacker heaven, and then, suddenly, Taipan's there. Got no idea where he came from – one minute I'm making pretty with the girls and the next there he is, shaking sand out of his hair and saying, what's this then, and Kala says, he's good with cars, and Taipan says to me, can you fix that heap of junk? Of course I can, right? I get the old clunker to the next town where they can trade up, so to speak, and the very next night the gang's all there and I'm in.

'They're on the road all the time, the Night Riders. They need a good mechanic, more than anything, and I was – am – a bloody good mechanic. But I never got Kala and I never got Penny, just cups of brew. For months. Years. Just brew.

'And then Taipan turned up at that farmhouse doing that shadow walk shit and said he'd got a new fang coming in, a mechanic – that'd be you, dude – and that's when I knew my time was up.

'I had to pick a side that'd pick me. So I made a call. You were the straw that broke this camel's back, man. I just wanted you to know that.'

Nigel leaned closer, a hint of desperation in his eyes.

'So how about it? Tell me where the Riders are and I'll put

in a good word with the boss. Because at the moment, you haven't got any friends at all; you're just bait.'

'If you think they're coming for me, you're wrong. I left 'em. I came here for my mum and none of them would help me. So it's all been for nothing. But thanks for the story, Nige.'

'I heard you had Kala with you. They're out there now, hunting for her.'

'They've already had their shot at her and it got them nothing. She's got no more idea where Taipan or Danica is than I do.'

'That's too bad.' He poked Kevin's chest, making the freshly puckered scar of the stake wound pain. 'The Strigoi sure put a hole in you, didn't she? Taking its sweet time healing, too. You must be one hungry dude right about now.' He looked at the window. 'She'll probably put a few more holes in you before sunrise.'

Nigel slumped back into the chair.

'You ever wonder why Taipan didn't just shadow walk in there the first time? Maybe straight into his sister's brain, even? I'll tell you. Coz he wanted to get caught. He wanted an end to it. He's suicidal. Too much sun. That's why I reckon he's gonna come after you. Revenge is a great excuse for suicide. Noble sacrifice and all that.'

'I think you're giving him too much credit.'

Nigel snorted. 'Maybe.' He stroked his chin. 'So what's she like, that Kala? You must've bagged her if she came with you.'

Kevin turned away, not wanting to give the surfie the pleasure of seeing just how much he wanted to tear his heart out.

'Bet that pissed Taipan off, her running off with you. Got a real problem, hasn't he? First his sister, then his moll. Yeah, I bet he's real pissed. Maybe enough to do something stupid. Something heroic.'

'You'd better hope he isn't, because I figure the guy who sold him out will be right on top of his shit list.'

'Maybe. I wonder if that puts me before or after you?'

The surfer cackled and Kevin turned back to the wall, and after a bit, Nigel took an mp3 player from his pocket and plugged in.

'Just wiggle a toe if you change your mind about saving your hide,' he said before turning up the volume. Indecipherable warbling hissed from the headphones.

At least Kala had got away. Kevin prayed that Meg had listened to him and was already on the road to somewhere safe, too. He had to hand it to Taipan, though; he'd had his doubts about Nigel the whole time and turned him into a self-fulfilling prophecy. He'd needed a new mechanic and, even there in the servo, with a stake in his chest and Hunter holding a gun on him, he'd been planning ahead. Too bad it had all come to a dead end.

FORTY-SEVEN

The door opened. Mira. Now he was for it. She signalled with a toss of her head for Nigel to leave. The door slammed shut. The lock clunked home. Mira whisked her hooded 'Bone from her shoulders and folded it neatly on the chair. She'd exchanged her armour for a long skirt and singlet, too flat to need a bra but shapely just the same, and excited, too, if those headlights she was high-beaming were any gauge. Kala's earring dangled in her left lobe. She swaggered over and stroked his cheek with the back of her fingers. She smelled fresh, lush. He saw himself in her eyes – a corpse in a television cop show, waiting to be sliced open.

'Have a good chat with young Nigel there?'

Kevin kept his mouth shut.

'He didn't hurt you? I'd be upset if he had.' Her fingers trailed across his chest. 'You are way over-dressed, Grease Monkey.' She snapped the pendant from his chest. 'So out of date. Here, have you seen mine?' She reefed down one side of her singlet to reveal a five-pointed star inside a circle tattooed on her left breast. The tat had the same silvery-iron colour as those of Bhagwan's offsiders. The ink seemed to move, like coolant through a clear hose. 'Traditional pattern put to a new use.' She traced the shape with a fingernail.

Kevin looked her in the eyes. 'Your tits are quite small.'

'I don't think you're the man to be making size insults.' She smoothed her singlet to cover the ink and tucked his pendant into her slight cleavage, then leaned over him.

'Of course, it's not what you've got but how you use it.' She stroked the wound her stake had left in him, like trailing her fingers through water. 'Does it still hurt?'

Kevin shook his head.

She pressed down on the scar. 'How about now?' Fresh blood welled where her nails sliced the skin.

Kevin squirmed, making the manacles rattle.

Mira licked her fingers, wrinkled her nose in distaste. 'Cow. It never does the job. Don't you agree?' Her fingers trawled across his stomach, his hip, his thigh. 'I suppose Nigel filled your head with ideas of what we might do with you. You're probably imagining yourself like a grilled steak; or maybe your mother dead and drained, or worse.'

He squirmed, aware of the response her actions were eliciting from his traitorous body.

'Still some blood in the system, then,' Mira leered. Her nails scratched through his pubic hair, stroked his swelling cock. She bent to lap droplets of blood from his chest, then stepped back, reached under her skirt and slipped off a pair of black knickers, stumbling once as they caught on the heel of her boot.

'Don't misunderstand me, Grease Monkey; I'm all in favour of the stick. But there are times when the carrot can also be effective.'

She climbed upon the table and straddled him. One hand teased his cock to full erection, the other kneaded her breast, then slid up her throat to her mouth. She sucked her fingers, then bit down. He glimpsed the curve of fangs in her upper jaw, then could focus only on the scarlet winding down her fingers into her palm. She dripped blood on his face. For a long, long moment, he managed to resist, keeping his lips tightly shut. The blood fragrance swamped him as the drops sank into his starving flesh.

Her other hand gripped the sides of his mouth. 'Don't play hard to get it. Not after all that we've been through together.'

Against his will, he opened his mouth, hungry to swallow. She let him lick her fingers, then thrust them into his mouth like bloody lollipops. He sucked hard, trying to get down to the bone. Felt his gums pinch as his fangs extended. She pulled her fingers away before he could munch them.

'No biting the hand that feeds.' Her hand locked on his jaw, making him stare up at her. 'Not when I'm being so kind.'

Mira impaled herself on his cock. Kevin groaned as she closed around him. Her fingers stroked his hair, his face. She buried him inside her until their groins rubbed against each other with delicious friction.

Her breath clouded over his face, the reflection of his own desire looking back at him, distorted and foreign in her chartreuse eyes. She kissed him hungrily. The musky aroma of sex enveloped him; sex and blood. She gave him her wrist and buried her fangs in his neck. Her flesh parted under his teeth and bliss, boiling and fervid, exploded through him. And inside his mind…

A door explodes into splinters and a flock of razor-winged seagulls with blood-dripping beaks fly out like bats leaving a cave, all backlit by a deep purple glow. Mira's poppet hobbles out on bird-like legs, glorying in her freedom. Swollen storm clouds race in, looking like cancerous lungs riven with violet lightning veins.

'Give me all you've got,' she shouts, and the clouds tear open. A thousand shrieking faces trailing intestines swoop at him like kites driven by a hurricane. Blood rains down. The poppet swells, grows, opens its mouth and lifts its elongating arms to embrace the deluge. Mira dances like a ballerina, fully fleshed and coated in crimson.

She sees him, then, and drops to all fours, fangs glinting, but she turns her back and opens her legs. 'You know you want this,' she says, her words like thunder. 'Blood calls to blood. Give me all you've got.' Fangs snap like scissors inside the wide pink lips of her cunt.

Naked, he runs, his hard-on banging against his thighs, blood dribbling into his mouth where the rain has left him saturated. She pounces, a jaguar in scarlet with maroon eyes, and Kevin screams. He's on his back and his legs and arms are bound and she fucks him and...

drinks herself

drinks Kala

drinks Taipan

drinks Danica

His blood drains into Mira, squirting with every twitch of his cock, pumping with every beat of his heart. All his secrets, his very essence, emptying into Mira, who clings to him like a tick. His climax is the vilest sensation he has ever felt, not because he doesn't want it, but because he does.

And all the time, she's laughing at him, coz he's so very easy.

Back arched, Mira rammed herself on to his dying prick until she shuddered her last. Rivulets of blood ran from the corners of her mouth, spotting her breasts where, sometime, she'd torn her singlet down and left deep scratches in her chest. Her tattoo was a vivid, liquid logo on her tit. His chest was a mess of bloody cuts; his neck throbbed with bites.

Kevin's senses reeled, Mira's voice indistinct through the maelstrom of lives swirling in his bloodstream. But the threat penetrated the riot. He tried desperately to focus.

He was on the bed at Whitby Downs, a prisoner; no seagulls, no storm, no blood rain. But Mira...

Give me all you've got

You're only young, Kevin

It was perfect

I'll be at the gorge till the end of the week

'Well, that was interesting. What is it about you boys and your mothers? Your mothers and your girls. And your fathers.' Smiling, so smug, she wiped a droplet of blood from her chest and licked it from her fingertip, then nodded to herself before asking him, 'Now which gorge would that be?' She slapped his face. 'I'm talking to you, *Kevvie*. Pay attention.'

He spat at her, a globule of sticky crimson that splattered against her chest.

'Don't go changing the subject,' she said, 'as tasty as that might be. Tell me about the gorge.'

He turned his face away, shame and despair ushering him back into the crazy carousel of Mira's lifestream. He hoped for some truth to emerge, for some weapon with which to destroy her, but all he tasted, all he experienced, was death. Pointless bloody death.

She scooped up his spittle and licked her finger, then did the same for the tendril of drool on his chin. 'No, he must think I'm stupid. Why would Taipan tell you that, when he must've known you'd be caught. That I'd find out. It's either a trap or a feint. And Mother – *Mother* has given me *nothing*.' She slapped him again, seized his chin so she could stare into him, their noses almost touching. 'You have no idea where they are, do you?'

Kevin strained, but he couldn't break free.

Mira chuckled as she sat back, her weight uncomfortable on his thighs. 'So what do I do with you now?' She tapped her jaw with one finger, pursed her lips as though considering the conundrum. 'What ever will I do with you *and* your mother now that you're both expendable?'

He tugged against the cuffs, desperate to get his hands on her. 'Don't you dare hurt her!'

'What if I did? They're just cattle, boy, ours for the taking. On that score, Taipan is right. If only he'd learned some prudence.'

Mira slowly stepped off the table, a rider dismounting after a long day in the saddle. She pulled her singlet back into shape and retrieved his pendant from where it had fallen. Her face was bloated, the whites of her eyes heavily veined, her lustrous lips full to the point of bursting. If only he could pinch one between his teeth and pop it like a cherry tomato, taste that juice she'd stolen from him. Take back all the lifestream that she'd absorbed.

A hesitant tapping on the door sparked a frown. Hunter. Poker-faced as he took in his blood-splattered mistress; surely the myxo could smell the sex, so strong it was gagging. Nigel peeked around Hunter's side, grinning like a sideshow clown.

'We have a visitor.' A nod at Kevin, the hint of a wince, so fast Kevin thought he might've mistaken it. 'The girlfriend.'

Kevin's despair threatened to drag him through the floor. If it was Meg – God, it could just as easily be Kala – if it was either of them, or his mother, even, and they brought her here to see him like this.

'She's alone?' Mira said.

'So I'm told. Turner's put her in with the widow.'

'Quite the collection we're getting.' She looked at Kevin, considering, stroking the blood bracelets on her wrist. 'I didn't think she was coming, not after her surprise meeting with the grease monkey. Unless her delicious little talk with Don Juan here has left her upset and confused. I can just imagine her, can't you? In her bedroom, pacing, her tender heart breaking. Her beloved with some wild woman, ranting, raving – until finally she can't stand it any longer. So she grabs a bag of goodies for mummy dearest, as requested, and comes out to see what the grease monkey was so upset about. Could that be it, I wonder?'

Kevin begged. 'Don't – please – just let her go. Let them both go. You've got what you wanted.'

'Trust me, this is most definitely *not* what I wanted. Well, let's go have a chat with young Meg.' She wrapped her cape around herself. 'And here's me, all out of carrot. Just the stick left.' She bent slowly, her face ruddy with his blood, and picked up something from the floor. 'Here, something to remember me by.' She stuffed her knickers in his mouth and sauntered out. The door shut. The lock turned.

FORTY-EIGHT

Kevin rode the black horse of despair through the fragments of lifestream that tried to enfold him. He had failed utterly; had given up the Night Riders, had caused his mother and Meg to be captured, had left Kala in the bush to face Mira's hounds. Mira had broken him and taken everything. Why had Meg come out to Whitby Downs? What would Mira do to her? And how much time had she already had to do it? He had no idea how long he'd been here. How much frustration would Mira want to take out on them all now that she knew Taipan wasn't coming? The phrase 'cut and run' kept cycling through his mind.

Again, he jerked against his bindings.

Useless.

'Pale, ain'tcha?'

It took a moment for Kevin to realise Taipan wasn't just some splinter of past life memory, but was actually standing by the bed, staring at his naked body. 'And cold, too, by the looks,' the biker said with a full grin.

After a bit of huffing, Kevin managed to spit his impromptu gag on to the table. 'What are you doing here, you bastard?'

'In maybe a minute, that door there is gonna open and you're gonna get a chance to get outta this place. Thought you'd like some warnin' so you could make yourself presentable.'

Kevin shook his chains.

'Oh well, as nature made you then.' He walked over, sniffing. 'Glad to see you bin enjoyin' yourself, though. I reckon that Mira, she's taken a shine to you. Our little secret, eh?'

'Fuck you.'

'You sure you got the energy after all that moanin' and thrashin' you bin doin'?'

'Why are you even here?'

'That Mira, she was right 'bout one thing, eh. I did reckon you'd get nicked. So I hitched a ride in ya blood here so I could take a good gander 'round the place.'

'You arsehole. You set me up.'

'I think of myself more as one of them *opportunists*. Anyways, I got some stuff I gotta do. Oh, there was one thing that bloodhag got wrong, but. If it does all go to shit, we *are* all meetin' up at the gorge. Kala knows the one and I reckon you do, too. I'd like to say I was bein' a clever dick, tellin' you mob the truth and expectin' that psycho bitch to think it was a lie, but the truth is, I just kinda fucked up. No matter. Mother'll be gone soon as you can spit, so it's just us if ya new girlfriend decides to take a look.' He winked, chuckled again at Kevin's nudity, and walked through the wall.

Kevin blinked, trying to work out if the biker had even been there at all or if it was just some weird hallucination.

The door opened and Kala entered. Behind her, Acacia stood beside Nigel, a hand gripping his arm at the elbow, a handgun pressed to his nape. He didn't look happy.

'Jesus, Kev, are you all right?' Kala asked.

'No,' he said, aware of his soiled nakedness.

She picked the panties up between thumb and finger and raised her eyebrows at him.

'Not mine,' he mumbled.

She laughed and threw them on the floor. 'I didn't think they were your size.'

Underneath the levity, he could see her concern, her doubt. What could he say: it was torture, honest? Covered in hickeys and his spent cock still glistening and sticky pink.

'C'mon,' Acacia said, 'time for a group hug when we're outta here.'

Kala began undoing the shackles. 'You can tell me about it later.'

'I'd rather not,' Kevin said, sitting up and rubbing his wrists. 'What the hell are you doing here?'

'Was hoofing it back to town when I saw a car comin'. Took a risk. Turned out it was your girl and, amazingly, she didn't run me down. Gutsy, that one; comin' out to see for herself what you were on about. Drove me back to town so I could call Mother, only to find that this mob' – she jerked a thumb at Acacia – 'had been followin' us. Your girl agreed to sneak us in.'

'A set up,' Kevin said.

'A back-up,' Acacia said. 'Besides, I wanted to make sure this girl here didn't do anything stupid.'

'Didn't do a very good job, did you? Lucky for me.' Kevin slid off the table, his knees weak. Mira had taken more than she'd given.

Kala hugged him, her body warm and reassuring. He gripped her tightly and nodded over her shoulder at Nigel. 'You found a friend, I see.'

'He's been very helpful,' Acacia said. 'Your mum and young Meg are in a room at the far side of the house.'

'Let's hope Mira hasn't got to them yet.'

'You gonna go like that?' Acacia asked.

He turned to Nigel. 'You're about my size, eh?'

They stripped the surfie – his pants and shirt fitted Kevin reasonably well but the shoes weren't happening – and threw him on the table, then snapped the cuffs shut. Nigel whimpered, offering no resistance, but gave a little gulp as Acacia threw the keys out the window.

'You're not gonna – you know?' Kevin drew a finger across his throat.

Acacia sniffed. 'He's made his bed.'

'You were almost right, back at the Crawfords',' Kevin told Nigel as he forced Mira's knickers into his mouth. 'It is easy to work out the difference between master and servant. It's all about who wears the panties.'

Kala grabbed Kevin's arm. 'Sorry to break up the reunion but we're on a kind of schedule here.' She held up a set of car keys with a miniature surfboard hanging from the ring. Nigel stared painful death at them.

'Surf's up, eh.' Kevin followed the women to the homestead's back verandah.

'This way, I think,' Acacia said, jerking her head toward the right. She listened at a closed door. Shook her head.

They crept around a corner where the verandah had been enclosed to make more rooms. Light shone from under a door. Kevin heard voices; Meg's, definitely, as nervous as hell if the quaver was any indication. He took a breath and turned the handle as Acacia kept watch. Kala pressed close, her pistol poised.

He pushed the door gently, the gap revealed Meg, sitting, legs pressed together, hands clasping a tea cup, looking every bit the debutante. His mother came into view, looking exhausted in a chair, her face drooping, eyes dark, skin waxen. Jeans and cardigan, tea on a table beside her, hands in her lap. Neither of them had noticed him yet, they were staring at the wall Kevin couldn't see. Relief washed through him. They were both okay.

The door swung open to reveal the rest of the room; a small one, crowded with two chairs, a sewing machine and – Jasmine Turner.

She stood by a curtained window at his mother's side, looking, if anything, impatient as she placed a hand on his mother's shoulder.

'Well don't just stand there in the doorway, young man. Come in.'

'Kev!' Meg's cup crashed to the floor. 'Run! It's a trap!'

His mother looked at him, trying to focus, her expression one of pure confusion. What the hell had they done to her? 'Kevin? You're back already. Did you win?'

Kala pushed Kevin from behind. He stumbled into Meg as she stood, an awkward bump of groping hands and overbalancing. Kala levelled her pistol. Jasmine lunged, a blur in the corner of Kevin's vision. Kala cried out as the sound of the slap cracked across the room. The gun thumped against a wall, then bounced across the floor. Jasmine pushed Kala in the chest. It seemed the slightest of gestures, but Kala flew backward out of the room.

Jasmine slammed the door shut, then grabbed Kevin by the throat and spun him around. The door shuddered with his impact. 'Does Mira know you're out? She promised me no hassles.' Her eyes narrowed.

'Let them go,' he said, his voice barely escaping her grip.

'That was never going to happen.' Jasmine slammed Kevin into the door again, drew back a hand that glinted as though her fingers were tipped with diamonds.

Meg threw tea in Jasmine's face. The woman spluttered. Her backhand smacked against Meg's cheek like a whip. She reeled over the chair and crashed into the wall.

Kevin punched Jasmine. And again. Like hitting a sack of flour.

Gunfire sounded from outside.

The door pushed against him as someone tried to open it. Jasmine forced him hard against it.

Jasmine's face filled his vision, her eyes blazing with fury, lips pulled back to reveal her rottweiler fangs. He just got his hands up in time to stop her from tearing out his throat. It was like pushing against a steamroller.

'I like your mother,' she told him. 'She tastes of sunshine.'

An explosion deafened him. Blood sprayed his face.

Jasmine stared through him, the slightest wrinkle of confusion dimpling her forehead. Her grip relaxed and she crumpled at his feet.

His mother stood to one side, Kala's handgun in her grip.

'Mum! Mum!' He crushed her to him, feeling bones. How had she lost so much weight? Over her shoulder, he saw Meg, sprawled and moaning.

'She was not a nice woman,' his mother said. 'Did she hurt you, son?'

'I'm fine, Mum.' He knelt beside Meg, found a pulse. Started to lift her.

Acacia and Kala burst in and slammed the door.

'We heard a shot,' Kala asked. 'Is she–'

'Just knocked down. Mum did for Jasmine.'

'Nice going, Mrs Mum,' Acacia said, then prodded at a wound in her own shoulder. 'Fuck, that stings.' She ejected the clip of her handgun and replaced it with another from her jeans pocket. 'You right to go, handsome?'

'Meg's hurt,' he said.

'Can she walk?' Kala asked, then said to his mother, 'How about I take that?'

'Be careful, dear,' his mother said as she handed the weapon over. 'They aren't toys.'

'She'll be all right,' Kevin said as he helped Meg to her feet. 'Let's get outta here.'

Acacia hauled the sewing machine table in front of the door, then shared a glance with Kala. 'Window.'

'Nailed shut,' Kala reported after giving it a shake.

They smashed it with a chair and cleaned off the glass. Kala glanced out. 'Short drop. No-one out here, yet.'

Shoulders rammed the door. Acacia fired three rounds into the timber.

'You first,' Acacia told Kala.

'I'll hand Meg to you,' Kevin said. 'That all right?'

'Sure. Of course.' Kala clambered out and dropped to the ground. 'Pass her down.'

With Meg deposited, he got his mother to the window. 'Kevin? I was worried about you. They asked about you, sometimes; but mostly they just did things. And gave me tea.'

She frowned in confusion, as though cruelty and politeness should not go together, as though of all her unspoken trials, that was the thing that offended her the most.

'You'll be all right, now, Mum. Jesus, what've they done to you?'

'Blood bag,' Acacia answered. 'Get a move on, eh.'

Automatic fire ripped through the door. He folded his mother under him as they huddled against the wall. Acacia returned fire and was rewarded with a shriek.

'C'mon, Mum, we have to skedaddle, okay. Can you get through here?'

'Hurry up!' Acacia glanced at Jasmine. Her hands were twitching. Acacia shot her again.

Kevin's mother winced. 'It's very loud here, Kevin. Sometimes they come and they – they kiss me. Your father wouldn't like it. *I* don't like it.'

'Get down there, Kevin,' Acacia told him. 'Kala's got her hands full; I'll pass your ma down.'

'Sure. Don't worry, Mum. This will all be over soon.'

He hopped down. Kala knelt nearby, keeping a nervous eye on the corners of the house. Meg leaned, dazed, against the wall.

Shoulders thumped the door again. The sewing table screeched against the floor.

'Pass her down,' Kevin said, reaching. Acacia stood by the window, trying to help his mother through.

A raw tearing sound, the splintering of wood.

Acacia swore and turned to face the door.

A machinegun barked.

Acacia toppled backward, half diving, half falling through the window, tearing down the curtain and nearly taking Kevin with her as she landed in a boneless heap.

Kala shouted her name, but she didn't respond.

Kevin jumped for the window, got his elbows over it, only to see two men in the doorway in black uniforms, silver flashes at their lapels, brutish snub-nosed guns in their hands. His mother huddled on the floor, hands over her head. He reached for her, one-handed and desperate. The jackals fired and he dropped back as timber splintered from the sill where he'd been hanging.

He grabbed Acacia's pistol and got it pointed up in time as a man ducked out of the window, a gun poised. Kevin fired and the man spun away out of sight.

'Mum!' he shouted, but there was no answer.

'Go, go,' Acacia said, her words bubbling. Her chest was a mess of blood and cloth. 'Help me up, damn it.'

'My mum–'

'She's gone, boy, for now, and we will be, too, if we don't get our arses out of here. Out the front – get to Nigel's wagon.'

'What's happening?' Kala yelled. She was firing a shot or two at a time to stop jackals from coming around the corner of the house.

'Kevin?' Meg looked groggily at him.

'Get her up,' Acacia shouted, and took her pistol off him. 'Let's roll.'

'I can't leave!'

'You have to.' Acacia grabbed him around the shoulders. 'Now help me. Across to that garage, first. Then we'll try for the Sandman. Run! And don't get shot!'

Kevin supporting Acacia, Kala helping Meg, they crossed

the house yard to the split-rail fence in a shambling three-legged race. Kala and Acacia snapped off shots to try to cover their flight.

Earth spouted. Wood splintered. Rounds thudded into the garage on the other side of the fence.

They scrambled through the rails, buzzed by bullets but unhurt as they huddled behind the thick timber.

'That's a lot of open ground to cover,' Acacia said with a wave at the Sandman, so close but yet so far. 'Be nice if we could take that chopper instead; fly out in style.'

'Could you fly it?'

'I might be a bit rusty, but sure, I reckon. Kala, how we lookin'?'

'Troopers are sneaking up; I got 'em staying shy but we won't last long here.'

'How's the girl?'

'I'm okay,' Meg said, her determination pushing up through the concussion.

Back at the house, jackals hunched at the rear corner; others sniped from the window they'd fled from. Mira and Hunter and a squad of jackals in vests and helmets thundered on to the verandah.

'We are completely screwed,' Kevin whispered.

Acacia winked. 'Oh ye of little faith.'

The lights went out.

FORTY-NINE

Voices rose, sparked by the blackout. Then came the sound of a generator starting up, the chugging getting louder and more rhythmic. Lights flickered, glowed, blazed.

'Something moving, out past the fence,' one of the jackals shouted.

'About time,' Acacia muttered. 'But if he's brought Cassie with him, I'm gonna kick his arse from here to Cairns.'

Kevin peered past the brightly lit mesh, and he saw what the jackal must've spotted – a speckled mass moving in the gloom.

Quickly resolving into a herd of cattle.

A stampede.

'Bush tucker,' Kevin whispered.

Two gunmen at the gate lowered their guns and ripped a series of bursts into the herd. Some animals dropped, some fled, but the main body stormed onward, a ram of flesh and bone that hit the gates like a Mack truck. The guards scuttled clear. The mesh held for a moment, and then the gate tore loose and crashed to the ground in two misshapen sections. The cattle scrambled over and around mangled carcasses as they streamed into the compound. Behind the bellowing and the gunfire came the sound of motors. The two guards at the gate collapsed inexplicably. Over the cacophony, Mira's shout: 'This is it, get to it, bring me that black bastard.'

Bikes appeared among the tail end of the stampede, and then a Jeep with its lights out. Teams of two on the bikes, Mohawk and Lions among them, the pillions spraying bullets, and the Jeep lit up with muzzle flashes as though it was hung with Christmas lights.

Hunter and a man in leather sprinted for the chopper.

Acacia handed her pistol to Kevin. 'Cover me!' She ran after Hunter.

Kala fired toward the house, working her way from one group of gunmen to the next.

Kevin raised the handgun. He felt a strange shift inside of him, the inherent knowledge bequeathed by Taipan and Kala and even Mira guiding his instincts, on top of the few occasions he'd had to handle pistols. The first shot put a jackal down as Mira's troops spilled along the veranda rail and down along the front fence. Explosions thundered and flared as the jackals returned fire.

'Damn it, they're coming, I can't hold them,' Kala said.

Two jackals at the back of the house sprinted toward them, a big gap between them. Guns sparked from the window. Chips flew from the fence.

'Back to the garage,' Kevin said, dropping one of the charging men. The other went to ground. 'Go!'

Kala and Meg crabbed backward. Kevin's magazine clicked empty. He ran, chased by gunfire, and slid into shelter at the open doorway of the garage. His spirits lifted. The Jag!

'Flat,' Kala said, kneeling at the corner, snapping off shots. 'Back tyre. Even if we could get it started.'

And no sign of Meg's Suzi. Kevin checked for Acacia. He couldn't see her, but there were two mounds near the chopper.

Taipan's attack had bogged down, a confused riot of gunfire and cattle and vehicles.

'Gimme the keys,' he told Kala. 'I'm going for plan B.'

'You'll never make it.'

'Oh ye of little faith.' He bolted, a mad zigzag. He was near the chopper when a bullet smacked his leg out from under him and he tumbled in the dirt.

Part of the house exploded.

Pieces of timber rattled down.

The Jeep ploughed across the battlefield like a deadly turtle, covered in slabs of metal sheeting. The word "Ned" had been painted on the front. Taipan drove; someone Kevin didn't know manned a machinegun bolted to a mount on the roll cage, and Hippie hefted a bazooka. They'd dropped their gunmen off to spread out across the yard, finding what cover they could behind saplings and machinery, the bodies of dead cattle. The raiders were pouring fire into the house, scattering Mira's troops. Everyone had come, he thought. All of the Night Riders. Everyone but Danica herself and Cassie maybe.

Hippie fired again and a section of fence erupted in flame and noise. Had he taken the bite, Kevin wondered? Was Hippie on the night shift now?

By the dying glare of the explosion, he realised it was Hunter and the pilot on the ground nearby. The rotor was moving with painful slowness. That black cockatoo knew her stuff!

He had a moment of indecision: back to the garage with Kala and Meg, or to the chopper, or to the Sandman? No gun meant he was useless to Kala; equally so with the chopper. But with the Sandman, he might run distraction; he might do more than simply wait to be airlifted out of this mess. Who knew – with the chopper putting down some serious kick arse, he might even be able to get to his mother. Stick to plan B; Kala and Meg were waiting for him.

Keeping low, he staggered on, and managed to reach the Sandman without taking any more wounds. He spared a sorrowful look for the Monaro – if only he had the keys – but the panel van was more practical anyway.

A revving engine caught his attention and he watched as

Mohawk's motorcycle raced past the house. The pinion fired from the hip. Two jackals manning a machinegun fell under the barrage. The bike disappeared around the far corner, only to reappear shortly after, followed by an almighty explosion from behind the house. A mushroom of smoke rolled above the roof line; a drum arced high, trailing a streamer of smoke like a weird flare. The lights along the fence, on the chopper pad, at the house: all died. Darkness flooded the battlefield and this time there was no generator to resurrect the light.

We're really gonna do this, Kevin thought as he reefed open the Sandman's door. They'd wipe out Mira's bunch and get his mum and drive home or even fly home and everything was gonna be just dandy. Somehow, everything was gonna work out okay.

Making the most of the darkness and confusion, Taipan's men advanced toward the homestead. The remaining two bikes scribed misshapen helixes as they laid down fire. Kevin blinked away memories, loud and fear-stained, of the attack on the service station. Over the top, the whoosh of Hippie's bazooka blended with his memory of Molotovs exploding.

He told himself to concentrate. To get into it. To do his bit.

Kevin edged the Sandman forward, just in time to see one of Mira's jackals stand up by the thick lintel post at the gate. The man bowled, nice action, smooth. It was as if the guy was a sorcerer casting a spell, because no sooner had he finished his toss and ducked back behind cover than there was a blast of flame, and Lions' motorcycle was lifted and thrown. The rider and gunman were hurled in different directions. The motorcycle landed all out of shape, its front wheel in the air, turning pointlessly. The pinion hit the ground and didn't move.

Two jackals ran out. One was shot down but the second reached Lions where he was trying to pick himself up out of the dirt. He turned in time to see the swing that severed his head from his neck.

That started the hat-trick for Mira's team, and Kevin could

only sit and watch in stunned despair as his team's attack was torn apart.

Mohawk came roaring in. Timber flew from the gateposts as bullets ripped into it, but the bowler was hunkered down, fully defensive. A jackal rose from behind the carcass of a bullock and swung, a massive pull shot, blade flashing in the uncertain battlefield light. As neat as you please, he lifted Mohawk's head and knocked the pinion from the saddle. The bike drove on under the influence of the dead hand till it realised it was rudderless and spun out. The head bounced along behind. The jackal stabbed the injured pinion to death.

A rocket flashed and the swordsman vanished in a blast of flame.

The Jeep was still in action. Hippie loaded again as Taipan brought them in closer to the house.

The bowler at the gate sent another delivery down. The Jeep jumped over a tongue of fire. Hippie tumbled clear and lay still. The vehicle trundled on, smoking from the nose, hit a crater and toppled sideways. A long green box bounced near Hippie's body and the lid flipped open, as though he'd brought his own miniature coffin. Taipan rose, groggy. He grabbed the tube Hippie had loaded and hefted it. The jackals opened up. He stood in the hail, valiant, an armourless Ned Kelly figure till finally the weight of lead bore him down. The rocket fired off, up and over the house, the explosion coming distant and wasted as Taipan lay in the wavering light of the burning Jeep, a huddled shape barely moving.

The bowler shaped up once more to deliver the coup de grace, but there was a blowtorch whoosh and both he and the gate were reduced to nothing as the chopper evened the score.

But Kevin knew the game was done. They were out of batsmen and there was nothing for it but to leave the field. The chopper was out of the question. The paddock was way too dangerous. Already Mira's men were fanning out, encircling the Jeep and advancing warily on the hovering chopper. Bullets sparked on its windshield and body. It wouldn't be able to take that punishment for long.

He floored the Sandman, tyres spitting dirt as he carved around the windstorm where the chopper was advancing at little more than head height. It was up to him to get Kala and Meg to safety. It was up to him to save his mother.

Shit!

Mira stood silhouetted as the homestead burnt, pointing at the van, and men near her swung around.

The chopper's guns stuttered, and streaks of light sped from the nodules on either side of the machine to scythe down Mira's jackals. The chopper rose higher, belched flame and smoke. A rocket blew the homestead's front steps to pieces. Had Acacia been aiming for Mira? Had she got the bitch?

Fuck: his mum was still in the house.

By the time he reached the garage, the van had been pinged; he had a bullet in his gut and cracks webbed the windshield. He all but fell out the door.

'Acacia can't land for us,' he gasped to Kala. 'You'll have to drive. Drive like a fucking demon.'

'What about you?'

'I'm not leaving without Mum.'

'There's a difference between suicide and bravery, y'know.'

'She's my mum.'

Kala gave him her pistol – 'You're down to maybe six, last mag' – and kissed him, pushed Meg in toward the passenger side as another burst of gunfire rocked the wagon. 'I'll wait at the silo till dawn. After that–'

'The gorge,' he said. 'If not there, the gorge.'

'Be at the silo,' she said.

Meg reached for him. 'Kevin – aren't you coming, Kev?'

'I can't. You have to go with Kala and be safe. I'll catch up soon as I can!'

Kala slammed the door, gave him a desperate look, then accelerated away. One jackal, reeling out of the smoke and shock of a nearby rocket hit, got clipped by the van and was thrown aside with a heavy crunch. Acacia did what she could to keep the jackals' heads down. The vehicle swerved around a dead bullock. Bullets sparked on its rear doors, then it was clear of the gates and vanished into the night.

Near the blazing jeep, Taipan staggered up and waved at the chopper. It hovered low, dust and smoke whirling in its vortices. A four-wheel-drive drove out from behind the house, a jackal firing from the passenger window. The chopper swung, fired a rocket that blew the vehicle to hell. Another rocket followed, hitting an outbuilding, and a third, throwing up a geyser of earth and flame near the corner of the homestead.

Taipan jumped, clung to the skid, and the chopper flew forward and began to climb.

Mira jumped from the veranda and sprinted toward the Jeep.

Kevin fired at her. Three shots and the pistol clicked empty. Mira kept running. He swore. No chance of getting to her in time, even if he wasn't wounded.

Taipan dangled from the skid like a possum under a wire as the chopper flew toward the fence, its engine noise rising.

Mira dug a tube from the green box thrown from the Jeep

Even got us a splinter to stick in their eye in the sky

and raised it to her shoulder and pointed it at the chopper. The tube belched fire. A swirling line of smoke traced the missile's path. The helicopter exploded. Once, twice. The second fireball engulfed the machine. Taipan vanished. Rotor blades speared off into the night. The wreck dropped like a cut elevator in a mass of flame and twisted metal.

Kevin stared, unbelieving, and realised there were jackals, not many, but enough, spreading out from the house. A couple of people not in uniform were spraying garden hoses at the burning house. Mira stalked the battlefield, pointing with her distinctive sword and shrieking, 'Find them all. I want their blood. All of them.'

Kevin sheltered by the garage wall.

Jackals approached, checking bodies, shining torches. Some wore bulky goggles. He didn't think they'd seen him yet, but it was only a matter of time. He stripped and hid his clothes behind a stack of ceramic pots heaped along the inside wall of the garage, then dropped to the ground.

Driven by desperation, Kevin called to the earth. Taipan's blood sang in his body, a didgeridoo wail; his heartbeat was measured by clap sticks. The voices of men were buried by the calls of birds, the crackle of flames, the sigh of wind and the groan of layers of ancient rock. Gritty warmth closed around him and he felt a moment of suffocation, of entrapment, but the didgeridoo played louder and the blood surged and the sounds faded to a gentle whisper of welcome and he was at peace in the dark embrace. Time stretched out behind him and ahead of him and through him. He felt Taipan inside of him, a phantom:

You're going outside?

Goin' to ground Wink

The earth is your friend

As the biker's thoughts swirled through his own, he found himself making a connection he had never expected. Kevin's desperate bid to save his mother found an echo in Taipan's life, but this girl was young and beautiful and dressed in white. She was the reason beyond all reason, the one saving grace, the one driving need. Lying in the embrace of the earth, Kevin thought he felt the planet quake with the intensity of Taipan's love for his sister.

FIFTY

Reece stood in the kitchen, washing down painkillers with rum. The rogue bitch had clocked him a beauty. If he'd been mortal, truly mortal, the blow would've killed him. But the laugh was on her, right?

Boom–crash.

Maximilian von Schiller wasn't laughing. The Big V's rant crackled from the telephone Mira held at a distance, as though he might reach down the line and rip her brain out through her ear.

Felicity leaned against the door jamb. She'd been disappointed to have missed the battle and now she was doing her damndest to ignore the body still leaking blood on the floor. The light from the kerosene lamp on the bench softened her features. She gave him a raised-eyebrow look as Maximilian hit a high note. The gesture made him feel so very old.

Mira clamped a hand over the mouthpiece and whispered, 'He loved his helicopter. I have to buy him a new one.' She rolled her eyes and Reece and Felicity shared a conspiratorial grin, but they both knew the shit was dripping from the fan. Mira hung up and walked over to Reece. 'Well, that went well. Pour me one of those.' She swilled the rum, spat it into the sink, leaving a pink tinge. Not his, thankfully, and he hadn't been game to ask her for a top-up. He'd have to rely on paracetamol to fix his aches.

'Now, where was I? Oh, yes.' She'd been interrogating a wounded red-eye when Maximilian had rung; she'd killed the hippie through distraction or irritation, but not before she'd found something in his lifestream. Mira scribbled an address on a notebook. 'Send a squad to check this place. The nest. Near Stonehenge.' She gave Reece a smile.

'We don't have a full squad, Strigoi.'

'Then send *someone*, Reece. I need to find Mother!' She stood, locked in desperation and fury, the change of mood so sudden and dangerous that Reece dared only nod and say, 'Of course.'

'Is there *any* good news?' Mira asked.

'I just got here with the swag from the mechanic's car,' Felicity said. 'Nothing in it to suggest where Dani– where Dee might be hiding.'

'Get the judas or someone to get rid of the grease monkey's gear. No trace. And this, too.' She kicked the body on the floor. 'Reece?'

'We still have Matheson's mother, though she's in rough shape. Took two to the chest. The Night Riders have been largely eradicated, but it's cost us. Also, we've lost an outrider during the search outside the fence – dead, bike stolen.'

'So at least one got out, other than the two in the panel van. The grease monkey?'

'Haven't found his body yet.'

Mira took a pendant from her pocket and dangled it in front of her, then turned around so Felicity could tie it at her neck. 'You won't. He's still alive, I'm certain of it. I can't get a lock, though. We've got no idea where he might be headed. Unless – hit me again.'

Reece poured her another shot. She swallowed this one, and tasted it for a long time, nodding to herself. A slow grin twisted her tight lips.

'Is there a plan?' he prodded eventually.

'Oh, yes. Our lord and master wants us back in 'Bane, as fast as we can drive. Us and all our men.' She snorted. 'With a kiss on Jasmine's arse on the way out, for all the trouble we've caused.'

'She can't stay here, surely?' Felicity said. 'Someone must've noticed all this kerfuffle.'

'Like who? Anyway, it's Jasmine's choice,' Mira said. 'We're footing the costs. You're staying here, my dear, to oversee the grand kiss-and-make up.'

Felicity looked away in a huff.

'Trust me, you're better off. My advice would be to make the clean-up take as long as you can, certainly till the dust has settled back at Schloss Unhappy. You'll probably end up being promoted. God knows there's enough vacancies.'

'I'll make a start now,' Felicity said. 'Make sure Smithy's hunt for Matheson doesn't come this way. I'm meeting him at the Commodore once the tow truck from Nancy has arrived.'

'Nancy? What's that?'

'En–Cee,' she said. 'As in North Collinsvale. The nearest shithole to this one. Barlow's Siding seems to have lost its only garage.'

'"Nancy",' Reece said. 'You going native on us, Flick?'

'Don't call me that. And not bloody likely. I haven't heard a tune more recent than 1960 since I got here.'

'Get yourself a player,' Mira said. 'And stay in touch.' The girl left and Mira turned to Reece. 'Gets into your blood, doesn't she?'

He shrugged.

'Give the men their marching orders while I make nice with the lady of the house. Keep a car for you and me.'

'Just us?' He tried not to let his depression show. It was going to be a long trip without a relief driver. Mira didn't drive. She'd done pretty well at keeping herself updated, but that skill set was one she hadn't mastered. Word was, Maximilian couldn't even use a smart phone, let alone an ATM. And they fancied themselves the top of the food chain.

'Don't be like that, Reece. *Vater* said we had to go home but he didn't say which route to take.' She fingered the pendant dangling above her breasts. 'You and I will take a small detour. We should be able to get there by dawn.'

'By dawn?' He checked his watch. 'How far away is this place?'

'Not that far. This one's personal; just you and me. Of course, if that makes you uneasy, I could take *Flick*.'

'Where are we going, Strigoi? What should I expect?'

'Pack a full kit and a good pair of hiking shoes. There's a gorge I want to check out.'

FIFTY-ONE

The earth grew quiet. No explosions. No voices. No footfalls. How much time had passed, Kevin had no idea. It could've been centuries. It could've been seconds. But he couldn't stay. Up there, the enemy had his mother, and Acacia and Taipan and everyone – everyone – was gone. He was the night watchman – it was up to him.

He rose, quietly, dirt sloughing from him, his body aching where wounds remained tender, where hunger clawed at his hollow gut. Cool night air wrapped around him, the ground at his back, stars overhead. Silence; no birds, no licking of flame, no engines or conversation.

Wait.

A creak of timber. Muttered words. The spark of a lighter and the burst of cigarette smell. Not Taipan's noxious roll-your-owns, but the more cutting reek of a tailor-made penetrating the smell of blood and burnt timber, gunpowder and guts. He ignored the memory of another razed ruin, of emerging from the earth at the rear of the service station to find his world in ashes.

Someone was close by, and Kevin was lying on the ground, naked.

He rolled over to take a better look around. None of the

spotlights were on; there were no lights at all, just moonlight masking the battlefield in shadows and, at the house, one window glowing orange. The people he'd heard were there, two of them, on the shattered remains of the veranda. He crawled into the garage and found the clothes he'd stashed; he'd be barefoot, but at least he wouldn't be creeping around with his old fella swinging in the wind.

Once he was dressed, he sneaked over to the house, then stood to squint through the gap between the veranda floor and bottom rail. Two guards stood at the front door – a man and woman in denim and checked shirts; him with a pump-action shotgun, her with a rifle. Bhagwan's myxos. That glow in the window – candle or lantern, he guessed. The front stairs looked as if someone had taken a giant sledge hammer to them: a jagged hole, timbers strewn everywhere, the roof sagging, the iron twisted out of shape.

'How much longer?' the woman asked.

'When she says,' the man answered, words a blue cloud driven by stress, the gun cradled in his arm as he took another suck on his flaring cigarette.

The woman reached to share a drag. 'What if the neighbours heard the battle?'

'There's no-one within coo-ee.'

'Noise travels at night.'

'We're fine.' He took his cigarette back. 'Better than that lot, anyway.'

'Jesus,' she said. 'Couldn't they have buried them or something before they left?'

Kevin edged around so he could see the front yard.

Jesus indeed.

Hippie lay there, buried in a tangled pile of bodies; the man's sightless eyes stared at the sky from a face caked in ash, dirt and blood. Kevin recognised a Lions footy jersey thrown on the mound, but there was no body. All that remained of the front gate was a crater, lopsided posts and scattered rails. The

Jeep was a smouldering beetle frame, the chopper little more than a dead bonfire stack outside the fence. The carcasses of cattle littered the area. Bizarrely, one grey-skinned bullock munched on grass in the far corner of the yard, oblivious to the destruction.

Kevin wondered how to get inside. Could he jump the rail and get to the guards before they gunned him down? A single shot would bring all manner of hell down on him. Would the rear be guarded? The windows? His gut churned, his vision blurring momentarily. The two guards radiated heat. Human heat. He could all but hear their hearts. He realised just how tired, how hurt, how *hungry* he was. He needed a distraction, just to buy him the time to get to them.

He sifted through Taipan's blood memories. He had the earth; what about the shadow walk? Taipan appearing on the road, and again in the hut where Mira had kept him trussed. Could he – yes, he could do that.

His heart beat to the rhythm of clap sticks, his breath was a didgeridoo. He felt a piece of himself break free and appear out by the Jeep. His doppelganger advanced slowly, jerkily. His vision doubled, making him reel: watching himself walk toward the house, watching himself watch himself walk toward the house.

Christ, but it was hard work.

Finally, he managed to separate the images, to focus on controlling the doppelganger without being in its head.

'Who's that?' the woman asked, the words jagged, the gun coming up to her shoulder.

'Markson?' the man suggested, taking a firm bite of his cigarette as he hefted the shotgun. He walked cautiously to the ruined stairs.

'What would he be doing back here?'

'Markson?' he called, but quietly, too quietly to carry the distance.

The woman walked to his side, rifle held in readiness. 'That isn't Markson. Jesus, who is that?'

Kevin lifted himself over the rail–

'Where'd he go?' the man asked, alarmed.

–hit the floor with a soft *thunk* of bare feet.

'He just vanished!' The woman, nearer to Kevin, gasped in confusion, and turned, acknowledging that sound, that movement behind her–

Kevin jabbed her in the chin. A crack. Her gun clattered on the floor as she tumbled off the veranda and thumped into the ground. The man stared at her. Kevin snatched the shotgun away, then slammed the butt into the man's face. The myxo landed hard on his arse up against a veranda post. Blood dribbled from his nose.

Kevin swayed, his mind floating from the effort of summoning the doppelganger, from the adrenalin rush, from the elation. He slumped to his knees in front of the myxo. The man's hand rose, feebly, lips forming a 'who' or perhaps 'what the fuck', but the words never came.

Kevin swallowed them.

He opened that man's throat and he feasted, barely tasting the fear and the pain and the anguish. Not caring that last night this man and that unconscious woman had been in love, planning how best to fully stock Jasmine's property, to milk the herd of its blood and transport it to Brisbane to feed the insatiable Von Schiller machine.

In the myxo's blood, Kevin found that Bhagwan had reportedly been dusted, that Mira and what remained of her troops had left an hour or more ago in separate vehicles, that this pair were in fact the last of Jasmine's retainers on the property. It was only their fear of Mira, of Jasmine, of age, that had kept them here.

And the blood told him what he most wanted to know –

that Jasmine and Willa were still here; that the old girl was acting weird, sitting in the lounge with her living dead doll, the judas surfie and the boy's – *Kevin's* – mother.

Kevin managed to stop before he drained him.

He did not want the man's soul inside of him.

The hunger led him down to the woman. He opened her throat, too. When he was done, when he could move again, when his body was fat and warm and no longer aching, with his fangs retracted and the bloody smears cooling on his cheeks, he fought back the pressing need to piss, his bladder distended so tightly it felt as if it would burst like an over-ripe fig. But all he could think of was being caught beside these two bodies with his cock in his hand. He sneaked, sluggish but alert, with the shotgun to the front door to listen, and realised only then that he could've sealed those wounds he'd made. A little dab of his own blood would've done the job. But he didn't want to be in them, any more than he wanted them in him. He locked their phantasmal lives into rooms in his mind, as Danica had taught him; locked them away with his guilt and wondered which would fade faster.

Taipan would be proud; Kevin would figure out how he felt about it later. Once he'd rescued his mother. Once he'd put all this far behind him.

FIFTY-TWO

One wall of the lounge room gaped open, jagged edged, the ceiling fallen, the window shattered, the curtain a burnt rag. The piano lay at an angle, the stool kicked into a corner with a pile of broken, blackened wood. The stench of burnt things made the air thick; a dusty halo glimmered around the kerosene lantern sitting on the mantel.

He gasped as he saw a pair of legs sticking out from behind a chair. Sandals. Bare legs, the hem of board shorts. But he didn't dare move to get a clearer look. Not his mother, that was the main thing. The only thing.

His focus was on Jasmine Turner, seated in one of her antique armchairs. She wore some kind of mustard-coloured poncho. Willa stood by her side, dressed in jeans, work shirt and joggers. She wore a long, wide-bladed knife in a sheath on her hip and held a familiar rifle – his father's .243 from the Commodore. Another slice of his past stolen from him. She held it casually, barrel pointed at him, stock against her side. He had no doubt she'd loaded a round into the breach. At this range, it'd leave a hole in him the size of a cricket ball. Shotgun versus rifle: he favoured the pump-action, but she had the drop on him. And then there was Jasmine. Let it play, he decided, until he knew the score.

'The *Strigoi* wouldn't wait,' Jasmine said by way of greeting. She made Mira's title sound like something unpleasant; fair enough. '*Couldn't* wait. She wouldn't say where she was going. She did say you were still alive.'

'How could she know – ah.' His pendant. He was back to square one, Mira having unrestricted access to him once again.

'I didn't think you'd leave,' Jasmine continued as though he hadn't spoken. 'Not while she was still here.' She pointed to a couch. A lump lay stretched out under a blanket. He walked around so he could see past the couch's obscuring arm, and recognised the pale face framed by mussed hair. His mother, silent and still. He ran to her, folded to his knees on the timber floor at her side, uncaring of Willa tracking him as he dropped the shotgun by his side.

'Family – I know its pull. Stronger than gravity.' A hand at Willa's elbow. The girl kept the rifle trained on him. 'Where might our Christopher be, do you think?' Jasmine asked.

He looked at her, then at Willa. Held her gaze. 'Taipan's dead,' he told them. 'The chopper–'

Jasmine waved away his words as though erasing something written on a blackboard. 'You are of his blood, and he is of mine. We would both know if he had been destroyed, and we both know that he has not. So, son of my son – where would he be?'

He felt again Taipan's love, his implicit trust even after her betrayal, and something in him broke. Maybe it was the fact his mother lay there dead, and he hadn't realised it. Surely part of him should have felt it, that moment when she'd gone? Why should he be able to sense Taipan's passing and not hers?

We'll be here for you. Always.
Always.

'He's at the gorge if he's anywhere,' Kevin said.

'Gorge?' Jasmine looked worried. 'Not Carnarvon, it's huge.'

'No,' Willa said. 'Not that far east; just a couple of hours from here. I know the place. From this side, you can only get in by foot. There are rock pools, palm trees, caves; I've never been there, but I *know* it. We both do. I'm right, aren't I?'

Kevin shrugged. But he knew it, too, her description conjuring vague impressions from deep in Taipan's lifestream.

'Well, this will be interesting.' Jasmine stood, elegant but quick, and for a split second he thought he had made a big mistake, that she was about to kill him, but all she did was adjust her serape. Under it, she was dressed for travelling in slacks, long-sleeved blouse and rugged shoes. 'We'll leave you to your farewells. We won't be back. I have no desire to explain all this to anyone.'

'All of this, because of a brother's love for his sister,' Kevin said.

Willa grimaced.

Jasmine gave the slightest shake of her head. 'Love should not be confused with obsession.' She turned to Willa. 'Bring the car around, my dear. We have a drive ahead of us, but we should be able to make it before dawn if we don't tarry.'

'What about him?'

'I don't think the young man will trouble us. He has his own family issues to deal with.'

'I don't trust–'

'Leave the firearm. Bring the car around, there's a good girl.'

Willa hesitated.

'We have no need of such base technologies,' Jasmine said. 'Not where we're going. I've never liked them. Dishonourable things; they cheapen us.'

Willa yanked the bolt open with an angry gesture. The bullet clanked on the floor and rolled away. She dropped the magazine and threw it onto the jumbled mess of the veranda, then extracted the bolt and left it on the mantel where a long, thin stake with a blackened tip was the only adornment. She propped the rifle in the corner, careful to avoid the body on the floor.

'Now the car,' Jasmine said.

Willa gave Kevin a stare that was part plea, part warning, and left.

Jasmine frowned as she watched the girl leave, then walked to the mantel and lifted down the timber spike. She tapped it in her hand as though it was a policeman's baton.

'Family,' she said, more to herself with a half-smile. 'Our greatest hope, our deepest despair. You know, I did warn Maximilian. I told him his daughter's appetites weren't sustainable. And once Danica left, well, it was only a matter of time. Sad, really.'

She paused at the door and pointed to the body on the floor. 'We found him trying to sneak off. Help yourself to a drink, if you can wring any more out of him.' Jasmine walked out, as though from a ballroom rather than a ruined house.

Kevin checked the body. Nigel, stripped to his shorts. A duffel bag lay nearby, its contents tumbled on the floor: clothes, a dagger in a sheath, and a resealable plastic bag of what looked like dried grass. A set of car keys on a silver key ring showing sun and moon combined. Kevin snatched them up; he took the dagger as well. Nigel's chest barely rose, his throat and arms marred with fresh wounds. His wrists showed raw patches where he'd fought the manacles Kevin had left him in. Someone had let him go, but he hadn't got far. Kevin wondered what had happened to Mira's knickers.

Kevin sat back down beside his mother. Wished to God that she could tell him what to do now. She'd been drained, he realised. Maybe she'd been shot, too; there was a suspicious blood stain high on her chest where the blanket was pulled back a little. But her pallor was recognisable to him now, and what a comment that was on his life, that he could even know such a thing. Exsanguination, they called it. Bled to death.

Someone – Jasmine or Mira or someone else entirely – had finished her.

She tastes of sunshine

That was never going to happen

You've got time, Kevin, you're only young

Someone had taken her life and her memories.

Takin' somethin' and keepin' it are two different things

On her dead body, he promised her that he would have her back. How, he wasn't so sure. Clearly he was no match for Jasmine, nor Mira. Not yet.

FIFTY-THREE

He'd found his gear from the Commodore scattered across a desk in a nearby room – bargain, to be wearing his own clothes and boots. Nice to be well dressed for a funeral, a procession of one.

He drove north, his mother's body on the back seat, buckled down with the sash belt.

Ahead, he saw flashing lights and he slowed. His Commodore was being winched onto a flatbed – called in from EnCy, most likely, since neither he nor his father was able to take the call. The scene was painted in orange from the tow truck's lights; red and blue from a cop car, the four-wheel-drive from the Siding.

He saw Smithy yawning as he wrote in a notebook. The constable – he'd been in the cricket team, medium-pacer and handy with the willow in the middle order – watched the Monaro drive past but made no attempt to stop him, and was back talking to someone sitting in the cop car's passenger seat when Kevin accelerated away.

If Smithy had stopped him...

His stomach growled.

He drove faster.

He'd feasted at the homestead on those two myxos, and yet

his hunger was already stirring. It was as though, now that he'd plunged into it, he couldn't go back. Like trying to drink cask after a diet of fine wine, he supposed. *Hey Smithy, how about a bottle of red to go?*

Once he'd got his mum in the car, once he'd searched the house and satisfied himself that it was empty, once he was ready to leave, then he'd gone to check on Nigel. That's what he told himself. To check on him. Just to check on him.

Help yourself to a drink, if you can wring any more out of him.

But the surfie had gone. Crept away like a dying dog, under the house most likely; God knew there were enough hidey-holes with all that damage. How long would it be before someone went out to the abandoned station to find, well, that would be the question, wouldn't it? What headlines would explain the inexplicable?

He drove.

Déjà vu struck as he steered the Monaro over the train line.

You're a vampire
Piss off
BANG

He shrugged off the past and drove on, around to the rear of the silo. The Sandman was parked out of sight of the road. The passenger's door was open, the cabin light off, but he didn't need it to recognise the shape of Meg sitting in the seat, leaning against the doorframe, her feet on the ground. Kala stood, arms crossed, against the bonnet. The urge to stop, to reverse, to turn around and just drive, seized him, but all he did was slow and then pull up near the panel van.

The girls walked over. Kala waited near his door, Meg a little behind her. She looked scared, hunched inside her coat.

He took a moment to find some calm, then stepped out of

the car. Kala glanced at Meg, then off into the dark then back to him.

'Brought you somethin',' he said, handing over the keys to the Monaro. Their fingers touched as she cupped her hand to take them. She wrapped her arms around him.

'Didn't know if you'd make it,' she murmured.

'I did.' Taipan. Hidden in the shadow of the shed, standing with a motorcycle – a rugged dirt bike covered in dust. A match flared. Taipan's face looked like black marble as he lit his cigarette.

Kala pulled back.

'Kev,' Meg said. One side of her face was swollen into an almighty bruise, her eye a puffy slit.

'I didn't know what to do with–' Kala said, but he cut her off.

'It's okay. How you travellin', Megs?'

'Wake me up when we get there?' Her voice sounded fragile, like the rattle of glass from a broken windshield.

'I tried to explain what I could,' Kala said.

Kevin imagined the two women in the car together. Meg, human Meg, dumped into the deep end with her life on the line, had acted – she'd distracted Jasmine and saved him, even though it meant she'd been smacked down, hurt. She was a hell of a girl, Megs. She would be safer without him.

'Did you find Diana?' Meg asked.

'She's in the car.'

Kala quizzed him with her look, the concern in her expression making him ache, then checked inside the Monaro. 'Oh, Kevvie. I'm so sorry.'

'What is it?' Meg asked. 'What's happened?'

'She – they – she didn't make it.' And he stood there, a statue in his grief, and Kala's hand was on his shoulder.

Meg took a single step forward. 'God,' she said. 'These people.' And turned away as Taipan joined them. His jacket was little more than rags of leather over his bare chest; he wore a pair of baggy GS trousers rolled up over his boots. His flesh showed fresh scars and bald burn patches. His skin was pulled taut across his bones. Meg's instinct to stay away from him was on the money.

Taipan looked in the car, then across the roof at Kevin.

'Jasmine or Mira?'

He shrugged a dunno. 'Does it matter?'

'It should. Know where they are?' He looked over his shoulder, toward the highway.

'Mira had already left. Jasmine and Willa have gone, too.'

'Any idea where?'

He hesitated, then admitted, 'Jasmine, to the gorge. Mira, back to Brissie, I think.'

Taipan swore, threw his cigarette and ground it into the dirt with the heel of his boot.

'What does it matter? I thought you said Danica wasn't there?'

'She insisted on waitin' till dawn. Then that girl of 'Cacia's gonna drive her out.' He swore again, muttered, 'Even if we lost, I didn't think they'd go there tonight.'

'What about the hotline?' Kala asked.

'Dead since you called home,' he said, 'even if she was in range. I can't shadow walk, either, coz I made her shield me out, just in case I ended up on the table like Romeo there.' His green-glowing eyes fixed on Kevin. 'How much head start they got, you figger?'

'Mira, a couple of hours, maybe. Jasmine, not long before me.'

'So we still got time. How many guns with Jasmine?'

'Just Willa, I think. But there's somethin' else.'

A nod to continue, clearly braced for bad news.

'Willa knew the place; she knows where to go. Mira had her fangs in me, Tai. She might know about the gorge, too.'

'What is it with you and that woman, eh?' He sighed, rubbed at his hair. 'So, that old bitch for sure, the bloodhag maybe.

Gonna be almost dawn by the time we can get there, but it's plenny rough. That bloodhag mightn't find Mother before we do. Whaddya think, Kay?'

'Kevvie?' Kala asked.

'My mum's in there.' He pointed at the car helplessly.

'Kev, what's happening?' Meg stood by his side. 'What are they talking about?'

He looked at Taipan, pleading.

'My mum–'

'Ain't goin' nowhere. But them what did this – they'll be gone soon. Back to the big smoke where we can't get at 'em. Scott free. With Mother's – with Danica's – head on a spike. And your mum in their veins, eh.'

'Can't I just–'

'She ain't here, fella. She'll be long gone by now. But here's a question for you: what's more important – who buries her, or how well she rests, eh?'

She tastes of sunshine

Kevin nodded, once, a single acknowledgement, a statement of intent.

'Kev, come back with me.' Meg gripped his arm, pushing herself against him. He smelled that mix of scents that was Meg. He smelled her fear. Her blood, there in that still-healing wound in her throat where the veins bulged dark blue, and there where it stormclouded around her swollen eye. 'We can start over – in Brissie, maybe. Plenty of garages there, Kev. A fresh start. Please.'

'Sounds like a good deal, fella,' Taipan said, but he was looking at Kala, whose mouth was set in a firm line as she stared at her boot. 'Of course, that Von Schiller mob runs the joint. You'd hafta bend over for 'em eventually. Maybe catch up with that Mira, eh? Get a cosy little threesome goin' with ya girl there.'

'You are so disgusting,' Meg told him.

'What do I do with Mum?' he asked, and turned to Meg. 'Can you take her? Keep her safe for me, till I can come back and bury her? Can you do that for me?'

'And what then, Kev? What are you going to do then?'

'I have no fucking idea.'

'Stay with me, baby. Please. We can bury her together. We can–'

'I gotta stop them, Meg. The ones who did all this. So you'll be safe. So no-one will have to go through this again. Do you understand?'

'You're going with him? With her?'

'I'm going for Mum. For Dad. For me and you.'

She studied him, and he thought for a moment she was going to say something else, a new argument, maybe simply a 'fuck you'. But she pulled herself straighter and looked at him square and said, 'Sure. What do you want me to do?'

'Kala, do you mind if Meg takes the Monaro?' He didn't want to touch the body again. Didn't want his mother out here, in front of them all, a piece of luggage, dead meat, to be manhandled into a storage shed till they found some use for it.

'Sure.' Kala handed him the car keys with all the solemnity of a priest dolling out a wafer.

Taipan cleared his throat. 'Prob'ly for the best that we take the shaggin' wagon anyway. Should make it by dawn, but still, plenny comfy in the back, there, if we get caught out.'

'I can do the dirt thing,' Kevin said.

Taipan nodded. 'Still, we'll take the wagon, eh? Gravel road most of the way. Don't wanna knock that Monaro round too much. *It's a classic.*'

And that, Kevin thought, was called sinking the boot in. The three of them all locked inside each other's blood. No secrets. Where could Meg possibly fit inside their sad, sick triangle? Who better than these two to go charging off with on a suicide mission?

He climbed in the Monaro and leaned over to his mother,

kissed her cold cheek. 'I'll be back,' he vowed. 'Just got some chores to take care of, okay?' He grabbed the rifle from the back seat.

'Nice gat,' Taipan said.

'It was my father's.' He held it tight.

'I shoulda grabbed somethin' from that fella who gave me his bike, eh. Couldn'ta bin thinkin' straight. Guess gettin' blowed up'll do that to a fella.'

Meg got in and fired up the Monaro. She looked up at him, her face so wan in the dash light. He squinted as she switched the headlights to high beam. By the time his eyes had adjusted, she'd turned around the silo and was headed for the Siding.

'Good woman, that,' Taipan said.

'Yeah,' Kevin said.

Taipan took the keys from Kala and told them to get in. 'It'll be rough road once we leave the bitumen, but if we're lucky, they won't find Mother before we get there.'

'And when we get there?' Kevin asked.

'Well, that'll be interestin', won't it?'

Kevin shrugged away the unsettling echo with Jasmine's comment, barely an hour old. This was not the time to tell Taipan that he sounded like his mother.

They pulled into a servo closed for the night and stole fuel and jerry cans. There was no petrol, no nothing where they were headed. Kala took food and toiletries and a fresh T-shirt with a crappy tourist logo on it; she tied it off around her waist. She nabbed a shirt for Taipan, too, but he tossed it, intent on rolling a cigarette. Kevin didn't protest. Next to the things he'd done, this theft barely rated. He cleaned his teeth with a gargle of Coke. Morning was mere hours away.

'This is gonna be tight,' Taipan said as they headed east, bouncing along a gravel road toward a hazy line of hills hunched along the horizon. The moon, only the barest of slivers short of full, hung low in the west, as though lingering to light their way till the sun rose.

'She might have left already.'

'She said she'd wait. Might even hang 'round till tomorra, knowin' her.'

'Well, they might not find her straight away,' Kevin said. 'She might see them coming and find a place to hide.'

Taipan concentrated on the road through his cigarette fog. 'Not from the likes of us, she won't.'

'Better than bloodhounds, huh? God, I don't understand how someone with your sense of smell can stand that stink.'

'What stink?'

There was no radio reception out here and Kevin had already thrown out the few CDs he'd found in the Sandman, as though they were contaminated rather than just plain shit. Nigel's taste was in his arse. Should've nicked some new discs from the servo; too late, now. Wished he had his mp3 player, but he hadn't found it with his gear at Jasmine's; it had either gone up in smoke or been impounded with the Commodore.

'I don't think she'd hold it against you,' Kala offered.

'Who? Mum?'

'Mother, I was thinking. Danica. If you'd stayed behind with your girl. Not your fight and all that.'

'But it is. It became my fight the moment Hunter pulled up in the driveway.'

'I'm glad you stayed,' she said.

'I never even seen where me dad's buried,' he said softly.

Kala squeezed his shoulder. 'We can go later, with your mum, yeah?'

'Later,' he said.

'Later,' Taipan snorted, and coaxed more speed from the shuddering vehicle.

FIFTY-FOUR

Mira had lost the plot. What had started out as a simple police action aimed at apprehending a bunch of Rogues had turned into some kind of vendetta – may, in fact, always have been a vendetta masquerading as some kind of justice. She'd played him, had played him from the first day they'd met and she'd asked him if he thought he, as a detective, could find her mother, and he'd said yes because he'd known that to say no was to die there in that West End flat.

'Can't this bucket go any faster?' Mira asked. The four-wheel-drive shuddered across the corrugation of the gravel road.

'We aren't exactly doing the school run here,' Reece said. 'But we're not far away.'

His satellite phone shrilled and he twisted in his seat so Mira could pluck it from his belt.

'It's Felicity,' she told him as she listened intently, her expression growing angrier by the minute. Finally she lowered the phone, gripping it so tightly he thought she was going to crush it.

'Someone is playing clever and it isn't us,' she said.

'What's up?'

'Felicity says she was out with her policeman friend and

the tow truck, getting the grease monkey's car. What does she see drive past other than the Monaro – the one that up until tonight has been sitting in Jasmine's shed. So she rings the homestead to check who's driving it because she knows no-one is meant to be.'

Bloody oath, they weren't. He'd locked the keys away himself.

'And there's no answer. So she drives back to the homestead and everyone's gone. There's no sign of Jasmine or Heather and the Jag's gone. She's about to leave and she sees a movement, over in the shed where the farm vehicles are parked, and she finds the judas there, all bled out. And he tells her, without any persuasion at all, that the grease monkey came back to fetch his mother. Came back, bundled his dead mother into the Monaro and left.

'But before he left, he had a pleasant chat with Turner and Co., and Nigel thinks, he *thinks* because he was bleeding out on the floor at the time, but he *thinks* he heard them talking about the gorge. Saying that Taipan isn't dead. That that sonofabitch is on his way here.

'Now, what do you make of all that, Reece?'

'I think we pull over and wait for reinforcements. If Taipan or young Matheson are on their way – Jasmine, too, for that matter – this is the most likely way they'll come. We could take them out here on the road before any of them get within coo-ee of the gorge, leaving Danica, if she's even there, stranded. Dawn is only a couple of hours away. We can call back our men. I can lead them in during the day. Jasmine, Taipan, Matheson – none of them will be able to interfere as long as the sun is up.'

Mira rubbed her forehead, as though weary and a little disappointed. She held up a finger, indicating a eureka moment. 'Or, I can ring your new partner and tell *her* to call back those men of ours and have them all meet us at the gorge, but you and I can make sure we get there first. So that when Taipan,

Kevin, Jasmine Turner or fucking Saint Nicklaus arrives, all they find is us with Mother on ice and a firing squad coming up behind. How does that grab you?'

Reece digested the information. New partner, hey; well done, *Hunter* Felicity. Out with the old, in with the new. 'With all due respect, Strigoi, I like my plan better.'

'That's what I like about you, Reece – you aren't afraid to speak your mind. And you know who's boss.' She thumbed Felicity's number and, for the first time, he noticed a fifth blood band around her left wrist. Mira's dance card was getting mighty full. 'Now drive. This time, there will be no escape.'

FIFTY-FIVE

They pulled the Sandman up only minutes from the gorge, taking advantage of a low crest to survey the road ahead. Stars filled the cloudless sky; the moon hung bright and round and low in the west like a mighty fluorescent bulb, bathing the landscape in washed-out grey. It reminded Kevin of nights spent spotlighting pigs and roos, back when they'd been pests, before the drought had culled them out. Tonight wasn't so different, he supposed – hunting vermin in the bush.

'You were right about the bloodhag comin' this way.' Taipan jumped down from the roof of the van and handed Kevin the rifle. 'Good scope, that.'

'What've we got?' Kevin asked.

'That old bitch's Jag and what, I'm guessin', is a VS-issue Toorak tractor.'

'Guards?'

'Nope. That mob's playin' this one close to their chest. Or maybe Mira's sent a goon squad up to the northern road there, tryin' to beat the bushes to flush Mother to her.' He snorted in amusement. 'Them bastards'll get a shock if they find the Rover.'

'How's that?'

'Mother's got them bloodhounds of hers mindin' the fort. Give them Gespenstenfucks a run for their money.'

355

'I don't get it.'

'Byely and Cherny are bloodhounds,' Kala explained. 'Hellhounds–'

'Doggy myxos,' Taipan said.

'Fed on Mother's blood,' Kala continued.

'Better than that tinned shit,' Taipan said. 'How else you think them mutts put up with the likes of us, eh? Rather tear ya head off otherwise.'

'Mother's milk,' Kevin joked. He hadn't thought anything of the dogs cleaning out the cups at the powwow. Dogs being dogs. Just when he thought he was getting a handle on things. 'So we drive up and then what?'

Taipan dug out his tobacco, swore, rolled a final cigarette and tucked it away behind his ear before scrunching up the packet and dropping it.

'Don't litter,' Kala said.

'Piss off.'

She picked up the packet and threw it in the Sandman. 'It's country. Have some respect.'

He seemed to be actually chastened. 'Fair 'nuff.'

'Well?' Kevin asked.

'Mother's got no chance against Mira and Jasmine together, even if they ain't got none of them jackals with 'em. We'll split up: you two head for the caves, and I'll work across the top and see if I can't track them bitches.'

'Is that a good idea, splitting us up?' Kala asked.

'You wanna come with me, Kala? Do some rock hoppin'?'

'I'll go with Kevvie.'

'Thought so.'

'Whatever,' Kevin said. 'Let's just do it before we all get roasted.'

He drove up, expecting an ambush, but nothing happened when they reached the two vehicles parked unattended near the lip of the gorge. There was an information board that might as well have said *Abandon Hope*, because it was a list of hopelessness – no roads, no power, no phones, no phone coverage, no water. The smelly septic toilet was the last chance to take a dump inside four walls.

'Take that path there,' Taipan said, pointing to a depression in the cliff edge where the slope arced away toward the floor, hundreds of metres below. The gorge was narrow here, a long rifle shot across, but it widened to the north, the cliffs glowing like bone in the moonlight.

'I'll work me way 'round to the north and meet you on the other side. With a bit'a luck, one'a us will find Mother.' There was a pause, the sense that someone should say something other than good luck, which seemed insufficient. 'Keep the rifle,' Taipan said. 'It'll only slow me down.' He ran off into the dark.

Kevin and Kala watched him go. The gorge was thick with trees along its floor and lower slopes, cliffs rising from overgrown scree. In the natural light, it looked tangled and foreboding.

'This is pointless,' Kevin said. 'It's too big. Danica could be anywhere.'

'We'll start with the caves,' Kala said. 'On the other side, near the waterholes. If nothing else, they'll be good places to hole up if we don't get back in time.'

'In time?'

'Before dawn.'

'Gimme a minute.' And when she looked at him quizzically, he explained, 'Just in case.' He wrenched the aerials from the four-wheel-drive and threw them into the gorge. The vehicle's alarm splintered the silence; its flashing lights strobed the scene in amber, wrecking his night vision.

'What a racket,' he said, wincing, and pulled out the knife he'd taken from Nigel. He squirmed underneath the Jag and then the four-wheel-drive. Vandalism suited him, he decided, at least in the mood he was in. He had to exert all his strength to get past the metal underbellies to perform his brutal surgery.

Nigel's knife was ruined by the time he was done, but neither vehicle was going to do anyone much good.

'What'd you do?' Kala asked when he re-emerged, and then gave him an exasperated, 'Kevvie' as he hurled the useless knife way out over the edge of the cliff. 'There's a bin, eh.'

'Yeah, well. They'll get a few kays before they're left with nothin' but shanks's pony. Not much cloud, either. Should be a nice day for a long walk.'

He lifted the bonnet of the Sandman. 'Here, you know what a distributor is?'

'Is the Pope Catholic?'

He took it off the motor and held it up to her, showing her where it connected anyway, before hiding it amongst the rocks piled around the base of the park's sign. 'Now I'm ready for this wild goose chase.'

'We probably should've told Taipan about that.'

'He doesn't need to worry about the sun.'

'Mother might.'

'She's got her own wheels, up that northern end somewhere.'

She nodded. 'You know, Mother has been in both our bloodstreams lately. She'll probably find us.'

'Shit. If she can, than Mira probably can, too.' He moved to touch his pendant, but was brought up short by the memory that Mira had taken it. 'Almost definitely, in fact.'

He picked up the rifle as he surveyed the area, feeling very vulnerable indeed. He tried to detect Mira with his senses, his mind, but he felt nothing but cool air, heard nothing but the stillness of the bush waiting for the day. No leaves whispering, no birds calling, no *thump thump thump* of a retreating kangaroo. Just stars and earth and his beating heart and the presence of the woman at his side.

'Let's get going before that alarm gives me a migraine,' he said, and started walking.

'Or brings them jackals runnin'.'

'That, too. But I guess we never had much chance of taking them by surprise, eh?'

'You never know,' she said.

'I wish we had more guns.'

'A flame thrower – that'd be handy.'

'A *tank* would be handy.'

'You've got me,' she said, slipping down the slope a pace or two behind.

'Next best thing.'

They followed a rough trail, stumbling past boulders and the slender trunks of gum trees, brown grass swishing past their knees. To Kevin's ears, they sounded like a column of elephants clumping down the slope. So still, so deeply quiet, the last hour before dawn. The setting moon was hidden behind the rim of the cliff, leaving them in dark and misleading shadow. The world was greys and olives and blacks, and a hundred shades of brown.

He stopped often, ears scanning for signs of ambush or pursuit, but he heard nothing other than the distant klaxon of the car alarm. A sense of futility rose with the scent of dirt, hopelessness arcing over him like that remote starry sky. They walked around the base of a slab of granite, its rough face mottled with fungi and moulds. A clump of grass sticks congregated nearby, like a little tribe of campers seeking shelter. There was the sound of something scraping against stone, a foot or a boot scuffing.

He turned to Kala.

A shape landed behind her.

She had no chance: her mouth an O of surprise, eyes intensely bright and wide.

An arm gripped her across the chest, pinning one of her arms against her side. Her free hand flew to loosen that grip, then stopped as a blade bit into her throat. Blood trickled, as dark as tar. Her eyes found Kevin, her expression desperate.

Willa looked determined. She would kill Kala; of that he

had no doubt. She was dressed as she had been back at the homestead, but had lost her shoes.

He lowered the rifle from where it had found instant, reflexive perch against his shoulder. He didn't trust himself, this close, hampered by the telescopic sight ranged for targets much farther away. Willa was a vampire, quick and tough. Kala could not trust her red-eye nature to save her from a bullet to the head or a blade to the vertebrae. Willa's knife was wide-bladed and curved; a butchering knife. It'd cut deep.

'Where is he?' Willa asked.

'Not here,' Kevin said, holding the rifle in one hand, away from his body, the other hand up as though he could somehow make Willa not jerk that blade.

'Tell him to go. Just go.'

'I told you: I don't know where he is.'

'You're his spawn. Tell him to leave me alone. To leave us alone.'

'Anyone would think you cared, Willa.'

'Why won't he just leave me alone?' Tears glistened in her eyes. Her grip on Kala loosened slightly, and then, realising he'd noticed, she tightened it again.

'Because I love you,' Taipan said.

Kevin started. He hadn't heard Taipan approaching through the grass sticks behind him.

Willa shook her head slowly. 'You don't know what love is, Chris.'

'I'm your brother, Willa.'

'Don't call me that! You are not my brother!'

'I'm the only blood you can call your own. Now let that girl go. Let's talk, eh?'

'Just run, Chris. Far away from here. Don't you get it? There's nothing for you here but death.'

Taipan shrugged. He was level with Kevin now, but his gaze was fixed on his sister. 'Some things – some people – are worth dyin' for. But not killin' for. Let her go.'

'I warned you. And I'm not that stupid. Like you said: blood relative. I know all your tricks.' She twisted Kala around in a clumsy dual stumble, but maintained her grip.

Kala cried out at the sudden movement. The doppelganger vanished and Kevin realised the biker was flanking Willa, had been the whole time. Still using Kevin as bait. But Willa was turned away from Kevin now. He could–

Willa's right hand jerked. Something tore. Willa pushed Kala at Taipan.

Taipan caught the woman in mid-flight. Willa flung the knife to the ground and jumped away, leaping metres. She stuck to the granite with hands and bare feet, scrambled up it as though it was a ladder.

Kevin tracked her but was too slow, too surprised. She vanished over the top before he could get a clear shot.

'Help me,' Taipan shouted.

He was crouching, Kala propped up in his arms. She faced Kevin, terror filling her eyes. Blood spilled from her throat. He could hear Kala choking. Drowning. Suffocating.

'Quick, fuck ya!'

Kevin dropped the rifle, knelt.

'Ya blood, idiot. Quick!'

Kevin snatched up the blade Willa had dropped. Dirt crusted to its sticky blade. He slashed it across his wrist, crying out with the sudden pain.

'Make it bleed,' Taipan urged, and Kevin did, willed it with all his heart, and the blood flowed out in a torrent. He held it over Kala's throat and mouth. Her red-eye body was trying to repair the wound but it was vicious and she was losing. They sat there, the three of them, a bloodstained sculpture. Kala's eyelids flickered. Her hands pawed at the air.

'No,' Kevin whispered, and heard Taipan's echo. He swayed, giddy from blood loss. His hunger stirred, a slithering thing coiling and uncoiling in his gut, in his veins.

The wound in Kala's throat began to knit. She gasped for

air, chest heaving. Taipan lowered her to the ground, rolled her on her side while she coughed and spluttered.

'Stay with her.'

'Why?' There was panic in his voice, panic at being left here alone with her, alone with her and his hunger and the danger waiting out there in the dark. 'You're not leaving?'

'Got a family reunion to see to,' he said, looking in the direction Willa had gone.

'What about Mira? About Danica?'

'You get to that woman. Keep her safe. It'll be dawn soon; that bloodhag won't be up to much durin' the daytime. Give you a chance to get Mother away.'

'Wait,' Kevin said, but Taipan was on his feet and wiping his hands on his trousers. He took Willa's knife and stuck it in his belt.

'A lotta gecko in that girl,' he mused. 'Me, I always took after the snake.' He ran up the slope beside the boulder and scrabbled up its side, neither as fleet nor as sure as his sister had been.

'Kevvie, am I alive?' Kala asked, her voice husky and weak and trembling.

'Yeah,' he said, and caressed her forehead. He helped her sit up – she coughed as he leaned her up against a nearby gum tree. 'Are you okay?'

She felt her throat, testing the new skin. 'Thirsty.'

'Me too.'

'Tai?'

'I reckon he's plenty hungry, too.' He paused, listening. Definitely another footfall. Taipan coming back? Too soon. And the smell – no, not Taipan. Different cigarettes, but a stench he'd smelled before. 'Stay here,' he whispered. 'Trust me.'

He ran to the rock Taipan had scaled, and traced the handholds, hauling himself up with surprising ease, boots scratching at the rock. He crouched on top of the boulder, watching over Kala's still form. Shit, he should've brought the rifle. Could've slung it and climbed, but it was too late now, the stalking footfalls on soil and in leaf and twig too close, coming up the slope, cautious.

One distraction, coming up.

Kevin concentrated. His blood burned; his head ached. His thirst scraped at him as if he'd swallowed sand. He struggled with double vision as his doppelganger materialised below. He was watching the scene from his high view as well as from where he – it – crouched over Kala. She reached out to his cheek and he pulled back, realised he had mirrored the shadow walker's action and cursed silently. Not a sound, he told himself. He didn't have enough blood to save her a second time.

FIFTY-SIX

Reece's family used to go camping. One thing about Brissie, there was no shortage of forest to get lost in. The tent was always too hot or too cold. There was dirt and twigs in the billy. The smoke stung his eyes, you had to shit in a hole, there was nothing to do other *than* shit in the hole and get sunburnt. It just wasn't natural. The worst thing was the noises, especially at night. Irrational, he knew; there was nothing in the Australian bush other than, heh, taipans and other snakes, some spiders maybe, to hurt him, and yet, when the dark came down, you never knew what was out there, scratching and screeching. He hated the bush then and he hated it even more now. Traipsing through the shitty pre-dawn forest on one more search and destroy mission. He supposed it always was going to come to this, from the moment he pulled into that servo, from the moment he'd pulled up at Turner's and collected Taipan, from the moment he'd faced Mira in West End and said yes. He sounded like a dozer pushing through the bracken. He climbed up the western side, the uncertain light making every stump and half-concealed log look like a biker with a gun aimed at his heart.

He and Mira had been crouched on the far side of the gorge, at the base of a spur that rose up along the cliff. There was a

Swiss cheese cluster of caves up there. In one of them, after more than an hour of creeping around through the midnight scrub, they had spotted movement. 'Red-eye,' Mira said. 'I can smell her from here. Mother won't be far.'

Before he could comment, she'd said, 'The boy's here,' and then the car alarm had gone off, echoing down the gorge.

'Deal with the grease monkey,' Mira said. 'I'll take care of the bloodbitch and her pet.'

He'd wondered then, and he wondered yet, if Matheson was even here. True, he'd heard motors, and the alarm made it likely that *someone* was here, but for Mira to send him away on this fool's errand when she was hunting a vampire even older than herself? No, that was on the nose. That stank to high heaven. Would the four-wheel-drive be intact or had some opportunistic bastard just stolen the wheels? If he climbed up the slope would he find it there, ready to take him right the fuck away from this?

Away to where?

He stopped in his stride. Hardly dared to breathe.

Voices.

A slab of granite projected out from the cliff – he could just make it out through the trees. The path they'd come down, the one he was more or less following now in his less than stealthy attempt at being clever, led right past it. He crouched, thumbed off the Steyr's safety and crept forward. He'd come in around the rock, use it to protect his flank. Sweat trickled down his back. He pushed through the trees and saw the girl, Kala, propped up facing him against a tree at the far end of a clearing big enough to park a car in. She looked distinctly worse for wear. Looked like her throat had been cut. Now who had done that?

And then he saw Kevin Matheson, bending over her. Where had he come from? Behind a tree, a bush? In this light, he could've been there the whole time. He crept forward, wincing at every footfall, and then he was standing over a hunting rifle lying discarded on the ground and pointing his Steyr at the lad's back.

'She said I'd find you hereabouts.' Should probably have gunned them both without a word, but he couldn't do that. Not from behind. Not the kid. But the kid wasn't a kid anymore, was he? No, he was a bloodsucker, and his sire was one of the most vicious there was. Like father, like son? And where was Taipan? He couldn't see anyone. Just the kid, on his knees, facing him, all impassive, and the girl, scared out of her wits beside him.

'Don't make me do anything I'll regret,' Reece said.

'Where's Mira?' Matheson asked, his voice thick and low, almost a whisper.

'Family business,' Hunter told him. 'Doesn't involve you or me.'

'We've got our own family business, don't we? *My* family's business.'

'If you want.' He adjusted the Steyr, to make sure the kid could see he was serious. 'Or you can just let it go. Like I told you – could've been Taipan, could've been me, could've been the two of us. Whichever way, your old man's still dead.'

'And my mum.'

'Don't know anything about that, sport, but it'd be a damn shame if she was.'

Matheson stood and Reece braced himself.

'Don't. Ask yourself: can she make it without you?' He indicated Kala with the barrel of his gun.

'Can Mira make it without you?'

'Of that, I've no doubt. Where's Taipan?'

'Gone to see his sister.'

'Sounds about right. So what's it gonna be, sport?'

Matheson smiled. 'I like your sword.'

'Don't!' He fired, point blank, as Matheson charged. His bullets blew the kid to mist, and he heard the noise, on the rock above him, and he realised he'd fucked up in a big way.

FIFTY-SEVEN

Kevin landed on Hunter, knees smacking him to the ground. He rolled to his feet, cat-like grace, cat-like speed. His blood surged. Time froze. The world narrowed to Hunter, just Hunter. The man rose, seeking to bring his assault rifle to bear but Kevin attacked, punching, a hammer against concrete. A burst from the gun blew fire and death past his shoulder and then the rifle was gone, hurled out into the bushes. Hunter was up against the rock, eyes unfocused, blood pouring from his mouth and nose. Kevin bit into him, bit hard, and he sagged against the limp body, pinning it to the cliff as Hunter's lifestream flowed. His life and his knowledge. Mira knew where Danica was. Danica and Cassie. She was going to kill them both.

Kevin tore himself free. Leaned, gasping, against the man's blood-drenched shoulder as he assimilated the knowledge, locking Hunter's experiences away behind a door in his mind. Hard to stop when he'd been so empty, so thirsty. Revelling in the man's sad, sorry life. A pawn, just another helpless fool floating on life's slipstream, trying not to go under. In over his head. So alike, him and Hunter, in their own way. It was true – Reece didn't know who had killed Kevin's father. But the shot had come from his pistol. Two fingers on the trigger. His father dropping. 'Sorry' falling from Hunter's lips, but not sorry enough to drag him out, to save him and Kevin as the flames roared up. Already knowing his father to be dead and believing that Kevin deserved to be. Nobody to save. *Pragmatic cunt.*

Kevin thumped Hunter in the stomach for good measure, then let him slide down, moaning, to lie in a pile at the base of the rock.

Kala's voice cut through his fug. 'Okay?' She stood nearby, his rifle in her hands.

'Okay,' he confirmed. 'We have to get to Danica. In a cave, like you said. Up the cliff a bit, on the other side of the gorge. We gotta hurry. Mira's closing in. She sent this bastard to stop us. She can sense me, so she'll know her man here has failed.' He nudged Reece with the toe of his boot, none too gently.

'Can you warn Mother? Can you reach her through the blood?'

'I don't think so. She's so shielded.' He looked up at the cliff on the other side of the gorge where he could just make out a smudge of grey stone through the tree cover. The sky was lighter there, the stars dim to vanishing. Somewhere in the gorge, a kookaburra cackled awake, an alarm clock for all the early birds. A new day was dawning, but there was still enough darkness for murder. Kevin unbuckled Hunter's belt and examined its pouches – sword in scabbard, pistol in shoulder holster, spare ammo, HeartStopper with spare gas cylinder and stake. Medical kit. Canteen. He passed the latter to Kala and she rinsed, spat, drank. He took Hunter's satellite phone from its pouch and smashed it against the boulder. Hunter wouldn't need it, and Kevin had no-one to call. He buckled on the belt and tested its balance on his hips. Passed the pistol to Kala. 'Swap you – you're better with handguns.'

She checked the gun and pocketed the clips he gave her, then asked, 'What about him?'

Kevin looked at the prone man through an overlay of memory and allowed it to fade under the urgency of the moment. 'Good luck to the bastard. I've got all the blood on my hands I can cope with right now. I'm more concerned about saving Danica.'

They made their way down the slope, heading for the caves where Danica and Mira waited.

FIFTY-EIGHT

Reece pushed himself to a sitting position, then used the rock to prop himself up as he stood. The kid had done him over but good. Quick learner, the little bastard. The wound in his throat: pulsing painfully but no longer bleeding. Jaw mending. Ribs cracked, maybe broken. Stomach a massive bruise despite his vest. Vision a little dodgy still, the combination of swelling and concussion. He checked his equipment. The kid had taken his Glock and utility belt, so his broadsword and staker were also gone. So too the first-aid kit – could've used a hit of go-juice and a couple of painkillers about now – and his canteen. It was gonna be a long, long day. But he still had his car keys in one pocket and his back-up revolver strapped to his ankle and a dirk sheathed on his inner arm.

He looked up at the rim of the gorge. There was go-juice and a two-way radio in the four-wheel-drive. It was a hell of a climb to get there. He'd make the most of the morning cool while he could. The sun would hit this side of the gorge first. He'd be plenty thirsty by the time he got to the vehicle. If he got there. Magpies trilled and he could've wrung their cheerful little necks. Cockatoos screeched and that rasping call felt a more suitable accompaniment to the state of his broken body. The kid had taken a metric shitload of blood. It was all he could do to stand. And then step. And then again. Eventually, he fell into a state of numbness that allowed him to put one foot after the other, using saplings for support. He could see his shadow growing darker as the world lightened, night slowly filtering to day. Behind, the eastern sky had faded from black to grey and the silhouettes of trees lined the cliff edge on the other side of the gorge.

Assuming Mira survived this little operation, she wouldn't be going anywhere before sunset. That gave him a good twelve hours of distance to put between them. The kid was right. There was enough blood on everyone's hands. Flick was welcome to it.

What now? He stopped his plodding, gasping climb. Voices. From his right. Through a veil of scrub. Golden wattle buds, birds already flapping about them. Wrens and some honey eaters with curved beaks. They darted away as he approached.

The voices again. Male and female. Familiar.

He could keep walking. Should keep walking. And drive.

He pulled his pistol and pushed through the undergrowth.

Back in his day, the police motto had been 'firmness with courtesy'. Special Branch had always been more about the firmness. Justice had failed, but revenge was a distinct possibility.

FIFTY-NINE

The air grew cooler as Kevin and Kala descended. Bracken carpeted the ravine floor. A creek gurgled its twisting, intermittent way through the gorge. Here it was reduced to a series of smooth-rocked pools, overshadowed by slender gums and bordered by thick hedges of ferns, cycads and palms. The eastern cliff towered above them, sheer and smooth in places, a tumble of vine-shrouded boulders in others. The caves showed as dark maws in the shadowed cliff, long and shallow, as though some mighty giant had carved footholds in the distant past.

Kevin's sense of urgency increased as they got closer. He couldn't tell if he was feeling Mira's anticipation or Danica's anxiety, or perhaps some feedback from Taipan or even Hunter.

Kala stumbled.

'Maybe you should stay here where it's cool,' he said. 'Rest.'

'No.' She sagged against a fibrous fern as tall as she was, its drooping fronds a strange umbrella above her head. 'I'm okay.'

'You've lost a lot of blood.'

'I said I'm okay. I'll see it through.'

'You don't have to,' he said.

'I was there at the start and I'll damn well be there at the finish.'

They sat by a waterhole, shallow and clear, and washed the worst of the muck from their faces. Her throat was still livid with the scar of the cut, her shirt dark with blood. 'Shoulda nicked another one, eh?'

'And a brolly. It's getting light.' Kevin wondered if that was the source of his rising unease. He paced as she scooped up a drink.

'The cliff looks steep. A hard climb.'

'Hunter's lifestream showed me – he and Mira were hereabouts when they saw someone in one of those caves about halfway up. There's a spur, there, on the right, see it? We can go up that. Kind of a ledge where it joins the cliff.'

'Can you see anyone?'

'No-one. At least we know she and Hunter are here by themselves. Reinforcements are on the way, though, so we'll have to do this fast.'

He shouldered the rifle and helped her up.

They crossed the stream and headed for the spur, the ground rising, the ferns thinning to be replaced by sparse spiky grass and blue gums. Bird song filled the gorge – darting parrots and slow-flapping cockatoos, crows and magpies, a whip bird. The kookaburra laughing again. Above, the edge of the cliff was clearly visible, the sky paling into the grey-blue of pre-dawn.

Kevin felt the threat of the approaching sun looming over him with all the solidity and menace of the cliff itself, trying to grind him down.

They finally reached the ledge he'd spied, some inner sensation drawing him, telling him this was the spot. No sign of Mira – that didn't inspire confidence.

'Oh fuck,' Kala murmured, and he followed her gaze through a gap in the treetops and saw figures on the cliff opposite. Taipan had found Jasmine and Willa.

SIXTY

From where Reece crouched in the underbrush, Jasmine Turner looked like a matron who'd just had her picnic interrupted by ants. She wore pants and a long-sleeved blouse, with a shawl or something rumpled on the stony ground at her feet near a wide-brimmed straw hat. She looked absolutely furious, but it was a cold fury, contained and focused. A splash of fresh blood marked a tear in Jasmine's blouse over her left breast; a smear dotted the lace cuff at her wrist. The picnic ants had been particularly fierce but the old girl was still standing – they'd bitten off more than they could chew, it seemed.

Turner snapped her hand out, palm up, toward Heather, who stood nearby in her denim work clothes. The younger woman gripped a black-tipped timber stake in both hands as though it were a snake, liable to bite her if she let it go. It was the same one Reece had seen displayed on the mantel at the homestead; the one he'd taken from Taipan's back a week ago when this debacle had begun at Whitby Downs. Heather wasn't responsible for Turner's wound, however. No, the offender in question crouched in front of the two women with his back to Reece, but unmistakable nonetheless.

Taipan held a curved dagger low, his other hand out for balance, knees bent. On the rock between him and the women lay a three-foot length of sapling spotted with bright spots where branches had been stripped. One end had been roughly hewn to a sharp point; it was tipped with blood, making it look like a massively oversized pencil. Reece didn't need a DNA test to work out whose blood it was. Should've led with the knife, he thought, even if it wasn't a stabbing blade.

Turner snapped her hand at Heather again, but the girl ignored her, clutching the stake close.

'God, Chris, please, just go! Turn around and go,' Heather pleaded.

Taipan shook his head, not taking his eyes from Turner. The winged skull on the back of his jacket grinned at Reece through the rips and scorch marks. Reece raised his pistol; from here, he could hit it right between the fiery eyes. Jasmine Turner was an important asset. Saving her might buy him some grace if Mira failed. It might buy him a pension or at least a clean getaway.

'No more chances, Chris,' Turner said, and Reece thought she glanced at him, gave him the slightest of nods. The old girl was in control here. The biker had taken his shot and missed; he was unlikely to do her any lasting damage. Reece lowered his pistol, but kept it at a point from where he could bring it to bear quickly. Neither the biker nor his sister, too caught up in their own drama, had acknowledged him. He could afford to wait. He owed Dave at least one good shot into the bastard, but he'd let Turner have her fun first. One thing he'd learnt in his long career: don't piss off the bloodsuckers.

'This ends, right here, right now,' Turner continued. 'My patience has been exhausted.'

'Then let Willa go,' Taipan said. 'Let her choose.'

'She has chosen, Chris. Time and again. It's you who can't let go. You who can't accept. You who are bound to a past you can't even remember or possibly know.'

'Because you stole them!'

'Nonsense. Without me, you'd be dead now, nothing but

bones and lost potential, just a waif in the petrol fumes and alcohol that have choked the life out of your kind. I saved you from genocide, boy, and how do you repay me? Betrayal. Treachery. Violence. The slaughter of people dear to me. The destruction of my home.'

'Please, Jasmine, let him go,' Heather said. 'For me.'

He stood, slowly, the knife gripped loosely at his side. 'But we all know that she can't. Because I can't let you go.' He glanced at his sister. 'Sorry, Willa, but I can't.'

Turner swooped. Reece lifted his pistol but Taipan was quick, darting to the side, the knife flashing out and up. Out and up and into Turner's stomach as her hands clawed for his throat.

Reece stepped out, pistol levelled. 'Okay, that's enough. Let her go, Taipan. Step back. Step back right the fuck now.' Taipan let Turner fall and turned to face Reece. Heather ran to the woman's side and pulled the dagger free. Didn't look like a heart shot, but it was damn close.

'You're like one of them bad pennies, ain'tcha,' Taipan said, inching closer.

'Dave says g'day.' Reece shot Taipan in the chest. The biker dropped to his knees, coughing, as the sound of the shot reverberated down the gorge. Reece stepped forward to finish him, one through the head, and then a stake to ice him till Turner came around – he had two to choose from, lying side by side on the ground.

A bullet sparked from the stone at his feet. He looked up, unable to see the shooter. Began to duck, to find cover, but an impact threw him down, rolled him across the rock, earth and sky cycling across his vision. He pulled up, dazed and snarled in bushes. The revolver was gone. It didn't have the range, anyway. Even if could see the sniper. Matheson of course. Lucky the light was so shit, the range long. Reece squirmed farther into the undergrowth, clasping the bullet wound, wondering if the hole in his side went all the way through.

Wondering if he had enough of Mira's blood in his veins to save him from this latest hit. Yet again he cursed the grease monkey for having taken his belt and the attached med kit. He eyed the vampires on the rock. Any one of them could heal him. He needed Taipan to lose this. Lose it bad.

Heather stood, looking surprised, the dagger clutched like an afterthought in her hand. Taipan and Jasmine were getting to their feet, a race of two cripples to recover enough to kill each other. Automatic gunfire rolled down the gorge, but there was no incoming. Had Mira engaged with Danica? Had she killed Matheson? Reece checked his wound. Blood a mere dribble, the flesh torn and ugly. He might survive it.

On the rock, a shout, and he looked in time to see Taipan snatch the blade once more from his sister's hand and reverse it, overhand, coming in to plunge it into Turner's face or throat. But the old girl, on her knees, plucked up the sapling stake and thrust. A wet impact. The blade fell from Taipan's hand. Reece couldn't believe the biker had fallen for that – how desperate must he have been?

Taipan staggered backward, a shuffling one–two–three steps, back toward the lip of the rock with the length of timber dangling from his chest and blood dribbling from his mouth.

'End of the line, my boy.' Turner grabbed him by the collar and forced him to his knees. Taipan clawed at the timber stuck in his chest, robotically trying to extricate it. Turner retrieved the knife and grabbed Taipan's chin, reefing his head up straight, exposing the throat. She hefted the knife for a backhand slash. 'Goodbye, Chris.'

Heather grabbed the stake from the ground and smacked Turner across the back of the head. Turner lurched into Taipan. The biker grabbed her around the knees and threw himself forward, knocking her off her feet. The knife rang on the rock. She lunged for it. Heather shouted, 'No! No!' Taipan crouched over Turner as she scrabbled for the knife, just out of reach. He hauled the stake from his chest. Her hand found the knife.

She twisted under him, blade flashing. Taipan stabbed down. Put his whole body behind it, driving the stake all the way in. Turner heaved once, twice, then lay still, the knife dropped by her side.

He tumbled off her and lay there like a shipwreck survivor washed up on a beach. 'A miss is as good as a mile, eh,' he laughed sardonically – to himself, the stunned Heather or the iced Turner, it wasn't clear.

Reece slowly drew his dagger and considered his chances. The biker was moving slow; he was badly hurt. Could Reece take him in a knife fight? Not his strong suit. Not with more bruises than skin and a new hole in his hide. He was in worse shape than Taipan.

'End of the line,' Taipan said, and this time the comment was definitely directed at Turner, making the old girl eat her words. *Smart arse.* Tiredly, like a man of straw, Taipan clambered to his knees and reached for the knife.

Heather stood on it. 'Don't kill her.' She clasped the stake like a rifle across her chest.

'She was gonna take my head, Willa.'

'She's still my mother.'

'She was never our mum.'

'Our "mum" is either dead or lying toothless in a gutter somewhere.'

'Is that what you think of us mob? You bin hangin' 'round with this ol' colonial bitch for too long.'

'That old colonial bitch is the only mother I've ever known. I love her, Chris.'

'And I love you, little sister. So here we are, eh.'

She kicked the knife away. Then she sat, more like deflating, her legs tucked up underneath her, shoulders slumped, facing Taipan across Turner's prone body, the stake sticking up like a barren flagpole. All they needed was a white flag.

Reece looked for the best way out. They seemed to have forgotten him, but sooner or later – preferably sooner – he'd have to move. Get up to the car. He eyed the eastern sky. What were these two playing at? They'd have to find shelter before he would.

'I'm very tired, Chris. Aren't you tired?'

'Plenny.' Taipan gave a half-laugh, an exhausted snatch of pain. 'So how you bin, anyways?'

'I've been better.' She forced a smiled. Wiped a tear. 'There's no going back.'

'Ain't no goin' forward, either, eh.' He looked at the washed-out sky turning from the thinnest of grey to the lightest of blue.

Birds called. Jackass and crow, magpies, parrots, cockatoos. Reece mentally joined the chorus. *Run, you dumb shit. While you can.*

'Do you remember this place?' Taipan asked.

'I don't think so. And yet, I seem to know it.'

'Maybe it's home, eh?'

'I don't know where home is anymore. You kind of burnt down the last one I had.'

'That wasn't ya home. But this is as good a place as any.' He dug in his jacket pocket – the action made Reece grasp his dagger tighter – and swore and reached to his ear and then looked around until he crawled a couple of feet to pick up a crumpled cigarette. He returned to his spot and straightened the ciggie out and lit up. He reached across Turner's body to offer it to the girl, but she waved it back.

Reece pulled himself up, expecting – he didn't know what. The knife hilt was slick with sweat in his hand.

Taipan looked over his shoulder at Reece. 'You still there, Gespensten-shit?'

'Still here.'

'Pity.' He blew smoke. 'Thought 'Cacia mighta done for you, back there at the homestead.'

'I've got a hard head.'

'You myxos usually do.'

'One of the fringe benefits.'

'Worth dyin' for?'

'No. But then, what is?'

'Family.'

'I'll leave you to it.'

'That'd be good.'

'Haven't seen my gat, eh?'

'Don't push it, Hunter.'

Reece's ravaged body complained in every muscle. The bullet wound felt as if maggots were crawling inside it, nibbling at the torn flesh.

The sun broke through the trees lining the gorge, fringing them in gold and orange.

Last thing he heard as he shuffled away was Taipan talking to his sister.

'Looks like a nice day comin', Willa. No cloud.'

'Yeah,' she agreed. 'Nice day comin'.'

SIXTY-ONE

Kevin's chest filled with pain as the sound of gunfire faded away, replaced by the squawking of birds. He'd shot Hunter, had been about to put a bullet through Jasmine, too, to give Taipan his chance. And then he'd had his legs knocked out from under him. His breath stolen. His heart stopped.

Kala lay by his side in a spreading pool of blood. She looked surprised, a dog kicked in the guts and winded.

He tracked Mira as she slid down the slope above in a shower of pebbles and dirt, an assault rifle just like Hunter's held high. She was dressed for war in combat boots and black cargo pants, a tight, black long-sleeved top under her fancy vest. Protective collar and armguards. The hooded Driza-Bone flapped at her ankles as she stood above Kevin. She lowered her head so she could see him over the rim of her mirrored sunnies, and said, 'Bleed for me, Grease Monkey.' She fired a short burst into Kevin, like bricks hurled into him, his body jerking as though electrocuted.

The gun clicked empty.

She threw it away.

She wore a pistol and a long knife and a sword with a curved blade. Scimitar or a sabre, something like that: a chopping blade. His pendant, the one Danica had made for him, glimmered on her vest. She still wore Kala's earring. Trust Mira to not miss the chance to rub salt in the wound.

She kicked his rifle – his father's rifle – over the cliff, then drew Hunter's sword and threw it out of easy reach up the slope she'd come down. She stalked over to Kala – panic pushed aside Kevin's agony for a moment, but Mira merely lifted Hunter's pistol from Kala's limp grip, checked it, then tossed it to land up near the sword.

'Did you kill him?' she asked Kevin.

He couldn't answer. It was all he could do to keep his eyes open as his heart faltered.

Mira held up her left wrist and spoke to it as though it was a radio. 'Still kicking, Reece? That's my boy. Though you might wish you weren't when I catch up with you.' She looked at the sky, then back at Kevin. 'Getting light, Grease Monkey. Do you think she'll put in an appearance before I or the sun put you out of my misery?'

Movement caught his attention. Near the cave mouth at the far end of the ledge. Behind Mira.

Cassie!

She aimed a submachine gun, a short black thing with a curved slab of ammo case hanging under it.

Mira barely looked at her, just a glance along her gun arm as she drew her pistol and fired three rounds into the girl's chest. Cassie dropped.

Shit, Mira had taken them all out, just like that. What chance had they ever had against someone who'd been fighting wars for centuries? The weight of his wounds held him down, his body burning with its feverish attempt to heal the massive damage.

The air rippled. A gush of heat far above. Brightness in the trees, as though aflame, and the silver trunks on the opposite crest turned to orange in the dawn light.

'Morning,' Mira said. Greeting or statement of fact, he couldn't tell. Pistol reholstered, she walked to where Cassie lay gasping and hauled the girl to her knees. She held her by her hair to stop her falling. 'You red-eyes can be such pains in the arse sometimes.'

Kala moaned. Her fingers moved, as though looking for the pistol Mira had taken.

Kevin had no guns. No guns, damn it. Just Hunter's wide-bladed knife and the HeartStopper. He fumbled the staker from its holster but knew he had no chance to use it, to save Cassie; to save himself.

'Come out, Mother!' Mira drew her sword. 'Or are you going to sacrifice these fools as well? What will it take to make you give a damn?'

'Enough, Mira.' Danica stepped out from the nearby cave. She pushed the hood of her cape down. She wore jeans and a lace-up shirt hanging loose. No weapons. 'Why are you doing this?'

'You really don't know?'

'It's been so long.' Danica approached Mira, her hands out as though trying to soothe a snarling dog.

Mira faltered, the sword tip dropping. Cassie swayed in Mira's weakened grip, then cried out as Mira pulled her straight, the sword lifting once more.

'Out of my head, *Mother*. You've given up your trespass rights.'

Kevin pulled himself into a sitting position. Caught Danica's eye. She shook her head at him, and Mira, following the action, turned to him and said, 'Sit, there's a good puppy.'

'You still haven't told me why you're doing this,' Danica said.

'*Vater* sent me to clean up the trash out here. It was as good a reason as any to track you down.'

'And now that you've done so?'

'I get a clean start. Your power. My inheritance.'

'You assume you can take my power without taking me.'

'Ghosts can't hurt me–'

'Then why are you falling apart in front of my eyes? There are too many doors for you to keep shut. You're in bedlam, and the more you take, the worse it gets.'

Cassie clawed weakly at Mira's grip. 'Where's 'Cacia? What have you done with my Acacia?'

Mira shook her, like a cat with a dead rat. 'Who?' She looked at Kevin, her eyes going distant, and then she blinked herself back. 'Ah, the *cockatoo*. The pilot. The lover. Unusual, that level of loyalty. Of love. Among our kind.'

'For you, perhaps,' Danica said.

'I'm not the one who abandoned her child.'

'You were always your father's daughter. Never mine.'

'So you gave up and left me with him.'

'It seemed the only choice, if I didn't want to kill anyone.'

'Weak,' Mira said. 'Even weaker than I imagined.'

'What happened to Acacia?' Cassie asked again, her voice dissolving into sobs

My country is wherever her feet are touchin'.

Kevin closed his eyes, drawing on the memory, on the love in her voice, in her eyes, tapping the well of his own loss, of his own rage. He was on his knees, his body responding, finally, but clumsy and heavy. He twisted the hilt of the staker to arm it; kept its long, shining length hidden behind his body.

'Your cockatoo couldn't fly so well,' Mira said, and Cassie sagged, a deadweight that pulled Mira off-balance, that made her jerk the girl's head again, allowing Danica to take two steps closer.

'What I want to know is,' Mira said, pointing her blade threateningly at Danica, 'is how you could do it. How you could choose these *untermensch* over us – your own family.'

'I found a place to belong. Have you?'

'What, here? Look at you, grovelling in the dirt, feeding off animals too stupid to fuel your dreams. You left your family for *this*?'

'Some family we have by blood, Mira. Others, by choice. Blood is not always the thicker.'

'And no regrets about the daughter you left behind?'

'I regret the creature that she became, but what was my choice? To destroy her? I could never do that. Maybe that was my mistake.'

'Creature? Creature!'

'How else would you describe yourself?'

'I am *Strigoi*. I am what you made me.'

She swung the sword. It sliced into Cassie's neck.

Danica screamed, 'No!'

Kevin forced himself to his feet. Mira swung again and the blade went all the way. The body fell, fountaining blood, and she dropped the head, shaking her hand to loosen the hair entwined in her fingers. The head hit the rock with an empty thud and rolled a few paces till it nestled against the torso.

'I won't fight you, my daughter,' Danica whispered.

'Then you can watch these two die. Tell me, did you have any pet names for them?'

Danica knelt by Cassie's body, then reached out, her hands bloody. 'Please, Daughter – enough. You can have me, if that's what you want. We'll be together, just the two of us, family again. But leave these people alone. Leave them to be free.'

'Free? Free to pillage and rape? To burn and destroy and bring us all into the light?' She glanced up, paused to reef her hood over her head. Then she stalked toward Kevin.

Behind him, Kala's breathing was shallow, her fingers curling and uncurling. He staggered to meet Mira, the HeartStopper behind his back, knowing he had only the one chance.

'Stop!' Danica reached for Mira, fingers clenched as though pulling on reins.

Mira paused mid-stride, stiffened, then pushed through with a shake of her head.

'Assume the position, Grease Monkey. It'll be easier if you don't move. Necks are tough, you know.' She drew the sword back.

He lunged.

She caught him, holding him one-handed against her chest as he fell against her, and reversed her grip ready to plunge the sword into him.

He reefed at the rim of her vest, then stabbed the staker into her side, angling upward. The staker bucked as it fired.

Mira stumbled back and he sagged. The sword clanged to the ground as she clutched her side

– the inch of steel in Taipan's chest –

and stumbled to one knee. She clawed at the buckles of her vest until she was able to hurl the flexible carapace away.

Kevin's blood burned as he fought to reach her, to stand, to finish this.

'I will kill you for this, Grease Monkey,' Mira told him through gritted teeth as she dug at her flesh. 'I will make you eat this spike.'

Danica reached out to Mira as though holding her head between her hands.

Blood trickled from Mira's eyes, her nose, the corners of her mouth. A stain spread across her groin. Her skin glistened with a red sheen. She clawed at her chest. Her top tore under her nails; she pressed her palm against the bubbling crimson and silver on her left breast.

Kevin picked up Cassie's sword and advanced, one leaden step at a time.

Mira reached for him, for his blood. She clasped her left wrist with her red right hand and one of the scar bracelets turned fluid, an evil worm squirming under her flesh. He saw through Mira's eyes:

His mother on the couch, fighting futilely, as his/Mira's fangs opened her flesh and her life flowed into him/her

Himself through his mother's eyes, attacking Meg
Fleeing, bloodstained and monstrous, with Kala

And he felt:

That horrible dagger in his heart of a child turned to monster.
Of a child he still loved

That incredible depth of hate for this woman who was killing
him/her

He shrugged out of whatever spell Mira had cast, surfaced from his mother's second-hand lifestream, and stumbled forward, and heard Kala shouting so faintly, and heard Danica, felt her inside his mind pushing at him, trying to stay his hand, but his hate was a bushfire and he blazed through it all.

He thrust down at Mira, thrust down at the woman who'd killed his mother, who'd consumed her life's memories. He would drain her, drain her to the last drop, and he would have his mother back.

He stabbed – stabbed through the resistance of flesh using all his desperate strength.

When his vision cleared, he was looking at Danica, transfixed on his blade.

Dark blood poured from her mouth.

Mira grabbed him from behind. 'Like mother, like son,' she snarled as she bore him down. 'Little rays of sunshine.'

Her fangs sank into his shoulder. He fought to stay upright, his eyes locked on Danica's as she toppled backward, her hands working to remove that great iron weight from her body.

He'd kill Mira for tricking him. He'd tear the bitch's head off. If only he could get her off him! If only she didn't kill him first.

'I will take you as I took your mother,' she said in his ear, her arms locked tightly around him. Her gory fangs flashed in the corner of his vision. 'And then I will *consume* your precious Danica and even your little half-breed whore over there, if she's got anything left, and we'll all be together. Forever. Won't that be *nice*.'

Her teeth found his flesh again and he screamed.

She jerked sideways. Her fangs ripped a chunk out of his flesh as she was dragged away. Her momentum carried him with her, knocking him to the ground as she lost her grip on him. Kevin rolled free; rolled free in time to see Mira and Kala locked in each other's embrace. They reeled in some sick dance as Kala, her dagger in Mira's back, steered them over the edge of the cliff.

And where they fell, in the space they left behind, he saw sunlight bathing the cliff opposite. He saw two people sitting there on a rocky projection, holding hands over the body of a third. He saw them crumbling like sandcastles in the surf. Then he was screaming, screaming, screaming…

SIXTY-TWO

When Kevin came to his senses, he was on his knees being cradled by Danica, her bloody wrist to his mouth.

'Better?' She pulled away, leaving him swaying.

'A little. What just happened?'

'Blood calls to blood,' she said.

'Taipan?'

'You tell me.'

Where Taipan had been, that shadowy presence inside his head, there was nothing. A sensation of lightness, but also of emptiness. He shook his head, then levered himself to his feet. 'Kala? Mira?'

She pointed to the cliff.

Swearing, he lurched past Cassie's body to the edge. Sunlight bathed the other side of the gorge. The cliff where he'd seen Taipan was bare but for a few piles of clothing. Vertigo struck. He was high up, very high. Could even Mira have survived a fall like that? Maybe she'd hit a dead tree, was lying impaled down there by a sapling through the chest. Or maybe Kala was. Movement caught his attention. Mira, like a giant fly, crawling up the rock wall, scrabbling from hand hold to hand hold. She called, inside him; she wanted him so!

Step forward, come to me.

He gritted his teeth with the effort of resistance. Could feel Danica in his blood, that fresh infusion sparking the lessons she'd taught him.

Lock her away. Lock her out. Do not take a step.

Mira was closer, her eyes shining purple, her face ruddy and sheened with bloody sweat.

A bullet took her in the shoulder. For an instant, she held on. Then gravity peeled her away. She arced down, swallowed in the trees at the base of the cliff with a distant crack and thump.

Kevin shook himself free of her influence and stepped back from the rim. Danica stood beside him, Reece's pistol still pointed down the cliff, his sword in her other hand.

'Can you see Kala?' she asked.

'No.'

'Take it,' she said, passing him the pistol. 'I hate these things. And this.'

He sheathed the sword and holstered the pistol. 'How do I get down there?'

'Climb.' She glanced at the sky, so light, so hot, and considered dead Cassie for a moment. Then she crouched on the cliff edge and lowered herself.

'Trust the blood,' she said. 'Let it guide you. Try it without your boots.'

Awkward. But he did as she said and followed her, letting his instincts guide his feet and hands despite the sword swinging from his hip, the ground threatening to rise up and smack him like a cockroach. They reached a scree slope dotted with boulders, wrapped in vine, peppered with saplings that offered darker shade. His muscles ached, his face felt as if he was running a fever. Danica slid down nearby. Her skin was pulled tight across her cheekbones; her eyes were black pits lit by green embers.

'There,' she said, pointing.

Kala had landed in a young tree and snapped through its branches to lay crumpled at the base.

Mira stood over her.

He pulled the pistol. 'Leave her alone!'

'She's got nothing I need.' Mira leaned against the tree trunk, one arm dangling limply, squinting with the loss of her sunglasses. She looked like a bug bounced off a car windshield. But she had her pistol pointed at them, however unsteadily.

'You can't beat both of us,' Danica said. 'It's over.'

Mira shook her head and lowered the pistol with a look of relief, as though she'd been lifting a great weight. 'Looks like you've got a choice, Grease Monkey. You might be able to take me. You might be able to save her. But you certainly can't do both.' She backed away, hobbling down the slope where the trees were thicker. The vegetation quickly hid her from view. For just an instant, he felt Mira's rage, her despair.

'She's gone,' he told Danica, and scrambled to Kala.

'For now,' Danica said.

'Kala?' He felt for her pulse. 'Still alive.' He looked at Danica where she pulled up behind him in a flurry of pebbles, a nearby vine tearing at her cloak. She pulled at it angrily and adjusted for maximum shade.

'Can you help her?' he asked.

'She's too badly hurt to heal. Only one of *us* could come back from that sort of injury.'

'I don't know if she'd want that.'

'I am the last person to advise on who to save, if saving is the right word. You knew her best. It's your decision.'

'Kala? Kala? What should I do?'

Breathing so thin, so soft, her bloodstained chest barely rising. In her fist, his pendant, clutched so tight he was afraid to open her fingers to take it. Holding on, he thought. *She's holding on. To me.* He opened a fresh cut on her arm with his dagger and fed, taking her into him in small, careful slurps. He had to fight to keep his hunger at bay. Danica's powerful blood had got him up and moving, but he was badly hurt. He needed more.

'She must have a foot in both worlds,' Danica cautioned. 'Not too little, not too much.'

He felt Kala's life, its myriad joys and pains, felt her energy fading. Heard the birds so loud, the crows raucous and echoing; he wanted to swear at them, but his mouth was filled with her blood, his lips were sealed to her flesh, his teeth buried in her. She faltered. Her heartbeat losing rhythm, striving, striving, then failing.

He bled for her. Willed her to live. *Live.*

In the corner of his vision, he saw Danica nod. 'The seed has taken. You've done well.'

Kevin collapsed, exhausted.

'We need to get her out of the sunlight. The Rover's too far away, more's the pity: we could use the decant. She'll be hungry when she wakes, too.'

'I got nothin' left,' he said. 'Let me at least bind these wounds. She's bled enough.'

Scratches. This is heavier kadaicha. All the way to the soul.

He opened the first-aid kit he'd taken from Hunter. Bandages, but nowhere near enough, and two vials, metal, stoppered. He opened them cautiously. Blood. The scent thickened, achingly familiar. Mira's blood, stale but unmistakable. Emergency rations for her Favourite.

'Not for her,' Danica said, a restraining hand on his shoulder. 'Not while she's in the change. Yours and yours alone.'

He drained the vials. And saw, as through a fog:

Mira stumbling through the bush

Huddled under her coat

Desperation and panic driving her as the sun lashed her

Still running. Good.

He shut her out.

He had to get Kala to safety, and then he had to go home. Home to bury his mother. To work out what he was going to do next. He looked at Kala, bruised and bloodied and bandaged, one foot in death and one in the unlife, the half life. Would she thank him or curse him?

They had to go the long way, clambering like drunks back up the ridge and across to the cave. Handprints in white and ochre, outlines of kangaroos and more obscure animals, decorated the walls. He retrieved Cassie's body – so horrible, carrying her severed head, those eyes and the dust and the blood, her lips open in a sigh, a glimpse of tongue. It was a relief to cover her with his shirt then crawl as far away as he could.

They made Kala comfortable far at the back where the musk of animals and dust enveloped them, the air cool and dark. The three of them spent the day there, each in their own private world of hurt, waiting for the night to fall so they could start again.

SIXTY-THREE

The dusty ochre ball of the rising sun blazed low in the east. Reece squinted against the glare as he dug the first-aid kit from the glove compartment and swallowed both vials of decanted Type O. He thumped his head against the headrest as the rush filtered through him. Nowhere near as good as straight from the vein, a little vinegary due to the anti-coagulant needed to keep the blood viable, but still, better than nothing.

He found the water bottle, rinsed and spat.

What a fucking disaster.

He lit a cigarette. West, to the main road, and then – north to Cairns? Would that be far enough away from Brissie to be off VS's radar? What about Darwin, those long monsoon summers? Perth, all on its lonesome on the west coast. If Mira was alive, she still had his blood in that bracelet of hers. She could find him, no problems at all. He'd thought occasionally about cutting that hand off, but then, the fucking thing probably would've choked him to death all by itself.

He started the engine and hit the air-con, then the radio. Nothing but static. He'd seen the aerials torn off, he remembered now. No matter. He could always stop in a town and phone it in: sit rep and retirement at the same time. What about the Jag? The shaggin' wagon? Turner had the keys to the Jaguar; if Matheson and Co. survived their run-in with Mira, they'd earned their ride. If Mira won out, well, at least she'd have a shady spot to wait for Felicity to turn up with the troops.

The four-wheel-drive rolled forward and he turned the wheel, bringing it around in an arc to head west.

And there she stood, a wraith silhouetted in the dusky light of dawn, huddled inside her hooded coat like some kind of monk stepping out of the mists of time.

A blackened hand emerged, fingers spread: Stop.

He thought about driving past. He thought about ramming her. But what he did was pull over and push the door open.

Who had he been fooling?

Mira dived into the seat and stayed down, cowering below the level of the dash. She'd lost her breastplate; her top was torn and stiff with blood. She was little more than a skeleton wrapped in flesh the colour of old headstones. He'd seen vampires like this before, usually at the end of a long hunt when they'd burnt up every drop they had. Reduced to animal instinct, just one big parcel of teeth and hunger.

'Drive,' she whispered, that one word carrying pain and thirst and such bitter determination. And something else, unless he was mistaken; something he'd never heard from her before. Despair.

'You found her then?'

'We danced, ate cake: it was lovely.'

'Did you get satisfaction, Strigoi?'

'Just drive.' She manoeuvred to open the dash compartment but he pulled her up.

'I've used it, and I've still got holes in me.' In other words, if you don't want to drive yourself, keep your fangs off, bitch.

She punched the dash. Something cracked. If it was her, she gave no sign. 'I could take it back,' she said. 'Penance for letting the grease monkey get the best of you.'

'The pup's alive, then.' He felt a curious mix of satisfaction and foreboding at the thought.

'For now. Him and his red-eye bitch, it seems.' She rubbed her left wrist. The blood bracelet second highest on her arm looked like a savage case of rope burn. Ouch.

He surreptitiously made sure his door wasn't locked. Just in case he needed a quick departure. Jumping from a moving vehicle would be safer than being locked in the cabin with a starving, pissed-off Mira.

'No word from Felicity?' she asked.

'Radio's out and I've lost my phone. We might meet her, if she's taking this road.'

Mira gave a short, sharp cry as she scrambled over to lay prone on the rear seat, out of the sunlight pushing through the window tint and the dust plume behind them.

'So where are we headed?' he asked.

'Nearest town. I need breakfast.'

'And then?'

''Bane,' she said. 'To face the music.'

'At least the Night Riders have been wiped out.'

'But the head remains.' She huddled inside her cloak. 'Wake me when we're there. I'm famished.'

'Oh, shit,' Reece said only minutes later.

'What now?' She sat up, a silhouette in the back seat against the sun beaming through the rear window.

'We're overheating.'

'You think?'

He tapped a gauge. 'I mean the truck. The grease monkey's nobbled us.'

'And this means?'

He pulled the four-wheel-drive up and reached for another cigarette. 'It's gonna be quite some time till breakfast. Unless Felicity turns up with takeaway.' Reece smoked in the light of dawn, waiting for the night or for rescue, whichever came first, while Mira lay in the back and fumed.

SIXTY-FOUR

Hunched wattle trees dotted the graveyard like praying mourners; gum trees kept tall, straight vigil. Jesus, angels and the Virgin stood amid the headstones, glimmering in the light of the full moon. His father's grave, too new for a headstone, was the latest in a row of ochre humps. It had been dry out here, the past couple of years, and the earth, it seemed, did not accept these offerings, though they were buried deep. It left these scars cracked and parched, like needle sticks along a junkie's vein.

Kevin looked at his mother's corpse. How could she be anything other than natural? She who had lived as best they could, in love with the land, now returning to it as totally, as wholly, as possible. His crimson tears spotted his mother's cheeks as he laid her body on his father's grave. He had wanted to say some words, to let them both know how much he loved them, how much he needed their forgiveness. But the tears were insistent and he could not talk.

He knelt at his mother's feet, his father's too, then slowly lowered himself until he straddled her body. He reached out, first to the body, then to the soil. He pleaded with the earth, prayed to it. Taipan had shown him that clothes couldn't go, but he rejected that. It wasn't right, wasn't proper. He felt his blood warm, glow with a dull purplish light, as he reached out through the corpse under him. Colder than him. The earth under it, cold, then warm. The whisper of wind, the call of cockatoos filled his ears as he reached for the warmth beneath him.

Gradually, he and his mother sank, clothes and all, through the crusty surface, the thick dirt, until she rested close to the coffin's timber. For a moment he stayed, reaching out, finding only earth and death, equally quiet and dispassionate. Mother and father were long gone. Earth, he realised, as warm as it was, didn't care. He rose, earth scouring through him and around him, and lay on the surface, smelling the dirt, feeling it beneath him, all but undisturbed. The air was cool, the night still.

Meg stood nearby, arms folded. 'You've kind of freaked me out,' she said as he stood and dusted himself off.

'Yeah, me too.'

Kala and Danica waited with the Sandman, parked a polite distance away near the Monaro. Byely and Cherny stood at relaxed guard nearby. There'd been no evidence of trouble when Kevin had fetched the Rover, an old, curve-roofed caravan hooked up behind it and – godsend – an Esky full of decant.

The dogs had been cautious, but eventually jumped in the back for the long, tense drive around to rendezvous with Danica and a subdued Kala at the Sandman.

They'd found the Jag still there, and on the drive out passed Mira's torched four-wheel-drive, but saw no sign of its occupants. They'd driven on to Barlow's Siding so Kevin could pay his last respects.

'So what happens now?' Meg asked.

'Your folks still goin' to Brissie?'

'I think what's happened, with the servo and that, yeah, I think that's decided them.'

'And you? You're goin' with them?'

She bit her lip then said, 'I don't see why I wouldn't. My neck's much better. And no, I don't want you to bleed on it, but thanks again for the offer.'

They shared a laugh at the absurdity that was now normal.

'Danica says Brissie should be safe enough – she doesn't think Mira will try the same trick twice.'

'Do I want to know?'

'Just watch out for them city boys.'

She hit him in the arm, and they hugged. He breathed her in, her and the cemetery dirt, and he knew those smells, this moment, would stay with him forever.

'I'll never forget you,' he said.

She cracked a smile, her face so close to his, her breath warm and tea-fragrant. She'd been drinking a cup when he'd turned up at her house to fetch the Monaro, to bring his mother home. 'You'd better not, mister.'

'I can't,' he said, and kissed her. 'You're in my blood.'

She shivered and stepped away. 'You're going with them, aren't you? Those *women*.'

'It's not like that.'

'I wish it was that simple.' She held his hand. 'So, do you know where you're headed?'

He glimpsed Kala over at the cars pulling at her ear lobe while she talked to Danica. 'Dunno, but there's a pretty good chance I'll end up in Brissie, too. Gotta see a woman about returning something that doesn't belong to her.'

As they turned away from the grave and began walking toward the cars, he heard Taipan, surfacing from his lifestream, saying:

Takin' somethin' and keepin' it are two different things

He smiled. Finally, he and his blood father agreed on something.

He gave Meg the keys to the Sandman, wished her luck and kissed her again, a peck on the cheek. Then he joined Kala and Danica at the Monaro. He opened the door and flipped the seat forward for Danica.

'You better ride in the back, Mother; keep those mutts under control until we get back to the Rover.'

He waited for Kala to take the passenger seat, closed the door and went around to the driver's side. Gave Meg a final nod over the roof and got in, hit the ignition.

He was driving.

ACKNOWLEDGEMENTS

This story has been more than ten years in the making and many friends have contributed to its development since those early days in Rockhampton.

To Philip and Gavin and the other members of our dice-rolling coterie, my thanks for their friendship and contributions at the point of genesis; I've given credit where I could, however oblique, in the text.

Various writing groups have seen iterations of this tale: Vision, the Edge, SuperNova, the QUT Specficcers. Particular thanks are due to Ellen, Stephen and Peter for their support and erudite critiques of this final version, and editors Keith Stevenson and Sue Abbey for assessments that gave much food for thought. Jack Dann, the eternal optimist; Kim Wilkins, the energiser; Alison Goodman, Sean Williams and Paul Brandon have also influenced this story directly with their feedback over coffee, wine and good times that have made the journey a joy.

My thanks to Selwa Anthony, the most patient agent ever, and the staff at Xoum for taking the first (digital) step with *Blood and Dust*, and to Clan Destine Press's Lindy Cameron for taking the story and its sequel farther down the road. It's wonderful to see both books in both paperback and digital formats.

And my love and appreciation to my wife and fellow writer Kirstyn McDermott, who makes all things possible.

Vampires

in the

Sunburnt Country

Vols 1 & 2

Clan Destine Press

Genre Fiction
Specialists

www.clandestinepress.com.au